Assassination

STEVEN VEERAPEN

First published in 2020 by Sharpe Books.

CONTENTS

ASSASSINATION

Prologue

UNCIL CHAMBER, WHITEHALL, MARCH 1606

Robert Cecil, Earl of Salisbury, moved with a quick, light tread. Past the tapestries and along the thick carpets he went. He did not slow at the sight of weeping women collapsed in casements. He did not slow at the sight of gathering guardsmen. He did not slow at the strange mix of sounds which had invaded Whitehall: crying, shouting, moaning.

As he approached the tall, polished oak door of the council chamber, the two guards who flanked it pulled up their halberds and bowed their heads. Cecil stopped. Diffuse sounds came from inside there, too: distant echoes of the woeful threnody that stalked the palace. He didn't enter, not just yet; instead, he turned to the scruffy, dirt-splattered man who was dogging his footsteps. He lifted a long, milky finger. 'Wait. Knock. In a little.' The man, his man, gave a sharp nod. Cecil's lips twitched in what he felt was a nervous, excited smile. He fought for neutrality. And then, without another word, he turned back to the door and pushed into the wails and grumbles of his fellow counsellors.

The room looked, on first glance, as it always did: the usher stood with his back to an arras; the clerk of the council was at his small desk by the door; tall wooden chairs lined the long debating table. Yet, on closer inspection, everything was just a little wrong, just slightly out of kilter. The tablecloth, with its embroidered thistles, was rumpled. Some chairs were pushed back, whilst others had counsellors in them, their heads bent, as far as their ruffs would allow, to the table. Papers were scattered, and quills lay dejected beside inkpots. Some men were standing, bunching up the wall hangings.

At his entrance, a dozen faces turned to him, each looking wan in the thin morning light which fell in, watery, from the huge window. And all at once, the scattered moans and sharp squawks fell. It seemed for a moment as though every man was gathering his breath. Then the entreaties started, the grumbling, panicked cries: 'treason!',' rumour?' 'sedition?', 'false news?' The words studded the inarticulate babble drawn from the dozen throats. To Cecil, it sounded like a kennel of dogs had all been whipped as one. He held up a hand and raised his voice above the din.

'Soft, my lords.'

His fellow counsellors fell silent immediately. As he crossed to the top of the table, taking his seat – the one to the right of the vacant throne – he felt their wide eyes following him. There was something pathetic in their gazes, as though they were lost children.

Cecil slid down into his chair, letting the silence spin out a little. He clasped his hands in front of him, almost, he thought, like a penitent. They sat in a knobbly, clasped bunch on the soft cloth. And then, when he felt he had held off his fellows as long as he could, he said, 'it seems, my lords, that you have heard. Please. Sit.'

As though ordered by the king himself, the privy counsellors took their seats. One of them, apparently unable to contain his excitement, said, 'what are we to do, Salisbury? What are we to do?'

His words opened the floodgates. 'We must flee!'

'All is lost!'

'We must look to our own, now!'

'There will be rebellion!'

'What shall we do?'

'What's to be done?'

And, above all, a shrill and pathetic, 'we are undone!'

Cecil snapped his head up, narrowing his eyes. Immediately, the hotheads closed their mouths. It was amazing, he thought. These men, the men of the king's government, had only yesterday been sat at the same table. Then, their voices had skimmed, darted, and droned. Something about the proposed union, and wouldn't the parliament make trouble about that? Ums. Ahs. Difficult, that one, and with the king away hunting, was it meet that it should be discussed? Cecil had told them that his cousin, the man-loving Bacon, had promised to report on the subsidy on Monday morning, and that was all well and good, matters proceeding as they should.

All had been orderly. All had been dull. Nothing in the world could have threatened it.

And now this.

This falling apart, like the sudden ripping out of a thread, leaving the whole to fray and fail.

Cecil began drumming on the table. So smooth, the cloth under his fingertips, so stable and steady. 'We shall not flee,' he said, raising his voice just enough. He did not let his eyes wander to the door, though they wanted to. Instead, he looked back towards his hands. He unclasped them, turning them over to look at the soft, vulnerable whiteness of the palms.

Voices drifted in from the hall outside. They were indistinct, unclear, but they were raised. Cecil felt his jaw muscles tauten.

Good man, he thought.

A sharp knock on the door of the council chamber. Each man's head twisted to it.

'Here's a knocking indeed,' said Cecil. 'Usher, see what this sudden matter is.'

The chamber's usher bowed, before sliding along the tapestried wall and opening the door. Immediately, the grimy messenger who had followed Cecil upstairs half-fell into the room, bringing the stink of the City with him. The counsellors began rising, a whole clutch of hairy knuckles grasping the edge of the table. Dirtying the cloth, rumpling it again, Cecil thought with a frown, as he rose neatly from his seat.

'What is your news?' he asked, without preamble.

'The king,' said the messenger. He came forward into the room, his head bent. A burble of muttering began spreading through the assembled counsellors. 'The king is truly dead. His Majesty is dead. The news is abroad in the streets. He has been murdered!'

The muttering became a kind of collective groan, the groan a shrill bark of pain. This was the news which had risen and run wild with the dawn, up and down streets, in and out of drinking kens, into palaces and through great halls. 'Is this true? Speak, man. My lords, pray listen, and we might have the truth of the matter. Not mere bruit. Usher, the man may sit.'

The messenger was set down in a vacant chair, and immediately he began babbling. Cecil barked, 'be calm. And tell us, truly, what has happened.'

'The king is slain, my lords,' the fellow breathed. His cap was pulled low over a face hidden in beard growth.

'This we have heard,' said Cecil. 'And what news of it do you bring?'

The man looked up. Cecil gave a slight nod. 'It was … done in Woking. A company of Scotch, my lord. Scotch men disguised as women broke in upon him and stabbed him, some say.'

Again, the counsellors groaned. Some let their heads fall into their hands. 'Disguised as women, indeed?' asked Cecil. He tutted. How unusual.

'Others say his Majesty was smothered in the night,' said the man.

'Ah. And so it seems this tale has many arms and legs.' Before he could go further, before the suddenly panicked, squawking counsellors could drown themselves in cries and shouts, Cecil banged his fist on the table. An inkpot jumped. He pulled it closer and reached over for a piece of fresh parchment and a quill. He began speaking as he wrote, his pen keeping pace with his tongue.

'What shall we do, my lords? What is to be done?' He coughed. 'Double the guard around Whitehall.' Ink danced across the page in tight, neat, black lines. 'Have the Lord Mayor levy guards. Every pass in and out of the City must be rich in arms. Send fresh guards to surround the queen and Prince Henry. No man in or out of their apartments. Allow no trouble or cares to reach either and assure them that this matter is being attended to. The Tower must be secured. Its keeper will raise the bridge, have the guns manned against trouble.'

His voice, smooth, insistent, as measured and calm as he could make it, seemed to have an effect on the other men at the table. Their cries shrank down again to jittery, heavy-breathed mutters. They were all, he knew, as he focused on the page, looking at him, listening to him, drinking in his voice. Like the crew of a ship suddenly told of the death of their captain – even as a tempest was brewing – they were lost, confused, leaderless. And here was he, Robert Cecil, Lord Salisbury, charting a clear course and assuring them that the seas might be mastered yet.

He looked up. The sheep-like faces were all staring at him, every eye a round O. He fought the urge to smile as he rose, stepped back from the table, sanded the document, and crossed the room. He helped the messenger up and guided him to the door. Cecil, as much as he dared, gave the man a wink, feeling it more to be a slight contraction of his eyelid. And then, after closing the door softly, he gave his paper to the clerk of the council. 'See to this immediately. Every item and with haste.'

'We must flee!' screeched an excitable voice. 'All is lost, it is.'

'Be calm yourself. We shall not flee. We shall remain with the queen and the prince until we learn the truth of this matter,' said Cecil.

Primly, the chief secretary of state returned to his chair near the top of the table. 'Ah,' he said, as he smoothed down his doublet and looked up. 'Those of you have no stomach for the business might return to your homes and your wives. Pray, go, those who will.'

No one moved. Cecil smiled.

They remained there even until noon arrived, and dinner with it. Few ate, yet Cecil helped himself to a hearty meal, served there in the chamber. Nothing of consequence was said; none of his fellow counsellors could offer anything useful, anything that might be done. None wished to leave the room. It seemed almost as though the City outside Whitehall had become a place of danger, as though the Powder Treason had been born again and might this time have succeeded. Eventually, a fresh messenger arrived and was shown in. This was not a man Cecil knew, but he was just as begrimed, even if less artfully.

'What news?' asked the chief counsellor.

'I come from the king.' The man's dirty stub of a chin rose. Every head turned to him.

'His Majesty is well?'

'Unharmed, my lord.' His accent was thickly Scottish. 'The false news is … false.'

A chorus of exhalations poured out, filling the air of the council chamber. In it, Cecil heard relief. Joy. Disbelief. He grinned. 'We thank you.'

'Yet,' persisted the fellow, 'none ken it, my lord. Or they'll no' believe it. In yon City, the people run wild. I've never seen the like ae it—loons yapping. The king will be infuriated. His Majesty bid me, and the others tae calm the place. But they're a' red-wud, hyte and gyte, the folk oot there, and drawin' a'the'gither. All dementit wi' the tale.'

Cecil nodded. 'Yes. I can imagine. You may go. Thank you.' When the messenger had left, he began speaking again, reaching once more for paper and ink. 'God be praised. We are delivered. And now, I think, my lords, we might cause a proclamation to go up condemning these seditious rumours and sending the more tumultuous spirits home to think again.' Already he was writing. 'Unless, of course, any of you wish us to take some other course?'

For form's sake, he paused, looking around the table. Of course, no one gainsaid him. Again, he set to writing. The proclamation was drafted, discussed, edited, signed, sealed, and passed to the clerk. 'We might also,' he said, as the text was carried away, 'arrange for some fireworks, some great spectacle, to entertain the people. The safe delivery, I think, of the king will warrant it.'

This time Cecil's pause was more honest. There was a risk here, he knew. Any man might have the wit to ask why money should be spent on celebrating the king's safe delivery from nothing more than a rumour.

The moment of potential cavilling passed without comment.

Lord Salisbury, leader of the privy council and chief minister to the king, had his way.

***

The room lit up in flashes of green, yellow and red. 'You ken, Beagle, how the people cry for me?'

'Yes, your Majesty.'

Cecil was standing; King James was seated. Both were in the council chamber, though the rest of the counsellors had long since departed.

In the wake of the false news had come James himself, riding post-haste from the country, eager to assure the frantic populace that he had not, in fact, been murdered. Cecil and the full council had ridden out to meet him, Prince Henry at their head, and together the whole body of politicians had come through the City to the joyous cries of the people. 'It a' passed off well enough,' said James. He raised a great golden cup and drank it back, before wiping his lips with his cuff. 'Aye, the damned churls. Came clutching at my horse like I was the risen Christ.'

'Yes, your Majesty,' repeated Cecil. He pursed his lips to avoid smiling.

'I shall give it tae you, Beagle. It was a plan of mighty great cunning. The fools truly thought me dead.' As he finished speaking, the distant sound of bells – hundreds, thousands of them – began again in a haphazard ding-dong-dong-ding-ding-dong. 'By God, listen tae them.'

'It will take,' said Cecil, smoothing the tablecloth and then regarding his nails, 'a little longer for the news to reach out into the shires. Bad news, I think, goes more swiftly than good.' His fingernails, he noticed, were ragged. Like his reflection in the mirror, they had grown haggard with cares.

'Aye, and that is the very truth.' James took another drink. Cecil averted his eyes. The king looked unkempt, ill-favoured. In fact, his Majesty looked eternally ruffled, no matter how good the cut and cloth of his greatcoats, doublets, and breeches. What James needed, his secretary thought, was a big, hulking body – fat would do if muscle wouldn't – to fill out his clothes so that he wore them and not they him. He made a silent note to see that more and richer food reached the royal table. 'I can scarce believe it worked,' said the king.

'The people, Your Majesty, will wax greater in their love than ever. And the parliament,' he added, looking up under lowered brows, 'more, ah … accommodating. At the thought of what, what …'

'What a guddle they might have fallen into wi'out me. Parliament.' The king spat the word and, growling, slammed down his cup. He brightened abruptly. His face, which had grown fleshier lately, even as a slight paunch had developed around his middle, split into a smile. 'I've been thinking, as I rode, man, on the flag.'

Cecil bowed, more to hide his face than out of respect. The king had got it into his head that he could achieve his goal of uniting England and Scotland – of, making Scotland English in its law and its religion whilst erasing the names of the countries entirely and replacing them with one 'Great Britain' – by giving the people a pretty new flag. Privately, the chief counsellor doubted whether the people were quite that stupid.

'I should have the designs made final in the coming weeks.' James waved a hand airily over the table. 'And these parliament creatures can approve it. And you lads in this wee chamber, you can see to it.'

'The people,' began Cecil.

'The people will like what they're told to like. They have their king here, alive, as safe as they could wish.' James patted his breast, his elbow upsetting the cup. Dark red spilt, as though from an open wound, pooling on the tablecloth before being drunk up by it. The king ignored it, raising his rounded nose in the air.

'As your Majesty wishes.'

'We do.'

'And the other matter, my lord – the death of that foul equivocator. The lecher priest. Garnet.'

'We would have him join the rest of the Powder Plotters in Hell.' Another abrupt change came over the king, his smile disappearing as he banged the table. The cup, on its side, rolled away, spilling more liquid to be soaked into the nap and weave.

'It is only … some slight delay … we might have it later than May Day. Lest there be troubles.'

James turned wolfish, leaning forward. 'Lest more filthy papists purpose at our destruction when they see their fat hero-priest die the death, you mean.' Cecil inclined his head. 'Bah! We tried to make Fawkes the author of that evil matter. And then, Catesby. And now, Garnet. The damned fool rabble is sharp enough to detect a confusing plot.'

'Quite, your Majesty. And so, it might be better to kill him – to be rid of him – a little later. When they have forgotten about the others.'

James sank back on his chair and folded his arms across his

bombast-padded chest. For a while, he seemed to stare out across the table, towards the door, his eyes hooded. At length, he said, 'aye. Aye, well, let the man die when he dies. Foul traitor.' He shook himself. 'It is too fine a night to talk of death, Beagle. Not when we are so safely and newly delivered back into life, when all thought us dead. Tell me, did you have trouble?'

Cecil gave the king a smile. He felt it creep across his face, a little shyly, mostly slyly. 'No, your Majesty. Some country justices paid to allow a criminal to escape on horseback, his sword drawn.'

'A criminal?' asked the king. 'A friend of yours?'

Cecil did not answer directly. 'And the constables cried treason. And so it went, like a ball of snow rolling downhill.'

'Aye, and a few men in each wee place around me paid to carry it, I shouldn'ae wonder.' James grinned, wagging a finger in mock remonstrance.

'Your Majesty recalls my man, Ned Savage?'

'Of course.'

'I had him disguise himself as a messenger. Begrimed from the road. And he brought to this chamber news of your murder.'

'And how your fellows must have shit themselves!' James threw his head back and laughed, loud and ringing. 'By God, what I would'nae have given to have seen 'em. Grey-faced pen pushers. Wet, the whole pack of them. Gutless and bootless. You did well, my dear Beagle, well. And your man, Savage. Reward him.'

'As you wish, your Majesty.'

'Now. I suppose I must see the wee wife.' Displeasure tinged his words, Cecil thought. He had grown to rather like Queen Anne, despite her feigned stupidity and her infuriating and dangerous sympathy for the Roman religion. James tutted. 'Ach, but we should have spared the woman's cares and told her of our wee complot. Had she an ounce of sense in her head.' He shook his head. 'She's senseless and loose-mouthed enough at the best of times. But with a wee one on the way…' Another tut. 'Women. Women, women, women.' The king's knuckles whitened on the armrests of his chair of estate as he heaved himself up. He paused in mid-air. 'Just one thing. This criminal, this man you had ridden about the country with his sword drawn. He is to be rewarded for his part in this wee guising, is he?'

'I could never,' said Cecil, 'reward a criminal.'

'Only, it seems the fellow knows a thing too much. A hanging offence, was it?'

A moment of pause spread out between them, pregnant, heavy with meaning. The room lit up again in red before fading back to candlelight. 'It might be, your Majesty. Yet, as you say, it is too fine a night to talk of death.'

'Quite.' James, apparently satisfied, stood. With one finger, he jabbed at the stain his spilt wine had left on the council table and tutted. 'Blood,' he said.

'Pardon, sir?'

'I was thinking of blood, Beagle. This, you see? It looks like the stain on the floor left by a murdered man. They say that there was sic a mark left on the boards by someone in the past. In our palace at Holyrood. Blood.' Cecil frowned, following his gaze.

'It will be taken care of. A slight mischance.'

The king continued looking at the mark for so long that Cecil began to wonder if he was drunk. 'The Powder Treason. People believing this wee jape. Believing me murdered.' He looked up sharply. 'Am I ever to be free of plots, real, imagined … papists, madmen, assassins, and all sic filthy persons. Will they never stop trying to murder me?'

Cecil knew the mood: morose, self-pitying. His father, the late Lord Burghley, had once told him that the king's mother, Mary of Scotland, had veered wildly between joy and sadness. It seemed the son had inherited her mutable disposition. For no reason he could account for, a small wave of sympathy and affection rose in him, washing up to encompass the boorish, gangly, awkward man he served.

'Yes, Your Majesty. And if they do not stop, we will stop them before they can touch you.'

King James passed him on his long, bowed legs, reaching out to clasp his shoulder. Cecil shrank from it, hating, as he always had, for his lowered shoulder to touched. 'Aye, we will stop them. You will stop them. Faithful Beagle.'

As the king left the council chamber, Cecil hoped that wishes might prove horses. Later, he would wonder if the mark on the tablecloth, which never would come clean, had been an omen. He would wonder, too, if the word 'assassin' had somehow acted as a charm, as a beckoning invitation.

1

I do not, at first, realise that anything is wrong. I am dressing, pulling on a shirt and tying it up; lacing up the hose and tightening the points of breeches; stretching out my arms and easing into a good canvas doublet, one which will be warm against the chill autumn air.

That air is then rent by the distant boom and crack of thunder.

And then I am falling.

My things – so many of them – clatter to the floor. Combs, jugs, little glass ornaments, spare buttons: all descend downwards in a shattering, tinkling hailstorm. The boards beneath my feet, beneath my hands, seem to sway.

'Faith!' I cry, forgetting that she doesn't live with me anymore. 'David!' I crawl, childlike, to the door of my chamber and push it open. No one is in the outer room. 'David!' The little cot is empty.

From outside comes another great crack. Cries follow it, discordant, noisy, frightened.

What is happening?

I gain my feet, unsteadily, still rocking, and wobble towards the door of my lodgings in Shoe Lane. It falls open at my touch.

Devastation.

Across the street, under the overhanging eaves of another house, a gaggle of old women huddle, all on their knees. Spilt baskets disgorge apples, some of them still rolling down the gentle slope of the road, others already having come to rest in the gutter. The women's cries soar upwards.

Another rumbling, deep and guttural, is born in the earth. The ground beneath me quakes with it. I totter again, one hand on the doorframe, nearly falling. More people begin screaming – the shrill, terrified voices come tearing from every window above me, from unseen houses and alleys. Suddenly it is as dark as night.

End of days?

Stillness, broken only by the shouts and cries. It is as though a giant, clawed hand has fallen before the sun. Looking up, I can see the cause. Like the tattered ends of a burnt shroud, smoke has drifted across the sun. And somewhere off to the right is a huge red column of flame, reaching up into the blackness. It gives off no light, though it is itself very bright. It seems as though, somewhere over the rooftops, Hell has opened up a portal in the ground and is spilling its evil out, upwards, to stab at God's celestial spheres. All at once, I can smell it, thick, choking and acrid. The desperate thud of feet comes, and I turn. A crowd is bustling up Shoe Lane, on its way to Holborn.

I step out into the darkness, into the smoke and swirling dust.

'What? What news? What's happening?'

A boy, his face black with soot, is running past. He stops, still looking up the hill, and remains standing in profile as the rest of his company of wraiths claw their way uphill, away from the river, away from the City. 'Death,' he says. His voice is queer, far too deep for one of his age. 'Fire. Powder.'

He turns, and I feel my bowels turn watery.

The other side of his face is gone, burnt away – it is a cruel mass of reddened, charred flesh. The creases in between the livid, glowing red, are packed grime and dust. An eyelid is missing, making the eyeball huge, naked, and rolling. He grins, before he hops off up the street, leaving me. Dogs emerge from an alley, their teeth bared, low growls coming from the pits of their stomachs. Slobber drips in long, glistening ropes from the corners of their mouths to the ground. And then they, too, join the mad scramble uphill, leaping about one another, biting at their fellows' backs. They must, I realise, wish to be away from it.

Away from what?

Fire.

'Has the bridge been burnt?' I shout to no one. There's something lodged in the back of my mind about that, about the danger to London Bridge, about a plot to blow it up. Yet I know – I know – I have already helped to prevent that. The creatures behind it are dead; they are drowned, they are

Burnt.

Immediately, more people come tottering up the lane. Politicians in black, their ruffs torn and hanging limply over their chests. Some are missing hands, others heads. Their going is slow. Suddenly a furious whinnying fills the air, and the politicians scatter, fall and some are ridden down. Into their midst comes a great black horse. No, it is a white horse, dyed with filth- little slivers of white show through its ribcage where the skin and muscle have been torn away.

And on its back, whipping it into a frenzy, is the old Queen, Elizabeth. 'Get ye gone, get ye gone,' she cries. Her voice is that of a young woman, and she raises and strikes out with a whip. It cracks and flashes, almost invisible in the gloom; only its sharp crack announces where it lands. The queen is grown ghoulish in death, her face white and her cheekbones sharp. Her flaming red hair seems to be on fire itself. The flames lick upwards, giving off a smoke of their own. 'Get ye gone. All are dead, and the end comes.' Riding on, she turns and offers me the same mawkish grin the boy had done. The fallen politicians melt into the ground.

But the king, I think. The king is alive.

The queen is dead.

The king is dead.

The queen is alive.

I launch myself into the street, into what has become a stream of the dead and the dying, and I cry out. I can scarcely recognise my own voice. Perhaps it is not mine, because the words are meaningless and confused. 'The Houses of Parliament are blown up! The end has come! Everyone is dead! Murder! Treason! Terror!'

Stealing a glance behind me, I see that my house, my little block of rooms at the butt end of a tenement, is gone, lost, swallowed up in blackness. Everything I own, I realise, is gone with it. The sky flashes for a second, and the nothingness is stark in the moment of brilliant red light. It as though my home has simply ceased to exist, and it is all wrong. The world is all wrong.

But look at it, I think. Look at that sky. Look at this scene, these Hellish creatures. No man has ever seen anything like it. It is a wonder – a mad, wild, glorious, terrifying wonder.

Suddenly I am in the thick of the crowd, being buffeted, smacked in the shoulder, wheeled around and thrown down. I can't see. I can't breathe. I can't speak. I only know that my end has surely, truly come. Something terrible, something monstrous and far bigger than I am has happened, and it has heralded this madness. I fall into the yawning ground as the great quaking comes again, this time splitting Shoe Lane, splitting the earth open.

When I am released from the nightmare, I find that I'm bathed in sweat, lying on the floor next to the coffer I use as a bed. My little blanket is tangled up around one leg. I'm shivering, but not with cold, for the summer night is appallingly hot.

It is not the first time I've had the dream and nor, I know, will it be the last. Cursing myself for a fool, I listen for a moment for movement. There is nothing: I have not woken David, who sleeps in the next room, with my night terrors.

Yet you know why you dream.

I push away the thought. My part, as small as it was, in the Powder Treason is over. I had done only as I'd been expected to do in those dark days: nothing more. I needn't bear guilt for doing my duty as an honest Englishman.

And a foul, ravening spy.

Stupid, stupid, stupid thing, I think. To calm myself, I move slowly, gathering up my blanket and lying back down on my coffer. Weak summer twilight falls in blades through the gaps in my wooden shutter. It makes tiny soldiers and sentinels of my collection of arcana – my suits of odd clothing, my cushions and ornaments, my trinkets and miniatures, some of the things come by honestly, some less so.

The Powder Plot had failed. Nothing had happened. The king and his parliament, his government, his queen and his children – all of them are safe, unharmed.

Why, then, do I dream so often of destruction that has been averted and a terror that has never come to pass?

In the darkness, I shake my head, hoping to free myself from the answer that forms in my mind: that just because one plot to kill the king and invite terror into my world failed, that does not mean that out there, in the secret City, others are not being plotted.

2

How do I describe the mood of the City in those months following the failure of the Powder Treason? It was an odd one, an admixture, heavy with relief and joy, strongly spiced with fear and suspicion. The plotters had been rounded up, tried, and executed. The threat had passed. Yet the thought of what might have been – what almost was – remained heavy in my mind. And a private war, strange, raged within me.

Thank God it is over, and no one was harmed.

That was my chief thought, and the one I let the world see.

But don't you wish you had seen it, see what would have happened if the world had been turned upside down so crazily and suddenly? Wouldn't it have been a sight?

The latter sentiment, which nagged at me like a secret shame, I kept to myself. Of course, I did not want to see the king, and his wife and son, and the whole government of England, blown into bloody chunks. I liked my life, and I had no taste for mad and dangerous insurrection. Yet, can you imagine the drama and spectacle if Catesby and Fawkes and the priest Garnet – all dead now – had pulled it off? It would have been the maddest play every conceived come to life.

It was a good thing a man's thoughts were still his own, and that Ned Savage could still go about his business, earn his money and keep his mean little lodgings on Shoe Lane without anyone suspecting that he might, just might, have lusted after the sight of a world turned topsy-turvy.

The failure of the Powder Plot, too, had left me busier than ever in my secret work. My master, who would have been amongst those dead in the explosion that would have torn a great, bleeding hole in Westminster, had immediately set me to report every scrap of information I heard on any who came into the City without cause. I had played my part, and if that had led to trouble for some … well, they should have had the wit to keep their mouths shut at such a time. They had only themselves to blame if they met trouble and punishment for their loose tongues.

And loose tongues are worthy of imprisonment and torture?

I had even been impressed into playing a messenger and conducting news to Whitehall that the king had been slain – a thing I would have been hesitant to do had the tale not already been spread about by others by the time I reached the palace.

Life was fine. Life was ordinary. Good cheer was even on the wind, blown in from Denmark, whose king had arrived to visit his sister, our Queen Anne.

Last night's nightmare had left, I hoped, no lasting impression on me. Still, I took extra care of dressing and washing my face in the morning. I had elected to wear a sober suit – grey and colourless, as though I were flirting with Puritanism. Using my old mirror, I absolutely refused to leave until I was satisfied that the bags under my eyes – ugly, purplish things – had faded as much as I could induce them to. Giving myself a smile, I set down my comb and left my room.

'Good morrow!' I announced. My smile froze on my lips, making my cheek jump. David, my ward, was seated at our table. He was not alone.

'Morning, Ned,' he said. He was no taller than he'd been when he was twelve, I thought. A good thing, if he wished to continue playing the female parts in plays. His red hair was combed, and he was dressed, his freckled face split in a grin.

'Good morrow,' I said again. 'And to you, Hal.'

Sitting at David's side was another lad – one of his theatrical friends, a boy who flitted between the King's Men and the dying Paul's Boys troupe. I had nothing against Hal Berridge, save that he was a year or two older than my boy's fourteen, and thus David had made something of a hero of him. And that, for some reason, irked me. I fancied that I, who had saved the boy's life – in more ways than one – should have been sufficiently heroic in his eyes.

'Morning, Ned,' piped Hal.

I frowned, considering whether to tell him to call me Mr Savage. No, I thought. Then I should be the arsehole, the old fuddy-duddy. I looked down and fixed an imaginary fold in my cuff. 'Are we ready, gentlemen?' I asked.

'There are a thousand ships there,' said David. 'All in gold. Like a fleet out of Egypt.'

'Ah,' I smiled. 'The East.'

Hal stood up, jogging the table so that the jug sitting on it wobbled. David reached out to steady it. 'I heard there's going to be a lot of folk going to see it. Do you think – will we be allowed? I mean-so many people.'

I crossed my arms over my chest. The boy was right. The plague numbers had risen again. It was odd – before the Powder Plot, the plague was the biggest disaster any of us could imagine. Now, the mortality bills held no more terror than a warning of bad weather. We ignored them, save those of us in the theatrical world who grumbled about trade drying up. When the theatres were closed, and large gatherings banned, I would have no manuscripts to ferry to my legitimate employer in the Revels Office and the players would earn nothing. The deadly pestilence was now a tiresome old visitor who came to London for summer and took a few dozen people – ideally fewer than thirty – with it. That number had climbed higher, and the theatres had closed.

But I was not about to tell him that he was right, the young pup.

'What do we care for the pest, or the old City fathers, either? You wish to see the Danish king's great ships – well, I can get you down to see them. Come, David. And you, Hal, if you are not too frightened of what the old men at the Guildhall will say.'

'But … if Hal says we shouldn't, maybe…' started David. A blush crept over his cheeks, making the freckles stand out.

'We're going,' I said, with a little more asperity than I'd intended. I swept towards the door, pausing only to scoop up the nosegay full of angelica that I knew to be a sovereign guard against the plague airs. 'Come.' I opened the door, letting the stifling July sunshine invade the room. 'Will Faith be joining us?'

Both boys erupted in giggles.

'What?' I snapped. Faith, David's sister, was my other ward, though she had worked for two years now as a dogsbody to a weaver's wife – all so that she could be near her dull little inamorato, an apprentice named Hopgood.

'Faith is stepping out with Nicholas today,' said David. 'They're talking about their marrying.'

My heart sank. I knew they were planning to be wed, and with his master's blessing no less, but still the thought saddened me. It felt like a breaking up of my world – of the world I had become comfortable with. Everyone, it seemed, enjoyed forging onwards in their lives, whilst I remained standing still, watching their backs grow smaller. I shook away the thought. I truly must be growing old, I decided, if I grew so maudlin over other people's good news. There was nothing to be done, anyway; the first banns had already been read. 'Well, good luck to them,' I said. 'Let us go then.'

Three abreast, we marched down Shoe Lane and across the wider thoroughfare of Fleet Street, making our way riverward until we reached the Whitefriars Stairs. Usually crowded with boatmen, there was a mass of people, and I had a time pushing my way through to the front. Thankfully, there was a boatman I knew, and I stepped, wobbling a little, into the wherry. Hal and David followed and, I noticed, sat on a bench together, leaving no room for me. I stationed myself instead near the head of the boat. 'Let us see the great ships,' I announced to our pilot. He didn't answer but used his oar to launch us, rocking, into the Thames.

As we bobbed downstream, I scanned the great river. It was alive with watercraft: wherries, private barges, barques. The water itself was alive and churning: it spread before and around us like a blue field, hung with the billowing white washing of sails. Most boats seemed to be going in our direction so that we were a little sparrow joining a great flock of doves, eagles, and hawks. As we passed under London Bridge – without incident, as our boatman was a good one – and emerged back into the sunlight, I turned my attention away from the jumble of crooked rooftops that lined the river and tuned my ear to the boys' conversation. They had not said a word to me I realised, but were bent in gossip like a pair of fishwives drawn from New Fish Street over to our left. I tried to form a jest around that, failed, and listened instead.

'Who said that?'

'Everyone. It's all the talk in Bankside,' said Hal.

'But a woman can't kill.'

A pause. 'Don't know so much. Heard she's like an artist in the act of murder. That she was alive in Roman days and is like immortal.'

I raised my legs and swung them over my bench, twisting at the waist so that I faced the lads. The waterman, behind them, was working his oar without expression, his cap pulled down. 'What is this nonsense?'

'Ned!' said David. Oh good, I thought. You remember my name. 'Hal says there's a woman in London who kills people.'

Hal nodded gravely. 'I should think there's a good many of them,' I said. 'Women can kill just as well as men.'

David laughed. At me, or with me? I wondered. But Hal frowned. 'No, Ned. This woman is the talk of Bankside. A murderer – like – an ancient Roman creature who strikes men dead.' He waved an arm in what might have been an imaginary dagger thrust.

'Who is talking this trash?' I asked, offering David an 'isn't he a fool?' smile. He didn't return it.

'It's the news across the river,' Hal insisted. 'That a woman has come to London and she's a notorious killer of men. Like it's her work, her - her … profession.' He folded his arms. Then, lower, he whispered, 'sent by someone to do wicked mischief.'

I sighed. 'Waterman, have you heard anything of a murderous woman abroad in the City?' I called. He grunted, spat, and shrugged.

'Nonsense,' I said. 'You boys shouldn't share such false news.' I heard the nagging in my voice, the querulous whining of an old man. And I closed my mouth.

'Look!' squeaked, David. He jumped up in his seat, making the wherry sway. Again, the boatman grunted.

We were rounding a curve of the river, near Deptford, I thought, judging from the sprawl of warehouses and cranes that clawed at the sky on our right. The Isle of Dogs loomed up on our left, though it was obscured by a row of pleasure craft rounding it. Some seagulls were skimming the water, their wings throwing up spray. 'What…' I began. And then I saw it, ahead of us, rounding the Isle and making for Greenwich.

The king's barge.

I had never seen the thing before. It was being towed by another ship, which it dwarfed in beauty. The vessel did not look like a barge at all, really, but a miniature aquatic palace. The whole thing seemed to be fashioned from gold and glass: its superstructure was a huge box of windows, carved golden statues on every frame holding up the roof. That roof was itself surmounted by golden turrets with glass pyramids, each tipped with gold, at the four corners. Everything sparkled against the crystal blue sky. Everywhere flew pennants with the strange new flag – the British flag, said to have been the king's design, neither English nor Scottish but both – and more of the things fluttered from the ship towing it towards Greenwich.

Hal Berridge whistled, joining David to stand.

Across the Thames, from every boat, came cheers. Some of the larger ships fired their cannons – I assumed into the air. People hung over railings waving streamers and handkerchiefs. Musicians were playing from dozens of vessels, their melodies gentle and merry.

'Do you think the prince is there, Hal?' asked David.

'I should think so,' I said before the other lad could answer. 'Though not the queen.' Sniffing, hoping I sounded like a court insider, I added, 'it is a thing of little taste, all this, with the queen so lately having lost her child.' Queen Anne, as all Europe knew, had borne a princess only a month before, the baby dying after barely a day's breath. 'Yet it is … impressive.'

I strained my eyes to try and see the two kings – Christian of Denmark and our King James – through the windows of the barge, but it was hopeless. Dazzling sunlight bounced off the glass, and then the thing was being pulled in a great wash into the protective maw of Greenwich's enclosed water gates.

'Well,' I said, 'what do you think of that?'

'What do the flags mean?' asked David.

Before I could open my mouth to answer, Hal spoke up, putting a hand on his friend's shoulder. 'They said in Bankside that the flag is peace between those Scotch and us.'

I folded my arms over my chest. 'Actually,' I sniffed, 'they mean the king hopes to make England and Scotland one country- ruled from England, of course. By his Majesty's own family. Forever.'

Hal and David exchanged a glance, and suddenly, ridiculously, I felt myself the class broadmouth, secretly laughed at for his knowledge by his fellows. Abruptly, I spat over the side of the wherry. I would not, I decided, by made to feel like a child by children. It was absurd, utterly absurd. 'I shall ask the king,' I said airily, 'what he truly means by it. If I should see him again.'

Again, the boys drew together, their arms around each other's shoulders, laughing at me. Why, you stupid little brats, I thought. 'Boatman, turn us. We've seen the barge. Take us home.'

Shrugging, the wherryman manoeuvred the little craft around. I gripped the bench to steady myself as we began to ply the waters home. The return journey was mostly unaccompanied; the majority of boats appeared to have continued downstream to see the Danish ships at anchor in Gravesend or else stayed to see if the sovereigns would deign to make an appearance.

There was little chance of that, I thought. I knew nothing of King Christian, but James, certainly, cared nothing at all for the public. And he trusted them even less than he cared for them.

I dropped the boys off, at their insistence, on the South Bank – I didn't like the idea of my boy chumming around there with Hal Berridge, but could not think of a reason to refuse that didn't make me look churlish – before crossing back over the river. After debarking at Whitefriars and paying the waterman more than I wished, I clambered up the crumbling steps, careful of the choke of weeds which sprouted to meet the sun.

I did not go home.

Instead, I took myself to the narrow building on Fleet Street, barely noticeable between two houses, which I knew to be a safe house governed by my master, Robert Cecil, lately elevated to the earldom of Salisbury. His method of managing his spies – his friends, as he insisted on calling us, the little weasel – was that we might leave notes at any one of his safe houses indicating if we had news or wished to meet him. In truth, I had little, but the enormity of the times, the coming of a foreign prince, had bred in me a thirst to be part of things. That, I knew, was something Cecil had long divined in me. I might grumble and cavil and profess to wish to be out of 'the service', but a far stronger part of me loved it. Yes, I loved the thought of being part of the dangerous, secretive current that ran below the surface of the government.

I knocked on the door of the crooked building and, without waiting for an answer, slipped inside. A counter stood against the far wall of the gloomy chamber, light spilling in from a doorway behind it. Immediately a heavyset man emerged from the room beyond, his eyes raking me. 'Message,' I said. He said nothing, but ducked down and re-emerged with paper, inkpot and quill. These he slid across the counter towards me.

Taking them, I wrote, quite calmly, though my heart began racing, for some reason: '710 seeks meeting.' And then I said to the turnip-faced man behind the counter. 'Mark this urgent, will you?'

He took it from me and glanced down. Frowned. 'You 710?'

'I am.' That was Cecil's little joke. Because I allegedly bore a resemblance to the late Earl of Essex, I had been codenamed 710: S for septa and X for 10. SX, or Essex.

'Master wishes you.'

'When?' I gripped the edge of the counter.

'Tomorrow.' His tongue wetted his fleshy lips.

'Greenwich?'

'Whitehall. After dinner.'

I nodded before reaching again for the paper. Briefly, I considered writing a reply – a confirmation that I would attend. There was no need, however. There was no doubting that I'd do as I was told.

I left the note to be burnt and stepped, blinking and whistling, back into the sun. Dimly, I wondered why Cecil should wish to see me in person. It had been months since our last meeting when I'd disguised myself and barrelled into the council chamber. Perhaps the great secretary was simply on heightened guard with the arrival, at last, of the Danish king. Probably he wished to know what was being said in the City about the meeting of two Protestant princes. It was only a shame that so many of the players were fled about the provinces on tour, what with the playhouses closed. Those fellows knew everything, more so even than the criminals who roamed the liberties, and they were far too vain to keep what they heard to themselves, as Hal Berridge proved.

It was small stuff, a rumour abroad in Bankside that a female murderer was stalking the streets. Yet, in the months following the Powder Treason, I had come to learn that Cecil considered nothing too small or unimportant. By God, I knew that…

And, as much as I distrusted the man, I knew that he had an uncanny ability to sort wheat from chaff and to divine secret plots where others would shrug their shoulders and cry, 'false news'.

It was all very silly, of course. The Powder Plotters had all been men – stupid, loudmouthed, fanatical men.

But they left behind them plenty of their women.

I quickened my step up Fleet Street, searching about for a pieman as my stomach began to gripe. All I could see were sagging-cheeked apple-wives hawking their trays of shiny red bumps. They lumbered about, crying, 'Who will buy? Who will buy?' One of them was hit in the back by an urchin throwing stones. In return, she launched a stream of obscenities that would have made a sailor blush. Women – especially London women – could have powerful tongues and stout hearts. But whoever heard of a woman murderer, a woman plotter?

Had I known what was in the wind, I should not have been so dismissive.

3

Security, I noticed immediately, remained tight at Whitehall – as much as it had been when the court was in residence and tighter than it ever had been in the days before the Powder Treason. I had left Shoe Lane early, as David had been expecting Faith and Nicholas Hopgood, and I had no appetite for discussing church porches and flower garlands. Afterwards, I had walked the streets, calling into taverns and old haunts, listening out for news from the criminals who skulked and whispered around and within Whitefriars.

I had learnt nothing I hadn't heard from Hal Berridge the previous day. A woman, reportedly beautiful, had come into the City and might have it in mind to threaten one of the underworld kings. It was useless tittle-tattle. When the time had come, I'd proceeded upstream to Westminster Stairs, along King Street, and into the precincts of Whitehall Palace. As always, the place was busy, even without the court in residence. Ugly, mismatched Whitehall, less a palace than a scattering of buildings thrown up by different hands and according to different tastes and styles, had become the unofficial, permanent centre of administration for the whole kingdom.

At every turn, I was questioned. These were not the weak, disinterested questions of yesteryear, which could be talked around, but sharp, searching demands. What is your name? Who do you work for? Where are your papers? Do you come in arms?

Thankfully, I had all in order. I was Ned Savage, servant of the Revels Office – mark you my livery? – and here were my papers signed by the Master of the Revels, Sir Edmund Tilney, and I have no arms. Passing muster, I was allowed into the palace and thus took my path through the maze of tapestried halls and corridors, passing into the administrative chambers. When I reached the large hall of writing desks, usually filled with clerks, I drew up short.

The doors to Cecil's double-storeyed office were closed. At the desk outside, where the secretary's secretary usually worked, there was no one. I frowned, biting at my lower lip. I turned on the spot. It was the right time, I knew. Cecil would be in there, expecting me. Shrugging to myself, I moved towards the double doors and put my hand on a polished gold ring. I was considering whether to push or pull when suddenly I was jerked off my feet.

'Who are you?'

I gasped choking. Someone had grabbed me from behind, right there in a usually busy room in the palace of Whitehall! The front of my livery rode up, cutting tight under my ribs; the creature was holding me up by the back of my clothes, as easily as one might lift a doll. I spluttered, coughed, wriggled. 'Lemme go! Lemme go! Help!'

Reason had fled me, sudden fear invading with the sheer abruptness of the attack.

I was thrown to the floor, just as simply as I'd been picked up from it. Rolling, I threw up a forearm defensively, letting my other hand slide to the knife in my boot (I had lied about being unarmed – of course, I had).

My assailant was too quick for me.

I saw him, bathed in the light spilling in from the windows to the outer courtyard: a tall, pale, well-muscled creature with expressionless eyes. A white falling band was just visible peeking out from under a long black coat. So fixed was I on trying to place him – he was new, I decided, unknown to me – I missed his hands flying to my own. Only when pain seared around my wrist did I realise that he'd got hold of me again. My blade bounced noiselessly to the carpet, and one of his huge boots dropped on it.

'Who are you?' he asked again. There was no trace of breathlessness in his voice. It was quite unmoved, as though taking me down had caused no exertion. I, for my part, was quivering like jelly and breathing heavily.

'I am the secretary's man,' I gasped. 'Lord Salisbury. He'll kill you, rogue.'

The giant smiled, showing good teeth. 'You are his noonday visitor?'

'What?'

He dropped suddenly, making me flinch, and swept me up, setting me down again on my feet. 'Didn't mean to be so rough.' I sensed no mirth in his smile. 'Can't be too careful. Not in these times.'

'Who are you?' I asked, brushing down my front without taking my eyes from him.

'His lordship's assured friend. Looking to the earl's security. His personal escort.'

A bodyguard? I thought. Cecil had always had men about him, but no great wolf loping about in his shadow, as far as I'd known. It was, however, probably a good idea. Other high noblemen certainly kept chief men at arms, and Cecil, whom I had known when he'd been a humble knight, had now become one of that mob. 'You might have been a little gentler.'

The man gave me a derisive look, his lips pursing, whitening. 'You might have surrendered your weapon as you'd been told to do. Outside.' He leant down and retrieved my blade. I reached out for it, and he tucked it into his belt. 'No naked blades in his lordship's presence.'

I contemplated saying something, challenging him, but I knew I was in the wrong. And I was not about to admit it. 'What's your name?' I asked.

Rather than answering, he stepped past me, making me jump, and rapped on the door.

At the same time, a number of other men seemingly melted out from behind desks. I turned my head from left to right, backing towards the wall. They each wore shorter black coats than my attacker. These I recognised; they were the rough London men that Cecil paid for dirty work. The coats were the earl's less official livery, granted to the crew of enforcers and bullies who served his secret and often violent proceedings. These, whom I would have thought he kept at arm's length, were now apparently subservient to the great ape who protected him.

'Enter,' said a voice from within. Rich, cultured, smug: I recognised it immediately as my master's.

Pushing the door, I stepped inside. The door jolted shut behind me, pulled by the close-mouthed bodyguard. I slid off my tall black hat, clutching it to my belly in one movement, and opened my mouth. 'Who, my lord, is that great ox–'

Cecil was not alone. He was seated at his broad desk across the room, his elbows resting on it; but facing him was another man in a chair. The latter leaned forward, turning at the waist to regard me. I closed my mouth.

'Come, Ned, come,' said Cecil. I stepped forward, trying to judge the new man's worth. He was dressed all in black. A clerk, perhaps, or lawyer, or justice. Early forties, curled greying hair, and a good short ruff. He was neither handsome nor ugly but had spectacularly dark, lively eyes, which made him lean towards the former. 'Cousin Francis, this is Ned Savage. Well. Does he look familiar?'

The man Francis stared at me for an uncomfortable length of time. And then he turned back to Cecil. The back of his head rose up as his face fell forwards. 'A cruel jest, Cousin Robert. Ay, I see some small resemblance. The late earl was taller.'

They were talking about Essex, I knew, and then I knew who this Francis was. A few years earlier – more than I cared to think about – Sir Francis Bacon, a lawyer and a first cousin to Cecil, had been a great friend and adviser of the doomed earl. People in the streets of London still spat at the name Francis Bacon for turning his coat and helping Essex to the block. It was said that the late queen had detested him, whether due to his betraying Essex, whom she loved, or because in her dotage she had become a tetchy old boot, I couldn't say and hardly cared.

Was this, I wondered, with a sudden jolt of anger, why I had been invited? Had I been dragged all the way up the Thames to let Cecil play a mean trick on a cousin? Perhaps my anger showed on my face, for Cecil tutted. 'You need not look so glum, Ned. Come. Sit by Cousin Francis. We have much to discuss.'

I stepped into the cavernous room. Bookshelves lined the walls, standing alongside portraits of King James and Cecil's father, the old Lord Burghley. I let my feet sink into the lush brown carpet as I moved. Bacon rose a little as I pulled back a stool that sat beside his chair, and I gave him a brief nod.

'Some slight resemblance?' Cecil appeared unwilling to let

his jest die. 'Does he not look like your old friend then, cousin, as I said? The very image?'

I tried to look away from both men. Yet I could see Bacon's eyes, gleaming like onyx, flashing at me. 'No,' he said. 'Have you not heard the ballads? The late earl was nine yards tall and bore himself on legs so stout and wide he could bestride the Straits of Messina.'

Cecil gave a derisive snort. 'Would that his brain had been so well-grown.' He turned his attention to me, and I met his gaze. 'Goodman Verney gave you no trouble?' asked Cecil. He was smiling nastily.

'Who?' I asked.

'My guard.'

'Oh,' I said, flopping down and setting my hat on the table. 'The great monster who devilled me out there.'

'I'm pleased to hear he is doing his job. He was well found, Francis,' said Cecil. Bacon inclined his head, his curls bouncing.

'I regret that in these whispering times we must all have our persons guarded. It did not use to be thus,' said the lawyer.

'Indeed,' said Cecil. 'He is formerly a porter at Gray's Inn. Yes, good Verney has brought some discipline to my men. It is needed now.'

A little silence fell across the room. Bacon shifted in his seat, folding his hands on the desk. Cecil leant forward and poured some wine into silver cups, one for his cousin and one for himself. He offered me nothing. Bacon, pointedly, smiled his thanks before offering his cup to me. I shook my head.

'You sent for me?' I asked, looking at Cecil. The secretary sank back in his seat, one shoulder rising higher than the other, as it usually did.

'I did. First, Ned, tell me. What news in London?' he asked. I sighed, using it to let my eyes slide towards Bacon. 'My cousin is well trusted,' Cecil persisted. 'What news?'

'There is some bruit on both sides of the river. About a woman, a murderess, abroad in London. And at this time, with the two kings meetings, I thought…'

The cousins, I noticed, exchanged a look. What it meant I

couldn't say, but I sat a little straighter. Cecil took a breath. 'For once, your news is stale, Ned. I have heard of this creature, this woman. And I have cause to think it more than mere rumour. It is why Cousin Francis joins us. Tell me, have you ever heard the name "Locusta"?'

I shrugged. 'I don't think so.' I was certain I hadn't. It sounded foreign. 'A Catholic?'

Cecil nodded at Bacon, and the little man licked his lips before speaking. 'Locusta,' he said, 'of Gaul. Her history comes to us from antiquity. And it is a lesson in several arts, she being loose of morals and notorious in –'

'To the point, cousin, before you run out of breath,' said Cecil, drumming his fingers on the table.

Bacon made a little moue. 'Locusta was a poisoner. Her age was that of Nero. You know of Emperor Nero?'

'Of course,' I said.

Bacon nodded. Animation began to come into his words. 'The wicked Agrippina, Nero's mother, hired Locusta to help her poison her husband and make young Nero emperor. Locusta was even then a wicked creature but skilled in the art of murder. During that wicked creature's tyranny over Rome, the woman, it is said, began to enjoy her deeds. To enjoy murder. And Nero saw her skills and, as his mother had done, he hired her when he sought…'

'When he sought his enemies done to death?' I offered.

'Quite so,' smiled Bacon. 'And so, in the annals of the Roman empire, we find a creature unparalleled. A woman who enjoyed murder and became so expert in it that she became an agent-for-hire. A murderer of men and women. An–'

'An assassin,' put in Cecil. He grinned wolfishly as Bacon frowned, apparently cheated of his climax.

'The woman began a school, training agents to administer poison. Or so great Tacitus, Suetonius, and Cassius Dio tell us. Until, of course, the tyrant's reign was ended. With it went Locusta's cruel and most wicked art.'

'What happened to her?' I asked. I was interested now if a little confused.

'She was done to death,' said Cecil. 'As all wicked creatures ought to be.'

'Just so,' said Bacon. 'She went to her death with Nero's other favourites. In her – and there were others, too,' he said, flashing a look towards his cousin, 'other wicked women. Martina, Canidia. The black she-wolves of Rome. In those days of empire … we see in the histories a turn from the honour and high dignity of the past republic and a turn towards vice, cruelty, depravity, and decadence under the emperors.'

'Have a care, Francis,' said Cecil. Warning, sweet and frothy, laced his words.

'I do not speak,' said Bacon, his chin rising as he matched his cousin's glare, 'of our own times. Nor of our sweet emperor of Great Britain.'

'Good. Though, I leave the field to you, good cousin, to discourse on depravity. Yet I own we have she-wolves enough in England. I understand your old friend's sister has returned to town. The Devereux whore. Hoping the Queen will call her, no doubt, the moment her Majesty is churched. And that Spanish wench at the embassy, she is well watched. Martina and Canidia indeed. I must say, cousin, it was wise of you to take a child to wife. There is little cunning or wit in a lass of – what is your good lady – thirteen?' At this, I noticed, redness began to streak across Bacon's cheeks.

I coughed, drawing both men's attention and defusing whatever was building between them. 'Sorry, my Lord. But what does this ancient history, this Locusta, have to do with these times? I mean the rumours I heard – they were nonsense. I didn't hear the name. Only…' I thought back on what Hal had said.

'Yes?' prodded Cecil.

'I heard it said that our woman killer – our assassin – was ancient, immortal. I thought it part of the nonsense. The bruit.'

'Who spoke these words?'

'A drunk fool in the Mermaid Tavern,' I invented. It would have been an easy thing to blame young Hal, to have him taken up, probably, or roughed up and questioned. But I could not.

I think Bacon might have sensed my discomfort. He leapt in. 'I came here to aid my cousin. I have studied those ancient texts.

And I repeat, this historical Locusta was a woman hired – an assassin, not a murderer for her own gain, nor any of her own agency save her enjoyment of the act.' I swallowed not quite following.

'What we do not know,' said Cecil, 'is whether there is truly a new Locusta in our City – an agent working on orders from the great. And if there is, then who sent her. And, naturally, if there is not, then who has begun these rumours. Who has…' He trailed off.

I shook my head as Bacon spoke again. 'Whether there is an assassin abroad or not, it is clearly a person of some wit and learning who has set the news in motion. I daresay this name Locusta is on people's lips – or the tale of a female murderer – without the common people knowing anything of the *Annals* or the *Life of Nero*.'

Cecil pushed back his huge wooden chair and stood. Standing barely made him taller. I half-rose myself, Bacon doing the same, and he swept a dismissive hand downwards, letting us keep our seats. He took one gulp of his wine, before staring awhile into its depths. Setting it down, he turned from us and moved to the fire. He went stiffly, I thought. Recently he had become an old man, spiked and bent, his carriage slow and his manner less humorous. It was stiflingly warm in the office, and yet a fire was burning. He prodded it with a poker, sending the flames leaping. His voice, when he spoke, was nearly lost to the crackling. 'I wish these rumours stopped. This woman found if she exists. And everyone behind the name Locusta dealt with.'

I said nothing, focusing on his hunched little back. 'A heavy blow with blunt tools. My cousin,' said Bacon, his voice loud, 'is a bureaucrat, like myself. He is better at carrying out policy than devising it.'

Cecil wheeled, his eyes flashing. The carpet at his feet bunched up, and his fists with it. I gasped. I had never seen anyone mock the man before, save the king with his hideous mock-jollity. Bacon, however, seemed quite unperturbed and began straightening his cuffs. 'Do becalm yourself, my dear Lord Salisbury. You know that I speak the truth. And in very great fondness. We all bow before your expert handling of this our realm.'

My chin sank into my falling band. I could see my straggling beard spreading out. 'What can I do?'

Cecil limped over to the picture of his father, looked up at it, and then turned. 'Do as was done in my father's time. In your uncle's time, Cousin Francis. Listen. There is some attempt here by the damnable Catholic scum to cause trouble. To breed fear and terror at this time of the meeting between the sovereigns. Mark me; it's the Catholics. They were filth in my father's time, and they are filth today.'

Never had I seen him so animated. Bacon raised a finger. 'You have lists of those with such sympathies from the late great buzz. You might–'

'And my friends will turn their houses round about if need be.'

'Now, cousin, their religion is false,' he said, 'but they are Englishmen and–'

'To Hell with their religion! They threaten the state and its security. I know it. You know it. Cats prowling the middens of London know it.' Cecil thumped on the wall panel, making the old Burghley jump. I had never seen him so angry nor so oddly jittery. He was the kind of man – admirable, in a way – whom I imagined retired at night and rose in the morning with his mind continually running through lists of things to be done and how best to do them. Yet under King James, I knew, any such list might now be unmanageable even by the wonder of all counsellors. The expense our jolly sovereign was said to be running up was the scandal of London and had been for three years. And so, my master had grown short in his temper, quick to anger, making great cares of everything. He had taken now to fixing on certain ideas and pursuing them doggedly: how to make the king loved; how Catholics were undermining him and the government at every turn.

How every man sympathetic to the late Powder Treason must be rooted out and tortured.

'Or perhaps Puritans who wish to disgrace the Catholics still further are behind the murder,' offered Bacon.

'Murder?' I rose from my seat, my hands on the desk. 'What

murder, my lord? What is this?'

Bacon coughed. Cecil padded back to his seat and, after patting the cushion, he sat. 'Ah. Yes. Thank you, cousin,' he said, the sarcasm heavy. 'I was coming to the point. Ned, this Locusta might be dismissed as air, as false news blown up by mischief-makers. Yet she has struck. She has killed already. Or so we think.'

I said nothing, focusing on the polished oak of the desk. Streaks of grey, reflections of Bacon's hair and beard, danced in it. Murder was something I tried not to touch. I was no coroner, no constable. My general rule of thumb was that, when a body appeared, it meant my cue to depart as quickly from the scene as possible. 'Who was killed?'

'We don't know,' said Bacon.

'What?'

'It is true,' put in Cecil. 'A body is being kept at the chapel at Gray's Inn. Sir Francis here has been good enough to allow it lodging there.'

'The chaplain, Mr Sturrock, is a friend,' said Bacon.

'Yes,' said Cecil. 'My men brought me word from the coroner's people when the cry went up about a corpse that did not bear signs of the pest. He was found dead in a tavern in Cheapside. A tavern at which, as we understand, a woman calling herself Locusta lodged. My men bore it through the City.' I nodded. An easy thing, in these times, to move a corpse from place to place. Rather than drawing attention, it would have caused every man and woman in the street to flee. 'That is all. You, Ned, will go there. Today. The tapster should be there – I have had him ordered to attend the place.'

'Am I – to find out who he was, the dead man? Or find her?'

'Both. The corpse was well dressed, as I understand it.'

'Sir Francis,' I said, turning in my seat, 'will you accompany me? To your Inns?'

'Me?' Bacon chuckled. Cecil, I noticed, also made a little snort. 'If I return soon, it shall be to sleep. I am no agent. No searcher of the dead.'

And I am?!

'Oh. The paper, cousin,' added Bacon.

'Yes,' sniffed Cecil. He reached under his desk and drew out a single sheet of old parchment. Holding it between his thumb and forefinger, as though it were dangerous, he dropped it and pushed it towards me. Looking down, I saw that it was a playbill advertising an old performance of *Eastward Hoe* at the Blackfriars theatre. A play, I knew, that had been written by Ben Jonson, a fat, opinionated blusterer who thought himself the premier poet in England.

'Jonson?' I asked.

'This was the only thing found on the dead man. Unless you find anything else,' said Cecil. 'Jonson. The untouchable,' he spat. 'Jonson, who dined with the Powder Plotters and got away without blot or blemish. This play itself was treasonous, banned.' I knew myself that the playwright had done a spell in prison for the drama, before being quietly released.

'Jonson is a fine man,' said Bacon, his voice low. 'I own a little loud, but–'

'It strikes me,' said Cecil, cutting over him, 'that this Locusta and her victim, if all is as it appears, has some connection to the theatricals. And the stage-men are none to be trusted. The King's Man, Shakespeare, he has neighbours in his country who lean mass-ward. And I understand him to be related to Catesby through his mother. His daughter, too, is suspected a papist. This whole strange business has Catholic plotting stirred through it.'

'Have a care,' said Bacon. Cecil flashed him a look, and he held up his palms. 'I mean only that you might set your hounds – I mean no offence, Mr Savage – your men to watch and learn. Do not fill them with pre-judgements. Let them discover the truth of this supposed assassin and her victim without setting out the truth for them to prove. For all we know, some sharp-witted wench has done away with her husband and invented this whole nonsense to evade justice.'

'Said like a lawyer,' scowled the secretary. 'Very pretty indeed. Ned.' My head snapped up. 'Get you to Gray's Inn. See what there is to be seen of this strange corpse and what there is to be heard from the tapster of his murderous guest. Keep your ears trained on the name Locusta. And when the acting companies return from their touring, I bid you keep a sharp watch. I do not trust them. They will be about the two kings much.'

He sat back, staring between his cousin and me, as though trying to remember if there were anything else. 'Yes,' he said at length. 'You have a free hand in this. Pursue any odd or unruly women. And follow up any rumblings from the papists if they should reach you.'

I nodded once, a little hesitantly. 'A murderess,' I said. I looked down at my hands, turning one over in the other. 'I … I do not say I fear any woman. Yet I confess, my lord, that I do prefer to sleep in a whole skin.' I tried to smile.

'You will be rewarded,' said Cecil, frowning. I swallowed. He knew me well enough.

'And do keep your mind open, sir,' said Bacon. Cecil rolled his eyes. 'Here is a riddle near at hand. Get at it by observation. Not by twisting what you see to fit what you have concluded.' He raised a scholarly finger and wagged it, before stifling a yawn. 'Oh, but it is late. Sleep in the noontime, Savage. It is a sure guard against ills.'

'I regret,' cut in the secretary, 'that the court shall be leaving for Theobalds within a week.' His chin rose. I'd never been to Theobalds, never even seen it, but his country palace was said to shame the finest of the king's houses. Rumours of indoor gardens with spurting fountains and ceilings painted with the constellations had long been current in London. With good reason, I thought, that whiskered chin was in the air. 'His Majesty wishes to take his brother-king hunting. Yet if anything should reach you – anything – have it sent to me without delay. In the meanwhile, my men will look to the Catholic rabble.'

'Or me, good cousin,' said Bacon. 'I am, of course, at your service. Mr Savage, you must feel free to call upon me if you cannot reach my esteemed good lord.' He grinned, his bright eyes flashing.

Again, I nodded. Then all of our heads turned at the whisper of the door opening. Verney, his face still an impassive slate, pushed a handsome young man into the room, his lawyer's robes brushed and shining. Light came into Bacon's face, I noticed, and he rose immediately, stepping around his chair and putting his hands out. He moved neatly, primly. 'My dear Roger,' he said.

'One of my cousin's lawyer friends,' said Cecil. Could I detect something in his voice – distaste? Dislike? Bacon ignored it, stepping over to the new man. To my surprise, they embraced. The fellow – Roger – leaned into Bacon's neck, for just a moment too long. 'If you cannot reach me quickly,' said the secretary, still seated, 'indeed, you might reach Cousin Francis. As you can see, you and he have much in common.' I felt scorn wash through the room and shrank a little. Cecil knew well enough about my tastes.

Bacon and his friend drew apart, their eyes still locked on each other, caressing one another. 'Ah, Cousin Robert. You have your guards of the body. And I have mine.'

Oh, I thought, my chin sinking again into my collar.

I fiddled with my hat, eager to be away from Cecil. And eager, I admit, to discover whether there was indeed a woman murdering anonymous men in the City and leaving playbills in their pockets.

4

People say that London stinks in the high summer, and they're right, it does. Yet I rather like it: sun-baked stone and overripe fish; hot spices drifting from the foreigners' quarters and stalls, and flowers gathered and sold from great open carts and boxes. There's always a searing heat in the air, and if you close your eyes, you might be in some great eastern City rather than a place that, in the less odorous winter months, smells wet and stale, like boots left out in the rain too long. Even the Thames reeks, to my nostrils, a good deal more pleasantly in summer, because I do so dearly love the summer.

I hopped a wherry for only a short trip downstream – and you can bet I only paid half fare – debarking at Temple Stairs. These allowed me to wander amongst the empty townhouses of the Strand, whose occupants had either flocked to live at court or else decamped to their country estates to avoid the plague. It was a tough choice for courtiers; I suspected: stay safe or stay relevant. At any rate, no doubt most of them would be taking the famous Theobalds Road out of London and direct to my lord secretary's house soon enough. I looked up as I kicked my way along the paved and sanded street, marvelling as I always did at the cupolas and turrets, the mass of shimmering, diamond-paned windows, the carved arms. Even deserted, the Strand's collection of palaces – for that is what they were – always gave me a stab of envy: a desire to carry one somehow away with me and put it behind bars, lock it up and own it.

Crossing into Fleet Street and left up Fetter Lane, I passed between less opulent but still comfortable houses: those of wealthy merchants, solicitors, and justices. Here, an unpleasant whiff of reality made itself sting. The street became busier, for one thing, and I found myself having to weave my way around unfortunates carrying plague wands. For another, I bypassed too many doors with painted crosses daubed across them. It was a relief, indeed, to reach the gentle slope of Holborn. Sticking to the middle of the road, just shy of the central sewer gutter, I made my way, wondering idly which was the house that David's sister, my little red-headed mouse, Faith, lived in. She and Hopgood had invited me many times to eat with them there, and for some reason, I had always found an excuse not to go.

Who needs to be reminded of how shabby and lonely their own home is?

Ahead, I could see the crumbling grey hulk of the old City toll gate. It was well guarded, I noticed, still. It seemed that every gate in and around London had at least one armed man, whether to assess incoming countryfolk for signs of plague or bags of gunpowder I didn't know. At any rate, I turned shy of it and made my way up the road on which Bacon's Inns of Court stood.

Gray's Inn rose on my left, unmistakable, an elegant palatial complex of buildings mostly in neat red brick. I had often wondered why the Inns were quite so rich in their dressing; it seemed, to me, a waste to turn such fine places over to roistering, lazy students, most of whom had no intention of ever thinking about the bar, far less being called to it. However, I knew the answer well enough. Most of the dunder-pates were useless second and third sons or bastards. Their parents would happily pay £40 a year to palm them off on a gaggle of tutors and masters, in the vain hopes, perhaps, that they might make a career or some useful court contacts. Mostly, I knew from experience, the student lawyers simply took advantage of being so close to the City to drink in taverns, gamble in gaming houses, watch plays, and turn poor whores across the river and more discreet ones this side of it.

Thankfully, there were few student lawyers about. Trinity Term was over, and Michaelmas not yet began. Most of the wastrels would have sloped back to the plague-free safety of their parents' country mansions or been decomposing in Southwark stews. Only those who were trouble at home would remain in their digs.

Decomposing.

I passed under the archway of the gate and looked around. On either side of the gravel path, buildings stood, gracefully watching like wise old elders. The sounds of those troublesome students laughing and kicking balls around drifted from somewhere ahead, carried on a cloud of their tobacco smoke. The wall immediately on my left, I could tell, belonged to the chapel, its sloping slate roof and small crown steeple giving it away. I followed the pale red walls until I found the doors and, hopping up the steps and without knocking, I pushed them open.

I was in a small chamber, the bulk of the building hidden to my left. Two men were talking, one louder than the other. Both ceased when I entered, until the more boisterous barked, 'here he is. Why it's Neddy Savage!'

'Good day, Rooks,' I smiled. Two things occurred to me at once. The innkeeper in whose place the body had been found was a friend – or at least a tapster I knew – and that inn was the Bull Head on Cheapside.

'Is it Savage the man you was waiting for?' asked Rooks.

I turned to the other man: a spare, unsmiling creature in clerical black. I slid off my hat and made a bow, the better to examine him. This was awkward. Rooks knew me, but he had no idea that I was anything other than a colourful man connected with the Revels Office and the players. And I wished him to know no more than that. I looked up, locking eyes with the chaplain, attempting to communicate as much as I could before speaking.

What was his name?

'Mr Sturrock.' Yes, that was the name Bacon had given me. The fellow inclined his head in my direction. 'Mr Sturrock is an old friend of mine, Goodman Rooks. He has told me about the unfortunate in your tavern and would have me help find his family.'

'Eh? You ain't no constable, Savage, nor nothing like that. You're having me on.'

Damn him.

'No, no. Yet with the plague in town- so many men occupied. Mr Sturrock said that he thought the man might have been connected with the Revels Office.' I was talking nonsense, and I knew it.

The playbill!

'I understand the fellow was found with a bill in his pocket advertising a play. Well, you know me, Rooks, a master of the theatrical arts. I know every player and playgoer from the Bull Head to the Blackfriars.' I forced jollity into my voice, and when I'd finished speaking, I held my breath.

Mercifully, Rooks seemed satisfied. He gave a broad, gap-toothed grin. 'Say n' more, young fellow-my-lad, say n' more. But I don't know why I'm here. Constable just ordered me be here for two of the clock. I dunno wherefore.'

I looked at Sturrock again. The man had an unsettling, sharp-eyed gaze. 'I'll speak with you in a moment, Goodman Rooks. Just wait here. My friend here will just let me see if I know the poor fellow you found.' I could see that Sturrock bristled at being called my friend, and so I put my hat back on. 'Well, come on, my dear friend. Do lead the way.'

Sturrock drew away from Rooks, his chin high, and sailed towards another door. He pushed it open and disappeared inside and, without another look at the tapster, I followed.

The nave of the chapel – I think one calls it the nave; I believe the little entrance chamber I had left was the narthex, but from then on I get lost in naves and transepts and apses: a chapel's a bloody chapel – was an open room with whitewashed walls. It smelt faintly sweet, like summer flowers. The ceiling overhead was crisscrossed with plain oak beams; the only nod to colour and cheer, was the red carpet underfoot. Halfway down the aisle – if one calls it an aisle – Mr Sturrock drew up and turned to me in profile.

'That man,' he said, his voice high and imperious, 'is not, I trust, the keeper of a bawdy house? I tried to divine that of him and met nothing but disporting.'

'The Bull Head Inn?' I laughed, and I could see his lip curl. 'It's as old as the hills, but you'll not get yourself a whore there.'

He wheeled. 'How dare you, sir. I have done my good friend the learned counsel Sir Francis a favour in this-this shameful matter of a corpse. I wish not to be spoken to thusly.'

I held up my hands. 'I meant no offence,' I lied. I truly disliked preachers of any stripe. 'Pray, continue. If I must look upon this corpse, I must.'

Without a word of acknowledgement, Sturrock strode on, his

black robes billowing. He made a sharp right, making for an old door sunk into the plaster wall. I followed, ignoring the pulpit – the stage, I always thought, for the world's most boring players to deliver the world's dullest soliloquies.

The tiny, vault-like room was low ceilinged, so that we both had to duck, him more than me. I did it by instinct; however, my attention fell and locked immediately on the table, on which lay the body, covered with a grey cloth but unmistakable. 'What do you hope to find?' asked Sturrock, almost making me jump.

'I …' had no idea. I looked at him and saw that, though I suspected he would never admit it, he was curious. I shrugged, before stepping forward and pulling back the cloth, throwing it over and away from me. Its weight dragged it to the floor on the other side of the table. No rotten smell rose, save a slight subtle sourness. And the musty smell of cloth, of leather.

His clothes!

I have always been a great lover of clothes and have quite a collection myself. Thus, my attention fell on the cut of the fellow's doublet. The buttons were good metal – not silver, but polished. I reached out and touched the thing, unable to resist. Velvet. I traced the circular line of a button and then hooked my fingers under the opening. Sarcenet lining.

I *want this!*

The breeches, too, were well padded with bombast, though they had been badly put on. The hose, even worse, were not tied to the points: he might have put them on blind, hoping the doublet would hold everything at one end and the shoes at the other. And good shoes they were too, leather with brass buckles. I moved down to the end of the table and looked at them. I could wear these, I thought; if this man were a cobbler, I could buy them. Then it struck me why: they were unworn. The soles were unscuffed, unmarked, lacking any of the annoying little pieces of grit and dirt that dug themselves into my own shoes and always refused to be teased out.

Strange, strange, strange.

I returned, unwillingly, to the middle of the table and glanced down at his head. His ruff, equally unblemished, was a little limp and squashed, sad looking. That might have happened if he were brought here on a covered litter, I supposed. I blinked, keeping my eyes closed for a moment, before turning my gaze to his face.

And I drew back in revulsion.

He was unmarked – unbloodied – he had not been beaten and mauled such as to turn one's stomach. No; rather, he was just as ugly as sin itself. His age, were I to guess, would have been past seventy. His cheeks were sunken, the cheekbones almost poking through the parchment of his skin.

A filthy old stinkard dressed up to look rich. Here, I'm rather good at this!

I did not draw too close, but I thought I could see dirt in the map of creases that lined the face. His hair was thin, sprouting mostly above – and out of – his ears, and he had an unruly thatch of beard. I made to lean a little over it.

'Don't!'

This time, Sturrock's bark did make me jump. 'What?!'

'I think … the poor fellow came with lice. I suspect they lodged in his beard.' The chaplain, I noticed, was pressed against the wall, as far away from the corpse as the small room allowed. I drew back a little myself. Rather than get too close to a lice-ridden beard, I looked at his hand without touching it. Broken nails were caked in filth. I shook my head, chewing on my lip.

'Well? Have you found anything? A cause of his death?'

'No, I … there is nothing in his pockets?'

'I have not looked. Nor touched him. I assumed Sir Francis's friends had done that.'

I scowled to myself. Grimacing, I forced myself to do a cursory search, hoping, at the least, that I might find a little perquisite: a ring or a miniature or something. I knew, though, that it would be hopeless. When I had finished my unwholesome pawing, I went around the table and lifted the cloth, covering him again.

'I am done,' I announced.

'And the corpse? Has Sir Francis told you what to do with it?'

'Mm. Have it buried.' I was on shaky ground here, I knew. 'Pauper's grave. St Andrew Holborn is the local parish, isn't it?'

I knew, because that, much to my well-expressed chagrin, was where Faith would be getting married.

St Bride's not good enough for her Majesty.

'It is.'

'Charge the expense to Sir Francis. The winding-sheet, and so on. Oh, and the clothing is to be laundered – there are still laundresses here?' He gave a nod. 'Mm. Laundered and sent to Mr Edward Savage of Shoe Lane. You have that?' Another nod. 'Now, I think, I shall speak to Mr Rooks.'

'I shall not join you. I shall lock this poor creature up and send word of what is to be done. After I check your instructions with Sir Francis.' He smiled with thin lips.

'By all means. Let the man moulder in this heat until you have checked,' I said. But my heart fluttered. Bacon surely lived nearby. It would hardly take long for Sturrock to speak with his friend and to learn that I was a grasping liar. I turned on my heel without another word and strode from the room, out into the nave, and down the aisle. I paused a moment before going back out into the narthex – just long enough to sneak a glance to make sure Sturrock wasn't watching me, and to transfer the fistful of gleaming buttons I'd torn from the dead man's doublet to the pocket at my belt. To hell with the chaplain. Whether I got the clothes or not, I'd got what I'd really wanted.

Outside, Rooks eased himself from the wall against which he'd been leaning. 'Neddy!' he boomed.

'Rooks. How goes it?'

'Well enough, my friend, well enough. Here, this ain't half a strange business, this. What's it all about?'

'Can't say,' I said, smiling, affecting an air of mystery I felt well enough. 'Poor old fellow.'

'It ain't plague, is it? Nor poison? He didn't have no plague marks on him. When he was dead, I mean, none of them botches. And he didn't come in afore he were dead, nor would I have let him in if he were rank with the pest.'

'What?'

'I don't let no one in with the sickness, rich-dressed nor poor, Neddy.'

'No, I – what do you mean, he didn't come in before he was

dead?'

'Just what I said. Didn't see him. It's a bit of mischief, all of this, a bit strange if you ask me. It's that woman what started it. She must have been a whore, pleasured him to death. I won't have none of that lark in my place; you know that. A bad business, if you ask me.'

I am asking you!

I shook my head, crossing my arms. Then I relaxed them, putting a hand out to his shoulder. He smiled, his few teeth showing in his broadcloth-sack of a head. 'It might be a fine thing, Rooks if you told me what started this whole business. From the beginning. As you recall it.'

Rooks removed his cap, scratching behind an ear. 'Well … well … like I told them men who come for the body – a hard lot, them.' He dropped his voice. 'Salisbury's men, I heard.' I said nothing but affected a wide-eyed look. 'This servant – a page, you know the like – he comes the other day. Nose in the air, you know?' I nodded as he demonstrated, turning his pulpy nose to the roof beams. '"My mistress commands you lodge her this night," says he. And I says, "and who is your mistress, lad?" and he says, "her name be Locusta of Rome". And I thinks, foreign trash. But them lot have the money, don't they? You don't get stiffed by foreign rich. But I don't say that, of course. I says, "then a room she shall have". And off he goes.

'And then at night – this was two or three nights ago now – in she comes. And a right grand piece she is.'

'Describe her,' I said. And then, when I noticed the frown lines begin to furrow across his brow, I added, 'please, what did she look like?'

'Well,' he said. Another scratch. 'About middling height. Oh, but right richly dressed. Like an Italian, was my thought at the time. But it might have been Spanish. Or French. I dunno,' he shrugged, giving me a man-to-man look. 'Women's fashions. Always changing, ain't they?'

'Her face,' I said. 'What did she look like?' I contemplated asking him if she resembled anyone famous, as I'd always found this the best way of describing people myself – he looked a little like Lord Salisbury; he had the king's nose. Yet I knew from experience that it didn't work with women. Everyone said the same thing: she looked like the queen. It didn't even matter who the queen was: she always looked like the queen. 'Pretty, ugly, black-headed, yellow? Old, young?'

'Well, Neddy, she was veiled.'

Bollocks!

'Not like a papist veil, mind you. Yet,' he went on, 'I did get a glimpse of her without it. When she went up to her room.' I held my breath, and he looked through me, into, I hoped, the past. 'Right pretty, she was. Reddish hair. Brown or red. Is there a colour in between them?'

'Russet?' I ventured.

He worked his jaw a second, his face crinkling. 'Ay, sounds about right.' He tried out the word. 'Russet. All little rings, curled like. I'd say about … I don't know. Under twenty. Not much under. Maybe over, but not by much.' I fought the urge to shake him. 'Hard to tell with the paint they wear these days, them apple cheeks. Pale, she was. But oh, carried herself like a lady born, right enough. And up she went to her lodgings, fellers whistling at her. A right crowd we had in, you know – since the news of that Dutch king on his way.' I didn't correct him. 'And she just sails past them, this Lady Locusta, quite the thing. I followed her up, showed her the room. And she lifted her veil and went on in.'

'And then what happened?'

He didn't answer at once, apparently gathering his thoughts into something coherent. 'So in the morning, I takes her up a little breakfast. Just some bread and a spoon of honey.'

'She asked for this?'

'No. Didn't hear a dickie-bird from her. Nor see her. Just her servant scurrying up and down. But, I thought to meself, she's a lady. And ladies likes their little comforts and such. So I takes up her breakfast and knocks on her door. No answer. And I thinks to meself; maybe ladies sleep in. So, I set down the tray and go back down. Well, the morning wears on, and I still hear nothing. Ups I go again and knock again. Harder, you know? And nothing. So I puts me ear to the door and have a listen. Wouldn't do that, you know, in the usual way of things. No sound. Not nothing. And I thinks, "leave it, Lancelot Rooks". It was the wife, Ned, that bid me bang down the door. Went downstairs and the wife says to me, she says, "is Lady Muck still abed?" and I says, "yes, sweet", and she says, "well get you up there and bid her rise. The lady had the room for the night". And so up I goes and gives a warning and kicks at the door. And open it flies. And then I finds me that poor bastard, dead as a doornail.'

'And the wench and her slave?'

'Nothing. No sign of either one. The window – that window opens onto the yard at the back – flung wide. It's but a short hop down. Easier if they'd used a rope or one helped the other. Both rogues gone and leaving that sod dead on the bed.'

'The man – the dead man – did you not see him come into the place?'

Rooks frowned, folding his arms over his broad chest. 'No, and that's the strangeness. Didn't see no rich old feller come in. You notice that kind of thing, you know? Feller comes in dressed up all in fancy silks and buckled shoes – you notice, and you think, "there's a man with money to buy the good stuff, the wines out of Italy we keep by special". But no. And I asked, Neddy – I did ask a few folks who stop by regular. None remember seeing a rich old man. Just the usual drift of trash like us.' He smiled, and then he covered his mouth. 'I shouldn't laugh. It ain't right.'

'And this is all?'

'Ay, all. Well, until I put out the word we had a dead man, then I couldn't get anyone to come in. Didn't go near the corpse myself, nor the wife. I just called out into the streets, and the constables come, and then them men in the black coats, and tell them as I told you, more or less, and the fellow is covered over and put on a board and carried off. And then I get assured it wasn't no plague – there weren't any marks – and to open as usual and come here at two of the clock. And then you appear.' Suspicion burbled under his natural good humour, I thought.

I shrugged. Two killers, I thought: a woman of substance with at least one servant to aid her. And one servant seldom satisfied a wealthy woman, any more than it did a rich man. I could see, also, how a feeble old creature might have been drawn in, lured upstairs unnoticed amongst a crowd of his fellow poor, and dressed up either before or after he was killed. But why he was killed, and how, I had no idea. I was no physician. There were no marks of violence that I could see.

An announcement. Locusta is truly in town.

I shivered. A woman who killed for sport and at command. An educated, evil woman with money at her fingertips. I felt my insides shrivel. An agent working on orders from the great, Cecil and Bacon had said. And if I knew one thing about the great, it was that they preferred to kill one another, whether by poison, the axe, or the paid assassin. The old vagrant dressed up to counterfeit the rich might have been the first course, a little sugared and decorated subtlety to whet the appetite for the boiled and roasted meats to come. A wealthy woman, to be sure, would know her way around a menu.

'Did she speak to you at all?' I asked. 'This great lady.'

'Just a gracious "thank you" and "I bid you goodnight".'

'And her accent – it was Italian, Roman?'

'Ay, it was that. Well, it was an accent, anyway. I presume it were Italian. Because of the "of Rome", you know. It was an accent,' he repeated. 'I've heard them all. I've heard it before. Just couldn't say where from. Some foreign dump, though.' He coughed, before saying, 'I thank you, Goodman … I bid you goodnight' in an approximation of Roman by way of Muscovy and Aleppo. I felt my lips tauten over my teeth, laughter and annoyance fighting for the sovereignty of my face.

Before I could speak, the door behind me banged open and closed as Sturrock joined us. 'If there will be nothing else, I should like to lock up the chapel. To deter thieves.' He gave both us a long look. I sensed Rooks stiffening beside me, but he said nothing.

'We thank you, then,' I said, giving the shortest bow I could manage. 'And bid you a good day.' I turned and held the outer door open for the tapster, who lurched through it. And then I looked over my shoulder. 'Now if it's whores you seek, you've to go south of the river. Must make a good wage here –the Holland's Leaguer has all kinds.' I skipped out on a wave of his sputtering protests, not bothering to close the door.

I walked with Rooks back down into the City but kept the conversation light, of no consequence, of cheap drink and Danish kings and the upswing in business with the theatres closed and no one going to Southwark. It seemed that in his innyard, amateur players would recite lines they could remember from the proper playhouses: drinkers came to hear their fellow drunks spit out mangled lines from Thomas Kyd. And what about this new flag? Is the new king against St George? How comes it then that a man can be born and raised English as they come and now set to die British, heh? And why does the great pest always come in summer – what is it about summer airs – does it come from those trashy foreign countries where it's always hot?

I let him rabbit on, hoping that his stream of chatter would bury any suspicions he had about my role in the day's grisly affair.

Besides, my mind was turning and turning on the sordid topic of wicked women.

We have she-wolves enough in England.

I already had an idea of whom I should have to approach and was toying with the means of doing it.

5

I had stalked my prey for days, enjoying the excuse to be from home, which was being invaded daily by two interlopers: Nicholas Hopgood, brought by Faith, and Hal Berridge, brought by David.

That morning, all of them had been crowded into my tiny parlour room, the boys seated on David's bed acting out parts from some trash called *Abuses*, and the lovestruck couple at my table, discussing wedding plans. 'It would be a good thing to have flowers,' Faith had insisted. 'In a crown.'

'Then flowers you shall have,' Hopgood had simpered.

'Cuckoo flowers and honeysuckle,' was her response. 'If we can find someone to bind them.'

'I thought marybuds and primroses, sweeting' he'd suggested, putting up a hand to touch her hair, which shone like copper in the light coming in through the open shutter.

'Why not daisies,' I'd said. 'And oxslip? That way neither of you will get what you truly wish, and you can each quietly resent the other. Just like a real wedded couple.'

Then I had slipped out, eager to be gone before anyone could question where and why I'd taken to spending my mornings and much of the afternoons dressed in sombre, patched clothing and with uncombed hair and dirty hands. My attire had raised eyebrows in the Revels Office, which I'd had to attend just to keep up appearances.

'What are you about, Savage? You look like a vagabond. And where is your livery?' Sir Edmund Tilney himself had asked. An ancient fellow with a long white beard, it seemed to me that he resented the new king. During the late queen's reign, he had seldom bothered coming to Revels in person, leaving the plays to be read, censored, and approved by those of us on his staff. Now, under King James, he had to make an impression – and look like he was fit for office – all over again. I had found him seated at his richly appointed desk, which was weighted down with curled and yellowing pages. Distaste and something like surprise narrowed his watery, red-veined eyes. 'No. Never mind. The players should return at the end of the month. I want their plays, Savage.' His bony finger tapped the desk, as though willing new pages to fall from Heaven. 'Some things that his Majesty and the queen have not seen. What was that old one about the Danish court?'

'*Hamlet*, sir?'

'Yes, that. The Danish king should like it. Bring me that.' I wondered if the old man had forgotten that the play depicted the murder of two Danish kings and a Danish prince. 'And whatever else the King's Men have that is new, when the blasted runagates deign to return to London. And all must be purged of bad language.' I'd bowed before leaving. New legislation had been brought in earlier in the year which banned profanity on the stage. The King's Men, I knew, had already been going back through their old works, assiduously scoring out and replacing all the "zounds" and "by God's". 'Heaven help us, all I have thus far is *Abuses*. *Abuses*! And with such entertainments to be staged. The like never seen before in the late queen's time. Go, Savage, and return when you have found me something to be played and the men who are to play it. Something clean. Go! And be suitably attired when you come here next.'

I had left the doddering Sir Edmund to his hot panic, and departed the office in Clerkenwell, as I'd departed my house: with a far more important and pressing matter on my mind. It did not involve scouring the streets of London for entertainments, but it did involve scouring those streets.

My mark was abroad, as she always was. I suspected she rose at dawn and descended into the City from where she lodged near the Barbican. I had found her, this time, outside St Paul's, where the poor men congregated to beg work. Every day she came here, after her tour through the Moorgate, Lothbury, Poultry, and along Cheapside.

She was not a young woman, and this I cursed, for I suspected that no amount of makeup could make an old dame pass for twenty. Yet she was attractive enough; I supposed if one liked women. She moved with a grace that spoke of noble breeding, her back straight, and her steps measured. She did not dress in rich clothing, to be sure, but clothing could be put on and off, as well I knew. Her favoured attire was a black gown and, to cover her hair – whether it was russet or not I had no idea – she wore a strange white hood and collar that made a snowy frame for her face.

Her name was Luisa, and she was a Spaniard.

That Spanish wench at the embassy.

This I knew because, as Cecil had said, the woman was well watched. In fact, on the first day I had taken myself up to the Barbican, beyond the City walls, to the neat, thatch-roofed building which housed the embassy, I had found one of the secretary's black-coats standing in a doorway opposite, staring up at it. I had introduced myself as '710', and the fellow had nodded. 'I'll be following one of the women who live here. I might make friends with her. Under false papist colours.'

He'd given me a long look before nodding. 'Right, mate. The wench goes out every morning. Collects strays. Name of Luisa de Cara- Carva … Mendoza – and some other foreign shit I can't say. She wanders the City. You'll find her.' He had described exactly the strange outfit I'd since found myself looking at from afar.

And which, now, I approached through the throng of St Paul's churchyard.

I fell, coughing, only a few yards from her. I had seen her tend to the sick before and prayed silently that it would work.

It did.

'Me poor man,' she said. Her accent was thick, like a jumble of belled instruments. Heavy on the tongue, I thought, with the syllables tumbling and tinkling over one another. The r became a rolling thing in itself: 'Me poorrrrra men.' Spanish, of course. It bore no relation to the accent Rooks had attempted in imitation of the Lady Locusta, but that meant nothing. 'Please to stand, let me help you.'

I allowed the woman – Luisa – to help me up, and I looked into her face. Clear blue eyes shone at me. Yes, I thought; her face was surprisingly unlined, the wrinkles thin and faint. Perhaps Rooks' eyes weren't the best – one never could tell whether to rely on a man's eyesight.

'You are gracious, madam.' I coughed again. There was, poking out from beneath the ruffle of white around her neck and breast, the foot of a piece of wood. A crucifix, I thought. She went about her business in the City with a papist idol hidden on her person – and not even hidden well. I stared at it and allowed my eyes to widen. She seemed to see this and drew back, her little white hands flying up to pull down the cloth.

'Madam,' I whispered, before casting a glance around the churchyard. It was the usual scene. Merchants, mainly booksellers, had set up stalls, and folk were standing around them, chatting in groups. City wives in tall black hats, some with great plumes of feathers, gossiped behind their vizards whilst their maids stood behind them, looking tired, hot, and bored, their laden baskets making them droop. Little boys darted between the groups, most of them filthy and probably on the hunt for low-hanging purses. Cries of 'will you buy?' and 'who will buy?' were suddenly drowned out by the church's bells, which were followed by similar sounds ringing out from all around us. Satisfied that we weren't being watched, I gave myself a discreet sign of the cross.

Luisa stood stock-still regarding me. 'Gloria a Dios,' she breathed. 'A Catholic.'

I gave a slight, but I hoped meaningful, incline of my head. She put out her hands to me, and I took them, squeezing. 'I seek comfort.' I had hoped to manage a single, crystal tear, but my eyes wouldn't accommodate.

'I … understand,' she said slowly, as though with difficulty.

'Might I speak privily with you? It is not safe here.'

'Si. Yes. This I would like. But later. I have work.'

Damn, I thought. And then, on the back of it, I realised that this might be a blessing. I wanted to get into that embassy, and yet, if I had leave now to pursue a friendship with her, I might observe her a little more easily. Hitherto, I had seen her wander the streets like a lost soul, speaking to vagabonds who lurked in alleys, strolling into companies of derelicts as though she had no fear. She would purchase food from vendors and pass it out, and here, at St Paul's, she would distribute small amounts of money to the men who cried, 'I am well enough and young.

Who will give me work? Fences built! Roofs mended!'. Never, from what I had seen – and I'd spoken to some of the men after she'd gone – did she press religion. And never did I see her meet with anyone who might have been in on a dangerous enterprise. If this woman was Locusta, or in league with her, she planned her murders in the safety of the Spanish embassy.

'My name is Ambrose.'

Luisa slipped her hands from mine, smiling. 'You come. You follow. You are welcome. Later.'

I nodded as she moved away into the crowd, her fingers now busy at the purse hanging from a string tied around her shapeless waist. She slipped out a coin, and immediately her lower half was lost as some of the urchin boys surrounded her. This, I knew as well as they did, was her custom. She handed out coins as though she were an old queen of legend, speaking gently as she did so. I could not catch her words, but she touched the little brats, cupping faces and laughing, ruffling hair. And the boys – foul-mouthed little wastes of skin, as far as I was concerned, such as one found lurking everywhere in the City – became children again, as though she was their mother.

This, I had always heard, was what the papists did to win foolish hearts and to buy their way into paradise. They believed that by giving away a little of what they had on earth, they could purchase a place in Heaven: as though, at the end of days, God would be sitting in His accounts office and saying, 'this one has given £400 in his last year and died with £1000. A two-chambered cloud for him. And this woman gave two shillings a week out of her weekly half-crown wage. The better part! A celestial great hall for her!'

Stupid Spanish cow, I thought. God weighed sins and souls, not charity. That money would be spent within minutes, lost forever. And she would win no converts amongst lads too stupid to know the difference between holy water and piss. If her game was the conversion of English souls, she was betting on the wrong ones.

I remained at a distance as she moved right up to the doorway of the church, where an old woman was sprawled. Luisa bent to her, before stepping away and purchasing a ladle of something from a vendor, returning with it and feeding the old crone. It was all, I thought, such a performance, such a damned pious display. Whilst she was busy, I moved into the crowd and, thrusting my hand out, gripped one of the boy's by the collar. He twisted and spat, kicking at my shins.

'Peace, lad,' I hissed. 'There's another penny in it if you cease. If you stop.' Pain seared in my ankle. 'Stop it, you little shit!'

The word finally seemed to sink in. 'What? I didn't do nothing!'

'That woman who gave you a penny. You know her? She has spoken with you?'

'Mama Lucy. She gave it me. I didn't steal it.'

I rolled my eyes, dragging him closer. 'Has she ever employed one of you lads in a job of work? Paid you to work for her?'

'No! No. Let me go.'

'I told you,' I said, looking up and over the rising and falling tide of heads, hats, and feathers towards the porch, where Luisa was still bent away from me, 'I will pay you. Has she taken up a lad as a servant? Dressed him like a page and had him play-act for her?'

'No! Mama Lucy don't ever ask nothing. Just gives us things. And says good times will come. Give me my penny and let me go.'

Mama Lucy!

Why do the rich, I wondered, cry upon sugar; here was sickly sweetness enough.

Frowning, I dug with my free hand for a penny and, loathing the act; I passed it to him. He grasped it in one dirt-caked, broken-nailed fist. And then, like lightning, that fist jabbed out, catching me under the ribs. I doubled, winded, sucking at the air.

Laughing, the boy was gone before I could strike back, lost in the forest of people. There was no hope of chasing him and nor did I mean to. Instead, I sipped at the hot air, getting my breath back, and refocussing my attention on the pious old maid who had finished with the fallen crone and was now wending her way back through the crowds. She did not acknowledge me, but continued, quite unruffled, as though I'd not spoken with her.

Clever.

The morning wore on, hot and sweaty, and I trailed Luisa Something Mendoza throughout it. The sun became unrelenting, though it did not seem to speed her passage. As I frequently stopped to cuff my brow and hide in the shade of eaves and alleys, she swanned on, refusing to rest, through swarms of flies buzzing around the indigent beggars who sought crumbs in Bread Street, back up to Cheapside and around the taverns, outside which more of the poor congregated in the hope of being bought a little ale. I cursed her industry, hopping over a man's rake as it darted in and out, clearing rubbish and flattening gravel.

The great thoroughfare was so busy I worried I might lose her, and so I stuck close to the bobbing black-and-white back. Everywhere there were people, chief amongst them workmen setting up railings and measuring out lengths of carpet, right there in the street. The sounds of hammering and banging echoed up and down. I had seen the like before when the king's triumphal entry was being got up. Now, it seemed, a similar show was being put on for his brother-in-law of Denmark. Near the Great Conduit, opposite the mercers' chapel, a great banner hung above the street, fixed to buildings on either side. On it were the words, 'WELCOME AND WELCOME FTILL FURTHER'. Despite the frenzied activity, my quarry – now my friend, or so I hoped she thought – went about her day, standing serenely by to let perspiring carters drive by, the carts behind them filled not with plague dead, but huge lengths of wood and rolls of canvas.

I thought I might have found her up to something when she turned up Wood Street – for here lay fine houses and businesses, where she might meet some wealthy criminal contact – but no luck. I was mightily relieved that she was simply making for the break in the City wall that led into the tangled streets of the Barbican.

As I followed Luisa to her home, I satisfied myself that if she were Locusta – or in league with the mysterious assassin – then she did not meet her partners in crime out on her morning jaunts.

From the few days I'd spent observing her, it appeared that she used these simply to play the role of the wandering friaress (I should say nun, but I had never seen a nun and assumed that they never left their convents). That must have been her cover, as my own was working for the Revels Office. Her true work, her secret work, would have been conducted indoors, hidden, of course, it would.

She paused briefly at the doorway to the house – a large two-storey affair, whitewashed, pretty – before the door opened and she was admitted. I stood, kicking at the ground outside, for a while. It was a broad street, fit enough for carts, and I should have been easily seen going in. Cecil's man – or one very similar to him – would be watching, undoubtedly, whether from a position on the street or from the window of another house. I did not look for him, nor attempt any signal; it occurred to me that the Spaniards might also have someone peeping out at me from a crack in a shutter above.

Thus, I was caught, between England and Spain, Protestant and Catholic, home and abroad. Someone had told me once that embassies were truly considered foreign soil, though I doubted that was true. Nevertheless, I was undoubtedly entering onto someone else's patch. In my head, I turned words over, trying out the accent I intended to use when required to speak at length, sounding out my false name. When I was ready, I went to the door of the house and rapped three times.

It opened immediately.

This servant – a page, you know the like.

It was a boy of about seventeen or eighteen, ripe for playing a page. Sallow. A little darkness around his upper lip and jaw which might one day graduate to a beard and moustaches. He regarded me through golden-brown eyes but said nothing.

'I am welcome,' I said, trying out my Scotch accent. 'Ambrose Adamson. At the invite of Mama Lucy.'

He drew out my discomfort, allowing no expression to pass his face. He did not turn to speak to anyone but continued staring at me. And then, at length, he pushed open the door. I stepped in, as he looked out over my shoulder, scanning the street, before pulling it closed.

The entrance hall to the embassy was wide and well-appointed, ending in a staircase. On the walls hung tapestries displaying the arms of Spain, every one the same. I stopped in the centre of the space. It was cool, despite the wall hangings and the carpet. I supposed that every shutter in the house was closed against the summer heat; they would be expert in keeping a cool house, being Spanish.

'There.'

I turned. The lad, in his good doublet and breeches, was pointing at a door set between two of the tapestries, on the right side of the hall. It was one of several – the first, in fact. 'You go,' he said. 'Inside. She comes.'

I hesitated.

Get out. Now!

'Aye,' I said, ignoring that little voice of instinct which dried my throat, rushed in my ears, and raised the hair on my forearms. My hat was already in my hands. I stepped across the hall and put my hand out the brass ring, keeping my ears sharp. No sound inside. No sound of anyone joining the boy at my back. Safe.

You hope.

I pushed open the door. The chamber was gloomy, and I squinted, stepping over the threshold. It smelt musty. A faint square of light marked out the cracks in the shutter. Very close, I thought – barely a hop from the threshold. It was a closet, I realised.

And it was the last thing I saw. Dull pain thumped into my lower back, and I instantly went to my knees, the bare black floor flying up to my face. Sharper stabbing pains jolted up each knee.

'Uuurrghh–'

My cry was cut off as blackness eclipsed me.

6

The lady straightened her gloves and pulled her mask a little more tightly about her lower face. It was difficult to keep the thing straight when walking, hard to feel where it was secured to the tall black hat perched on the mass of her hair. She had only just had time to return to her new lodgings to change before going out again in search of her prey.

And she had found him easily enough.

The fellow who had been pointed out to her was another vagabond, this one tall, spare, gangly, and red-faced. He was not so old as the last one – perhaps in his forties – and wore a scraggly beard and moustaches. He was bound, she noted with irritation, for London Bridge, and he tramped through New Fish Street with a surprisingly determined gait for a sot.

''Ello, lovie! Them's fair skirts. You got striped stockings beneath?' The fishwife's voice did not slow her, nor did the hooting laughter the woman drew from her fellow harridans. The lady tramped onwards, determined not to lose sight of her quarry. He was only a little taller than most but thankfully hatless; his uncombed tangle of greying brown hair was easy enough to spot.

The bridge was busy for plague times. The news being cried from mouth to mouth was of the Danish king's warship, moored somewhere downriver. Mercifully, no one asked her a thing about it or cried out to her; no one expected a little lady to have any interest in ships. And in her case, they were right. Her interest was fixed now on the drunk weaving alongside the carts and horses which choked the bridge.

At the far end, near Southwark, she thought she had lost him. It was almost a relief to see that a tavern's sign jutted out over the street. She could not go in, of course – it did not look anywhere near as respectable a place as the Bull Head in Cheapside. However, she did not have long to trouble herself; within a minute, the fellow was slung out, a chorus of jeers following him.

And on he went again, presumably to try his luck on the south bank.

Where to grab him? That was a question she had wrestled with. The problem with London was that you never knew who was watching you. Most people didn't see others, and the majority of the rest either didn't care or wouldn't dream of speaking to anyone important about seeing something unusual. Yet, as the sprawl of Southwark – the domed shape of closed playhouses, the wooded amphitheatres where the animals were baited, the white-fronted whorehouses – opened up, she began to give it more serious thought. There was always the chance that one of the minority – a constable or his wife; a lawyer; a nosy alderman or servant to someone of importance – might see, and that they might go home and say, 'I saw a well-dressed lady taking up with an old drunk. What does that signify?' Worse, there was the chance that some well-meaning idiot might interfere: 'madam, mark you, this here is a drunk and a scoundrel; keep well away' – perhaps taking her arm and trying to save her, whilst her prey shambled off.

Her masters would not like that. Play your part, they had said, and don't be seen.

She followed him as he bypassed the winding network of streets which abutted the gaming and playing places; apparently, he found it easier to follow the direction of the bridge, marching on. The great cathedral rose on their right, its shadow not quite reaching pursuer or pursued, and then fell away. He was attempting a drink again she realised: this time at the old coaching inn, the George. A wise choice. Such places were used to seeing folk in various states of disarray. He stumbled through the yard, making a desultory attempt to straighten his hair, and went inside.

The yard was swept clean, and so she waited outside, spreading her skirts on a low bench. An ostler's boy appeared, looked at her, cap in hand, and then backed away, apparently unsure what to make of a lady with no horse. He might be trouble, she thought; he might fetch or speak to someone and then she should have to make up a story. That might be enjoyable, but it would be risky.

She was spared it by the ejection of her nameless vagabond from the George. He fell out of the porch and wobbled for a second on unsteady legs in its shadow. Wiping sweat from his brow, he stumbled forward into the innyard. He was, she noticed, mumbling to himself. Mad, she thought. 'Dunno-bloody-thrown-no-good-no-place-all-the-same-bastards-town-bloody.'

As she was standing, looking around the yard – empty, thank God; not everywhere had returned to constant activity, uncaring of the pestilence – he lurched away. Her heart fluttered for a moment until, with distaste, she saw that he was relieving himself against the tavern wall, still hurling oaths and insults at it.

When he had finished and fixed himself – more or less; there had been some splashing backwards – she drew towards him, her head lowered as much as the hat would allow without tipping. 'Goodman? Goodman?'

'Eh?' The old wreck wheeled, a fist raised. Living on the streets to be sure, she thought. His red-veined eyes scoured her and, relaxing, he rested a forearm on the white-washed wall. 'What's you wantin', lady?'

'I need service,' she said. The trick was not to say too much, even to an idiot. Simple guile worked best. 'I am lost. I must return upriver. And I must have an escort. Will you do me the pleasure?'

'You wants me? For yer service?' He hiccupped and – she almost laughed at this – attempted to stifle it, as though he might have ruined his chances.

'If it pleases you.' She gave him a false address, and he frowned.

'Dunno it.'

'It is upriver. My husband will be glad of it. He might find a position for you. You are masterless?'

'Me, lady? Me, no, no, I ain't no masterless man, no. Your husband, 'e a constable?'

'No.'

'But I … I's lookin' for a new master. Ay, that's I am.'

'Good. My husband has a large house. A fair way up the river.

In good lands. I would have you walk ahead of me and keep the creatures of this City from me until I am home.' More clearly, she said, 'I would like that you take me there. To my home, far up the river and beyond.' She faltered a little here. It was true enough that she had been instructed to take the man to a quiet place, a grave place which had been pointed out to her, but she was not to give him too much information on how far it was or where it lay. It was imperative that he must not know to where he was going until he was nearer it, and he must not be able to locate it himself. In fact, the mysterious big house was to be understood by the victim only as a place upriver and requiring a great deal of walking. She would deal with him, she decided, in her own way, ensuring that he became lost enough until he had been deposited.

'You want me to walk yer horse afore?'

'I have none. We shall take the river.' And trust the wherrymen to keep their mouths shut for once, she thought. There was no help for that. 'What is your name?'

'Georgie,' he said, with a semi-toothed grin up at the tavern. The compact little female figure followed his gaze, making a note of the place. It would serve her and her masters well in days to come. 'Don't get me no drink in 'ere but.'

And so, with much bowing on his part, the strange pair left the George's innyard, unseen and unremarked. They might, indeed, have truly been a lady and a down-on-his-luck serving-man hastily employed to return her home. That was hardly unheard of and certainly not unseemly. She had taken care not to dress as anything too great – a gentleman's wife, with the tall, feathered hat and face vizard, rather than the tiresome Italianate gown she'd donned for the Bull Head. She doubted even if the oafish keeper of the Cheapside tavern would recognise her now.

They did not cross London Bridge again, but she had him hail a wherry at its water stairs. This was easy enough with her present, one hand patting at her waist. Together, they settled for the journey, she seated on the boat's bench and he with the wit to remain standing nearer to the waterman. She kept a gloved hand up to steady her hat as the little vessel cut a path through the glassy water, making its way deftly past and between larger, heavier ships and cargo boats.

Her fellow, transformed now into something resembling a servant, even began to whistle jauntily. She could hear him, chatting with – or rather to – the wherryman in tones she supposed he thought she wouldn't hear. 'Can't believe me luck, Sirrah – thought I'd be taken up and whipped and no mistake and now 'ere comes a bit of fortune from God's own 'and. Ain't it the truth that a man don't know what fortune 'olds, eh? This morning near to a beggar and now a proper gen'lewoman's man.' His bobbing voice lulled. ''Ere,' he shouted down the wherry, 'begging yer pardon, marm, but what does I call yer?'

She did not turn in her seat, but offered over her shoulder, 'my name is Locusta.'

***

Locusta pushed the blindfolded Geordie into the room. It had been an easy thing; once off the wherry at the most obscure stairs she could think of – 'pray, pull in here; I have forgotten something in the City!' – the tricky part had been getting him lost enough on the long walk which followed. That had been made easier by her giving him a coin to get himself a drink at every tavern they passed. After two or three, he had begun to grow insensible and, with her following sedately behind, he had rocked along the streets, bouncing from wall to wall, sliding into the gutter, swearing as women opened shutters and scolded him ('piss off,' he'd cry, before turning a bleary face to offer, 'pardon, Marm,' to his smiling new mistress).

Only when they were entirely alone, hard by the meeting place, had she fallen on him, pushing him to the ground and tying her mask over his eyes. He had barely protested, aiming punches at the ground rather than her. Then she had had only to drag him, thankful for his spare frame, into the building.

It was a tall place, echoey and ancient, with a hammer-beam ceiling and windows – real glass windows – embedded high enough to prevent eyes peeping in from outside. Paintings lined the walls, none of them of men she recognised – though one, she saw with surprise, was of the late Queen Elizabeth. The whole space stank of age and wealth, of beeswax and old rushes and good wine, spilt and sunk deep into ancient wood. Stationed along either wall were men in black robes, their heads bent so that the hoods obscured their faces – at least fifteen of the fellows in the large space. At the far end, a long table with a white cloth spread over it was set up on a raised area.

And there sat three more men.

Locusta swallowed, nervous. She knew they would be here, of course, but their appearances were altered by the strange masks they wore: white things, like vizards, but which entirely covered their faces. To add to the strange, mystical look, they were wholly clad in black or dark brown hooded robes – it was difficult to tell in the wavering light cast by the candelabra which anchored either end of the table.

'You have done well, my lady Locusta,' said the man seated in the centre. His voice was rich and earthy, seeming to come from deep within his belly. It was an educated voice, laced with amusement. And power, she thought. He might have been a prince or a governor. 'Remove the creature's eye covering.'

She did, leaning forward and tearing it from Georgie's face. The drunk, on all fours, tried to stand, and she pushed him back down.

'Pray, be gentle, my dear. We have need of him yet. Stand, man.'

Shaking, Georgie remained on the floor until Locusta pulled him – gently – up, wincing at the feel of his bones through his cheap shirt collar. They were jutting, sharp. Despite his paunch, he had not eaten in some time, she thought.

He stood, unsteadily, his weight first on one side and then the other, before the three seated men. 'Come forward,' barked the one on the right. His voice was not so rich but sounded more vicious.

Locusta walked behind the unfortunate man; her hands held out to catch him if he fell. The men who lined the walls did not look up, but remained statue-like, staring down at the floor. Georgie paused, still a good distance from the trio. 'I didn't do nothin',' he said. 'Just brought here, m'lords. Don't put me in gaol. I didn't do nothin'.'

'Be silent,' said the leader, not unkindly. He turned and leant to the fellow on his left, who kept staring forward, and then the one on the right, whispering each time. 'You please us. What is your name?'

He didn't answer, so Locusta cleared her throat and said, 'he calls himself George.'

'Splendid. Goodman George, we have called you forth not to imprison you.' The derelict began stammering, and the man at the table raised a finger – a flash of white emerging from the darkness of his robe. 'Silence. We are the head of a group of men. A group of men whose antiquity is of some age. Not as great as some, but great. Our brotherhood came together in the reign of our late and dread sovereign lord Henry VIII, by the grace of God defender of the faith and king of England, Ireland, and France. Do you know who that was?'

Georgie's head swivelled from man to man, and then from side to side, and then up and down. Locusta followed his gaze, looking again at the paintings. 'Ay, my lord,' he said.

'We are known as the Brotherhood of Augustus. Do you know who Augustus Caesar was?'

'N-no, my lord.'

The masked faces on either side of the leader twisted towards him before returning to Georgie. 'Never mind. Never mind. You may know us henceforth as the Augustans. We have hired the Lady Locusta to aid us. We would have you play a very special part, Goodman George. Do you understand?'

Georgie slid to his knees, clutching at the bottom of his doublet and the shirt front which had fallen, loose and ragged, from his breeches. 'Yes, m'lord. A part on the stage, sir? I ain't no player.'

'Ugh,' said the leader of the Augustans. His fellows chortled. 'No, not upon the filthy public stage. We have in mind a far prettier stage than that. My dear lady, you may go. We understand you have other matters to attend to. Leave dear George with us.'

Locusta turned with a swish of her City-skirts, just as Georgie turned his stupidly pleading gaze towards her. This she ignored, and yet, as she swept away from her delivery, she nearly collided with yet another of the Augustans coming in, carrying something covered with cloth. A chill ran through her. How many of these fellows were there?

'Ah,' cried the voice from the top table, 'another of our brethren. Come to induct you, Goodman George, into our company. Only for a short time, regrettably.'

Eager to be gone, Locusta swung her way from the room, her skirt moving bell-like. Once free of the great chamber, she smiled to herself. All had gone as planned; she had pleased her masters with the gift of the vagabond and now might turn her mind to other matters.

7

A bloody idiot, that's what I was: a bloody idiot. The room into which I'd been forced was a tawdry little closet. I had not been beaten or assaulted by any of the damned Spaniards, but one of them – I supposed the lad who had allowed me into the embassy – had knocked me down and put the sack over my head. This I had removed, only to find myself locked in the chamber.

The thing was that the wooden shutters in the little room were flimsy. I had not been tied up or restrained in any way and might have made an easy job of kicking them open and worming my way back into the street. Failing that, I could have opened one and cried out for help, drawn whichever of Cecil's men were out there watching the place.

But that's what they want you to do.

I did nothing of the sort. I had prepared my story well enough. I was Ambrose Adamson, a Scotch Catholic convert who admired the work of the Lady Luisa Mendoza, no more. If I were anything otherwise, I should try and escape, calling out for help to my fellow spies outside the window.

But Ambrose was an honest sort of a fellow. On being trapped and tested; thus, he would wear out his knees in prayer. Therefore, I remained quiet in my closet, stayed on my knees, and didn't grumble when even the floorboards began to jab and weave aches through my joints. I mumbled in Latin, over and over, 'Áve María, grátia pléna, Dóminus técum, Benedícta tu' – I didn't know the rest.

They didn't come to let me out, any of the bastards.

Gradually, the light outside weakened, and I shifted to sit cross-legged, wondering how long this little piece of theatre, this test, would last. I had heard that the papists were sticklers for punishment – hair shirts, self-flagellation, all of that strange and soul-whipping mortification. I drew the line at beating my back. Being locked in and left was quite enough, the boredom inclining me to give up and beat my way out.

The sounds of the City outside faded too. Although the streets had remained busy despite the plague, I knew that only the taverns made much of a trade. The watchmen were surprisingly active in shouting people home at night. Dimly, I wondered if the Barbican had its own officers. I thus occupied my time tracing my way home for when I did finally escape the place. There was a breach in the wall near Cripplegate, and I might sneak along near St Giles, hop it, and make my way home through the City. They knew me enough at Ludgate that I'd have no trouble. It might be a lark, avoiding the watchmen, something like the life I'd led when I'd first come to London and taken up with the gipsies and the cutthroats.

Where is the bitch!?

Annoyed, feeling suffocated by the darkness, I lay sprawled on the floor, no longer willing to pray. The woman, Luisa, had invited me. Test of loyalty or not, she was now presuming too much.

Did she go out again?

I cursed the question. To answer it, I should have to find the man outside when I was freed and ask him. And I should have to be careful; I could not destroy my cover story. I sighed into the blackness. I had thought the days of Spanish schemes were over. They had been before my time, in any case; my work for Cecil had begun after the hey-and-hurrah-days of Spanish-backed plots to blow holes in the old queen. Those I had heard about from some older men in the service when they had a drink in them, but I had never known of any serious Spanish agent sent into England to kill King James. He was, he proclaimed to the world, the great Augustus – the great peacemaker king, like Solomon, who settled the Borders between England and Scotland, who ended Elizabeth's never-ending war with Spain, who promised to tolerate the Catholics.

And who then persecuted them as wicked equivocators who lied in their teeth and did not respect princes.

Or was that your own dear Cecil, Lord Salisbury?

My mind, I knew, was unloosening, thoughts running hither and yon, arguing with one another. Such was the power of encompassing darkness. I did not doubt that the papists who had imprisoned me knew it. Surely they knew enough Jesuits and priests who, in their time, had been shut up in far darker and worse places than this.

Then, as smoothly as you like, came the snick of a key turning in the lock. I rolled onto my back and up to my knees, ignoring the throbbing that racked me and clasping my hands in prayer. Light spilt into the room, screwing my eyes shut. Framed in the doorway was an unidentifiable figure. It said, 'ven!' I did not know the word but recognised the voice as that of the young lad at the entrance. I wobbled to my feet, and he stood back, holding the door wide.

I understood well enough his invitation and moved forward slowly, letting my eyes adjust as I stepped out of the closet and back into the hall. More light washed the room, bursting out from wall sconces. I tried not to look around, not to look furtive.

'Señora Luisa?' I asked, testing out my accent. A little rough, a little hard. Perhaps that fit. I suspected that Spaniards would know no better.

Slowly, the young porter said, 'she is to see you now ready. You go. You follow.' And, with an almost military nod, he stepped away from the door and marched up the stairs at the end of the hall. I followed with my hat in my hands.

Upstairs, another hall curved to the right, leading to a warren of wooden doors. My host charged onwards until he came to the last of them. He knocked and waited a few beats before opening it. 'You're coming with me?' I asked. He did not respond but let blankness blur his features – though I thought he understood me.

I shrugged and stepped into the room.

You should know the Catholics' queer reputation for abstinence and opulence. It has long intrigued me about them, the idea that they build vast treasure troves of relics and idols and pretty things and yet live in poverty. So it was in the chambers of Luisa Mendoza. Dual-natured, I had heard said of them, two things in one, loving display and hating it, adoring pomp and ceremony and preaching austerity and poverty. The idea appealed to me, not in its religious nature, but in that notion of having two separate strands to the self. It was, after all, what made me: a man who was repelled by the nature of his work and yet wouldn't give it up for the world; a man who lived one life as a perfectly respectable servant and another as a spy.

And another as a deviant, haunting the taverns for unnatural acts.

The door softly closed behind me, but I did not turn. Instead, I stepped onto the bare floorboards, shining clean, polished with what I imagined must be back-breaking intensity. A desk – a box, actually, laden with books and with a cushionless stool beside it – stood against one wall, next to a flat pallet with no mattress. Candles were studded into the walls giving light to the cheerless space.

The lady, however, was standing in the low doorway to a private closet. She was framed in red, gold, silver, blue – though she was straightening her plain, black-and-white costume, which still looked like she'd draped a winding sheet around her head. The little room behind her, the jewel box of colour, was, I realised, a private chapel. As she stepped forward, I could see the little wooden lectern thing at which papists knelt to knead their beads or to do whatever it was that made up their devotions.

As Luisa swept towards me, her skirts brushing that perfect bare floor, I tried not to stare at the treasures in the room behind her. I had a brief impression of a huge crucifix – wooden, but inlaid with gold and silver, and with the Christ figure painted in hideously lifelike colours – and then my eyes fell on her hands. They were clasped in front of her shapeless bodice, a neat little knot of white.

'You are welcome,' she said. And then, with an edge of suspicion, 'you are Catholic?' Her eyes were narrow, her brow furrowed. I knew doubt when I saw it.

'I am that, aye,' I said. 'A Scot.' I tried to think of the Scots words I had heard before from the native speakers, from the king. I chewed my lower lip before saying, 'steek the door, madam. Ensure it is checkit to.'

Puzzlement wiped away her suspicion, at least for a moment. 'You speak Spanish?'

'Only English, madam. And Scotch.'

'This Scots, I do not know. English, yes.'

I smiled, openly, without guile, I hoped. 'Very good, madam.'

'Please. Sit. Tell me.' She gestured towards her stool, and I moved to it, keeping my eyes down, alert for any sudden movements, any incursion from her friends who might be listening outside. As I sat, I noticed that she remained standing, her arms crossed. Her face had become a mask.

Tell you what?

I supposed she was inviting me to make my plea, my entreaty or petition. I had, after all, accosted her in the street for a reason. As a Scotch convert, I must have some story, some reason, some demand or request. 'I'm a simple man,' I said, after a breath. This was the tricky part, alone in hostile territory with one chance to make an impression. 'My auld da, he was in service to the king's mother.'

Luisa's eyebrow lifted, but she said nothing.

'Queen Mary. Who was murdered by the late heretic, Elizabeth.' Still nothing, though I had hoped to elicit a scowl, a curse, a sign of the cross—anything but her passive silence. Clever wench, I thought. My throat was beginning to dry, narrowing, to betray me. I swallowed. 'In Scotland, the times are wicked. Heretics in the kirk.' I had been to Edinburgh – I had seen how the Protestant ministers had formed a church which poked its nose into men's lives, making itself the arbiter of what they should and shouldn't do. 'And now in England, our king killing good men.' Silence drew out between us. The air smelt clean. The candles were good beeswax.

'You speak of Father Garnet?'

Garnet.

Father Henry Garnet was one of the most notorious Jesuit priests. He had been implicated in the Powder Plot, though he had denied encouraging it. And, after his time in the Tower, he had been taken out to the churchyard at St Paul's and hanged, the people pulling on his legs to break his neck before his heart had been cut out and held aloft. That had been in May past. I had not gone, not because I had no stomach for executions – there were often plenty of fools with fat purses at them – but because I hadn't wanted to see one at St Paul's. I liked the place;

I passed the time of day there often. It was not, I thought, the place for such bloody revels. Better he should have been done in at Tyburn or Smithfield. I had no idea whether King James or Cecil had decreed my pretty churchyard full of booksellers and good cheer should become a killing ground.

'I know you knew him, my lady,' I lied, lowering my head and crossing myself for good measure. I squeezed out a tear, and it came, just one, wending its way down my dry and dusty cheek.

'Si.' This time she crossed herself. 'A good man of God. Most cruel, his murder. Most cruel. At his invitation, I come to this country. And no one touches me. I have God's protection.'

And Garnet didn't?

'Yes, my lady. I have seen you at work, amongst the people. Giving alms. Giving comfort. A noble cause.' I smiled up at her. 'You make our faith to sing.'

'I love the children,' she said, smiling back, I thought, despite herself. I was winning her; I could feel it. 'Yet why have you come? What do you seek, Señor Ambrose of Scotland?' She pronounced it as 'Scot-len'.

'I have heard,' I said, dipping my chin, 'of the lady set abroad. I wish to help her. I know of her work.'

Luisa frowned, her brow wrinkling under its snowy headdress. Genuine? I couldn't tell. I let my gaze slide to the books on the table beside me. Volumes, I saw, in Latin and English: history, philosophy. She was educated, and that meant cunning in any woman. 'I know no other ladies save my women,' she said. Her rounded chin rose up and over its white bedding.

'The Lady Locusta,' I said.

'I…' Her brow wrinkled. Her eyes widened. She knew the woman, I thought, or the name at least.

Because she is part of a plot.

Or because she is well-read?

'I wish to be of help,' I said. 'In the cause of the true faith. I offer you my service, my lady.'

Luisa smiled, appearing to gather herself. I could see that she was still thinking. 'Then,' she said at length, 'you are welcome,

Ambrose of Scotland. There are many to be helped. The poor. Those without letters or the knowledge. There are many in this City I see. Young and old.'

I grasped at the word. 'Aye. I know that an old fellow died. Rich, madam. In my lodgings in Cheapside. I think he was one of us?'

'What? I … your voice, I do not-' She made a little confused ball of her hand. 'You say a man died?'

'Aye, madam. An old man.'

'In the Cheapside?'

'The Bull Head. You know it?'

'A tavern, an inn,' she sniffed. 'Some of my poor men, those I feed, they go there.'

'This was the old man. Filthy but well dressed. I thought he might be a man set to watch us of the true faith.' I was throwing out nonsense then, and I knew it. Yet the Spaniard simply looked confused, as though our language was coming between us.

'I only know … old Lambert.'

'A creature of the heretics?'

'No. No. A sick old man. I tended to him, in the streets. He went much to this tavern. And others. I have not seen him these past nights. I thought the pestilence, perhaps he had palsy and a …' she beat on her breast, 'a canker in his chest. He had not long left. I thought …'

Could this Lambert be the unfortunate creature I had seen in the Gray's Inn chapel? 'If it is the man I saw, he was given lodging and dressed well. And then killed. I saw his body taken away by …' I lowered my voice theatrically, 'men of the king's own secretary.'

Luisa stepped away from me, backwards, her hands falling to her side. 'Old Lambert. He was a … this word you use, vagabond. A nothing. A poor soul.'

'Yet I thought perhaps more,' I said, attempting a meaningful look. 'I thought, mebbe, a plot was afoot. And so I wished to offer my services, as I said, madam.'

'I know nothing of any plots.' She gave a hard shake of her head, cloth brushing her cheeks. 'Nor of the great butcher Lord

Salisbury.' She almost spat the name. 'Nor of the king. Only the queen, God bless her. Your own Queen Anne.'

'What?' The word spilt out, partly in laughter and partly in surprise.

Luisa nodded. 'Your Queen Anne. We have hopes of her mercy and love. All of us. You wish to offer service?' I returned her nod. 'Then I pray you, Ambrose of Scotland, you trouble us not, but go to your queen of the Scots. She shall listen to a good man of our faith. We can offer you nothing nor suspicion of any plots. This is a place of refuge for the true. Come. See.'

Without waiting to see if I replied, she wheeled and moved into her little closet. I sprang up and followed.

'It is beautiful,' I breathed. 'Bonny.' She went into the room, which was lit by its own candle-tree, and leant over a silver-ribbed chest. As she fussed at something, I let my eyes wander the crucifix on the wall and down to a laden, crimson-clothed table at its base. Here were piled treasures: onyx beads and gold ones, more crucifixes, little miniatures of, I assumed, saints, set in gold enamel.

My mouth watered.

This was a treasure trove indeed. It was the kind of cache which pursuivants tore English houses apart to find. It was the accumulation of dozens of priest holes and hidden spaces beneath floorboards and under haylofts.

And every bit of it was proscribed.

I traced my finger around the rim of a miniature. Being caught with such a thing could be dangerous. Indeed, even if I said I was a man of Cecil's, an overeager watchman or constable might discover it on me and throw me in gaol. Then I should not be saved. Spies who got caught by the locals were useless, known, apt to be thrown to the wolves.

And yet my fingers closed around the damned thing unbidden, even as my gaze fell on the bent woman as she fumbled in her chest. And then the saint was in my palm, closed and hidden, turning warm.

'Here,' she said, rising and turning. From her hand was dangling a bulging stringed purse. 'This I would bid you take. It is not much.'

It looks much!

'Give it out,' she said, smiling and stepping over the carpet towards me. 'Take it. Please, take.'

You're goddamned right I will, I thought, reaching out with my free hand and letting the bundle fall into it with a musical jangle. 'Thank you.'

'I ask only that you share it amongst those in need. The people of this City are ill-fed. Unlearned and unlettered. They rely on good works. And go forth, Ambrose. A good name. A learned man was Ambrose of Milan. A man of Godly wisdom. Be like him. And go to the queen if you wish to do more. Be safe.'

I was, I saw, being dismissed a richer man by the silly pious papist. I smiled and stepped back, nodding and trying to match her look of sagacity.

'Wait.'

I froze.

'Oh. You must keep that little limning,' she said. I swallowed. The miniature was poking out from between my fingers. 'I like every good Catholic to take something. To remind him – or her – of the faith. We all need reminding of what we fight for.'

I did not answer but left her presence and thudded my way out of her chambers, into the long hallway, and downstairs.

I fled the Spanish embassy, not pocketing the stolen painting or tying the purse to my belt until I was out in the moonlit summer night. Not stupid enough to seek out one of Cecil's men – for who knew which eyes were on me from the building I'd fled – I began making my way through the Barbican and back into the City proper.

My mind remained fixed on what I'd learnt – what little I'd cultured – on the journey home. I followed the path I had set out, dodging watchmen as easily as a rat might flee a fat mouser of a cat.

And my mind turned.

The dead man might well have been this Lambert whom the busy papist lady had tended. And she might have been up to anything whilst my loyalty was being tested in the embassy: it was late indeed by the time I began my walk home, likely near to midnight. Even if she was not the mysterious Locusta, might she not have been in league with her?

I know no other ladies save my women.

She was educated, intelligent, and presumably of some good background. Such women knew other women. Wicked women, quite probably.

And the queen? It had been rumoured for years that Queen Anne was a hedge-papist, practising her secret faith, as it were, behind a hedge. I had no good hopes of approaching her.

My thoughts kept pace with my footsteps. Two words had taken to dominating them as I finally turned into Shoe Lane: wick (left foot) ed (right foot) wo (left foot) men (right foot).

It was no such woman who answered my door, but my own Faith.

'Time do you call this?' Her face was flushed.

'I'm home,' I said, pushing past her and scanning for David. He was already sleeping; I was pleased to see. Hopgood was not around. 'No need for applause,' I added, lamely.

'Thought I'd better stop the night,' she said, closing the door. She moved to the brazier and began dampening the coals. They fizzed, the herbal scent turning smoky and acrid. 'Since we didn't know where you'd gone. You shouldn't be leaving David alone. And your accounts are a mess again. What do you need a moustache comb for? A comb's a comb. And I don't know what bombast is, never mind half a crown spent on it.'

'He's fourteen,' I said, throwing my hat on the battered table. But I didn't press the matter. I knew she was protective of her brother, ever since he had been kidnapped and held aboard a creaking old ship two years before. Instead, I decided to disarm her. 'I'm sorry.'

Her eyebrow, red darkened to brown in the weak light, rose. 'You're always sorry about something, you are.'

'I'm sorry I was an ass this morning.' I held up my hands. 'No, don't argue.'

'I wasn't goi–'

'I was an ass and worse. I know it. And I'm sorry.'

'You weren't very kind to Nicholas.'

Am I ever?

Easing the buttons of my doublet, I took a breath before going to her and circling her waist. 'Get out of it,' she said fidgeting. 'There's something I wish to speak about, give over.'

'Ah, Mouse.' I pulled her closer. 'I haven't been very kind. You're right. Not about you and your young prentice.' I swallowed. The thing was, I didn't dislike the gormless lad. I hated him, in fact, less than I hated most people who crossed my path. And besides, as much as it stung me to admit it, my thoughts didn't matter. She was going to marry the boy. She loved him. I could either accept it and embrace him or crawl into my own little pit, spitting and hissing at them both and at a world that was passing me by. I released her but was pleased to see her shaking her head, chuckling.

Just like the old days.

'You're all dusty,' she said.

'By way of apology,' I said, tilting my chin, letting my eyes roll as I patted down the front of my breeches, 'I wish to buy you flowers for your wedding. On top of the dowry.' This I had already provided in the teeth of her arguments, not willing for my girl to be taken a pauper. She opened her mouth to protest, and I hurried on. 'And any other sundries, a feast afterwards, and the like.' I yanked free the purse Luisa had given me and held it out to her.

'Ned, there's no need, I …'

'Oh, no need to be gracious. Take it. It's yours.'

'But this. And I told you Nicholas's parents didn't even want a dowry.'

'Shush. Be married. Live well. Eat meat. Make his shirts. Drink sack.' I left the purse in her quivering hand and turned to my room. 'Goodnight,' I said to my door. A tear, twin to the one I had worked up for the Spanish lady, had fought its way out of my eye.

A bloody idiot, that's what I felt—a bloody idiot.

8

I was thoroughly sick of music. From dawn, the entire City had rocked with it, until the ceiling above me seemed to thrum. Occasionally cannon fire cracked the air, recalling my sometime nightmare. Lower than that, lower than the drums and trumpets, lower than the pipes and tabours, but just as annoying, was the constant hum of voices drifting up from Fleet Street.

The two kings had made their triumphal entry through London, and I had elected to stay at home. If some trouble was planned, if Locusta was hiding in a tavern window above Cheapside with her pistol cocked, then I decided that one of Cecil's army of cutthroats could discover her. Me, I had decided to wait the whole thing out, holed up whilst Faith and Hopgood took David and Hal Berridge down to see the sights.

At home, I should have been content to fold a pillow about my head, or perhaps to try on an array of outfits, perhaps even to rearrange my bedchamber full of treasures.

Naturally, I couldn't. I blamed the intrusion of noise, deciding that trying to ignore a din that was unavoidable served only to draw attention to it, to make it more irritating. The truth, I suppose, was that I simply could not resist going out to see what was happening. As much as I wanted to miss all the tiresome pageantry, I could not bear to do so. Besides, to stay at home was to think and think and come up with nothing. It had been two days since my evening at the embassy. In those two days, I had decided that the Lady Luisa was most definitely at the heart of a Spanish plot, the mysterious Locusta its agent. And then I had decided the opposite: that the woman was a well watched and well-known papist and nothing more, and that she had been as honest as any Catholic could be in her claims to know nothing of the female assassin. It was fruitless and bootless to remain indoors thinking myself round in circles any further. The only way to find answers was to be out on the streets, watching and listening: to do, in short, my job of work.

Thus it was that I managed to thrust myself in amongst the

music and laughter and drunken cheering. The procession, with the two kings in the state as its greatest part, had passed on to Temple Bar by the time I left Shoe Lane, locking my door against drink-emboldened looters. The carpet along which the whole troupe had ridden was already gone, torn to pieces by the people. Yet I was in time to see the aftermath.

Halfway along the broad thoroughfare, two great orbs were set up, each bigger than a man. I could not say what they were made of, though the numerous spikes driven through them, of something gold-coloured, made them appear to be giant mace heads. Both were hollow and still had fires burning within.

Two suns, I realised. Two great suns, of equal size: King Christian and King James. A group of people dressed as shepherds and shepherdesses was standing near them, being toasted and clapped on the back by some of my fellow citizens. Those who were clustered near the suns were lounging in the shade of porches and awnings, tankards and cups in their hands. The singing rose up and down the street in raucous waves. I shook my head, smiling in spite of myself, before turning and heading down towards the heart of the City.

St Paul's churchyard was a vast sea of people, some hanging up like monkeys on the vacated scaffolding that must have held dignitaries. Locusta, I thought, carrying on past, had come to the right place. Here was imperial Rome come again. The environs of Cheapside were no better. I had intended to go to the Bull Head, to ask questions of Rooks again perhaps, or even to search the room in which the body had been found. I drew short, however.

Cheapside was a bedlam: a muddled, confusing scrimmage of people of all classes, from recorders in red to vagabonds in patched grey. Despite the sunny day, much of the street was in the shade. Finally, I discovered what the scaffolding and work that had been jangling and banging and shouting for days had betokened. No mere triumphal arches, these, but a great canopy resting on pillars set up either side of the thoroughfare. On each pillar was carved a giant. The canopy overhead must have been wooden: it was gilded to catch the sun, and, stepping back to see what sat on top, I saw the points of pyramids and the rounded outline of great rocks painted with the arms of England and Denmark. The whole thing was bizarre, huge, and almost threatening. Had it collapsed, it would have crushed the street below. No red carpet – or remains of one – here, but instead the tattered remnants of billowing blue tissue, folded and turned so that it looked like bobbing waves. I passed through it – waded, I might say – ignoring the abandoned hulk of a green-painted wooden sea dragon. My heart fluttered as I missed a step, catching a foot on a puff of blue tissue, and passed on again into the light.

At the Great Conduit, a strange bower had been erected, with real – I supposed – trees and bushes, their limbs meeting over the fountain in a tangle of wood, leaves, and fruit. The beauty and wonder were someone diminished by the sight of nine cupshotten boys dressed as Greek muses, their white gowns splattered with the watered-down wine which spurted from the fountain. Everywhere voices bombarded me in a babel of languages. Amongst them, I noticed, was a great deal of Scotch. An odd thing: I had always thought the Scots an abstemious race, an army of scholars forever harping on God's cruelty. Perhaps they were, and these were the defectors who had deserted south to lick up the wine of London.

It was all too much, I decided. It was gaudy, mad in its splendour. My fellow Londoners, drunk with revelry, seemed to have taken the Danish king's visit as the beginning of a general festival, and I suspected that that feeling would stretch on as long as the fellow remained in London. I cut away from the madness, from the wild, happy, madcap airs of Cheapside and made my way down Bread Street in the direction of the river. The royal revels had reminded me of my legitimate work. Though I had not seen the procession, I realised that the King's Men must have taken part in it. The players, in short, must have returned to town. And that meant I might recover whichever plays they had and deliver them to Revels.

I had little trouble catching a wherry to cross the river. Everyone, it seemed, was enjoying the delights of the City, which on such a day outstripped even those of Southwark. Further, I knew that the players would have no part in any great banquets or feasts; if they had taken part in the procession, it was to march. Thereafter, they would have been dismissed. And that meant they would have gone on to drink.

The Tabard in Southwark was, to my mind, a rather meagre affair. However, it had unaccountably become a part of the players' circuit of drinking dens: a sign, perhaps, of the strange new rakehell air which had come to blow through the new reign. Debarking near the southern end of the bridge, I passed through the quieter streets of the south bank until I passed the more pleasant George and came upon the sagging wooden structures ranged around a sparse yard. Nodding at some men I vaguely recognised outside, I stepped up to the porch and went in.

Immediately, a man was at my elbow. I cursed, oaths fighting one another for expression, expecting to see a music-man begging to play. Yet the little man was no pipe-peddler. He was, in fact, a fellow I recognised, and relief washed through me.

'Armin,' I said. Robert Armin was the chief clown of the King's Men. I had made the right choice by turning my back on the thick crowds north of the river, and the players had shared my thoughts.

'I dinnae ken nae Armin,' he growled. 'A porter, am I. Knocking, were ye, at thon gate?'

'I … what?'

The man broke into a smile before jerking his chin over his shoulder. 'Mr Burbage is amongst us.' I looked over him – not burdensome, for he was not a tall man – and saw, across the room, a jumble of players seated around a large, battered table. The tavern was not busy and their usual hangers-on, those men who loved to gather crumbs of wit from men who loved to toss them, were not present.

'Burbage,' I said absently, spotting the big, blonde, bearded fellow hunched over the table, still in his red livery, his hands clasped around a tankard. The great tragic actor, I knew, was famed for remaining in character even when backstage. They must have been rehearsing, and so he had become whichever poor fellow he was playing. On his right, his thinning forehead shining in the weak light from an open shutter, was Will Shakespeare, the player-poet, and, at his elbow, to my surprise, was Hal Berridge. The brat must have been seeking to join the company, hoping to make a mark, since his own band of boy actors was dying. And the principal boy of the King's Men was not a role I intended he should have. Only one woman was present – the old seamstress, Mrs Cole, who made the company's costumes and was a notorious blabber-spout.

'Well, porter,' I said, 'take me to … to whom am I paying court?'

'Tae Macbeth, who will be king hereafter,' said Armin, again adopting the accent that I now realised was meant to be Scotch. It was not a patch on my own efforts but a sight more pleasant than his usual bouncing Theatre English. He winked. 'Ye ken, a writer tells. A players shows, and feels, and is.' He turned his back and, head down, scuffed his way towards his fellows. I followed in his wake, nodding at the tapster to fetch me a beer.

'Good morrow, and what news, gentlemen,' I said, taking off my hat and essaying a bow. 'And good Mrs Cole. *Macbeth* then, is it? By Christ's bloody cross, I hope you shall have swept it clean of those ungodly oaths and curses.' In truth, I didn't know if the play breached the new rules by having any. It was new and had been performed only a few times when the theatres were still open. It had never been played before the king, and I had not been the one to deliver it to Revels for approval before those public performances.

Shakespeare made a little moue and looked set to speak, but Hal Berridge jumped in. 'Mr Savage! Have you brought David?'

'Indeed I have not,' I said, scraping back a stool next to another man, the round-faced John Heminges, and replacing my hat as I sat. 'His sister has only just got over her hatred of stage-wrights and all things theatrical. Taverns, she will not abide.'

The boy looked downcast, and I felt – I almost felt – bad. '*Macbeth*,' I said. 'Your tragedy of *Hamlet*. And something else. Have you a comedy to lighten the air after those weighty tragedies? Perhaps a little masque.' I cocked an eyebrow at Shakespeare. He did not, as far as I knew, write masques. Those were Ben Jonson's art.

'Masques,' piped Heminges, 'are the worst things to happen

to drama since the pestilence.' He looked at the playwright, I noticed, for approval after speaking. Armin, who had taken up a position at the far end of the table, leapt onto his stool, balancing on one foot. Performing, I thought, always performing and tumbling. It was sad, really.

'Ben Jonson, our English masque-fashioner. Would that he might fashion something great enough to mask his belly.'

A ripple of laughter ran over the table, more polite than genuine. Jonson, the man who continued to make Shakespeare's plays look like yesterday's weeds, was that rarest of creatures – a man so rude and objectionable, so utterly uncaring of what men thought of him, it was difficult not to like him, however grudgingly.

'But such costumes as they have,' said Mrs Cole. 'It's not like in my day, not at all. In my day, a lady was content with a good kirtle and skirt. And ladies taking part. In men's work. Good for those noble ladies, I say.' No one answered her. To do so would be to encourage the cracked old wench in her wild claims of adventures in Italy, France, and Scotland.

I sniffed and addressed myself again to Shakespeare, whose muddy brown eyes were clouded. 'So, King James and King Christian shall have two plays about falling crowns and swaying sceptres. Tell me, Master Word-wizard, how many times do you intend to go to *that* well?' I smiled; I hoped achieving a sarcastic one. The playwright had cast about often enough that he was unimpressed by our living courts, first of Queen Elizabeth and now King James. He was a man above palace intrigues and the trifling toys of courtiers, or so he claimed. Yet his plays gave him the lie. He was, I thought, an avid lover of royal wickedness and Machiavellian schemes, albeit only those of the distant past. 'Well, Mr Shakespeare, Sir Edmund, asked for *Hamlet*. If you think this *Macbeth* will do well…' At the name, Burbage lifted his head and stared at me through narrowed eyes. I shifted in my seat.

'Ye dare tae speak of crowns?' he asked, in a fair Scottish accent.

I swallowed, unsure of what to say. I had no desire to share the fellow's odd humour and habits. Old Mrs Cole saved me, announcing, 'I know something of Scotch crowns myself, you know. Served the king's own mother, in her first days in England. Then she was uncrowned, of course. I shall dress the ladies of the play as they truly dressed, those Scotch women of the olden days.' She drummed her trim little fingers on the table.

'Oh! And David can be a nymph! One of the seeing-sprites,' said Hal across the table. I folded my arms before leaning back as the tapster delivered my drink.

'This Macbeth who will be king must have a wife who will be queen hereafter, then. Perhaps,' I said, licking my lips, 'my boy…'

'A queen Ah have,' snapped Burbage. 'But … a guid imp tae personate ane weird sister tae promise me much. Aye. Aye. Perhaps.'

'And I shall dress him,' added Mrs Cole. 'You send us your boy, Mr Savage, and I'll make a weird sister of him.'

'What is this play about?' I asked, looking again at its author.

'A dark tale,' said Heminges. I cursed the man. I would rather hear from the one who wrote it. 'Of the death of a king and the rise and fall of another.'

'The death of a king? How is that?' I asked.

'He is done to death with daggers,' said Mrs Cole.

I snorted. 'A fine thing to play before a king who fears being done to death with daggers!' I lifted my cup to take a sip and, as the yeasty warmth filled my mouth, I saw Shakespeare's eyes crinkle and gleam over the table at me. Before drinking, I held the drink to him for the briefest of salutes.

You sneak-minded country bastard.

The playwright's palms were flat on the table, but his fingertips danced upwards. 'I study histories. Not always are they pretty.'

'Study, ay. As he should!' burst out Burbage, making my beer fall down the wrong pipe. I hacked and coughed to right matters, as the man thumped the table. 'Frae dusty histories dae our lessons come. The murder of a king is an act founded in Hell.'

'As the Powder Plotters will now know,' said Heminges. At that, silence fell amongst us all, awkward and unpleasant. I tried again to clear my throat in a scratchy growl.

'A thing not to be imagined or encompassed,' I said at length. A general murmur of agreement met me.

'A thing to be tabled only in the chambers of meditation,' said Shakespeare, tapping a sausage finger to his forehead. I frowned.

What is wrong with "to be imagined"?

'Quite.'

'We play before the kings, the seventh day of August,' he added.

'Hmm.' I thought, so the seventh had been settled upon. It was the last day of July already. 'I will gladly carry the play to Sir Edmund for half the purveyance fee if my boy can have some part. A nymph or sprite or sister or whatever you call it.' I belched and finally felt my throat clear.

'Oh please, yes,' said Berridge, looking around the others. 'Then we can play together.' I regretted my demand suddenly and drained my beer. Immediately, the tapster was on me, looking to recover it in case I should be a thief. 'Tell me,' I said aloud to the company, 'have you heard of a woman calling herself Locusta? A woman who took rooms in the Bull Head. A great lady, she passes herself off as. With servants.'

Glances were exchanged around the table, murmurs, and I was so intent on trying to read them that I did not at first realise that another voice was intruding. It came again, blasting over us. I spun on my stool, its wooden edges cutting into the fabric of my breeches.

The tapster, a husky little man, was only a few yards away, his apron pulled up and doing service in wiping the inside of my cup. 'Master Tapster?'

'I said, sir, that this woman, this – what did you call her, sir – Loca…'

'Locusta!?'

'If it pleases you. Heard from my mate over at the George, down the road – you know it?' I nodded impatiently. 'Heard from my mate that a woman, a great lady with a servant, took a room over his place. Odd thing. He hadn't seen her, but her servant came and took the room and paid a pretty penny in advance. She might be there by now, though, this wench you seek. If it's the same one.'

I was on my feet, fumbling at my purse before he finished. I paid for my beer – which I had hoped the players would do – and gave him an extra coin for his news. 'Gentlemen,' I called over my shoulder, 'an honour. I will have your plays anon. I will seek you out. Remember no fucking profanity.'

9

As soon as the words were out, I was flying across the chipped floorboards and out into the light, across the innyard, and down the street. Houses and shops passed in a blur.

Is she in there? Has she been in there whilst you were merrily passing the time of day wandering London and drinking beer with foolish actors?

Never have I moved so quickly, my heart racing. I skated over broken cobblestones from which weeds sprouted. I leapt over beggars slumped in doorways, their legs protruding. I ignored the catcalls of whores and thieves and other assorted denizens of the south side.

The square bulk of the George Inn rose on my right, its yard sprawling before it. I stopped and drew breath, trying to think. Now, at least, if she was in there, I should see her.

And then what?

This was the problem I had delayed dealing with.

This woman, whoever she was, knew what she was about. She had either taken on or been given the name of a notorious Roman assassin for a reason. Perhaps foolishly, I still thought that I might take her, for a wicked woman was still just a woman. If she turned out to be the Spanish Luisa or one of her maids – well, I could easily enough force her down.

Yet if she were skilled in fighting, if she knew foreign tricks, or worse, if she or her servants – or whoever had hired her – were to appear, to surround me…

I cast a glance around the street. It was like any Southwark thoroughfare, jammed with thatch-roofed houses, most lacking any whitewash or windows, some with crooked overhanging balconies one storey up; shops with sad faces and meagre wares; a central sewer channel about which wound pedlars bent by packs, women carrying baskets, shoeless boys without hats, their faces red from the sun. I could scream for help in Southwark, and someone might come. Then again, I might be ignored.

But there is one face you won't see out there.

I scowled away the nagging voice. He had been from Southwark, the man I'd reported. I didn't need reminding. His shop might very well be one of those I was looking at. Despite myself, I tried to see if any were entirely abandoned. And then I gave up.

I was wasting time, looking for reasons not to go in, not to put myself in danger. The wise thing to do would be to send someone for some of Cecil's hire-hacks and have the place surrounded with black-coated rogues. But vanity prevented me. I would fight, if I had to, although my cardinal rule is that running is sovereign and fighting to be done only when you have an advantage, you can cheat, or someone will listen to your screams and call up help.

Forcing one foot in front of the other, I crossed the yard, passing a bench, and went to the door.

The George was somewhat grander than the Tabard, as befitted a coaching inn. It occupied two storeys, and the upper one even had white painted shutters for the guests' rooms. Like a whorehouse, I thought, and I supposed that, unlike Mr Rooks, the owner of the George might well turn a blind eye and an open palm to those who would take a tumble with a willing man or woman.

Inside, the taproom was spacious: in addition to tables, it boasted benches along walls covered floor to ceiling in ballad sheets. Already, a music-man was singing in a corner, some dreck about the meeting of two giants. He had drawn a crowd, the men – and a couple of women – perched on stools and tapping their feet on the packed dirt floor in time with his voice and lute. For once, I was grateful; he was keeping the drinkers occupied.

I knocked on a low bar, bringing the tapster from his backroom. He was a flinty man, sallow, with a crooked smile. 'Can I do you for, gentle?'

'Good morrow. I come in search of –'

'Been up to see the two kings, 'ave you?'

'No, I–'

'Lots gone north, over the bridge, like, see the two kings.'

'I'm looking–'

'Gentleman, are you?' His eyes roved my hat and doublet. 'Come with the court?'

I sighed. I knew the type well enough: whatever he had to say and ask was more important than anything out of my mouth. I did not, therefore, answer in words, but pulled free my purse and held it up. His mouth closed just as he was about to speak again.

That's got your attention.

'I come seeking a woman. One of your guests.' He made to speak, and I hurried on. 'I know she has taken lodgings here, so you need not deny it. I would speak with her. Her name is Locusta.'

His eyes left the purse and returned to me looking; I thought disappointed? I couldn't tell, for they glazed quickly. I wished, if possible, to find out which room was hers without paying him anything. 'Them's private things, mister.' He smiled again. I did not match it. 'Private. Not to be told out to no one. Them's stopping here don't need no snooping men come to disturb 'em.'

Dearly, I wished to tell him that I was in service to Robert Cecil, Lord Salisbury. But that was out of the question, of course. Grudgingly, I drew out a penny. 'Here. Where is she?'

He grasped the coin without giving thanks. 'True, a lady has taken a room. A great lady, by my reckoning.'

'Which one?' I turned my head back into the taproom, seeking the stairs. 'Which room?'

'Peace, lad. Now, for a penny, I shall tell you all.'

I didn't argue. The first coin had already disappeared. I would simply be sure to reclaim the balance from Cecil or one of his chief servants when next I saw him. 'Here.'

'Good lad. Friendly.' He stowed the second coin and coughed, a knotty hand demurely held to his lips as he turned his head away. 'Now. I don't know any Locusta.' That look of disappointment again. My own was about to reflect it when his eyes widened with relief. 'But of course. You're a friend. Locusta.' He drew the name out, snapping it over his teeth. 'Odd sorta name, that. That must be her Christian name then, like me wife is a Nell.'

'Yes,' I said, perhaps too eagerly. 'That is so. Her Christian name is Locusta.'

'So Johnson is her married name, is it?'

Johnson?

'Johnson?'

'That's the name her boy give me. Mrs Johnson.' Something stirred within me, a memory, like a stick being swirled in a pool of water. Mr Johnson, Mr John Johnson, had been the ridiculous false name the Powder Plotter Fawkes had given to his captors when he'd been caught under the Houses of Parliament tending his gunpowder. All London knew of it.

'That's it,' I said, my voice sounding distant in my ears. 'Locusta Johnson. A great lady. She is upstairs?'

'She ain't here.'

'What?' Relief and disappointment made uneasy companions in my mind.

'She still ain't come.'

Hope flared. 'Well, when is she coming? When are you expecting her?'

'Dunno.'

'I'm not paying anymore.' I leant over the bar towards him, as menacingly as I could. 'When?'

The tapster did not look frightened or even surprised. Instead, he grinned his odious grin again – a grin that spoke of fights with better men, of a whole multitude of Southwark broils. 'She ain't never come, this grand lady. She sends her imps.'

'How do you mean?'

'Just as I say. First day – ah, three days since – her page comes and takes a room. For a week, says he, and I'm not saying nothing, till he produces a great purse of coins, much like yours, sir, but fatter, and says again "a week". So I'm keeping the room free.'

'And since then, you've heard nothing?' I looked up to the shadowy beams of the ceiling.

'Not quite. I mean, not me. My wife, she tends the place sometimes. When she ain't making the ale. To give me a bit of time to meself.' He leered, and I chose not to pursue whatever he meant. 'And she tells me that a servant of the lady what took rooms but never yet come, come.'

'Who was he? This same page?'

'I don't know. I wasn't here, was I?' In irritation, I spat at the ground. ''ere, watch that. No, but I don't reckon it was the same slave. The missus, she said this were a soft maid, not a page. Like a maid of … what's it?'

'Honour? A female servant?' Another woman, I thought, as he nodded. This Locusta was certainly not working alone, but neither was she the only wench involved. 'Where is your wife?'

'Out to buy bread, sir. If you'd like to buy a drink and wait…'

'No. So it was a maidservant who came.'

'A well-dressed maidservant,' he corrected. 'This was yesterday. And she has the key what I gave the page. And up she goes, she tells the wife, to make things ready, like. For herself coming.' He shrugged again. 'That's it.'

I took a breath, my thoughts cartwheeling. 'Very well. I thank you, goodman.'

'That be all, sir?'

'Yes. I shall come back another day when the lady arrives. If you could leave word at the Tabard, I might be found there.' I made a show of huffing and puffing, and fixing my purse back to my belt, before bowing to him and making my way to the door. I did not turn, though I let my eyes swivel towards the group of drinkers, still being entertained. The music-man had turned to his pipe and was interspersing a song about a jolly old king of the Danes with blasts from it.

I stepped back out into the light, counted to twenty, and then did a tour of the yard, looking up as I did so, tracing the upper storey. And then I slid back into the George.

Had he still been out at the bar, I should have invented something I'd forgotten: what was the colour of the maidservant's hair, did your wife say? This page, did he give any other name than Locusta? Or perhaps I might have said, 'I have changed my mind. I will wait on your good wife.'

But, as I'd hoped, the stringy-haired old creature had slouched back into his private room, to whatever entertainment kept him there. Keeping to the walls, so I didn't jog a table or attract undue attention, I made for the stairs I'd spotted as I'd left. They lay on the far left of the room – a steep wooden flight which disappeared into the darkness. As though I belonged in the place, had taken a room myself, I stepped lightly up on the balls of my feet.

This was a risk. I did not know which was the lady's room. Yet, from my brief survey from outside, I could see which room had the best shutters, those which were of horn rather than wood. There was only one pair, and the thatch above looked relatively fresh. It stood to reason, I hoped, that this betokened the best room the place had to offer and that a high-paying lady should have been given the best – and the most expensive.

I moved along the dim corridor, trying to place myself in what I had seen from the outside, ignoring the whispering scurry of mice in the walls and keeping my tread soft, padded. I passed over what I thought must be the area of the tapster's quarters below with an especial softness. And eventually, I reached the door. It was thin-looking, but polished and made of good wood. Gently, I rapped on it with my knuckle.

Nothing.

Again, more insistently.

Still nothing.

I cast a look the way I'd come. The top of the stairs was lost in darkness; there were no windows or shutters up here. If someone was standing on the stairs watching me, I couldn't know of them. And so there was little point in worrying. I put an ear to the door and heard nothing, no soft movements, no whisper of voices.

And then I put my shoulder to it once, hard. Pain trembled through me. The door shook but didn't give. After another cautious glance, I put my back to the wall opposite the door and kicked across the short hallway, my boot connecting with the middle. At first, I thought I'd failed again. But the door had been breached, its lock broken. It remained standing only by the determination of its hinges. Without looking to see if I'd made too much noise, I pushed it open and went in.

The room was not as dark as it might have been, the thin horn admitting some of the summer sun. Still, it was dim. I stepped in, avoiding the shape of a flock bed, and opened one, allowing the place to bloom. As I turned, my breath caught in my throat.

The wall next to the door was the only part of the room which had been panelled, the rest lost to greying plaster. Across the wood, however, someone had daubed letters, each the size of a man's hand, in white chalk. Together, they read:

VENGEANCE

I stood, staring at them awhile. She's not coming, I thought. She never intended to come. On the wings of that arrived: but she, or whoever employed her, knows that she is being searched for. I shivered. This was a message from an assassin, and it had been intended for me, or one like me, who might dare to hunt her. If she was a step ahead of me, luring me, inviting me, that meant I was in danger. How typical it was of a woman to do nothing but by sinister craft.

Eventually, I remembered that I was intruding, that I had broken in upon the place. The realisation set me to work. I overturned the mattress, no longer caring about noise, digging my hands into the fluff, looking under the stringed frame, feeling around the floorboards for a loose one. The air turned thick with straw and feathers – the cheap bastard of a tapster must have sold the room as having a feather bed and saved money by mixing in the straw. So intent was I on finding something hidden that I missed something in plain sight. Against a plaster wall, almost invisible, was a sheet of paper. It was placed neatly, deliberately, so that it could be read if one discovered it. I bent down, snatching the thing up.

It was a page from a book, I realised, as my eyes travelled over the dense script. The paper was thick enough, of quality. A good edition, then, of whatever the book was. I read it silently:

Now, when nothing might quiet them, at length they met thus in a pitched field, where after great slaughter &c murther made of a huge multitude of people, the king being put to the woorsse, fled into a mill, whither being fiercelie followed and found therein, he was cruellie slaine, and vnreuerentlie left stark naked. A notable mirror to all princes that calling to remembrance such a pitiful and most dolorous sight, they may take heed by what manner of persons they suffer themselues to be led and abused. For if this prince king James the third had not followed upon a wilful pfetense, and obstinat mind, the counsel and advise of vantperlors, and such as (being aduanced from base degree vnto high authoritie) studied more to keep themselues in fauor, than to give true aduertisetnents, and faithfull aduise unto their prince, he might haue reigned longer by manie daies & yeeres, in great and higli felicitie. In which conflict was on the kings part slaine (as saith Buchanan) Alexander Coningham, earle of Glencarne. He was thus slaine neere Striueling, on the seuenth day of lune, the yeere after the incarnation, 1488, being also the 29 of his reigne.

Now then, after that the barons of Scotland had thus slaine their souereigne lord and liege king James, the third of that name: his eldest son James the fourth was crowned king of Scotland, and began his reign, the 24 of June, in the yeere 1488, being not past sixteen yeeres of age, who notwithstanding that he had beene in the field with the nobles of the realme against his father, that contrarie to his mind was slaine; yet neuerthelesse afterwards, hee became a right noble prince, & seemed to take great repentance for that his offense, and in token therof, he ware continuallie an iron chaine about his midle all the daies of his life.

It meant nothing to me. It was a history of some sort, of Scotland obviously – ancient stuff. I folded it into my belt and continued searching the room. Sweat began to pop out on my brow, and I could feel lengthening wet patches forming around my shirt, clinging to my skin. A weapon, I thought – a gun, a sword, a dagger—a hidden cache of powder.

Nothing. The place was empty, untouched, a hollow shell.

But for that one word: VENGEANCE, sworn by one Locusta, calling herself Mrs Johnson as Guy Fawkes had named himself John Johnson, and the strange sheet torn from a history I didn't know.

On whom would the remaining Powder Plotters – if there were any – want revenge?

The answer was obvious enough: on the loafing Scotsman whom they had failed to kill and who had then wiped out the better part of them.

And those who dared speak sympathetically of them in your company.

The king.

The king being put to the woorsse, fled into a mill, whither being fiercelie followed and found therin, he was cruellie slaine after that, the barons of Scotland had thus slaine their souereigne lord and liege King James.

Could some relative of the Powder Plotters have hired a woman – a kinswoman, perhaps – to do as the barons of Scotland had once done and killed a King James? My heart began to pulse again, to thud in my ears, in my chest. This was a matter too big for me, I realised, too big for any one man. I had no hope of getting to Cecil, who would be entertaining two kings. However, I remembered, I did have hope of his cousin, the clever lawyer who was already involved.

You must feel free to call upon me if you cannot reach my esteemed good lord.

Sir Francis Bacon might have been a place-seeker, a man of little repute but for his canny and unloved lawyering, but he knew of the Locusta madness and, perhaps more importantly, the chance to be part of ending it might well help his star to rise.

10

To my disappointment, if not surprise, Sir Francis Bacon was not living in a fine house full of pretty things. His home, I learnt on the streets, was a little cottage called Twickenham Lodge, many miles upriver from London. There, however, his child bride lived a quiet existence. The lawyer himself was living in a large building called Fulwood's Rents, not far from me, up in Holborn. I took myself up and, opposite Chancery Lane, found that the place was a passage between Holborn and Gray's Inn, abutted on either side by white-washed lodging houses several storeys high and topped with triangular slate roofs. It was a fine enough place for student lawyers, but for a cousin of the great Salisbury, it seemed mean.

I was directed by an usher to the fellow's chambers and found them, up three flights of stairs, in the middle part of the block of buildings. With a gloved hand, dressed soberly, I knocked.

Movement rustled inside. Voices rose and fell. Giggled.

I frowned and knocked again. This time, the patter of footsteps sounded, growing louder as it approached the door. I thought I heard whoever was there call something softly, as though over his shoulder, to someone else, and, before the door opened, there was a gentle bang.

Before me stood Sir Francis Bacon, a furred gown pulled about his shoulders, covering a nightshirt. He came up to about my chin and his dark, jewel-like eyes rose up, first in annoyance, then confusion, and finally recognition. 'My Savage,' he said, standing back. 'Good morrow, sir.'

Removing my hat, I bowed. 'Sir Francis. I apologise for coming upon you so early.' It wasn't particularly early, but I intended to concede something to his nightgown. 'I would have your help, sir. In the matter, my lord of Salisbury set me to work on.'

Bacon's brow wrinkled, and he cast a glance over his shoulder and then back at me. 'I … it is early, quite.' His little pink tongue swept his upper lip. 'Savage. Savage.' He seemed to be working something out. 'Oh. Yes, of course. Please, come.' He stepped back, giving me passage.

What are you hiding?

The room was a parlour which seemed to be counterfeiting a study. Two strong desks stood against the far wall, just below open wooden shutters. Each was stacked with books, papers, inkpots, rolled scrolls with squashed middles. Chairs stood at either one, their backs to the door. Stupid, I thought – anyone could walk in whilst the sitter was at work, anyone with a grudge. Lawyers must make enemies enough, especially those whose fame came from helping Essex to the block.

'What news, Mr Savage?'

Briefly, I told him about my visit to Luisa Mendoza first, my suspicions of her as a wicked woman, and my being locked awhile in a closet in the embassy. I did not mention my business with the dead old man, lest he frown at my charging him for the burial – or worse, that he asks for money. 'My good cousin watches the lady,' he said. Throughout my summary, we had both stood, and now he gestured to a seat, waiting until I was settled before taking the other. He tapped his chin with a finger. 'And there is no proof that the Spanish woman has done anything ill?'

'Beyond her being a papist and seeking to convert others?'

'Yes,' he said, rolling his eyes a little. 'Beyond that. You found nothing to tie her to an assassin?'

'No.' Before he could speak, I launched into my discovery of the day before, of the room in the George with its chalked message. With a final flourish, I removed the page from my coat pocket and handed it to him.

For the first time, Bacon seemed excited, interested. His eyes widened at the page, and he set it down on the soft leather top of his desk, smoothing it out and touching only the edges. 'Ye Gods,' he said. He repeated it before reading the whole thing aloud. His voice was fluid and clear, lilting – the voice of a man of the courtroom.

'What is it?' I asked, almost ashamed of my bluntness. 'Where's it from?'

Bacon bent again over the page, very close. Then he pulled

his head back and cocked it from side to side, a little blackbird examining a crumb, before darting in again. It was extraordinary, I thought, how intent he was, and truly how much he resembled a sharp little bird. No blackbird, I decided, but a raven.

He opened his mouth to speak before closing it again. His eyes rested on me briefly as he frowned, one finger again tapping his chin, where the beard grew silvery black. He tutted, swivelling, and using the edge of the desk to haul himself up. I remained in my seat as he fluttered across the carpet and knocked on the door to an inner chamber. It opened immediately, and the fellow whom Bacon had embraced at the conclusion of our first meeting emerged.

He, too, was in a nightshirt, and just before he closed the door behind him, I had the impression of a bed's hangings. 'Mr Savage, this is my friend Roger Delamere, student and, I hope, soon to be a steady man at law.'

I bowed, fumbling with my hat so as to get a good look at the fellow. Roger Delamere was young, noticeably younger in the morning light than he had looked in Cecil's stuffy chamber. And he was handsome, too, every feature of his face coming together in bland perfection. He was still possessed, I could see, of that fresh, smooth skin that seldom seems to last – to my eternal annoyance – past eighteen. Delamere smiled, showing perfect white teeth. 'Mr Savage,' he said. 'It is a pleasure.'

I merely returned his smile, unsure of what to say. I understood Bacon's slight awkwardness at letting me in. I understood, too, his odd look after he'd looked at the paper; he'd been weighing me up, deciding if I was a safe man to let know of his arrangements with the handsome young student. And, apparently, I was.

'My dear friend Roger hopes to be a student of the law's history. And he has a love of history in its general terms. I, alas,' said Bacon, with a rueful rub of his chin, 'confine myself to the theory of history, how it can be divided into the ecclesiastical, the history of letters, ideas, civil works and political thought. You see?'

I saw but didn't care, and so I nodded.

'Roger here,' he went on, clapping his lover on his white-shirted back, 'has a mind tuned to the reading of histories themselves. Chronicles, and so on. This page, I suspect, has been clipped neatly from just such a text. By the printing, I suspect a bound volume. And such volumes are the preserve of the great. Universities, royal palaces, and so on.'

I thought of the pile of books on Luisa Mendoza's table and cursed myself for not having paid attention to their titles, their condition. Without speaking, Delamere stepped around me and lifted the paper, holding it easily and smiling as he read. 'You are quite right, Francis,' he said. 'Chronicle indeed. This is from Master Holinshed's Chronicles of these islands.'

'Holinshed,' echoed Bacon. I knew the name myself. It was the source of almost every history play every written and seemed to have been available, in various editions and runs, in every bookshop in London for years.

'I cannot account for which volume. But Master Holinshed wrote of the history of Scotland, and I should say this page is drawn from it.'

'How do you know?' I asked, somewhat brusquely.

Delamare did not seem offended; instead, he beamed. 'Because, sir,' he said, 'I know the tale of the third King James. And I had read some of Holinshed's history of Scotland – when the old queen died, I read it. Yet I have read no other chronicle of that nation's history. And therefore,' he added, glancing impishly at Bacon, 'it is logical that if I know this chapter of Scotch history and have read only one book on Scotch history, the knowledge comes from the book.'

Bacon grinned, moving over and reaching up to ruffle his friend's already-tousled blonde hair. 'You do well, Roger, very well.'

Something like jealousy made hot little pinpricks across my forearms.

How dare that old goat have a lover. How dare he live happily.

'This is all very well,' I said, tapping the desk before me with a finger, before pointing at its stack of books. 'But what does it mean? Why did she leave it?'

Bacon's brow darkened. 'A threat, Mr Savage. A threat against our king. What could it be else? She is an assassin, judging by the name. And she uses the example of history to warn; I might say to brag, of what evil she intends. One theory of history at least holds that it serves as a series of lessons to us. We might learn from past occurrents or repeat them, at our pleasure and according to our wits.'

'But why? And how did she know to leave it there?'

'I daresay she knows she is being hunted,' said Bacon.

'I guessed that,' I snapped. 'I'm sorry.'

Bacon waved a hand in the air, dismissing my rudeness with a mumble. 'No, you are quite right. The matter is strange. The woman is not working alone. As the true Locusta didn't. She has Masters, paymasters. And she has servants, too. To call herself also Mrs Johnson, to speak of vengeance…'

'What is this?' asked Delamere, flopping down on his chair. 'Vengeance?'

'I suspect this has something to do with the plot … the late Powder Treason,' I said.

Bacon paled, looking towards Roger. 'That, I had hoped, was over and done with. A thing of the past. A lesson now to be written in the histories.'

'And yet what if it isn't?' I stood. 'What if it isn't?'

Bacon went to his friend's chair and put a hand on Delamere's shoulder, squeezing it. 'We neither of us are pursuivants, Mr Savage. We are not my cousin's men. I am a humble lawyer. That is what I'm good at. And as a man at law, I can offer you only one thing.'

I searched his face, the greying hairs, the rounded features, those black eyes, hoping to communicate desperation. In truth, I had no idea what to do next, where to go. I might tramp about London, searching every tavern, and finding that the bitch had eluded me, was mocking me again. 'What? What is it?'

'A good lawyer will interview witnesses. Including those, he holds under some suspicion. You mention the Powder Plotters…'

'I cannot ask severed heads and burnt entrails anything,' I said.

Bacon's cheek twitched, and it was Delamere, I noticed, who paled this time. 'I see, Mr Savage, that neither my cousin Robert nor good Mr Sturrock spoke falsely of you. Your tongue is a cocked weapon.' I raised my chin, lowering it when I saw he was smiling. 'They are not all dead, sir. Not all of them. Only those found to have been deeply in the murder plot.' His eyes clouded, seeming to see through me, before sharpening. 'You … yes, my good cousin told me that you took part in the great to-do after the plot. During the whispering times this last year.'

I felt my throat narrowing, drying. Into my mind came again the deserted shopfronts of Southwark. 'I … I did my duty. That is all.'

'What was it?' asked Delamere, his youthful voice full of happy ignorance. I could have punched his handsome face.

'Yes, I recall.' Bacon was no longer looking at me, but regarding the carpet, nudging at it with his little slippered feet. 'A butcher, was it?'

'A baker,' I said, my voice a husk.

'What became of … ah. No. Perhaps it is not meet that we speak of such things.'

He did not need to. His little show of discretion, or prudence, or whatever it was, however, was wasted. I knew well enough what I'd done. In the days following the trials of the Powder Plotters who hadn't been killed in the capture – Fawkes, Digby, Keyes, Garnet, the Wintours, and who cares for the rest, all dead – there had been a great buzz about London. Bad times for the people, who were for the most part, scared and skittish, like horses whipped too close to danger – but good times for an agent. The City was a veritable fruit tree, just as the bower set up over Cheapside had cheerfully proclaimed, for us. I had been sitting in a drinking ken at the Southwark end of London Bridge, wearing an old woollen cap pulled low, when I'd heard two men talking.

'The king lives, then, and all the counsellors and parliament men with him,' said the prentice.

'Ay. And for a farthing I'd have seen some of them lot gone up to the clouds,' said the master baker, raising his mug.

There had been laughter.

I had remained there, watching, learning who the baker was, his name, until the shadows grew, and the tapster lit the place. And, when he and his prentice left, I'd followed them out and saw them disappear into the dancing lights and ribald songs of Southwark. And then I had returned home and filed my report, my dispatch, a jagged scrawl betraying the loose-lipped baker for his careless jesting. I had nothing against him, didn't know him, but was quite willing to collect my reward – for Cecil had made it clear that there would be a reward for turning in such fools. He might hang, I knew, but I convinced myself that it was unlikely. He might instead just get a little fright.

It was only later that I'd heard a baker accused of spreading sedition, of treasonous talk, had died. Of what, I never asked – probably an ague caught in the Fleet or the Newgate. If he had a family, a wife, children, I had no wish to know of them.

That was my connection with the great Powder Plot. I was one of the shadowy creatures who profited from selling men's lives to Lord Salisbury and the king.

And I had learnt nothing but shame and earnt nothing but enough for a new coat.

Bacon coughed, shaking me out of the memories I'd been trying to ignore, and which he had dredged – was dredging – up, like a rotten corpse from a stagnant stream. 'There was a fellow,' he said, 'that the Star Chamber could imprison only on lesser charges, though much was suspected of him.'

'Of course,' said Delamere, thumping the desk. 'The wizard earl.'

'Quite so,' Bacon said, giving a watery smile. 'Percy, the Earl of Northumberland. He is lodged in the Tower, at the king's pleasure. Vengeance, Mr Savage, is a cause found in every history of murder and plot. I understand that the earl is well kept in the Tower and has built himself a vast library.' Delamere and I both looked at the little man, and he inclined his head to me. 'And he has many servants. Many friends. A wife, indeed, who lives freely. Any one of whom – all of whom – might seek vengeance. And any one of whom might seek to attain it through an assassin who could strike today, tomorrow, next week. In a pitched field, anywhere.'

'King James III was taken with daggers,' said Delamere, frowning. 'The first James of Scotland was driven into his own privy by his thanes and done to death likewise. King Duncan was slain by Macbeth and Banquo at someplace called … ah, Botgosuane. All in Holinshed, whether true or not.'

'I suggest that you act with haste, Mr Savage. This lady has advertised her presence twice now for a reason. She means to act. Go you to the great prison and discover if Locusta, Mrs Johnson, dances to the tune of vengeance played by our captive plotter. If you find anything, you must write up some dispatch, or whatever it is you are commanded, I -No. No, I should take it straight to my cousin Rob – to my Lord Salisbury. I will send word to him to expect you at Whitehall tomorrow morning. Every man according to his genius, I think – and I regret that bloody matters are his lordship's.'

I bent a little, shaking my head.

I did not relish a visit to the Tower of London.

Turning, barely bowing, willing my feet to carry me over the carpet and out of the parlour, Bacon's voice caught me in a gentle net. 'Oh, Mr Savage?' I turned, hoping for some reprieve. Already I was considering what extorting information from a Tower prisoner might mean, based on what I'd heard from those who had had that ugly task.

'Yes, Sir Francis?'

'Why not wear that fine suit of clothes you took from the corpse of the lady's victim?' Laughter burbled from behind him, from the seated Roger Delamere. 'A more costly funeral I have never been so pleased to give. Your dead man's weeds should be with you today at Shoe Lane. I pray you enjoy them. And that they bring you better luck than their last owner.'

11

Low growls rumbled from the pits of the creature's stomachs. One of the beasts – a female or a youngling – circled the large, flea-bitten old male, before, extraordinarily, sniffing and biting – yes, biting – his bottom. The old fellow looked nonplussed, giving what sounded like a resigned grumble in return, before dragging his bony body into the shadows of the sandy, circular yard. Loud slurping sounds drifted up to the viewing gallery as he refreshed himself in the cistern fed by the moat. The female, if it was indeed a female, flattened herself in the centre of the yard, oblivious to the little white round ovals of we who looked down on so much captured Majesty. There she remained, looking treacly, the muscles in her back occasionally rippling, like an old stained rug whose weave is rocked by a breeze.

The lions were the great attraction of the Tower of London, greater even than the occasional sight of the imprisoned Sir Walter Raleigh taking his walks. I leant back from the railing and straightened my hat. A warm breeze seemed to swirl about the top of the Lion Tower.

I had come straight from the lawyers' quarters of London, taking a wherry downriver all the way to the fortress. You've heard of the Tower, of course – who hasn't? It has existed, so they say, since the time of the first Caesar, who was done to death with daggers. I daresay that most of Europe has heard of the Tower and associates it with those infamous bad men of England.

And those wicked women- Anne Boleyn, Katherine Howard, the Grey sisters…

The Tower is death; it is imprisonment, it is terror and fear, bare stone and strong bars, scaffolds and blood-soaked greens and always the dull, heavy crunch of a bone-splitting axe.

True enough.

Yet, I thought, as I descended the stairs, nodding absently at a party of well-dressed men and women ascending to see the beasts, it is also a place of coronations, of the beginning of festivals, of cannon being fired in celebration as well as doom, of the merrily clanking steel of the Mint. Only the day before last, the kings of England (or is it Scotland, or Great Britain) and Denmark had begun their triumphal progress through the City from here, just as King James and his family had lodged here before the great coronation entry back in '04. The Tower is the element of London, whipped by its winds, forged from its grey stones, lapped by its Thames, bristling with guns lit by its fires. It is an odd sort of place, being all kinds of opposite things at once: death and life; joy and sadness; hope and terror.

I found myself rather liking it.

Once at the foot of the stairs which curved down the Lion Tower, I took myself over the small bridge towards the Gate Tower, stopping for only a moment to look up at the grey bulk of building which stood, almost defiantly, before me: a jumble of parapets, curtain walls, turrets, spires, and everywhere those curious Union flags blown stiff by the summer wind. After showing my papers to a yeoman – I had carried papers with Cecil's seal to Bacon, in case I met trouble reaching him – I was told, 'through the Bloody Tower ahead. Big arch. Can't miss it. And then to the left beyond the garden.' I nodded my thanks. There it was again: a garden and a bloody tower, beauty and ugliness.

Beyond the gate stood a clipped green, and I set out across it, enjoying the feel of grass beneath my feet – it's something one rarely gets in the City, especially during plague times, when going out into the marshy fields dotted around London is an invitation to death. On my left, the grey wall stared down; on my right, across the green, another turreted outer wall kept the moat at bay. The Bloody Tower itself was clear enough, a rectangular block with an arch cut through it. I slipped under, engulfed for a moment by its gloom, before emerging back out into the Tower precincts.

A great courtyard spread out before me, ending in the distance with a chapel and more buildings enclosed by the wall. This was truly, I thought, a place from the past, from the histories of chivalry and the days when kings and knights had to build their little words behind great curtains of stone. My way, as the yeoman had pointed out, was to the left, and there indeed lay a pretty little garden, with trees set at intervals. Rather than marching through, I skirted the edges, keeping my head down, and made for the series of slate-roofed buildings nestled against the wall beyond it.

It was the constable's lodgings I'd asked for, and been given, with a cockeyed look, these lieutenant's lodgings. I supposed they were the same thing, unfamiliar as I was with the place's governance. They were not bleak or gaoler-like but bore a resemblance to Bacon's own Fulwood's Rents instead, bearing the same jagged roof. If anything, they were better kept, fresher. I found the door, knocked, and was escorted by another yeoman through an open, rush-matted hall and eventually to a large private chamber.

'Good morrow. You come from Lord Salisbury?' The voice boomed from a compact old man with a forked beard, who was warming his hands at a fire despite the heat. 'Come in, man, come. My men can send messages faster than your feet can carry you, I'll warrant. Come!'

I stepped into the room. It was well furnished, not only in its appointments but with meat and drink. Cabinets lined the walls, standing between tapestries, and every one looked ready to spill its cargo of jugs, bottles, cups. I wondered, for a moment, if the good lieutenant might be a drinker, until I caught sight of another one of those wretched flags hanging from a wall panel to my right, next to an indifferent painting of the king. Another flag, bearing a red cross on a white background, had partly fallen down on the other side of the portrait. It was easy to forget the revelry that was infecting London and had begun only the day before, with the procession leaving from this place. I locked eyes with the lieutenant, turning my hat in my hand. 'My lord, I …'

'Sir, only, alas,' he said, his florid face crinkling. 'A humble knight am I. Sir William Wade. Help yourself to a drink, man, if it pleases you.' He took his own advice, leaving the fire and crossing to a large table in the centre of the room. I felt sweat moisture beginning to glisten on my forehead. The room was an oven. 'So, from Salisbury. Salisbury. A fine title. In the service, are you?' I gave a tight nod. He mirrored it with a more emphatic one. 'Know it well. I began in service to the young fellow's father, the late Lord Burghley.' I looked up at this to find the old man beaming as he poured a gurgle of red into a silver goblet. He began to swirl it before taking a little sip and an appreciative breath. 'Ah. Fine stuff. So, is it Raleigh the fox you've come to see? I had a hand in putting that rogue in ward myself.'

'No. I'm in search of a wicked woman, sir.'

'Woman, eh? No women prisoners here.'

'Perhaps she is a relative, this she-wolf, of one of your prisoner's.'

Wade's hand froze in mid-air, still grasping his goblet. 'A she-wolf, eh? By God, I know something of them.' I said nothing, realising he had more. 'Dealt with the wickedest of them all.' He glanced over my shoulder, in a furtive little way, before smiling. 'The king's mother,' he said in a mock whisper. 'Oh, yes. The deadly and mischievous Mary. Went down to Chartley myself back in those days, whilst the wench was taken out to hunt. Or so she thought. Warded her pestilent secretaries and tossed her cabinets, her secret papers. Took all back to good old Burghley. And Walsingham, of course, was much in favour then. Thirty pounds, if I recall correctly. Thirty pounds English to deliver that sovereign lady up to justice.' His voice trailed away for a moment, lingering on the past, on his successes.

Sending a woman to her death for money.

Just doing his duty.

'And still, his good Majesty knighted me when he gained the throne, what.' Wade raised his goblet in a salute towards the painting of the king before taking a long draught. 'So what is this matter with this woman? Sheltering those pestilent papists, is she? I know a thing about discovering those creatures myself.'

I cut in, uninterested in any more of his brags. 'She might be connected to the Powder Plot.' He looked set to speak again, so I hurried on. 'I understand that the Earl of Northumberland is resident here. And he was… something to do with that plot. Perhaps a female of his is the woman I seek. She has killed once, we believe. And threatens to do so again in the name of vengeance. And to kill the king,' I added, bending my head towards the portrait.

Wade whistled. 'By Christ. Plots within plots. I remember the old days, the plots against the late queen's Majesty. Did something of the searching and seeking out of such plots myself, what. How they did stretch across all Europe. Northumberland, then. Martin Tower. I'll take you. A strange one, that. Married, too, to one of the Devereux wenches.'

Devereux...

Before I could demur, Wade was fixing his belt around his ample waist and waving his hands towards the door. 'Well, boy, well, go.'

Together, we emerged into the glittering light of the yard. 'By Christ, but there's a chill in the air,' he said. I did not reply, instead letting the warm breeze dry my perspiring brow. The good smell of the cut grass drifted from the garden, and the little trees shook their bows saucily, enjoying it as I did. 'This way.'

We set off across the courtyard, keeping the enormous White Tower, with its four flag-bearing, gilt-domed cupolas, on our right. Its short shadow fell over us, shrouding us; it was still morning, if only barely. The chapel I had noticed earlier began to take shape – a neat little building. Wade, I thought, moved with a sprightly step for an old man. 'Here,' he announced, with pride, waving one arm at the open ground before the chapel, 'is where the scaffold is set when traitors meet their ends here. A good space, a good place from which to see.' He did not break his step, but continued on, curving right so that we fell behind the White Tower. 'Now, my boy, Martin Tower. Built into yonder wall of the inner yard. Protected by the Brass Tower beyond.' He halted suddenly and raised a palm against the sun before turning to me. 'Ah, that is better. Not so cold in the sun, what.'

'Yes, sir.' I looked past him, towards the expanse of grey, the slate of roofs which lay over the buildings before the Martin Tower. It was difficult to tell where exactly that tower was. Roof seemed to crowd against roof alongside the curtain wall.

'Yet hold a moment, my boy. Yet youthful blood cool.' I

frowned down at him. 'Peace. I am sure my lord of Salisbury has trained you well. Yet you are never too skilled to learn of an old man. Have you thought how you might approach yonder caged beast?'

'I will approach as a friend. I had thought the man is a Catholic, is he not?' Wade shrugged. I felt my confidence rise. Though I had never been willing to engage in such work, I knew how the ugly side of the trade operated. Once an agent had been granted access to the prisoner, he was free to use his own wit and wiles to gain information. The common practice was to pretend to be a sympathiser, to win confidence, perhaps to feign a shared faith.

To my annoyance, Wade chortled. 'That old caper, what? "Good friend, I have gained entry under false colours. In truth, I am your good friend, and I love you. Now please tell me the secrets of your heart and betray your conspirators. Here is a pen if you should like to write their names for me." Ha! The wizard earl is no fool, young fellow-my-lad. No fool. You will get nothing from him but by greater craft than that. Such tricks might work on men facing the rack. Desperate creatures, seeking a way out, seeking a friend with their hearts even when – in their minds, you know – they know they're speaking to a false fellow.'

'What,' I asked, frowning, 'do you suggest, sir?'

Wade shrugged. 'How did we get at the Scotch queen? Season your bait with a little truth. See if he takes it, as she did. See if he tastes it, I might say and read on his face whether he likes of it or not.'

What does that mean?

But I thought I knew. I thought, in fact, that a direct – or a slightly direct – approach might well work on this wizard Earl of Northumberland. I looked again at the fine blue sky. One pillowy cloud was chasing another across it. 'Sir,' I said, 'it must be time for dinner. Tell me, are the earl's meals brought to him?'

***

A whole string of keys was needed to unlock the door in the circular Martin Tower. I stood well back, the silver meal tray held in both hands, as the yeoman attended to each brass lock. I had reached the place through the network of buildings that seemed to cling to the tower, like warts sprouting from a blunt finger. I had learnt from Sir William Wade that a liveried yeoman usually brought the meals in, and considered dressing as one, before realising that such subterfuge wouldn't work. How then should I explain how I'd gotten the uniform – had I spent months, years, training to become a yeoman simply to have a word with the earl? No, my strategy was fixed.

The door swung open easily, and the yeoman called, 'dinner for the prisoner.' Not 'his lordship', I noticed. I stepped inside, and the door was immediately pulled closed behind me, so skilfully it did not even bang.

The room was semi-circular, its far wall curving. That wall, too, bore fine glass windows, though the diamond panes were marked out with stout steel bars. But for a prison, it was not Newgate, nor the Fleet, nor the Clink. It was, instead, the room of a palace. I was standing, just inside the door, at the top of a shallow flight of steps. At their foot began a Turkish carpet, weaved in a rich shade of red. Similar carpets blanketed the whole space, which was otherwise tenanted by tables, cabinets, strange instruments – I recognised a seeing-scope set up beside a window – and everywhere books, books, books.

Was Master Holinshed's Chronicle of Scotland amongst them, I wondered.

The room was not devoid of people. Rather, it was fairly well filled, with a group of gentlemen seated on cushions before a huge fireplace, others seated at tables, reading to one another, and still more at work brushing down tapestries. For a moment, I was lost. This, I had not envisioned. I had instead seen myself entering into a dank cell, where the man sat alone on a cot – perhaps not manacled, but still, a secret Catholic left hopeless and popeless.

'His lordship's dinner, first tasting,' I announced, taking care as I descended the steps. I had been given only the first course. Apparently, the fellow was fed well, even if not in the state to which he must have been accustomed. Under my covered tray, boiled pork steamed merrily, and from it drifted the apple-heavy scents of various little sauce bowls. Not that I intended the earl should eat immediately. If he tried to, in fact, he would be rather at a loss. Already I had secreted the pretty little solid silver sauce spoon up my sleeve.

Some heads turned in my direction, uninterested at first but curious when they saw that I was not dressed in the usual livery. I paid them no heed. 'I would speak with his lordship,' I announced.

Whispers slithered around the room, hissing with suspicion. Eventually, a tall man rose from a settle, his finger marking a place in the book he'd been reading. 'What is th-th-this?' He cocked his head, narrowing his eyes. Immediately, another fellow was at his elbow, speaking to him. The taller man, I noticed, bent to listen, but kept his eyes on his fellow's mouth. Deaf, I thought, or getting there. He nodded, before running a hand over his receding forehead. 'M-m-master server. I will s-s-talk with you.' He settled himself down in a smoothing of black velvet and tapped the empty space on the settle beside him.

I crossed the room, feeling the stares of his men following me, and set the tray down on the nearest table I could see to the man I realised was Northumberland himself. As soon as my hands were free, I removed my hat and got down on one knee, bending my head. 'My lord,' I said.

'A f-f-f-fine server you a-a-'

Spit it out!

Deaf and with a stammer. Both things I could not abide, feeling unsure of how to proceed in conversation when either was present. 'I am a stranger, my lord. Yet…' I let my eyes slide, noticeably, over my shoulder – towards the door, not his men. 'Yet I have news from without.' I looked up. The earl was lounging, his long legs kicked out.

'News and f-food. I am blessed.'

'News of the lady without. She who bears many names.' I looked up. And saw…what? My plan had been to toss out news of Locusta and see if he wore a look of recognition or complete ignorance. By either, I should know if her promise of vengeance bore his support or was intended in his cause.

I saw neither.

Northumberland's long, rather horsy face looked, if anything, disgusted. Annoyed, I might have spat phlegm on his fine black satin. But it was something. I waited. 'The lady can go h-h-h-hang. I find I can shift for myself without her. Nor can I d-d-do anything to save her wretched sister.'

I had no idea what he was talking about. But no matter. 'The lady will be most disappointed, my lord, to hear this.' I bowed my head. 'She and her good sister have sent me with such hope.'

'T-t-together?'

Shit.

'Yes,' I said.

'Hmph. She blames the king, m-m-my wife. No, sh-sh-she blames Cecil, does she n-n-not? The little pot. She blames him for th-this,' he said, waving a padded arm about the room, 'and f-f-for her sister's disgrace. Two w-w-women, alike in hatred. A b-b-bitter gall.' His foul humour seemed to dissipate. His wife, I realised. He thought I had come from his wife

one of the Devereux wenches

and her sister.

I had lied myself into a corner, I knew. I could not pretend to be anything other than a messenger from the countess of Northumberland. I could not now pursue anything of the Powder Plotters in any manner of cunning, could not offer feigned service or friendship.

But perhaps I did not need to.

I had come in search of a female relative of the earl who might be working for him and found one – even if he claimed he wanted nothing to do with her. I had come in search of a wicked woman, and I had been given two of them. For I knew well enough who the other Devereux girl was. Cecil had mentioned her, in fact, in the same breath in which he'd condemned the Spanish woman living at the embassy. I could not recall his exact words, but I had no need for them.

I did not know the countess of Northumberland, whatever her Christian name was. But, like all of London, I knew the name of her sister, the Lady Penelope Devereux, sister also to the late Earl of Essex, whom I so much resembled – allegedly. Everyone knew her, indeed, as the wickedest woman in England: a whore, an adulteress, a liar, and almost certainly a traitor.

'I will tell my lady of Northumberland,' I said. 'And her sister.'

As I rose and began to bow my way from the room, I remembered what it was Cecil had said about the she-wolf Devereux woman, who apparently seethed against King James and my own master.

She had returned to town.

12

'Should be ready in a day or two, my lady.'

Locusta frowned into the pomander she was holding up to her face, a guard against the thick smell of oil and wax, of vinegary paint and cut wood which filled the air of the large, open-roofed warehouse. But the thing was useful as more than a sweetener. It was important now, more than ever, that she leaves no trail save that which she had been instructed to scatter. She and her masters knew who was chasing her, and they had encouraged her to play a little with him, daubing messages, leaving notes. And she would have time enough to play with Mr Edward Savage yet. One day, when all else was accomplished, she would enjoy laughing in his face just as he realised that she had got him.

Though she had not seen him that day, he might well be lurking somewhere, waiting to pounce. This, she had been instructed, would be a grievous thing. If she should be caught, there would fall out many great disasters. Her masters, those white-masked great men who ruled the world from behind the curtain, would be furious. 'A day. It must be ready by the third. At the latest. My husband wills it.'

She looked at the bizarre contraption. She had seen them before, of course, but never at such close quarters, nor even in such a state of not-yet-being. It sat, still with naked axles jabbing outwards. The body was black and looked like an immense, hard-shelled beetle. Even in the dusty air of the building-house, even unfinished, it was a sight to behold. But unfinished it undoubtedly was. It was just as well, she thought, that the last old fellow she had cozened, the Bull Head creature, had not been fit for purpose; but this was really stretching matters. 'Just the wheels to be finished, ma'am, up from the wheelwrights,' said the master maker of wagons, carts, and coaches.

Locusta looked at him sharply, her eyes narrowing over the pomander. 'And the paint. And the…' She gestured vaguely, sending rosemary scent out to battle the dry whiff of sawdust.

The coach-maker did not take up the thread, not at first. He sniffed, his red-veined nose inflating. Something rattled in his chest. 'Mmph. Ay. That.'

'My husband is a man of the court,' she said slowly. 'A great man. This will be his gift to the king, and it must be fit. This is why we chose you, good Master Coach-maker. The thing must be gilt and girt about with the royal arms.'

'This husband, my lady,' said the old man. 'Will he pick up the coach himself? In a day or two?'

Locusta frowned. He was sharp, this creature. Suspicious. 'No. We shall send a boy. And a fellow with horses to ride. Tomorrow.' This seemed to relieve the fellow a little. Despite his reputation as the finest coachbuilder in Clerkenwell – in London, indeed – Mr Webster, whose son was becoming known as a stage-wright, was not a good man of business. He asked far too many questions, and he had been skittish since the first mention of dressing the new coach she had ordered as a royal rig, with detachable arms to be hung on its sides.

But her masters had been quite clear. The coach must appear to be one of the king's own. Otherwise, the thing would not come off. They had not apprised her of the full plans for it, and she did not greatly care. It was another of their little games, and she had her part to play, as no doubt she would have more in the coming days.

Locusta took one last look at the half-finished beast and nodded slowly. She would have to return to the men who called themselves the Augustans and inform them. Probably she would have to find good horses too. 'I shall tell th- I shall tell my husband that all will be well. He would have his gift finished and ridden from hence to our sovereign lord the king. It shall be a delight to his Majesty. A great delight.'

13

'Hunting, hunting, hunting! And drinking, drinking, drinking! I had always heard that the Danes were men of Bacchus. I did not think that their sovereign should outdo that old pagan.' Cecil settled down in his seat. I had not, on my way through the paper-rustling gauntlet of Whitehall, in which the kings were thankfully not in residence, been delayed in making the meeting Bacon had engineered. Nor had I been assaulted by the new bodyguard, Verney, though the creature still insisted on my turning out my boot-tops and even looking inside my hat, as though I were the interloper, the threat.

It seemed that the trip of the week before to Cecil's country house of Theobalds had not gone well. I had, in fact, heard scraps of information on it about the town, though I did not intend to report them. The Children of the Revels had apparently put on a masque titled *The Queen of Sheba* and, though the rumours blowing down the Theobalds Road had probably been spiced, it had been a great spectacle for all the wrong reasons. I had had it from David, who had had it from Hal Berridge, who had said it was common currency amongst the stage-wrights: the lady – yes, a real lady rather than a lad – who had played the role of the Queen of Sheba had got drunk. Her part involved giving gifts to the two kings, but she had stumbled on the steps leading to their thrones, dropping her load into the Danish king's lap and falling, sprawled, at his feet. Christian, being an honourable king, had risen to help her, to lift and lead her into the dance gallantly, but he had fallen himself into a drunken stupor to rival her own and been carried off to a bed of state. The rest of the masque might have been carried off well enough if the other ladies listed to appear hadn't been busy spewing in the lower hall.

The images flashed through my mind as I stood in Cecil's office. He had not invited me to sit and had been pacing and cursing to himself when I entered. The man was rattled, drawn, and utterly despairing. I wondered at the costs of the whole royal visit and how much he had shouldered in entertaining the kings in their wine-fuelled revelries in the country.

Good!

It always helped, whenever pity for my master threatened, to remind myself that he had chosen his course. He had brought King James to the throne, and he had sought ultimate power. If he was now being crippled by it, then good.

'Well, then, Savage, I understand you were in the Tower yesterday. My cousin has told me all that has passed. I cannot understand this business. I hear a plot against the king, some precedent of a dead King James. I hear of an assassin sworn to vengeance, I –' He lurched forward over the desk, gripping at his side. His lopsided frame had graduated to the full crookback reputation which haunted him. He had become, I saw, a hunchbacked and overworked old man. And the work, the toil, which had always driven him, was now killing him. I sprang forward, leaning over the table.

'My lord!'

At the same moment, the door behind me flew open and Verney burst in, dagger drawn. Before I could speak, he had flown across the carpet of the office, moving in silence. I was still turning from the stricken Cecil when pain jolted up my arm as he twisted it behind my back. 'Argh, get off –'

His dagger was at my throat, pressing into the flesh. His face remained impassive. 'Touch Lord Salisbury, and you die,' he hissed.

Laughter burbled behind me, pained sounding. The dagger fell away. 'Peace, good Verney,' said Cecil, his voice scratching its way over phlegm. 'Ned has not touched me. A little – a little pain in the back. No more. I am quite well. Yet I thank you for your vigilance.'

Verney, to my surprise, smiled at me without guile and bowed, before backing from the room. I remained standing, eyes popping from my head as my hands wandered up to circle my neck. 'A porter, you said he was? Rather at a bear-baiting pit than a lawyer's school.'

'You think there is a difference?'

To my surprise, I laughed myself. Without asking, I slid into one of the chairs across from him. He reached for a cup of wine, already poured, wrinkled his nose at it and sipped. And then he pushed it away and, for good measure, gave it one further little jab away, as though the sight of it offended him. 'So,' he said, blinking, and then working his jaw until colour returned his face. He looked down at his nails. 'First. Tell me in your own words what has passed.'

I did, beginning with my stalking of the Spanish Luisa. At her name, he grimaced and said, 'that wench is well watched. Yet I think her no great plotter. She is the very worst of papists – the one who inspires others by playing on their poverty.'

I nodded and did not tell him that she had spoken of him as a butcher. I did, however, add, a little timidly that she had spoken well of the queen. At the look on his face, the sharpening of his eyes, I stopped, before launching into my account of the corpse, its strange significance as a signal of arrival, and of the lady's promise of vengeance and the page from Holinshed. Along the way, I sweetened my narrative with an account of the players, but he waved this away with impatience. Of the Tower, he was more interested, and he questioned me hard on the Earl of Northumberland's conditions, his belongings, the rough number of men in his train. I answered and ended on the earl's words about his wife and her sister, the ladies Devereux. Again, Cecil's face wrinkled in disgust, until he looked like an aged tortoise.

'It strikes me,' he said, again focussing on his nails, 'that the lady we seek – and I think we must put aside who commands her until we can have it from her own tongue. It strikes me that she is a lady of wit and cunning.' I said nothing. 'Consider. You had so little knowledge of what she left that you had to run with it to a learned counsel. And he, in his turn, had to turn to his … well … a friend.' Again, I held my peace, wondering where he was going. 'Tell me, what do you know of the Devereux woman. The sister to Northumberland's wife.'

'She is … she married, my lord. Became the countess of somewhere, I –'

'No!' Cecil's hand descended on the desk so hard it made his cup quiver. 'No. No. No. She is the countess of nothing.

Nowhere. The king has undone her pretended marriage. And it was not her first. She wed Lord Rich in the late queen's reign and led him a merry dance, cuckolding him with her lover, the Earl of Devonshire. Produced a fair number of bastards in her lusty doings, too.' A leer crossed his face and was gone. 'And when the Rich marriage was dissolved, she continued with Devonshire. Oh, both had the favour of the king and queen well enough, until they wed against all decency. And against his Majesty's command. And against the law of the Church. Both were disgraced. It did not stop them living in sin until the weight of it drove Devonshire to his grave. The king blames the lady. And yet she persists, accusing me – me – of poisoning his Majesty against her.' He gave a flicker of a smile. 'She is, you know, sister to the late Earl of Essex.'

'I know that, my lord.' I held his gaze a moment and then looked past him, to the low fire which sent up transparent flames.

'Did you know that, before he lost his head, Essex claimed that she had been the very mover in his treacherous rebellion?'

If I ever had known it, I'd forgotten. I put my fingers on the edge of the desk. Its top was fine, cool leather and they sank a little, pressing down. 'He … tried to blame his sister? I remember no trial. I…she might have lost her head.'

'He did. That fellow that is cried in taverns as a hero of chivalry tried to blame his pretty sister for his destruction and sought hers in doing so. Would that that were better known amongst those who cry "sweet Essex, brave Essex, our English hero Essex".' His voice had taken on a sing-song at odds with his scowl. I swallowed, wishing I might bite my nails, might light my pipe and have a smoke. 'Yet,' he went on, sitting back, relaxing, 'perhaps the fool spoke the truth. The woman is a born intriguer. A she-wolf, as her mother was in her youth. And probably still is, for the old woman lives still in the country. The Lady Penelope – she has no other title, mark you; she is a pretended countess – the lady … in days long ago, she tried with her brother to court the king when he was but the king of the Scots. Sent him her picture, as though a lady's picture would excite …' He cleared his throat, shaking his head a little before reaching for another drink. 'As I say, she is a viper. And a viper with a grudge against our king and his court.'

'But an assassin…'

'She would not bloody her own hands. Yet wolfish women might find one another. She – and the sister, Dorothy, wife to Northumberland – both have reason to seek vengeance on the king. I noted a moment ago that this woman, whoever she is or whoever employs her, is educated. The Devereux wenches were learned enough. Less sense than they think they possess, but books, reading … educated.' He drummed a brief tattoo on the desk.

'Do you think, then, that … I might have something, my lord? Some conspiracy of assassination against his Majesty? Involving women, indeed?'

'Yes,' he said flatly. And then, after a pause, he frowned. 'But … I think, Ned, that we have been friends long enough that I might speak freely.' I attempted a smile. Friendship was a concept alien to the great Salisbury. It was a concept belonging to men, not snakes. 'You know that I can smell a plot. Strands, threads. I fancy I can see these little things scattered and draw them together.'

'Yes, my lord.' He spoke truly, but he did not thrive on flattery.

'Here, I see something—a plot. But, there is something wrong, something we are not seeing. And that is what I cannot fathom. We find rumours of a woman killer, and we find a strange body, yet otherwise very little. My friends have looked into the papist families about the City and beyond. Nothing. All quiet. So who is this woman that your tapsters have seen? Who are her servants and her masters? It is all … this ill-humour of wrongness. It unsettles me more than the thought of some fool woman loose with murder on her mind.'

I licked my lips. 'Perhaps … perhaps that's it.' He raised an eyebrow at my words, one dark slash arcing upwards. 'That it's a woman, I mean. It's hard to take- to take seriously the idea that a female might truly be a danger. A threat. But it is so. I've seen the corpse. She demands to be taken seriously. And yet she demands not to be, playing these games. I've run about all over

London chasing her, and she gives me a fillip, the bold minx. Every time.'

Cecil appeared to consider this. At length, he said, 'yes. Yes, I grow lax and tired, and old. And I fail in my duty in not taking a threat with enough weight because it comes from rumours of a woman. You are quite right, Ned. Good man.' He reached under his desk and brought out a stack of papers, before stretching beyond his cup and pulling an inkwell and a quill towards him. It was my turn to give him a questioning look. 'I intend to write down all you have said. I have some time. Yesterday, good King Christian demanded to be taken to see St Paul's. A rest from King James's eternal hunting, I should think. They quite cleared Eltham before they came to me at Theobalds. And after four nights at my home, it too is stripped bare. And now Greenwich must suffer the like depredations. King James demands they hunt again on the morrow. They are quite safe out there unless our wicked lady has a coach and horses to carry her thither. For now, I shall do as my father did.' He cast a look, involuntary, I thought, towards the tall painting of Lord Burghley which hung on one wall of the office. 'I shall write down all we have learnt. And see if a pattern emerges, some spark of thought. And I shall ensure that those charged with the security of King James are alert to danger from gunshot or dagger. Or, God help us, powder.'

'And I…?'

'And you,' he said, already writing, not looking up, 'you shall go to Wanstead. Ride. About eight miles out of the City. Not far. Take a horse from our stable here.' He frowned down, blotted a line, and continued scribbling. 'The Lady Penelope spends her summers with her mother in the country. Hiding from the plague, you see. Yet she has recently returned, in hopes that the queen might receive her when Her Majesty has been churched on the morrow. And my eyes tell me that she is still fighting at the law, trying to get hold of the late Devonshire's money and lands, using her pretended marriage. Nonsense, of course. She is notorious as a jade and a schemer.' He stopped writing and looked up, smiling. 'I understand the lady uses her wiles on men. Bends them to her will. She is a great beauty. Yet

I think, my dear Ned, that you will be safe enough from her charms. You look like her late brother and you … well, I think any lady who intends to seduce you might find herself a little unarmed. Go now.'

I neither smiled nor frowned but rose and, after a bow, I set off to meet England's most wicked woman.

14

And, in the mid-afternoon sunlight of the 2nd of August, I found myself waiting in the antechamber of the wickedest woman in England. I had taken a middling sort of horse from the stables at Whitehall – the kind of beast I supposed might not be missed or chased up if it went missing. I had no need for a horse myself, and certainly had no intention of paying for one to be fed and stabled, but the creature could be sold and the money happier in my pocket. And then I had ridden hard for Wanstead Hall in Essex. It was a fine place: three multi-storey blocks each facing a courtyard, the whole house set in a great green blanket of parklands, orchards and hunting grounds. Once it had belonged to Queen Elizabeth's favourite, the Earl of Leicester, and I had no doubt that the old queen had been no stranger to its beds.

On arrival, I had handed my horse off to a groom and been shown by a steward into the great hall, and from thence handed to a maid and led into the antechamber. The pretty little maidservant had asked my business, of course, and I had professed myself a lawyer of Gray's Inn offering service to her mistress. I had been wearing the same rig I'd worn to see Cecil: a suit of dark blue. I would have worn my new outfit but had only just received it on returning home from the Tower the previous night; Faith had still to tailor the dead man's gear for me and replace the buttons, probably because I hadn't yet asked her to.

And so I waited on my audience – if she granted it – with the not-a-countess Lady Penelope. The antechamber was musty; its shutters closed tight against the sun. Cobwebs clung to most corners of the room, some with bits of insects trapped and wizening in them. The place was evidently largely shut up for the summer, as Cecil had indicated. Perhaps in the interests of economy, the lady would have sweetened only those rooms she needed until she was either called to court and embraced or forced back to wherever her mother lived in the country.

There had been no time to learn any more of the woman, and so I had to rely on what Cecil had told me of her and what I had heard over the years from the London news-merchants and singers. All sources were unanimous on her being intelligent, cunning, beautiful, and wicked. I had a theory about the last two. Beautiful women, I knew, fell into two camps: the virtuous fair maidens and the wicked temptresses. A handsome man – oh, a handsome man was always a fine, strapping thing, endowed with all God's blessings. But a beautiful woman – there was a creature that men loved to fear. My suspicion was that they distrusted their own powers of resistance; too many of us became idiots in the presence of female beauty. In that, my affliction was perhaps good fortune; I was immune.

I had no idea of what her relationship had been to the late Earl of Essex and hardly cared. What I did care about was whether I might use my appearance to cow or surprise or intrigue her. Lately, I had taken to wearing my hair to my shoulders, brushed back over my forehead. It waved naturally, in a way that pleased me. In addition, I had lost interest in maintaining a heavy beard but did cultivate a pencil-thin moustache. I could not recall what Essex looked like, though I had seen him riding about London in his lifetime.

My thoughts were interrupted by the chamber door. The maidservant slid out, her eyes on the bare wooden floor. 'Her ladyship will see you, Mr Delamere,' she said. It had been the first name I could think of on proclaiming myself a man at law. I bowed, before following her as she turned and entered the inner chamber.

'Mr Edward Delamere, sergeant-at-law,' she said. I had given myself the promotion along with the false name.

The room into which she'd taken me was also shuttered, though it bore no traces of the penury of the antechamber. Instead, the lady appeared to have had her staff build for her a temporary treasure chamber of a parlour. The air smelt far less stale, for one thing – in fact, the soft blush of roses hung in it. Tapestries were already hanging, carpets covered every inch of the floorboards, and cushioned settles lined each wall. More cushions were scattered about the floor, presumably for guests who might or might not come. The only oddity was the number of bare places on the walls, which were themselves panelled up to the waist and then whitewashed. I assumed she did not carry her portraits around with her, though the ghostly rectangular outlines whispered of their places when the house was in full residence.

The lady herself sat on a great carved chair on the wall opposite me, next to a door that must have led to her bedchamber. I took a few steps towards her, just as the maid slipped out, and went down on one knee, removing my hat and observing her. She was veiled, the reputed beauty, and wearing a fairly simple day dress of white lawn. Its sleeves were only slightly padded, and little ruffs stood out at the wrists. Her hands were clasped demurely in her lap, innocent of rings. 'Come,' she said. 'You may kneel on a cushion.' Her voice was soft and lilting, rather like small bells. I moved forward and took her up on her offer, my knee sinking into a cushion. 'Your business, Sirrah?'

'I am a sergeant-at-law, my lady,' I said. 'I have come to offer my service in your troubles.'

'Is that so? And wherefore should you do that?'

'I was a –'

'Look up at me, man,' she said. And then she partly rose from her seat, lifting her veil and letting it fall back. She was, indeed, a woman of rare beauty. I could not tell her age, though I knew she must be past forty. She might, indeed, have been twenty, so unlined was her face. The features were small, the eyes very dark in the low light. Only her hair betrayed age. It must once have been a rich red but was now sprinkled with grey, as though dust had settled deep in the roots. She could not be, I decided immediately, the one who called herself Locusta, though she was age-defying enough. This was not a woman who could creep the streets of London nor give up the dignity required to do so.

But she might employ that woman.

I had a sudden urge to turn towards the door through which the little maidservant had gone. It was easy enough to resist, for Penelope Devereux' eyes had a terrific pull. They widened a little and then narrowed, and an expression fell upon her that I didn't like. It was something like sorrow. 'You,' she said.

'My lady?'

'Nothing. No. I thought … only for a moment.' Her voice turned dry, as though she was running out of words. 'Why should you come?'

'I was in service to your brother-in-law, the Earl of Northumberland. In legal matters.'

She sniffed. 'And much good, then, that you did him.'

I fought a smile. 'And I learnt of your plight, madam. Of the cruel courses of your life.'

She folded her arms over her chest. 'Did you leave your manners at home, Sirrah?'

Did you leave your head out to rust?

'Madam?' I lowered my head, setting my hat on the carpet.

'It is no business of yours or any man's which courses my life has taken. I will accept no discourses on myself from a stranger not known to me.' She raised her soft, round chin in defiance, her eyes set. Dark lashes fringed them, looking like spiders' legs.

'I apologise if I was forward, my lady. Yet I have some knowledge of matters of Chancery,' I lied.

The lady smiled. 'Chancery. My case is altered from the common law, I admit, my man. But Chancery? Really? You would not hazard any such nonsense if you had a sharp legal mind. My case rests on the Star Chamber.' I cursed my own stupidity. Her suit, which I assumed was to have her marriage acknowledged and to be given her late husband's property, must have been advanced to that great court. It, I knew, was simply the Privy Council acting as a judicial body. And Cecil, as head of the Privy Council, was thus its arbiter.

Well, you're *fucked, then.*

I blinked away the irreverent thought. And then I began to talk. 'My lady, I confess I came here under false colours. I'm a student of the law only—a mere prentice in the legal arts. Yet I heard of your case. It so moved me, I … I wished to offer my services, meagre as they are. I'm not a rich man, but of good family and prospects. I heard of your great beauty and the cruelty you have suffered. It so – it so outraged me,' I cast a furious look at the carpet and jabbed at my hat, 'that I purposed to come hither and see you. And pledge my service.' I looked up at her again, an attempt at appeal painted across my face.

Again, on looking at my face, she got that look of sorrow. I had her, I thought. Her brother had famously been a man of great passion, of sudden doings and a stout heart. And here he was, come again. She said nothing, content to let me wait there acting, acting with my features for all I was worth. At length, she said, in a cold, distant voice, 'I have learnt to be unmoved by the passions of men. Passions today are forgotten tomorrow. All men are inconstant.'

'Perhaps,' I offered. 'Yet … my lady, I … I know that the king has ill-treated you.' At this, her hands clasped, claw-like, on the ends of her armrests. She drew breath in a sharp intake.

'You speak treason, sir. I know well enough who my enemies are. And who they have been for a long time since. And they are not his gracious Majesty, but the counsel that surrounds him.'

I said nothing. I knew who she meant, of course. But it was mere policy. No man – or woman – of breeding would ever speak against their sovereign. Instead, they would sheathe their wicked intents, their jealousies and rages, in attacks on royal counsellors. It was a far safer thing to plot against the monarch whilst claiming only to oppose a wicked counsellor who had misled them. Her brother, indeed, had done the same, riding against Queen Elizabeth whilst crying to the world that he meant only to rid the court of Cecil.

'It might be,' I said eventually, 'that vengeance is sought against those who have done you wrong.'

'What is this?' She looked over my shoulder, I noticed, towards the door the maidservant had gone through. Perhaps she thought me a madman now, a danger. I was, after all, a stranger alone with her. 'Speak you of vengeance?'

'Ay, madam. It is bruited about the street that there is a plot laid against wicked men of the court.'

To my surprise, she laughed. 'Then I suggest, Sirrah, that you take these bruits to the men fit to discover them.'

I bit at my lower lip. She was too clever to be trapped, too shrewd to open her heart and mind to a stranger.

To hell with it.

'Go with what I've heard to the king's minion, the crookback? Never. Never. I should die before I turned to that man.' I raised my hand to my heart, hoping I might put those words in her mouth, might make her condemn herself.

She smiled weakly. 'Better born men that a poor student of the law have tried to turn traitor against the king's good servant. Sirrah, I shall offer you advice. Stay out of matters which are bigger than your little world. Meddle not in my affairs nor in any rumours you hear.'

'But I –'

'You will do me no service, man. I am set on my course. My trusted people serve me, and I will have no others.' She tapped the edges of her armrests. A faraway look came into her eyes. 'If you hear of rumours against my lord of Salisbury, then you hear rumours against the king. If you hear rumours against the king, then you hear treason. And I am no traitor, nor ever have been.'

'But …' I was losing her. I had lost her. 'Who would wish ill against the king, madam? I could not take news of idle rumour.'

She laughed, a hard, bitter little laugh, like bells, shattering. 'You come from London, do you not?' I bowed my head in affirmation. 'Tell me, is the queen yet risen to be churched?'

I looked up, frowning. 'Tomorrow, my lady.'

'Mm. A woman of wit, Queen Anne. With friends in the town, amongst the playing sort.'

What was she talking about?

'Quite, my lady.' But something occurred to me about the Lady Penelope. She had been rusticated, cut off from the world of gossip and rumour. That was the meat and drink of courtiers, I knew. And here was I, ridden hard from the City, and along with my lies and offers of service and passion I had brought with me a great feast of gossip. 'There is much news cast about the City, madam,' I said. Her eyes glittered, their focus landing on me.

'Oh?'

'That the two kings drank overmuch at Theobalds. Certain ladies fell about, mad with it withal.' At this, she openly smiled, leaning forward in her chair.

'Their names?'

'I cannot say. Only that Lord Salisbury's entertainments at Theobalds were no success.'

'Ha! I daresay his Majesty will covet that great house. Little Salisbury will not hold all for long.'

I licked my lips. There followed a full half-hour of my imparting every scrap of gossip I'd heard in the previous two months: about the liberties taken at the royal court; about the entertainments to be staged; about the distance said to be springing up between the king and queen; about the Scotch supposedly being furious about the new flag. Throughout, the Lady Penelope ate greedily, clapping her fine hands together in delight. If I do say so, I caught her up with the London news expertly, garnishing the tales with wit.

Eventually, she settled back, sated. I smiled, shaking my head and watching her. I finished by mentioning, as though it were an idle thing, tales of a female-led conspiracy against the king. By then, her wariness had abated; she was well-filled, contented, and eager to divulge what she knew.

'A conspiracy of women, they say? Now there is something.' Was she being playful, I wondered – or was she concealing her own guilt and knowledge? 'How seldom men of the state remember the women left behind when they have rid the realm of their plotting men.' My heart fluttered. I might, if I were minded, have woven this into an accusation against her sister, whose husband languished in the Tower. But I was not fishing for means to condemn, but for the truth. 'I have often wondered who might plot against men,' she said. 'And do you know, young Master Lawyer, who most gains when her husband – her lawful husband – is struck off?'

My eyes widened. 'You mean…'

'Ride back to London, Mr Delamere. You might offer better service to our gracious queen, and find it rewarded.' Her eyes glittered. 'When Queen Anne is returned to society … well, perhaps I shall see you there.'

***

That was two, now—two wicked women who had directed me to Queen Anne. And yet, as I rode back into the City, I could scarcely credit the idea.

I did not know the queen, had never done any more than seeing her abroad when she made appearances. About all I knew was that she kept Revels busy, demanding masques – strange, extravagant spectacles which were more show than story – in which she and her ladies could perform.

Ladies performing...

The queen certainly had lofty ideas about what women could do. As I rode up towards Ludgate, I considered the possibility. I had no idea if the queen loved or even liked her husband. For all I knew, she hated him. Though it was apparent that they still slept together – the recent daughter, dead after a day, proved this – I knew that King James's tastes ran according to my own, according to Bacon's.

And if King James were killed, the queen would become regent until Prince Henry came of age, with Cecil likely continuing to govern. I knew enough of history – real history, English – to tell that queen consorts of England often took the reins. Two of the old tyrant Henry VIII's wives had been made regents when he was alive. It stood to reason that a queen might rule, even if only in name when her husband died. And if it happened when her brother was in town, she could count on a foreign sovereign's support.

But could Queen Anne really be overseeing a conspiracy to be rid of her intolerable husband? She could not do it directly – she must have a team of men – or women – acting on her orders. A small army of them.

It could be - it could be ...

It could also be that the wicked Lady Penelope had just cozened me, manipulating me into looking in the unlikeliest of places, so I ceased disturbing her. As I turned into Fleet Street, about which people still milled and chatted and sang (the festival air seemed set to stay awhile) I tried to marshal my thoughts.

Luisa Mendoza had sent me to Queen Anne, thinking me a

Catholic who would find succour there.

Penelope Devereux had sent me to Queen Anne, laughing in her sleeve at the thought that the queen might wish to be rid of her husband.

A woman, most certainly, had threatened the king's life in the name of vengeance.

And that woman had to be part of something larger – she had servants enough of her own, at any rate.

And from there onwards I was lost in a sea of possibilities. The problem was, as I now saw it, that everyone I had met seemed to have a reason to seek revenge against the king. Could the Spanish be orchestrating a plot in vengeance against the bloody reprisals against Catholics? Of course. Could Northumberland have managed to get his wife or sister-in-law to seek vengeance on his behalf? Certainly. Could Queen Anne be a secret Catholic, as gossips said, and seek to be rid of the husband whose sexual adventures were descanted upon in every alehouse? It was said, indeed, that King James kept a room at the Holland's Leaguer brothel in Southwark, where he played bed games with floppy-haired and pimply-faced boys. Though I didn't believe this particular bit of slander, I knew that he held his marriage in no great sanctity, and any wife might resent that. So this was possible too.

I dismounted, my head swimming. Perhaps, I thought, they were all in it together, and I'd been set chasing one woman only to find that she was part of a network stretching from the Spanish embassy to Wanstead to Greenwich.

The potential of a web of a conspiracy was too great, too frightening. So it had been with the Powder Plot: that had threatened to enmesh everyone, from players and poets to Jesuits to nobles and gentlemen.

Could it – *could it* – be happening again? Could the Lady Locusta be controlled not by one puppet-master but part of a vast web of conspirators? And if so, had I met any of them and, like a fool, betrayed myself, made myself known to them?

The webs of Wanstead crossed my mind, their network of white, silken lines crisscrossing one another. Everything, it seemed, was connected. Even in my own little circle of London, my regular job, the players and the Revels Master were linked to the king; the king kept Cecil, too, and Cecil kept me dancing on his silken lead; the king and queen's court was full of courtiers – in and out of favour – like the Lady Penelope; Penelope's family web stretched and crossed over the Powder traitors; the Powder Traitors included the priest who had helped bring Luisa Mendoza into England; Luisa Mendoza's Barbican home was a weed-bed of the queen's secret faith. All connected, everything, lines crossing so thickly the whole became opaque. Impossible to unpick which of the spinners had set a baby spider out to eat.

Yet, I could remember it being said during the great buzz of the Powder Treason that the band of plotters couldn't have acted without at least one nobleman behind them. Perhaps Locusta and her minions could not act without the noblest of women…

I left the horse standing in the street and banged on my front door. Faith answered, and over her shoulder, I saw Nicholas and David, playing some sort of game with cards at my table. 'Hopgood,' I shouted, ignoring Faith's greeting. 'Would you do me a favour? Before I give you my Faith, I would that you would give away my horse.' I looked over my shoulder at the tired beast, and then up at the sky. Though it was still light, I could see the pale winking of stars. 'Take the creature into the town and get me a good price for it, will you?'

'Yes, Mr Savage, sir,' the prentice answered, bounding up and ruffling David's hair. He was a reliable, fellow, Nicholas Hopgood – too damned dull to be anything else. I stood back to let him pass, looking away as he kissed Faith's cheek.

'I shall see you on the morrow, sweetheart,' he said. She smiled in return.

'And see me on the morrow with a good price,' I said, watching as he took the horse's reins.

Faith began to mutter something about the late hour, but I burst past her and into the house, leaving her to close the door behind me. 'Mouse,' I said, wheeling on her. 'I have a favour to ask of you too.'

'What is it?' Wariness edged her voice.

'A good thing. A fine thing. That new suit of clothes that

arrived yesterday. I want you to help me fix it up. To fit me better. More, I wish you to make it fit for court. Just as full of bombast – yes, bombast – as we can.' I gave a flourishing bow. 'Her Majesty Queen Anne rises tomorrow from her confinement. I intend to be amongst the first to pay her court.'

15

Locusta gasped, in spite of herself, at the change she had effected in the man Georgie, whom she had stolen off the streets only a few days before. It had taken a set of skills she did not know she possessed, though she had seen it done often enough, of course. She had been dressed aplenty. Never had she been called upon to dress a man up, to make a likeness, save the limp old vagabond in the Bull Head.

Georgie was slumped, as drunk as a lord, on the carpet. She had cut his hair – a thoroughly disgusting job, which had required her to wash her hands in wine afterwards – and trimmed his beard. His tattered clothing she had cut away with a dagger. He remained insensible, thankfully, and did not cry out when she nicked him. And then she had folded his new suit of clothes onto him, slapping him about the face until he smiled like an idiot and grumbled, bidding him to straighten his arms and stretch his legs. It was an ugly, odd job, but she had done it.

Georgie, the pathetic wreck she had lured from the streets of London and delivered to her masters, had been transformed. All that was needed was the hat they had left her. She turned, reached down, and lifted it, plopping it onto his head.

And then she fought the urge to laugh.

If it had been legal to depict the king on the public stage – which, of course, it was not – Georgie would have done him justice. King James was no master of the regal presence; he was a stuffy looking old schoolmaster who ill-fit his clothes. And that, she thought, was what she had made of her charge: a fine, a more than passable, double for the king. In the candlelight, the similarity was really quite startling. She had seen the king often enough, at reasonably close quarters, and this creature might have been a cousin if not a brother. It was the clothes that sold it and, she fancied, the cut she had given the hair and beard.

It was just as she had been commanded: take this creature and clothe him as we provide, until he is a counterfeit king.

Now, she had to awaken him enough to get him out into the

alley behind the house and into his carriage. This she managed only with effort. Georgie could not walk in fine clothes and could barely stand in the drunkenness in which he'd been kept for days. Yet she managed to lift him under the armpits, as though she were a tapster and he an unruly patron, and stagger out into the adjoining chamber. The stairs would be more of a challenge, she thought, grunting.

But she would not have to do it alone. One of the Augustans was already waiting outside. He immediately came forward and took the fellow under one of his pits, and together they got him down and out into the street.

In the narrow alley, the carriage stood ready. It had been delivered the day after her visit to Webster's carriage-making house in Clerkenwell, complete with its wheels and its detachable royal arms. The horses were already bridled and ready.

'Magnificent!' boomed the fellow she knew as the leader of the Brotherhood of Augustus. He stepped out of the shadows; his black hood pulled low. In the darkness, his voice was disembodied, eerie. 'Exactly as we wished. This creature, can this be the same thing which has tossed and puked and soiled yonder chamber these past days?'

Georgie burped. The jerk of his head seemed to bring him to a kind of sobriety. ''ere,' he said. 'Wha' goes on?'

'Peace, gentle sir,' said the leader. 'You are to be carried from hence in some style. The good lady here has made you fitter for the journey.'

''oo said that? 'oo's there? 'ere, geroffa me!' The well-dressed wreck attempted to wrench himself loose, forcing Locusta and her fellow captor to hold him more tightly. The Augustan who had his other armpit eventually slapped him across the face.

'Remember your charge, you filth. If you do not wish your throat cut.'

'Gentle, brother,' said the leader. He moved across the cobbles soundlessly, until he stood in the moonlight directly before the captive. 'This night, Goodman George, you are to be taken from this place. Some distance, I am afraid. And yet you will be conveyed hence in good style.' He stepped away and patted the side of the coach. 'When you arrive, you will remain in this fair coach. Its driver shall not remain, though he shall dress it for you. It is well provisioned. The night shall be warm. There are beer and bread to see you through it.'

Georgie managed no more than a muted squeak, and Locusta could feel him going limp. Doubtless, he was beginning to see through the fog, to remember that he had been seized and was being forced into a game. 'Y-yes, master.'

'That is good. You understand.'

She released his arm, just as the Augustan did with the other. Georgie slumped forward, his hat falling askew. Its silver buckle glimmered. 'I … I ain't never been in no coach afore, sir, nor driven one neither.'

'You will be unharmed. The backroads, alas, a trifle bumpy. But you will be unharmed.'

The two Augustans, leader and follower, helped the man into the coach before the latter went to the front and climbed up to see to the pair of sleek horses. Locusta, looking at them, marvelled at the sheer amount of money that these Augustans must have. Enough for fine clothes, fine places to serve as meeting halls and gaols, fine horses, the carriage, even.

Only when the false king was seated in the coach did the leader turn his hood up to the open, wood-framed window. 'Now,' he called up, 'remember. You are to play a most important part in a joyful little game, dear fellow. On the morrow, the king will go a-hunting. We will seize him.'

In the coach, a jolt of good sense finally seemed to seize the man. 'Wha'? Seize? This is …' He gripped the window frame, his freshly clipped fingernails becoming little white half-moons. 'Let me out! Treason! Treason!'

Quick as a flash, the leader threw up a hand and struck him across the face. 'Quiet, you fool. If you cry so on this journey, your throat will be cut. Look at yourself. It shall not go well for you.' Georgie, like a whipped puppy, fell back on his hard-wooden seat, mewling, kneading his cheek. 'Good. Silence. There is no treason here.' The Augustan's voice had become honey, dripping and sweet. 'I promise you; this is a mere game, a toy. His Majesty wishes to play a trick on his brother-king, the Dane. We will seize him by his own command, and when the king's men look for him, they shall find you in this fine royal carriage. And you shall say, in your own manner, "why, I know no other king but me" and hold out your hand for them to kiss. It is a mere jest. Why the king is the very chief of the Brotherhood of Augustus, he is our own great peacemaker. We shall release him, and all shall be well, the two kings enjoying their mirth and merriment.' He went on talking awhile, until Georgie's mewling ceased, repeating over and over that the times were made for revelry, for jesting, for entertainments, and this was simply one of them.

Eventually, the coach lurched forward once, twice, and then was off, bouncing a little on the uneven ground. Locusta watched it go. It had disappeared into the blackness when the leader of the Augustans put a hand on her shoulder. 'That was well done of you,' he said. She did not answer. 'The king shall find much mirth indeed at Greenwich on the morrow.' A little chill ran through Locusta, though she couldn't account for it. 'The man, Ned Savage, now runs about the town and beyond, seeking you.' There it was.

'I left him the note.'

'Yes, we know. He must have found it. And he since has taken boat and horse in search of you.' Locusta swallowed. 'Let him. He seeks to hold the wind, my dear. He cannot touch you. Now, we think, he runs about blind, following the old trail of gunpowder long since blown away.' Then he leant in to whisper what she must do next.

16

I was one of many petitioners, but I had my own way in. That was a connection to the Revels Office. I had not told Cecil of my coming to Greenwich. If I were wrong about the queen – and, after spending a sleepless night on it, I was sure I was – I had no wish for him ever to know I'd even entertained the slightest suspicion of her Majesty.

I had never been to Greenwich before, but I was up with the sun. Faith even stayed over, and she and David helped fit me out in my dead man's clothing until I was fit for the royal court itself. I had then embarked downriver and been set ashore at the palace, as though I were Lord Edward of Farringdon Without, master of the Shoe Lane sewer channel and feudal lord of the cat and kittens that lived behind the broken wall edging Fleet Street.

The palace itself was a pretty enough thing, though I am not a man bowed by splendour and pomp. Old fashioned, I thought – as befitted the birthplace of the late Queen Elizabeth and her father – it rose beside the river in a series of tall windows, depressed arches, decorated chimneys, and those curious, thin, angular towers that seemed to delight men seventy years before. After showing my papers – Cecil's name was as influential in the queen's court as the king's – I was conducted through a series of equally old-fashioned long galleries and hammer-beam roofed great halls.

The queen, I was told by the various ushers who led me through each room, was at service. This was the day of her churching, which I understood was a woman's thing – a cleansing of the stain of childbirth by the Church. After the cleansing, she was free to re-enter society. From the presence-chamber – a large, densely packed room full of chatter and laughter – I was taken into a narrow corridor which led to the privy chamber. And there I had been left.

The approach to the queen's private rooms was thronged, well-dressed men and women standing shoulder to shoulder, jostling and barging for a better place. Most carried scrolls of paper, letters, little wrapped silver and gilt gift boxes. At the far end were stationed two stout guards, their halberds held across their chests. Every now and then the door was opened from within and everyone hushed, waiting to see who was called.

The early morning passed, and I suspected that I might not see the queen – if at all – before dinner. I had given my real name and shown my papers to prove that I was one of Cecil's friends, but my appeal to the ushers had been to carry forward news that a servant of the Revels Office wished an audience. Given her love of all courtly spectacles, I felt certain she would see me at some point. It was the best course of action; I'd judged, not only to win that meeting but because lying was far too dangerous. A queen was not a Spanish interloper or a disgraced courtier. If I offended my sovereign's wife with false lies, with suspicions, Cecil would not save me.

'Savage of Revels, tae see hir Majesty.' The voice – a woman's voice – cut over the landscape of feathers and hat brims which spread before me. I had been leaning with my back to a tapestried wall, and I slouched forward, relief and trepidation washing through me. A path was grudgingly cleared, painted faces and bearded ones frowning in my direction. I pasted on a dumb smile and walked through them, staring ahead.

I did not acknowledge the guards but was grabbed roughly by the forearm as I reached the door. The woman inside was unsmiling, her face very hard for one that only looked to be about twenty. 'Savage?' she asked. Her accent was Scotch. I nodded. 'Guid. Hir Majesty has heard of your coming. She wid speak with you.'

I passed into the privy chamber, the door smoothly clicking behind me.

No stranger to the private rooms of royalty – I had been in the king's bedchamber in Holyroodhouse – I was nevertheless surprised at the Greenwich apartment. It was large, for one thing, and I could see a number of doors set into the far wall, and several casements bordering window embrasures on which were sat ladies with fans. Queen Anne did not appear to have a privy chamber, indeed, but a whole set of private apartments hidden behind the more public presence-chamber. The first of them, the room into which I'd been shown, must have been a reception or gaming room, judging by the marble-topped card tables and chess boards covered in crystal and jet pieces. Every surface was covered in fringed red and white cloths and arrases shot with gold, and most of them rustled in the gentle, warm breeze from the open windows. I supposed the doors must lead to her bedchamber; her closet; her close stool; her chapel, perhaps, where she might keep a priest hidden.

'I am the Lady Jean,' said my young hostess. The woman who had conducted me into the chamber had caught me looking around. Rather than angering her, it seemed to soften her. Perhaps she was proud of her mistress's fine rooms, pleased to see a stranger gazing in what she took to be awe. 'Hir Majesty is willing tae grant you an audience. She shall be here directly and looks to hear of nothing ill, sir. Fair news of revelry, only.' Her tone had become that of a schoolmaster, and I found myself looking at a face stern enough to match.

'Yes, my lady,' I said, though my mind railed, 'milady gatekeeper'.

She stepped back, gave one hard nod downwards, and then retreated across the room, knocking on a door. It was opened almost immediately, and Queen Anne burst out, her arms swinging as much as her large sleeves would allow.

The queen was not, I admit, a raving beauty. She was, however, rather handsome. I knew her to be about thirty, or perhaps a shade over. She compared well to her husband, who was past forty and looked every day of it (and a few more besides). Her skin was remarkably fresh and her face long, dominated by a drooping, aquiline nose. It was apparent that she had grown weary of her confinement and had taken this, her first day of freedom, to dress the part. It was almost difficult to take her in all at once: her hair was a great dun beehive, laced through with pearls; her jagged standing ruff and the edging of her bodice were lacy geometric patterns; around her neck and down her bosom hung more pearls; her stiff, drummed farthingale was the colour of pale cream. She stood, framed in the doorway a moment, and bent sideways so that the diminutive Lady Jean could whisper something to her. As she did, I fell to my knees. My hat, already off, I held pressed to my belly.

'Staunt,' she barked across the room. Her voice was deep, brash, and confident. 'Staunt, zir!'

It took me a few seconds to realise that she was bidding me to rise. I stood, keeping my head down.

'We will walk a wee pace, doon the gallery. Aye, zir, come.' She reached out a thin hand, making a crook of her bony finger. And then she snapped it. 'Now!' She turned and moved towards another door. Jean opened it for and, after the queen bent through, she gave me a wide-eyed but unspoken 'hurry up'. I scurried over and through the door.

The privy gallery was a long room which seemed to stretch on into the distance. It must have been, I imagined, the place where she exercised away from men's eyes. Already she was partway down it, floating over the thick scarlet carpet, one minute in shadow, the next bathed in sunlight from the tall windows. I followed, a little lost now. 'You do not mind if I walk, zir?' she called without turning. 'It is good.' Her accent was odd. It was Scotch, to be sure, but stretched up and down and side to side by what must have been Danish. I hurried down the gallery, past enormously tall Flemish paintings, until I was a few paces behind her. Then I began to match her carriage.

'It is good to receive visitors once again,' she said.

'And so many, your Majesty.'

Queen Anne stopped, and so did I; she turned so that her long-nosed profile was winking at me. A dimple appeared in her cheek. 'Yes. There are many who have waited long for this day.' She began moving forward again, and I kept my eyes on the hem of her ruffled skirts as it bounced along the carpet, thick lace sweeping weaved wool. 'You, we think, are from the Revels?'

'That I am, your Majesty.'

'Guid! We must have the business in hand.' She halted again, pulling up a pomander that hung from her waist and tossing it in the air before catching it in her palm. 'We have heard of the revels at … what is the name of the place, again? I do not…'

'Theobalds,' I said, pronouncing it 'Tibbalds' as Cecil did.

'Yes. We have heard. And we hope that the next entertainments at Hampton Court – that they shall be well done by your Sir Edmund.' This, I thought, was a little unfair. Sir Edmund and the whole Revels Office were charged with approving plays for performance. It was not our job to ensure that the royals and nobles who watched and participated should refrain from getting pissed and acting like jackasses. Of course, I said no such thing.

'Yes, your Majesty.'

'Guid.' A little business-like clap of her hands and she was off again. I noticed that she never troubled to lower her voice. The privy gallery had several doors along one side, most of them open. Apparently, Queen Anne cared nothing for spies or listeners. 'And what plays, zir?'

'The King's Men's own tragedies of *Hamlet* and *Macbeth*.'

Finally, the queen stopped next to a tall window. She turned to me. '*Hamlet*. The prince of Denmark.' She gave a smile, showing good teeth. 'This, I know. It must needs be cut. The king, my husband, shall not sit the whole space, not again. And this other, this *Macbeth*. A Scottish play?'

'So I believe, your Majesty.'

'Guid. It shall go well. And perhaps a little thing to bring laughter at the evening's end? A light thing, I think, not by Mr Shakespeare. He writes of soiled souls well – like a woman – but his comedies ... My Mr Jonson is finer for mirth.'

'I have already requested it, madam. Some light matter, I mean.'

Anne gave another little smile. It dissolved. 'Who are you, zir?'

'I …'

'You are not the usual man who comes to us from Revels. You do not wear your livery but come to delight. Yet … it appears you serve two. Your papers,' she added, jutting her nose at my belt, 'speak of more than Sir Edmund Tilney of the Revels Office. They speak of one greater.'

I had not expected this. I did not fool myself that Queen Anne was an idiot, but I had expected her to be indirect, to be guarded and careful. Instead, I found a well-caparisoned charging bull. She seemed to read my thoughts. 'I know,' she said, 'that my husband the king thinks us all mumps and mops in this house. Yet we are not so. What are you, Mr Double-tongue of Revels and Salisbury? A poet, come with some small scribblings to crave our favour?'

'No, I ...'

Her eyes narrowed. 'No. No, I think you have not the look of a poet. Then tell me. What does my lord of Salisbury wish?'

I recovered, I hoped. 'It is true. I serve Sir Edmund and oftentimes, my lord of Salisbury.' That was a thing I had admitted to very few people, and here I was volunteering it to the queen of England. 'And my lord wishes only that the entertainments are passed off well. As your Majesty wishes.'

'Hm. Hm.' She raised her pomander again, tapping it against her chin this time. Her eyes were an unsettling pale blue. I could feel them, unblinking, boring into me. 'Does my lord fear some mischance?'

I looked up, my mouth dropping open. 'Mischance?'

'Some accident. It is his, ah- his obsession, is it no? That some stramash shall make a great disorder. We hear things, Mr ... what is your name again?'

'Savage, your Majesty.'

'Mr Savage. We hear that my lord of Salisbury collects bruits, as my husband collects good riding horses. And we hear that some lady is set abroad in London with evil intent.'

I swallowed. There was no point in guessing what she knew. 'Yes, Your Majesty. My lord fears for the king's safety.'

'It is but rumour, I am sure. Such tales attend on princes.' She shrugged, moving away from the wall and beginning her progress back up the chamber. She swept past me, tapping on the side of her narrow bodice. 'I have often thought my lord would be mair gainfully employed, you know,' she boomed, stopping almost immediately at the next window along, 'out there.'

'Madam?' I paused at her elbow. She was looking out through the diamond-paned window at a vast sprawl of greenery –

fields, parks, woods. Some men were leading horses about, the beasts already dressed for riding.

She tapped on the glass with all the fingers of one hand, leaving little imprints. 'My lord and husband is at the hunt again. Every day, every day, riding out. I fear my brother the king will not keep up with him. He takes small pleasure in the wearing out of horses, his dear Majesty. But my husband shall have his way again. Hunting! We had thought he might come to these chambers…' I did not reply but continued to look out, unsure of what she was talking about. I knew the king was a keen hunter – everyone did. What had that to do with Cecil? 'I mean,' she said, turning from the window to look at me, 'that his Majesty is more like to fall from a wretched horse than to be bitten at by some woman. This I cannot make him see. Nor Lord Salisbury. Perhaps you can tell him. If his lordship wishes to protect the king's person, it is by curbing this hunting.'

She was being serious, I realised. 'I shall tell him, your Majesty.'

'Guid. Every morning and afternoon, until the midges buzz about. He rides until his body of gentlemen cannot keep up and fall behind. If he should fall from his horse, he would be alone in the field. You tell my lord of Salisbury, Mr Savage. The king will listen to no woman. Cease this hunting by degrees, or, at the least – finer horses.'

I was no longer listening.

He rides until his body of gentlemen cannot keep up and fall behind.

If he should fall from his horse, he would be alone in the field.

In a pitched field, where after great slaughter &c murther.

'Mr Savage? You are gone white.' An iron band fell around my wrist. Queen Anne's hand had reached out, her white fingers circling it. 'Zir. Zir! We are speaking wae you!'

I looked at her, my mouth a wasteland. My teeth were sunken into my bottom lip. 'Hunting, where is the king, your Majesty, you said he is hunting, when, *now*? Cecil – Salis – I must get word!'

The queen, to her great credit, did not slap the sudden madness out of me. Instead, she released my hand. She, too, had lost the blush from her cheeks. In a low growl, she said, 'danger. We understand. The kings – both – are hunting in the parks here.'

Of course! Cecil had said that.

I began to move off, away from her, forgetting to bow.

'Wait!' she cried. I stopped. I could feel a trembling start up within me. 'We will send word to Salisbury. We know he has many men lodged within. They surround the king already, always. We will alert him that you have some suspicion. You, Savage – make no fuss. Say nothing to my people. Find your master's men – they will be, I think, about. They always are. Search, seek, find what you must.'

'Yes, madam.'

'Go now. The king will be going out, might be already abroad in the field.'

I fled from her presence, all suspicion that she might be behind the plot forgotten. It didn't matter. I knew – knew – that if an attempt were made on the king's life, there would be no better time or place than when he made a great broad target, set up alone upon a horse in an open field or secretive woodland.

17

I will never know how I managed to keep my head. Yet somehow I did, somehow I managed to refrain from running and shouting, 'the king is to be slain at the hunt! An assassin lies in wait!'

Instead, I went calmly from the queen's apartments and found my way through the palace, through the crowds of courtiers who seemed to spill from every doorway and tumble around each corner. Now that I was looking for them, I began to see Cecil's enforcers, in their Puritan-like weeds, everywhere. These were creatures who would once have been kept to the streets. Since the Powder Treason, of course, the secretary had stationed them everywhere the king was or might be, watching, spying, their black coats betraying that they were men of subtle security quite apart from the regular palace guards, who had failed so singularly to spot anyone filling the under-croft of Westminster Hall with gunpowder.

'Lord Salisbury – the queen – you must search the park. Search! An assassin lies in wait for his Majesty!' My words, jumbled, hectoring, and rude, were not ignored. Cecil's motley crew of dour-faced watchers were searchers and seekers by nature: the homes of Catholics, taverns and alehouses; I had even seen them lurk about theatres and executions listening and watching for a breath of treason. With grim nods, they fled the palace to coordinate their searches around the perimeter of the hunting grounds. To search for I knew not what – a person, a group, a woman, a weapon.

Gunpowder…

I moved too.

Out into park which spread behind Greenwich like a vast green sea, its waves trees swaying in the wind. Viewed from above, from Queen Anne's gallery, it was a pretty sight – a gentle swell in the dirty brown swamp outside of London. As I stood looking at the treeline, however, it became dangerous waters indeed. A man – a woman – might lurk in any sweet bower, pistol or bow primed. As far as I knew, the great royal parks were fenced, but a fence was not a wall. They were managed by keepers and wardens, but these were men set to maintain deer and frighten away night-poachers.

The stables stood to the rear of the palace, abutting a gravelled courtyard dotted with ornamental bushes. I flew across it, bits of grit flying up behind me, and skidded into the reek of manure. Pins shook loose from my ruff and sleeves; snaking laces began to wag and wave. Suddenly I was a moving mind, my body – a quaking, itchy thing – quite separate in its rapidly undressed state. 'A horse! A horse!'

His kingdoms for a horse!

I did not wait to be questioned. Instead, I scanned the bays of stalls, ignoring the confused stable lads who were wielding pitchforks like halberds. Most of them were empty, but a few still had tenants. I kicked my way over buckets and bridles, muttering and barking like a madman. One beast was dressed in saddle and stirrup, as though its rider had not turned up. I skipped over and released the bolt on its door, throwing it wide and leaping up to the mounting block.

''Ere, what the hell are you about?' This from a groom, woken from the stupor my wild entrance had induced. 'That's the Danish king's horse.'

Christian of Denmark, I realised, was either late to the hunting party or had got out of another tiresome day in the saddle. I said nothing, but shook the beast onwards, out of the stall. It went willingly enough, and the stable servants all jumped out of its path, some of them crying, 'treason!' How I hated that damned word.

From above, I cried, 'his Majesty is abused!' And then I was jolting and bouncing past a line of their white, round faces and white, round eyes, and I was gone.

I slapped and whipped the horse onwards and right, crunching over gravel and then grass. Suddenly, as though I were flying, I left the palace grounds and was swallowed up in a canopy of emerald.

I slowed the horse, whispering soothing nonsense, stroking it. Looking ahead, I could see a wide trail of churned mud and gravel. It had been years since I'd been hunting at my old family's home in Derbyshire. But I could remember the sport clearly enough. Barking was what I was must listen for. I must find the king and lead him away from the chase. And the hounds would lead me to his Majesty. I cocked my ear over the crunching of twigs and gravel under my horse's hooves.

It was August, I realised, the third day of August. In such a season, the king would seek the hart in coppices and near springs. The park's huntsman would have been up at dawn, looking for tokens – broken branches, fresh droppings – that signalled the late passage of the beast. I looked myself but saw only thick trees to my left and right, their trunks a succession of brown columns. The roots were lost in blooming, mossy foliage.

Ahead, the path branched three ways, snaking left and right into more woodlands. The direct path fell through a more open field of grass as high as a big man's waist. As I reached the fork, I reined in.

Left!

The path to the left was a mess, the others undisturbed. I leant forward, my breath rippling the horse's mane, and listened. Distantly, I could hear the furious rise and fall of barking, the thunder of hooves. The king and his party had certainly gone along the wooded left-hand path, and by the sound of the hounds, they had sighted their hart. I sat back, my mouth drying, and made to follow.

What's that?

It was just a glimpse, a fleck of something in the corner of my eye, something that didn't fit and gave me pause. I almost ignored it, so intent was I on listening rather than looking. I cast just a glance over to my right, along the path through the grass. The sun was glinting on something, shining white on … black?

I turned, tutting, to look again.

Yes, the great open field, which boasted only scattered trees above the wavering greenish-yellow, had something in it. Something that wasn't moving. My horse kicked at the ground, apparently annoyed by my irresolution. I ran a hand through my hair – my hat must have fallen off on the dash across the courtyard without my noticing – and darted glances between the woodlands and the field. Focusing on the latter, I tried to make out the black thing with its white edging of sunshine.

After a few moments, I began turning my mount, and struck off the short distance back to the fork, bearing left and into the field. I went slowly, warily, allowing the horse a bare trot. As we made our way along the path, the thing ahead began to take on a round, tall shape.

What the hell?

It was a carriage, I realised. A fine coach which had been left in a clearing in the middle of the field. It must have been brought in from the southern reaches of the park, along the same path I rode along, but in the opposite direction. I shook my head a little, confusion overtaking fear or caution, and for the last stretch, I shook the horse on to a canter.

When I reached the thing, I rode around it in a circle. It was a fine carriage, to be sure, a royal one, with its black shutters closed, and its arms hung up on them. I considered riding away, leaving it. Some mistake, perhaps, or something sent into the field by the king for reasons I couldn't comprehend.

A place for an assignation, I realised suddenly. The king might tell the world he is hunting when in fact he creeps off with one of his young friends to frolic and roll naked in the shuttered darkness of a carriage.

You dirty old bastard!

I was on the point of riding away when something struck me: the hounds, the sounds, the disturbed path that had lain to my left, something wasn't right. I reined in and slid down, pain shooting up my legs as I landed on the gravel. I chanced a look back the way I'd come. It was clear. I did a circuit of the carriage and looked down the rest of the path. Sure enough, the ground was disturbed. The thing must have been driven up here and then untied, abandoned. And recently, I thought.

From inside the coach came a low rumbling. I stepped back, struggling to place it. It rose and fell, rattling and whistling.

Breathing!

Snoring, more like. It seemed as though the coach itself was inhaling and exhaling like a giant, slumbering pig. The strange sound rose and fell, distinct over the myriad chirrups and rustlings and cracklings of the field. I stepped closer again, putting a foot on the step leading to its door, and I banged a fist against its side. 'Who goes there?' I shouted. If it somehow was the king and a lover, I had no doubt that I would be in trouble.

The snoring stopped. Muttering came from within, and I stepped back. I cursed myself for having no weapon – I would not have been allowed near the queen had I been armed. Instead, I made a fist. 'Come out, in the name of the king!'

At first, nothing happened. And then the muttering came again, too low to be distinct. I looked around the clearing again, seeing only the grasses swaying gently, and then I began beating on the door, crying over and over, 'open up! In the king's name!'

The door fell inward, partly from my blows and partially pulled from within. I leapt back, my fist up.

Oh, shit.

For a second, I thought I had indeed disturbed King James. The figure in the shadowy coach was dressed well, as well as I was – or had been – and he had the king's florid features and scraggly beard. I looked down, my head bowing automatically. At the fellow's feet sat a tall, silver-dressed hat.

And something else.

Empty bottles rolled about the man's fine, polished shoes as he shuffled them. The smell of stale wine wafted out in a stomach-swirling blast. I looked up into bleary, red-rimmed eyes. A counterfeit king, I thought. Perhaps it was some revelry organised by King James's fool, some game. But I knew it wasn't.

The creature in the carriage stifled a hiccup. 'I know no n'other king but me,' he said.

'What?' I stood back, looking around me once again for help, for support. 'Who are you?' Before he could answer, I barked, 'are you of the Lady Locusta's company?' Again, my fist balled.

'Oh,' grunted the man. 'That wench. Her.'

'Where is she?' I sprang up onto the first step. 'What is this?'

'A game,' he said. 'I know no n'other king but me.'

I threw myself into the carriage. The drunken fool fell backwards, unprotesting, as I pinned him to the small floor.

Only when I began fumbling with the loose laces of my shirt – my ruff fell away entirely – did he begin to struggle. In answer, I grabbed his skull by the hair and slammed it into the carved wooden seat. He went limp immediately. And then I set about binding his wrists and ankles. As I worked, I tried to find anything that might have been intended to slay the king: daggers, a pistol, bags of powder, poison. There was nothing other than the empty bottles and a fine carpet of crumbs.

When I was satisfied that I had him held tight, I emerged, bathed in sweat, back into the sun. I swayed on my feet a little, the summer heat and the madness of all that was happening, making me as drunk as the stranger. And then, all at once, noise surrounded me. I fell back against the coach, as the grasses began to part and hounds entered the clearing, their fangs bared and dripping. First one barked its high, shrill scream, and then another, and another. The ground beneath me began to quake.

Along the southern path came the horses, three abreast. Men's halloos and cries filled my ears. I felt myself begin to slide down the side of the coach. My horse – King Christian's horse – started to paw and kick at the ground, whinnying at the sudden intrusion.

'Hold!' cried a high, sneering voice.

I looked up and saw that the first trio of horsemen coming up the track boasted, at its centre, King James. 'Treason!' he cried. His horse halted, its front legs rising and kicking at the air, its head twisting to one side. Before I could speak, the man on his right raised a bow and fired. I felt the arrow cut through the air inches from my head, embedding itself in the painted black frame of the carriage.

'Fall back! Back!' cried the king. I saw, though the scene seemed to be tilting, spinning, James raise a hand to his heart in a nervous, fussy gesture. It righted itself, and I saw the king looking into my face. Fear drew uneven lines across his brow. The look was replaced with narrow-eyed confusion, then flaring red anger, and then purse-mouthed annoyance. And then the gravel under the horsemen became a cloud, and James and his fellows were departing, driven away by their surprise, by their confusion, by *treason!*

I fell to my hands and knees and hunched there, panting, for I don't know how long. At length, I crawled back to the carriage and used the spokes of a wheel to haul myself up. I sucked at the air awhile, letting it clear my addled mind, quell my disturbed humours. And then, as I began to collect myself, I realised that I was in no wise finished.

I had caught a man who knew Locusta, who had been sent by her – dressed as a counterfeit king, no less. What it meant I had no idea. But I had to find out.

Mercifully, my wavering legs did not have to carry me far; I did not even have to remount my horse immediately. Down the path which I'd travelled came one of Cecil's black-clad men on foot – one of the ones I'd spoken to in the palace.

'Trouble?' he asked.

I nodded, still breathing too deeply. 'Ay. Man captured. In the coach.' He looked up at the thing, shading his eyes with a hand, and whistled. 'Where is his lordship's nearest house? Safehouse? For interrogation?' My master, I knew, had such places dotted all over London – places where agents and informants could seek refuge and leave messages, to be sure, but also where I supposed less legal activities might be carried out. The man gave me a hard and knowing look, and then an address in Deptford. 'Good. I have to return this horse. A king's horse. Borrowed. Could you – your men – your friends – get this coach rigged with a pair of beasts ridden to Deptford?' I would have done it myself had I known how to drive a coach.

Again, my unnamed colleague in the service nodded. 'It will be done.'

'In all secrecy,' I said.

The man gave me a withering look. 'And his lordship?'

'I'll get word to him. When I know what we have here.'

As I began leading the royal horse away from the false royal coach, I noticed two more of the black-coats coming down the path, swords drawn. If I set off walking to Deptford – not a great distance – I should probably meet the coach and its cargo by the time it was horsed and ridden out.

18

I had time to wash off the worst of the grime and tidy myself up in the safe house in Deptford. It was an unassuming lodging house, to the outside world, and operated by a stout old woman, but she seemed to understand who I represented and knew to keep her mouth shut. She provided me with a washbowl and guided me to a private room, and in return, I told her to be on the watch for a great black coach which should arrive at any time with a prisoner of the state.

I had just about completed my toilette when the unmistakable clank and thud of a lumbering coach reached the little closet room. I dropped the towel into the murky depths of the bowl and left, returning to the meagre, plaster-walled chamber, out into the hall, and down the wooden steps. The lodging house was a plain place, utterly unremarkable. At the foot of the stairs stood a counter, where the old lady waited. I held a finger to my lips as I passed her, went into her back room – a place with shelf upon shelf of scrolls and papers – and through the postern door to the yard.

The light was fading to the grey-blue of summer twilight. Above, over the thatch, roofs, and pointed steeples that stood across the yard, pale white stars were already glimmering. Two of Cecil's men were unhorsing the boxy vehicle, which sat at an odd angle, as though it were sinking into the hay-strewn ground at one corner. I exchanged a few words of greeting with them ('sorry we're late, man – fucking thing has one broken wheel!') before moving silently to the coach door – its faux royal arms were gone – and opening it.

The counterfeit king was much as I had left him – bound on the floor. His new captors, however, had been wise enough to gag his mouth. Bruises stood out on his brow and cheeks, whether from a rough ride or some rough handling I couldn't say. He began mumbling immediately. I opened the door, making sounds in his throat and letting them fight their way over the tied rag. Ignoring him, I leant back. 'This thing has been searched?'

'The coach? Ay, man,' grunted one of the black-coats. 'Have to have these back to the palace. No powder, nothing in there.' He tapped a finger against the coach's side. I frowned. I had meant the man, not the carriage.

I stepped up and inside, grasping the creature under his armpits and hauling him up. Keeping my head bent low in the small space, I got behind him and, with one hard shove to his lower back, sent him sprawling face-first into the yard. With one last look around the shadowy interior, I bounced down after him.

After helping Cecil's men to mount, I half-dragged and half-helped the mumbling prisoner into the lodging house, me jerking and he hopping. He didn't fight, thankfully. I suspected that he'd drunk himself stupid on wine and was now paying for it. Together, we gained the hostess's front hall and moved past her. To her credit, she said nothing and did not look surprised. 'Just taking our friend upstairs,' I supplied, though I couldn't say why. Again, she ignored me and busied herself wiping her counter with a rag, or pretending to.

Once I had got the stranger into the larger upstairs room, I let him fall to his knees. I studiously ignored him, digging in a woodworm-eaten old coffer – the only furniture in the room – for a candle. I found a thumbnail of one, its wick torn, and managed to get it lit with my tinderbox. After shutting the lid of the coffer, I fixed the weak flame to it and sat beside it. The tinderbox I kept out; I fished for the pipe inside my coat, with its precious store of expensive tobacco, and lit it too, blowing the first cloud across the room and into the man's face. Only then did I bother to remove his gag.

For a few minutes, he spluttered, trying to breathe, trying to cough, and I smoked moodily. An odd fellow indeed, I thought. A sturdy beggar, I should have said, though dressed up in mighty fine clothes.

Just like the other.

And he knew Locusta, had met her, recognised the name. When I judged the time right, when something like sense seemed to have crept across his features – and fear with it – I began to speak. 'What is your name?'

'Georgie, sir,' he said. His voice was pure gutter, rusted and cracking. 'M'names plain Georgie.'

'And how did you come to be in the king's royal park?'

'Me, sir?' I raised an eyebrow and sucked on my pipe. 'It's the game, sir.' He frowned, appearing to remember something. 'I know no n'other king save me. That's right, sir, ain't it? You's one of them, ain't you?'

'One of who?' I set the pipe down on the coffer and moved over to him. 'What are you, man?'

'Just a plain serving-man, sir, just a plain serving-man.' He nodded the truth of his words wildly, his reddened eyes popping. 'I didn't want none of this. I did what you asked, your folks.'

I fought the urge to slap him. And then I gave in and let him have the back of my hand. He slumped sideways and began mewling. Regret flooded me, but I blinked it away. 'Stop speaking in fucking riddles, you filth. You were found, garbed like a king, in a false coach, in the king's great park. How does any honest serving-man come to be so, eh? You tell me that.'

Georgie didn't answer right away but lay there, his lips moving wetly. I reached down and hauled him upright, dragging him along the bare boards and setting him against the wall. He seemed to weigh less than his clothes. Remembering, suddenly, I began feeling for pockets, gingerly sliding my hands around his waist for a belt and purse. Only the latter was present – a single, tiny brown purse. I yanked it free and emptied it into my hand. One coin tipped out – a single one with the edge illegally clipped. I squinted in the weak light. I did not recognise it.

Foreign!

'What is this?' I held it before the man's face.

'It ain't mine, sir. Ain't mine. I ain't never clipped no coins.'

'And yet it was in your purse.'

'That ain't mine neither. You – they – dressed me up like this, sir. I'd never have the cash for no great weeds like these. It's all the game, sir. Didn't the king – didn't his Majesty – didn't it work?'

I slipped the coin into my own purse and balled my fists. 'You tell me,' I snarled, 'what this madness is about. You tell me.' I paused for a moment. 'You know who Lord Salisbury is? The king's chief counsellor? Robert Cecil? Do you know?'

Georgie's eyes widened. 'Ay.'

'Good. That's good. I'm a servant of his lordship. And you, my friend, have the marks of a traitor upon you. I suggest you tell me exactly how you came to be in that park, or you'll have a worse time of it, with less friendly men. You know what the rack can do? There is worse. Much worse.'

I let my words sink in, let them sober him further. And then, all at once, his words began to fall over one another. I bent down and pushed him back, just hard enough that his head hit the plaster. 'Peace. You make no sense. One word at a time.'

Georgie's breathing shallowed. 'I'll tell, sir, I'll tell all.' And then he began to unfurl his tale, of being out working hard when a lady – a good Christian City wife, so he thought, lost in the town – had begged his service. And he had gone willingly, quite eager to serve, as a working man ought to be.

'Her name?'

'It was that name what you said. Locust…'

'Locusta,' I breathed.

'That's what she said, sir. Took me on a boat upriver. And then off into the streets.'

'Where? Which streets?' I got down on my haunches next to him, my face near his. He was, I could see, well-groomed, as though recently shaven and barbered. Even that could not hide the broken veins across his nose and cheeks.

'Can't say, sir. Honest, I can't. She- she took me to houses.'

'Whose?'

'Taverns, I mean, sir, inns. With enough to … a drink, ain't it?'

I swore loudly. 'And then?'

'Then … she took me to meet … them. Her masters.'

I got up and moved over to the box. The nub of the candle was beginning to melt into its own pool of wax, drowning itself. The only light came from a small, rounded window cut right into the wall. Heat began to prickle through me, despite the rising chill in the air. I sat down. 'Who are her masters?'

'I ... the men of August, sir. Said how they was men of power, standing, and that. I thought- I didn't think. I don't know. And it was in that grand place I met them. Ain't never been in nowhere like that. Great big hall, like a king's palace.'

'What did they look like, these men?'

'I didn't see 'em.' He shook his head. 'Always wore them masks and hoods. Frightening like. But they spoke fair and soft enough of their- how they'd been around forever. Since the days of ...' he seemed to be thinking, 'of the old queen's old man. Henry. Since them days.'

I hunched forward, my elbow digging into my knees, and put my head in my hands. 'And this woman who took you, this Locusta, she knew them?'

'Ay, sir, worked for them, sir.'

'How many? How many of them?'

'Can't say. Stacks. A whole lot.'

Plotters, I thought—an army of plotters.

'And she – the woman – she came back. And they all – they kept me in ale, lots of ale. And food. And dressed me like you see here, sir. And told me, they did, told me I was to go in that big monster of a thing, that coach. It was a game, they said, sir – a jest. Said the king knew about it. A jest on that other king what's in the town.'

I looked up and over at him. He wasn't lying; I could tell that. He was a witless nothing, stolen off the street and forced into whatever bizarre plot was unfolding.

Organised by a whole stack of men, of plotters, men of lineage stretching back.

I tried to think, to make my mind run clear. Could it all truly be some game? Locusta, a group of men with a fine house in the town – perhaps some prank organised by the Danes and intended to be played on King James? I might have simply stumbled upon games indeed, planned and executed by the Danish king, he having sent rumours ahead to add spice to his planned revels. Absently, I reached down to my purse, fingering it until I felt the clipped coin through the leather. To what end – to seize King James, to allow him time to be spirited away to a brothel and have a pathetic old drunk take his place?

And then I remembered the dead man laid out on the table in Gray's Inn. Perhaps he had been these 'men of August's' previous effort; perhaps he had resisted more than Georgie and been silenced.

'What else were you told? What were you to do when you were discovered?'

Georgie slid down the wall a little. 'Just to say as I did, sir. That I were the king and didn't no know other but m'self. I- a jest. The king knew!' he persisted.

I rose and went to the man. He looked up with pleading eyes. 'You'll tell the king's man, son, won't you? I don't know nothing else or I'd tell you. I would, honest to God.' I didn't answer him but tightened the restraints around his wrists and ankles. As I did so, I felt something crinkle in his doublet. Frowning, not asking his leave, I thrust my hand in and drew out a small leaf of paper. 'That ain't mine!'

I moved along the wall to the window and held it up. No page from history, this, but a good quality bit of writing paper, torn along one edge. On it was inked one word:

ABEL

Cain and Abel? I wondered. I knew the story, of the former biblical brother murdering the latter.

A king set to murder a brother king, a brother-in-law?

Why tell me this; why announce it?

I folded the page into my doublet and made to leave the room. He began to cry after me, and so I scuffed back across the dim chamber and pulled his gag back up from his neck and into his mouth.

Stepping back downstairs, I found the old landlady hurrying back behind her counter. 'See that the old creature is given a bed if you have one. And kept restrained. Feed him, if you will.' She nodded. 'And fetch me some paper and a quill.' She disappeared into her back room and returned with both.

As the woman set about doing as I'd bid, I wrote out a brief dispatch for Cecil, detailing my interrogatory and the prisoner's answers. When I'd finished, I left it for her to send. I caught her just as she was leaving another downstairs room with an armful of lockram. 'See that his lordship is delivered this. Tonight.'

'Yes,' she rasped.

'I will see him on the morrow, I've no doubt,' I added, lest she dilly dally. And then I turned my back on her, moving towards the doorway. I paused, looking over my shoulder to find her still watching me. 'Oh, and you might find fitter garments for a sturdy beggar. The things he is wearing -send them to Mr Edward Savage of Shoe Lane, Farringdon Without. I should think his lordship will wish them retained.' I then slipped out of the house in Deptford and into the full darkness of the August night.

Men of August, I thought, as I wound my way through the warren of streets riverward. A whole company of men. I shivered at the thought that there might be a secret society of plotters, at that moment, watching me from the shadows.

19

We were quite a company in the office at Whitehall the next morning: me, Bacon, Roger Delamere, and the Lord Salisbury himself. When I was shown in by the taciturn bodyguard Verney, the other fellows were already seated. A low stool stood waiting for me, and I bustled across the chamber, my hat already in my hands.

'Thank you, Verney,' said Cecil. 'Ned, sit. The coin, please, and the paper.' He had, I was unsurprised to realise, already studied the dispatch I'd written the night before. 'We have already discovered the source of the coach. The maker in Clerkenwell. It was ordered over a week since, by a busy, pushing woman who kept a company of servants, the creature which calls itself Locusta. It then appears that the thing was sent with its creature aboard through the southern route to the hunting grounds. And there left.'

I folded myself onto the stool, nodding greetings to the pair who sat opposite Cecil and let my mind catch up with his words. 'Yes, my lord,' I said, fishing out the coin and the note and placing them on the desk. I slid them across the tight leather. Cecil half-rose and peered down, his bloodless lips curling downwards. 'The coin is Danish,' he said. 'A rigsdaler.' With one long finger, he pushed it back across, in Bacon's direction. 'Clipped.'

Francis Bacon did not touch the coin; instead, Delamere did. 'Clipped,' he echoed. 'As Mr Savage wrote.'

'Well?' asked Cecil.

Delamere looked at Bacon, as though for approval, and the lawyer nodded. Again, I felt that stab of jealousy at their intimacy. Delamere cleared his throat. He looked up and met Cecil's hard gaze only briefly, and when he spoke, he sounded very young. 'There was a Danish king. Eric V.'

'Is this coin from his reign?' barked the secretary.

'I … no, I don't … I cannot say.' He looked at Bacon, who shrugged. 'This King Eric lived long ago. Hundreds of years since.' Cecil's fingertips began drumming an irritated beat on the desk. 'I … he was known as Eric Klipping, so named, I believe, because he was a cheat and a rogue. I have read of him in the histories. He became lost, so the tale goes, and took shelter in a barn.'

'And?' Again, Cecil was irritated, excited, tense.

'And he was set upon in the night by assassins. Men dressed as friars. They stabbed him to death.'

I saw the colour drain from Cecil's face and imagined my own was no more sanguine. 'A dead Danish king,' he said. 'And whom but a Dane should have a Danish coin?'

Delamere raised a slim finger. 'It might have been found by anyone, anywhere, my lord.' Cecil glared, and I saw a blush creep up the man's soft cheeks. 'I've – I've seen King Christian's Danes in taverns about the town. Tapsters will take any coin, anything round and glimmering.'

'And then pass it off to customers to be rid of it,' said Bacon. 'Excellent, Roger. Well observed.'

'The note,' I said. 'The word. Abel.'

'My friend,' said Bacon, who remained looking fairly proud, his whiskered chin up, 'has the answer here too. Go on, Roger. Do not be afraid.'

Delamere's tongue darted over his lips. 'When Sir Francis told me about the note sir after he left you last night and came home,…' Delamere looked down at his hands, which were folded now on the desk. Cecil, I saw, gave a nasty smirk. 'When we spoke of the matter, and he said there was a coin and a note … at first, I thought of Abel, brother to Cain. But when he said that there was found a clipped coin, and I thought of Eric Klipping.' Cecil tutted, his eyes flashing a mute 'get on with it'. Delamere did, adding, 'I thought then of King Abel. Also of Denmark, king many years ago. It is said he had his brother, Eric IV, assassinated by his chamberlain, my lord. And so the Danes say, "Abel by name, Cain by deed" in their tongue. And so Abel became king. And then he too was assassinated. Killed by a wheelwright. On a bridge, I recall reading.'

I thought of the broken wheel of the carriage. Perhaps it signified, or perhaps it was coincidence. 'The coach's wheel was in need of a wheelwright,' I said, after a second of weighing the matter. 'It had been left so. It took some time to get to Deptford.'

'A message,' said Bacon. 'That the Danish king must need be killed.'

Cecil closed his eyes and kept them tightly shut. None of us spoke, and only the crackling of the fire sounded. At length, he said, 'Danish histories. Scotch histories. A great society of men. Secret men, employing a female assassin.'

I cleared my throat. 'And wanting us to know of it, my lord.'

He ignored me. Still, his eyes were closed. 'Who is in danger here? Who is threatened? Our king or his brother-in-law?' Before anyone could answer, his eyes popped open. 'But wait.' He focussed his attention on me. 'Ned. This drunken fool, this George – he told you something of this society.'

'The men of August, he called them, my lord. As I wrote.'

'Men of August. That is this month. Something is planned against the two kings this month. By some small band of fanatical spirits.'

'Or that is what they wish us to think,' said Bacon.

Cecil glared at him for a moment, before saying, 'you think this is trickery, cousin? Some lark, some jest?'

'The man Georgie thought it a jest,' I offered. 'As I wrote.' Cecil's hands became milky fists, and he beat both on the desk. 'A jest? You saw the man, Savage, the dead man. And you buried him, cousin. A jest! Is it a jest, think you, to counterfeit the king, to dress a nothing as him and deposit the false creature in a royal park? I had to soothe the king for near an hour yesterday, telling him that nothing was amiss, that there had been only some coach delivered in error.' I looked at my hands, settling them in my lap, and out of the tail of my eye, I could see my fellows doing likewise. Thus, chastened like schoolboys, our master's voice washed over us. 'It is high treason. Never could such a thing be taken in jest.' And then he added, his voice sounding suddenly wearied, 'do you know what his Majesty, our king, fears the most?'

I looked up. 'Naked steel?' It came out a whisper. But I had heard it said, even from the time before he became our king, when the great Elizabeth lived still, that James of Scotland was terrified of blades.

Cecil gave a weak smile. 'No. No, Ned. It is said, but it is not so. Our sovereign lord truly only fears the seizure of his person. It has ever been thus. Since he was a child in his native realm. Then, factions and factions and factions. Each intent on stealing him away, of putting him in ward. Some even succeeded when he was a boy.

'And that is what this is. Or was. These creatures intended to steal our king when he rode out in the field. And to leave in his place this counterfeit creature. It was no jest, but a means of causing confusion. Anger. To embarrass us, his servants, before the world. And to gain custody of our sovereign master.' He sat back in his carved chair and let his eyes wander over us. There was a challenge in them, I thought; he was daring us to question his view of the plot.

I had no stomach for it. Bacon, however, did. 'I cannot see it,' he said. 'These creatures would require too much knowledge. Too much of history and the movements of our court.'

'You need not see anything, cousin. I am telling you.' A false grin split the secretary's face. And then it faltered. 'They threaten assassination now. Vengeance against King James and now this.' He pointed at the coin and the note. 'An attack intended upon King Christian.'

'But who, my lord?' I asked. 'Who is they? These men of August, around since the time of Henry VIII. It cannot be, surely.'

'Bah! A band of plotters born yesterday,' he said. But doubt furrowed his brow. 'There can be no secret society, no brotherhood of such an age. I should know of it. I should have heard of it.' He glanced over towards the wall, towards the portrait of his glaring father. 'I should have read of such a thing in my father's time, in his writings. He would have known, would have heard whispers.'

Bacon's back straightened, and he leant forward. 'Pardon me, cousin,' he said. 'But … there have been such things in ancient times. In the days of Rome, there were men who met in secret. Ay, and women, too. To worship their pagan gods and- well, you recall the rumours about Raleigh.' My ears perked up. I had met Sir Walter Raleigh. 'The old tales about his mastering a society of wizards and such like atheistical men.'

'Raleigh is dead,' said Cecil flatly. 'Or as good as. The king willed it, and the fellow is now an unperson, a Tower-rat. Like Northumberland.'

Bacon appeared to deflate a little. 'Quite. But not, I think, quite dead. Still, he writes. Still, he has visitors. And I mention him only as an example. Men do meet in secret, cousin, and they do band together.'

'Then they are foul, treacherous plotters who must be hunted. The old drunk saw these men and heard their tales. He spoke, you wrote, Ned, of their having good property. But I cannot believe- I cannot conceive …' I watched my master crumble into himself, wizened and old. He reached out for his jug and glass and poured himself a drink. He really could not, I realised, envision there being any society of great men which did not include himself as its head. I looked down again as he drank. Afterwards, in a stronger voice, he said, 'we must deal as we find. A large party of plotters, a murderous woman, her servants included, have now threatened two kings. And those two kings must be protected. You all recall the horror that might have befallen if the Powder Treason had gone off. Two kings slain on our soil would be as great a misfortune. Ned, you are deep in the matter. My men are still searching taverns. This woman – whether she dresses as a City wife or a great lady – she must lodge somewhere. We shall find her. You, my friend, have uncovered plots before. With Mr Bacon and,' he gave a sniffy look towards Delamere, 'his friend's aid, you will put an end to this.'

I bit on my lip. 'You would have me discover and break this plot?'

'Discover it, yes,' said Cecil. 'Discover it and lay it before me.' Again, his ugly smile broke his neat features. I felt a weight drop within me. Silence, heavy with meaning, fell over the four of us.

I knew it.

Though I had never confirmed it, I had long suspected that

Cecil had known of the old Powder Plot before Fawkes had been discovered in the under-croft below Westminster – that he had let it ripen, let it come within a whisper of succeeding before he drew the net tight around the plotters. He had watched the stupid creatures leave their trail of powder, letting it grow just long enough that they would blow themselves up. And now, though this plot was still oblique, he was hoping to do the same: discover its design and then let it run close to success so that he and the king might have another holiday, another chance to make London glow red with bonfires and choke us all on their smoke.

You bastard, I thought.

'The rest of my men will assist you, should you have need of them again. I give you command of them.'

Before I could answer, the door behind us banged open. Cecil rose, looking past us, and the three of us stumbled up too. I turned in time to see Verney barrelling into the room, his face white, but his features neutral. 'My lord,' he said, bowing, 'you asked to be informed if strange women were sighted anywhere near to the kings.' Cecil nodded for him to continue. 'One of your men is come over from the Abbey. He says that a woman has entered, though the place is to be cleared. Well dressed. Veiled. Suspicious.'

Cecil lost no time. Within seconds, he was around the desk and at my side. 'King Christian and Prince Henry are visiting the Abbey this afternoon. A tour.' He looked over at Verney. 'This strange woman is there now?' The man shrugged. The bells of the palace chapels began ringing out the hour. Cecil swore – something he did only rarely. 'By God, I must go to the king; else he will suspect much amiss. Go, Ned, go. Find this wench and ward her close. The king should like to interrogate her himself, I think, when he knows what she has threatened and that she is caught. Go now! Don't let her escape.'

20

Westminster Abbey was, thankfully, not far from Whitehall; I had only to escape the palace precincts and hustle along King Street, through the great gates, and over the bridge that spanned the moat around the tiny town and through another gatehouse. Westminster itself was a little City, a little honeycomb of streets winding between lodging houses newly built to provide beds for the justices, lawyers, and army of administrators who had come to London to join King James's ever-expanding court. Above the ramshackle roofs, the broad bulk of the Abbey rose like a disapproving old bear crouched on its haunches. It loomed there, ahead of me, never seeming to get closer as I fought my way through the crowds of slow-moving apple-wives and carters, balladeers and hucksters.

I came upon the building nearest its north doorway. At the same time, bells began to chime from within, splitting the air with merriment. I paused, panting. I had not realised the speed at which I'd moved. The plain suit I'd worn to Cecil didn't come apart at speed in the way my prettier court gear had; I'd even saved my hat.

The road curved around the Abbey, like a broad brown arm cradling its western end. I could see, far down that way, the small figures of men in black. I did not need to go and ask them their business. Evidently, Cecil's men were expecting King Christian and Prince Henry to enter the place that way. Other men – and some women with their arms linked through them – were coming out. The place was being cleared of visitors, who customarily were allowed to come and gawp.

Would a black-coat have the wit to stop a lone woman?

One of them at least had known to run along to Cecil at Whitehall. Hopefully, the rest knew to keep her there, if the woman was indeed Locusta.

Probably you will apprehend some ale-wife looking to say a prayer in peace.

I didn't think so, somehow. I had not had time to speak to the man who had come to Verney; I had fled on the wings of Cecil's command. But I felt certain that the creature calling herself

Locusta had made a point of announcing her presence, of making herself known, in the Abbey. It seemed to be the style of both her and these men of August she served. They wanted us to know that they were leading us a good chase. They advertised.

I turned away from the activity at the far end of the building and let my eyes wander along the innumerable dark windows, projecting towers, and carved gutters of the Abbey's flank, all the way back to the huge doors directly ahead. They were set in a triangular stone arch, above which more windows looked sightlessly down on me; and above these stood the magnificent rose window, this one glaring like an angry cyclops. The main doors were shut, but a smaller door to the right stood open, and I crossed the lawn to reach the cobbled walkway leading to it. Casting one last look over my shoulder, I slipped into the cool gloom.

Size can be a threatening thing indoors. Palaces – Whitehall, Richmond, Greenwich – manage to be impressive rather than frightening, I suppose because they fill their vast indoor spaces with pretty colours, soft carpets, and furniture. The interior of the Abbey, though, is of a different scale. It is open right to the ceiling, no doors or cheerful galleries to be seen. To slip inside it is to slip inside not a giant's jewel box but the belly of a sea beast. A place of curtains and shadows, I thought, like all great religious houses. The space opened up ahead of me; the south side lost completely in the dimness. I could see as far as the sanctuary before the high altar, which was hidden ahead on my left, and I decided to press on for that.

Barely had I taken two steps when someone stepped from behind a column ahead and to my right. I froze, bending at the knees, ready to spring, to fight and claw. 'Who goes there?' I relaxed. It was not only one of Cecil's men, but the same one who had come upon me in the clearing at Greenwich. He seemed relieved too, his hand falling away from the hilt poking out from beneath his coat.

'I understand there's a woman come. Did she give her name?' I disliked how my voice seemed to bounce about the chamber, becoming loud. I whispered, 'Locusta?'

'No name. Didn't see her. But heard from one of the lads a woman made a show of coming, all veiled. Suspicious – we've been told to watch out for a strange woman and then one of the lads sees one, behaving right odd for a woman.'

I smiled absently and without humour, but I was no longer looking at him. 'Where is she?'

'Can't say. We haven't searched. We're still seeing folk out ahead of their Majesties coming.' As if the building had heard its royal visitors mentioned, the bells above began ringing again. 'Been going on all day, that. To welcome the king and the prince. Annoying, ain't it?'

This time my smile was more genuine. 'Very.'

'But the strange woman, man – she came in. Not come out yet, far as I know. Not unless she met a feller and went out with him. But its all old couples we've seen walk out.'

'Stay here. Guard the door,' I said, gesturing at the northern entrance. 'No woman to leave, on a husband's arm or not.'

I left him, striding on until I stood at the very head of the nave. Glancing down to my right, I saw more people than I'd expected milling about. From them came that dreadful echoing whisper that all churches seem to breed. Some, I could see, were women. None were veiled, but all wore either mob caps or hats of some kind. They were, as the fellow had said, City wives.

She knows how to counterfeit a City wife!

I bit at my lip, watching the crowd – who probably had hoped to be allowed to remain and gawp when King Christian and Prince Henry arrived to visit the place – fight the order to leave with the weapon of slowness and feigned stupidity. If Locusta were amongst that crowd, the men on the door would have to pick her out and detain her.

But for me, I thought she remained inside, hidden somewhere, waiting for the king. She had now, after all, threatened the Dane as well as the Scot – or her masters had.

I crept across the floor, my boots clicking until I stood directly before the sanctuary. I had no particularly superstitious beliefs, but I felt it invited ill-fortune to intrude upon the sacred space up those shallow steps.

And then I rolled my eyes at my own stupidity and did it

anyway.

Beyond the sanctuary stood the high altar, and behind that more steps rose to St Edward's Chapel, around which was banked a sea of tall, lit candles. Their light was not cheerful, I thought; it cast a sickly yellow on the tall stone structure. I kept the candles and the chapel to my back and began moving deeper into the Abbey. I froze. As I looked down into the gloom beyond the candles' reach, I saw a group of people, none of them moving.

My voice came out in a whimper, an abortive, 'who goes there?' And then I forced my legs to move. In the northern wall across from me, I realised, the people were standing within an enormous

cabinet?

Of polished wainscot.

Corpses!

I exhaled relief in a long, drawn out-breath, and fought the urge to laugh. The cabinet, taller than any man, stood between a column opposite that from which Cecil's man had emerged and a projecting wall. It was open fronted and ranged about its rush-strewn floor was a collection of effigies: those wooden and waxen dressed figures of long-dead kings and queens. The whole macabre collection must have been brought out to impress the king of Denmark. They were not moving because they were not alive.

Shaking my head, I ignored the display, but I stepped away from the lit chapel and onto the red carpet in front, which had been set up all around the ambulatory. I began a circuit, indeed, of that part of the Abbey which surrounded the high altar and its central chapels, swivelling my head this way and that. A couple of semi-circular apses jutted out on my left – chapels, I supposed, dedicated to saints or dead kings. Next, an open passage led into a long stretch of the building which seemed to extend the Abbey's eastern range. I stepped into it.

It was, I realised suddenly, a surprisingly airy chapel full of tombs. I walked part of its length and then turned, ready to leave – no one was hiding here – when my breath stopped. On my right stood the late queen's tomb. I had heard about its construction, which had only been recently finished. The thing was of marble with black columns and gilt edging. It was taller than I was, but through the columns, at about the level of my waist, lay a marble Elizabeth, her sceptre in one carved hand and her orb in the other. Her crown, which seemed to grow out of her white head, was painted red and gold. I couldn't help myself. I reached between the columns and touched her, racing my fingertips along the edge of her marble ruff. It was cold, hard, feeling eternal. My eyes wandered over her face, which had been carved to look aged and sagging, as she must have looked at the end. I shivered, before withdrawing my hand and arm.

I left the eastern chapel, still feeling the late queen's coldness on my fingers. To be rid of it, I folded my hand into my armpit as I stepped back out into the ambulatory and completed my circuit. No one, as far as I could see, was lurking in the next two little apses either.

It was only when I had passed the St Edward's chapel, this time on its opposite side, that something caught my eye.

Movement?

No, a shadow, I thought, a trick of the candlelight.

Yet there it was again, darkness moving against the darkness. I squinted. What I'd seen – what I thought I'd seen – had come from that ghastly cabinet. I glanced towards the cavernous nave. There, groups of people were still moving wraithlike, emitting their ghostly chatter. I straightened my hat and crossed the apse, skirting the sanctuary, my eyes firmly on the cabinet.

Stare at anything too long, look away and look back, and it becomes strange, shifting, and mutable. When the effigies standing in their wainscot tomb appeared to shift, I told myself I'd merely made the mistake of glancing down as I moved. Of course, it didn't help that the things were, by any man's measure, terrifying and strange.

They were, as I knew, the likenesses of kings and queens. But precisely who those kings and queens were it was difficult to tell, though the first I reached – and the rest, I saw, at a glance – had painted wooden heads so close to being real that even wrinkles and blemishes were nicked into them. No, it was not the painted faces and wiry hair that made them odd; it was that, like common players on the stage, they had been dressed weirdly. The first king and his queen were clothed in the fashions of our own time, more or less – their heads bobbed on ruffs – but with odd concessions to ancient times. He wore an open crown and an ermine robe; she a similar crown but over hair dressed as I'd seen Queen Anne's own. The others – two more kings and their queens – were the same: realistic heads skewered on ruffs over mingle-mangle fashions, the arms posed to show waxen hands in prayer or holding symbols of the state.

And here is Elizabeth.

The second to last in the display was the old queen herself. Her head must have been carved from the same death mask used for the marble tomb, for both were old-looking and spent. The whole thing, indeed, looked identical to the tomb carving, but in full colour, vibrant, come to stiff, unmoving life.

And, between her tall, golden sceptre and deep burgundy sleeve, a piece of paper was folded. I narrowed my eyes, focusing on it, before reaching out to touch it. Just as I felt it between my fingers, the whole effigy burst into life.

Argh!

I did not cry out; perhaps I yelped. I disturbed her! I thought. Vengeance for prodding at her tomb! The thing, Elizabeth, was falling forward, collapsing on top of me. I folded beneath it. Apart from the clothing, it was weightless, a cascade of cloth, pearls, and wood. Its breath – its reek – was of fusty cloth, and beeswax, and paint, a cloying and heavy brew.

Don't let it break!

My legs stiffened. My arms stiffened. The old queen was caught in my grasp, her white cheek icy against mine. My breath came out ragged; I began to shake, holding the thing there as though we were frozen in the middle of a dance.

And then the last figure moved.

The queen had no consort, I thought wildly, not like the others. But there was, to be sure, another in that cabinet

hiding

and now on the move.

'Stop,' I croaked, shifting, nearly dropping the false

Elizabeth, her red frizz falling into my face, into my mouth. It did not stop. I had the barest impression of a woman's shape, a cloak and veil about her, step past me. She was a blur; I could not see her face, but curling blonde hair flashed and bounced beneath its covering. 'Stop!' I said again. I made to pursue, to drop the old queen and let her shatter and crumble to wooden fragments, but I dared not.

Goddamn it!

Pushing the effigy back up, righting it, my trembling hands fought me in trying to make the old bird secure. Satisfied that she wobbled on her dress – which, I thought, held her up; I'd no idea what wire and wax base might lie below – I snatched the note away from her. And then I turned back towards the apse, the wings of the transepts, the nave, turning, turning.

I began to skip towards the nave and its crowd and had barely taken two steps away from the cabinet when I went sprawling forward. This time I did cry out, and, hissing, I reached down to see what had caught my boots.

At my feet was a great blonde wig, the veil still pinned to it.

'Are you hurt, man?'

I looked up stupidly. 'What?'

Over me, one hand out and the other on his hilt, was Cecil's man. I took his proffered palm, and he helped me to my feet. I shook my head. 'No, I … where is she? Where did she go?' And then, realisation dawning, 'the door! The door! You were set to guard that door!'

Wasting no more words, we both darted around the columns and up the north transept. The door was open, as it had been when I'd arrived. Out into the light, out of the suffocating air of the Abbey, we tumbled, trying to look everywhere at once.

If the woman had escaped that way, she was gone, melted into an enormous melee of people which had filled the main road leading to the church's western entrance. I could see, at the head, a group of brightly coloured riders – gentlemen pensioners. Behind them rode a long-faced man – Christian IV, I guessed – alongside a white horse bearing the haughty, handsome Prince Henry. And, behind them, the dean, a whole army of his canons, Danish gentlemen, English gentlemen,

Scottish gentlemen. If Locusta had darted off into the main road, she could not have chosen a greater party to lose herself in.

And, I realised, if she had jettisoned some disguise – she was russet, according to Rooks the tapster – she might easily have joined the throng and escaped out the other door. What was clear, though, was that I had lost her.

I looked out towards King Street and, beyond it, the uneven line of Whitehall's roofs. For once, I was grateful to King James for calling Cecil away. I should not have to explain my failure immediately.

The Abbey's bells began their mocking clamour once again. 'Shit,' said my colleague. Indeed, I thought. 'I have to go. Make sure the boys have cleared the place.' I did not reply, but let him dart back into the building.

Only then did I realise I was still holding the note. I dreaded uncrumpling it, dreaded reading it. But I had no choice.

What now, you damned slippery bitch?

Full five will be slaine,
Three watched, two watching,
Three crowns disdain'd,
Four nations falling

The doggerel was written in a neat script. It meant nothing to me. On the other side, in the manner of an address, it read, 'For the Seventh'. I despised numbers. I folded it into my doublet. For a moment, I felt angry tears threaten, and to combat them came the sudden urge to kick, to punch something, anything.

I looked again towards the procession, most of which had now disappeared from view.

Numbers.

Faith, my own little mouse, had a head full of accounts. She had, indeed, helped me to discover cyphers in the past, seeing immediately what numbers might mean.

Hardly daring to hope, I began stamping out over the cobbles, away from the Abbey.

21

Faith sat at my table, which was otherwise covered in flowers. The whole front room of my house smelt sweet and fresh. She had cleared a little space amongst the blossoms and was bent over the note.

I, however, was seated on the bed beside David, a thick sheaf of pages in my hand. 'It's good, Ned, really good,' said the boy. 'And I get to speak a lot. Not as much as in other plays but a lot.'

I smiled down and then put an arm around him, hugging him close. 'I shall take it to Revels on the morrow,' I said. 'When do you perform again?'

'The seventh.'

I repeated the words. 'Ay, at Hampton Court. A fine place.' I set the manuscript of the King's Men's *Macbeth* on the cot. The players had given it to David to give to me to deliver to the Revels Office. I might even read the damned thing, the better to take my mind off my own troubles.

I confess I was rather in the mubble-fubbles, at a low ebb. I could not understand the note, and so I felt like a half-brain. I had missed catching the wench Locusta, though I had been within touching distance of her. I had not even got a look at her, seeing only that she had wit enough to change her appearance.

In my dark mood, strange suspicions came upon me. On the ride upriver from Westminster, I had quite convinced myself that Cecil was behind the whole thing. He had hired the woman to play Locusta, perhaps with the king's knowledge. It was all some Machiavellian scheme, with me and even his cousin Bacon enlisted to discover it, and thereby to 'save' King James and King Christian from an assassination attempt, to the bell-ringing, bonfire-burning joy of all. He was capable, my master. So too was the king. Both were slippery as eels and cunning as foxes.

Yet I did not believe it.

Cecil had seemed too discomfited, so vehement at the thought that there might be some society of great men at work. And who might such men be? Friends and relatives of any of those women I had visited? I considered them. The foreign stranger who spent her time doing pious good works. The disgraced courtier and notorious temptress who made no effort to tempt. The half-brain queen who was as sharp and clear-eyed as any. I could see no society formed between these creatures nor any of their menfolk.

In truth, I did not know which was the worse: that I was an unwitting pawn, sent out to discover a plot of my master's own making, or that I was enmeshed in rooting out a scheme organised and carried out by a party of rich, powerful men – and women – who had hired a cunning assassin to play games with me.

Fuck!

'I don't understand this, Neddy.' Faith's voice broke in upon my angry, confused thoughts. I rose, patting the manuscript with one hand and stepping across the room. I leant over her shoulder and saw that she had circled all the numbers in the note. 'It's not a cypher; I don't think.'

'A code?' I offered.

'Maybe. Maybe. The seventh, I think, for the seventh. Of the month. The day before I wed.'

'Yes. I thought that.'

'But look at the words, not the number,' she said. 'On the verse side. Watched and watching.'

I shrugged. 'I don't know.'

'Plays are watched,' said David, his voice piping across the room. 'And heard.'

I half-turned to him, and then looked again at the page, frowning. 'Three plays … will be watched,' I said. 'On the seventh!' I kicked out at the wall, more of triumph than revelation or anger. 'By two kings, James and Christian. But, no- the line before, it doesn't- full five will be slain. Five what?'

'Men are slain in *Macbeth*,' said David. Faith and I both looked at him this time.

'How many kings? In *Macbeth*, how many kings, David?'

'Two,' he said. 'King Duncan with daggers and Macbeth. At

the end.'

I stepped back from the table. The other play I knew was to be performed before the kings was *Hamlet* – I had seen it more than once. 'Two kings die in *Hamlet*,' I said aloud. 'But that would make six, not five.' And then it dawned on me – the old Hamlet, the slain king, appeared as a ghost at the start of the drama. We never see him die – the only crowned king we see fall is the evil Claudius. 'Three kings die on the stage in those plays, during the action itself,' I announced. 'Full five be slain. Three watched: this Duncan and Macbeth, and Claudius.'

'Two watching,' said Faith. 'Our king and the Danish one.'

Could it be?

I snatched up the note, looking at her other circled numbers. 'Three crowns disdained, four nations falling. Which three crowns?'

'England, Denmark,' began Faith.

'And Scotland!' said David. He had risen to join us at the table. 'Macbeth's kingdom.'

'And King James's,' I said. 'By Christ, I think we have it.'

'Language,' said Faith.

Ignoring her, I said, 'just the last line, just the last. Four nations falling. Why three crowns and four nations, why?'

Faith rose from her seat and gently took the note from me, looking closely at it again. 'Well, we know England, Denmark, and Scotland.' Her lips moved silently. 'Ireland,' she said at last. 'King James is the king of Ireland, isn't he? I know Queen Elizabeth was queen of there.'

'Ireland,' I echoed. 'I'd forgotten about Ireland.' In truth, I thought it was every English gentleman's duty to forget about Ireland.

'It's where all them soldiers come from, isn't it? All pocky and sick, off the boats and into London.' She shrugged. 'I feel sorry for them.' I sucked in my cheeks. I didn't, particularly. Any man fool enough to go for a soldier deserved to end up rotting in the streets, bits of him missing. It was hardly unknown that only rich men profited in the wars.

'Why doesn't Ireland have a crown?' asked David.

I didn't answer because I didn't know and couldn't think of a lie. But I did know that the king had been crowned as a boy in Scotland and as a man in England. I had never heard of him going to Ireland nor of there being an Irish crown. Joy filled me, and I was about to clap my hands when I saw Faith's face. It was deathly pale. Her hand, gripping the edge of the table, was like chalk.

'What are you involved in now, Ned?'

'I …'

'Where is this from, this paper? Is it, is this a threat to kill King James? And the other?'

'Yes,' I said, and she slumped in my chair. 'But the king's secretary will know of it. He'll know what to do.'

'I hate this,' she said. 'I'm to be married in a few days and … it's the Powder Plot days come again. I've been hoping to speak to you about all this—your work. And having David here when I'm married. In these dark days, I mean…'

'Days?' I set down the note and felt my throat tighten. 'Mouse … I didn't … when is it again?'

'On the eighth. In Holborn.'

'But you didn't tell me it was so soon.'

'You haven't been around,' she said shrugging. Strands of red fell about her face, and she brushed them behind her pink-white ears. 'I know, I know – you've been busy with this … this secret business. I don't mind.'

I got down on my knees next to her. 'You will have a fine wedding, you and young Hopgood. I promise. These plotters I seek … we know now what they're about. Lord Salisbury will know. If they plan to strike on the seventh, during these plays, when the kings are watching them, well, then, I'll … I'll be sure he smashes them on the sixth!'

'This is dark work,' said Faith.

From her side, looking like her younger self, David's solemn voice said, 'foul and fair.'

She gave me a weak smile. 'I should get back.'

'No,' I said. 'No, I wish you to stay the night with your brother and me. I would have us all together these last nights before that Hopgood steals you away from us. Come. We'll read this *Macbeth* and see if David knows his lines.'

I felt good as the children – my brother and sister and son and daughter and best and only friends – gathered around me, warm in the cheerful light of my brazier in my own home. I felt certain, for the first time in days – that I had conquered the little riddle laid out by the men of August and their bitch-dog. And if I was right, if their plan involved an attack on the two kings as they watched their entertainments, then I could be assured that Hampton Court would be thoroughly searched and secured and flooded with Cecil's men. No one would come within shooting distance of either king. Their plot, advertised in its nonsense rhyme, was discovered.

As I opened the first page of Mr Shakespeare's neatly written manuscript, I chose to ignore the voice in my head.

But why have they told *you of their plot?*

What haven't *they told you?*

***

The sun was still climbing, promising another hot day, as I dressed in my livery, my shutters open to let the night out. When I emerged from my bedchamber, I found Faith and David up already, he sweeping the floor and she cooking something over the brazier. 'Good morrow, Ned. Will you eat?' The sizzle and pop of butter filled the air, and I saw a loaf of bread already stripped down to neat slices on the table.

'Perhaps later.' I began humming a jaunty little tune. I had slept well, satisfied with my interpretation of the note. And I had rather enjoyed the Scottish play, though it irked me that David would not be performing as the wicked lady. Still, he had known his parts – second weird sister, Lady MacDuff, third child, and gentlewoman – without peeping over my arm. Even Faith, I thought, had liked it, and she so set against dramas. 'I'm off to Revels,' I said, touching my cap. I planned to go directly to the office, hand the play off to Sir Edmund or an underling – along with my recommendation that it was clean, fit matter for the kings – and then descend on Whitehall in the hopes of catching Cecil there. If he was not, if he was with the king somewhere else, I could always have word sent to him.

There was time, I thought. Of that, I had convinced myself. It was only the fifth, and if the plotters of August intended to strike on the seventh, there was time enough.

Stepping out into the sour, burnt-smelling air, I struck off northwards. The crowds were sparse, but the place a dried-out mire. Poor folk were rooting about the gutters, looking for anything valuable that might have been dropped by revellers. As I had noticed on the return journey from Westminster the day before, the whole of London seemed still to be locked in its unofficial holiday. Taverns rocked with music and lights; whores of both sexes strode around with impunity, not even keeping themselves south of the river; ale- and pie-sellers were making a roaring trade. It was as though the City had taken a lesson from the king's court and all was licentiousness. I did not even spot any of the Puritan preachers out, ringing their handbells and crying doom. I guessed that, following the rain of rotten fruit and vegetables that would have met their cries in the first days of King Christian's visit, they would be quietly stewing, penning doom-laden sermons to be served when sobriety rode back into town.

The Revels Office was a fine building which resembled an old manor house – and perhaps it once had been. Inside, walls had been knocked away, and others put up so that it became a place of work, of desks and inkpots and tall wooden jars of quills. What might once have been a great hall had even been altered into a small playing space; prior to court performances, the players were often required to act out their plays before Sir Edmund so that he might be sure that the spoken word stuck closely to the approved written version.

I knocked on the broad wooden door and was admitted without question. I marched through the panelled entrance hall, ignoring the door to the reading rooms on my right and left, and turned right, climbing the staircase and going directly to Sir Edmund Tilney's office.

The old man was slumbering inside, and I coughed discreetly. Immediately he bounded forward in his chair, his bent hands darting towards the desk, fumbling about at nothing in particular. 'What? Eh? Oh. Savage.' He eyed me critically. 'Better dressed than the last time I saw you, what? Good man.'

'I have the play, sir. The King's Men's own tragedy of

Macbeth, written by the hand of Mr Shakespeare.' I stepped forward, searching for a clear space on the jumbled desk, and then I set down the stack of tied papers.

'*Macbeth*. Scotch. It was read, was it not? Before they played it at the Globe.'

'Ay, sir. But since the new rules…'

'Tidied, is it? Free of filthy oaths and curses.'

'It is, sir. I have read it. You will find no matter in it to be cut.'

Sir Edmund shifted in his seat, leaning forward and drumming his fingers on the manuscript. 'Splendid. Splendid. And the old thing, the Danish *Hamlet*. It has been cut.'

I coughed again. 'And the light thing, sir? To close their Majesties' evening?'

'What? Oh, quite, yes. Mr Jonson's *Volpone*. A sharp comedy, what. That should delight and soothe the kings after such tragedies.'

I managed to retain a neutral expression. Inwardly, I cursed Ben Jonson. The man was like the pestilence – he got everywhere. And, to my eternal regret, I rather liked that play, as smug and cutting as it was. 'Where are we today?' he asked.

'Sir?'

'The fourth is it?'

'The fifth, sir.'

'Oh, yes, quite, quite.' His tongue slid over his patchy, discoloured lips. 'Then we have little time enough. Have the players come in and give us their *Macbeth*. Before the seventh, what?'

'I will carry your order, sir.'

'Good man.' Sir Edmund frowned down at the manuscript I'd brought, his bushy eyebrows descending, as though deciding whether or not to bother reading it. 'Well, you may go, Savage.' I bowed. As I was turning to leave, I saw that the old fellow was settling back in his chair, his eyes already closing.

As I reached the bottom of the stairs, an argument reached me from around the corner. An adult voice was speaking over the excited chatter of a female one. No, I realised it was a child's. A child's voice I recognised.

David!?

I stepped around and into the entrance hall, to find my boy waving his arms excitedly, a piece of paper in one hand. In front of him, barring his way, was one of my Revels colleagues. David's eyes locked on me. 'There he is!'

'What is it?' I asked, stepping towards the pair. 'David?'

'This came for you, Ned. At home.'

I nodded away my colleague and reached out, my mind whirling. Cecil never wrote me at home, no one of importance did. 'Who left it?'

'Dunno,' said David. 'Faith found it put under the door after you went off. I ran up here with it.'

I took the piece of paper. On it was scrawled a script, I didn't recognise.

No more games. Come to the Duck and Drake this evening at six.

- Locusta

My heart fluttered as I balled the note in my fist.

I was being lured.

23

After delivering the note, Locusta fled Shoe Lane. She had been sure to watch until the rude fellow had departed, but she knew of the pair still inside. Thankfully, neither had opened the door whilst she'd been standing before it.

A strange kind of nervousness had come upon her since the previous day, she who had always been brimming with confidence. After fleeing the cabinet where she'd been told to leave her note – and, she hoped, evading detection by Mr Ned Savage – she had thrown away the disguise and escaped the Abbey quite unnoticed.

A magnificent relief.

But she had been told that the fellow was busy elsewhere. Had her employers lied to her, had they intended for her to get caught? Or had the matter been an accident? She had escaped, of course, but it was a close-run thing, and she had been told, repeatedly, that Ned Savage must not catch her, must not expose her or the truth. But how had he known where to go and when? True, her masters had been quite emphatic that she should be seen, but the man had appeared so quickly that she barely had time to slide into the cabinet and hide until – she hoped – he left. Instead, he had made for her.

As she strolled down through Fleet Street, her heart beginning to slow, she turned her mind towards the next job of work she must do. She ducked under the awning of a shop front, into the smell of leather, and watched the world creak by. Business was beginning to pick up, trade beginning to rumble along on cartwheels and opening shutters. Locusta watched the street as a shoeless urchin scampered by, a stick in his hand, chasing a gaunt dog. For the hide, she supposed. The aldermen were still offering money to anyone who killed the pest-carrying vermin. It was an ugly business, but it paid.

The leader of the Augustans had assured her that Mr Savage was blindly running after those Powder Plotters and that their own revelry might continue without him making trouble. Yet, as she'd reported to the leader after escaping the Abbey and making her way through London to their sanctuary, he was a persistent man and seemed to be violently set on spoiling their merriment.

She bit at her fist. For the first time, she was frightened, frightened of these smiling old men and their wealth and their power and their reach and their-

Their what?

She didn't know. In truth, she knew nothing about the Augustans save what they had told her: that their reach was great and their numbers high. That first meeting rose up in her mind.

We admire your work and would advance you in it. But you must take upon you a role for us – oh, it is nothing. Nothing. Merely you must play a great lady, a dangerous lady, named Locusta. We will direct your actions. It is part of a great revelry, a great game, to be acted during the visit of the Danish king. It will amuse you. It will amuse everyone. We will provide you with all you need – fair disguises, all.

The name had meant nothing. Her first doubts had been entertained only when she had been instructed to gain custody of an old drunk and to fashion him as a prince. To her horror, the old creature had dropped dead, and she had had to flee.

Her masters, when she had told them of the tragedy, had been amused. 'We shall find another, then. We have time enough.'

There was no sense of questioning anything. The pay was good, and there was a fine place to sleep. Work was work, however ugly it might get.

She would have to meet with them soon, to report on the next bit of rather unseemly, distasteful business she had been set upon. There were to be no more chases: Mr Ned Savage was to meet his reward. But first, he had to be lured to the place where it was prepared. When that was done, she decided, she was going to find out exactly what these games of cat and mouse were all about.

But first thing was first.

The grisly business of capturing a whore.

***

Her costume for the day was that of a Puritan Goodwife, black of dress and white of headscarf. She wore no tall hat – far too grand for such a creature, too decorous. It stood out in the tavern down by the river, for the place was a pit. It bore neither name nor sign but appeared to have been an old warehouse, taken over, perhaps, by hucksters and beer-men when the previous owner lost everything. The walls were neither plaster nor whitewashed, but the same undressed wood on the inside as out. There were no tables, only benches. And the men who drank in the place were sailors, by the sound and smell of them, men who spat phlegm onto the dirt-packed floor.

But it was the place, to be sure, which the leader of the Augustans had directed her to. It was a place apparently known for providing young flesh willing to take a tumble with lonely old men.

There had been wolf-calls as she'd entered. These she had ignored. Her masters had given her the address and told her exactly what she must say, and the type she must seek. Looking up demurely, she spotted one of them: a boy of about fourteen, his ear pierced. His doublet hung on him and his breeches were likewise too big, but they were of middling quality, good enough to catch the eye—he half-sat and half-lay on one of the benches.

Locusta crossed to him. 'I would buy you a drink,' she said, drawing out a penny and holding it to him. He grabbed it, bit it, and hid it, all before rising to a proper seated position, his back to the wall.

'What you after, lady?'

She blinked. 'I understand your work.'

'Eh?'

Gesturing an arm around the room, she said, 'the games you play with such men as these. For coins.'

No shame crossed the lad's face. He shrugged. 'Need to eat.'

'Would you not like a fairer life?'

'Ain't no fairer life in this town.'

Locusta frowned, paused. She had been expecting a 'yes' and

his complaint had thrown her. 'A fairer … a fair … my husband!' She grasped at the rope of a word and hauled herself back onto surer ground. 'My husband has … lusts … which I cannot meet. In my piety. And so I seek a fair youth to learn of him.'

'Puritan husband, yeah?'

She inclined her head and raised a hand to her heart. 'Yes.'

'Them's all the same. Preaching doom and looking for ones like us when the sun goes down. Seen it before.'

'Will you come?'

'How much and for how long?'

'I …' she began. 'For as long as you live, if it pleases you.'

The boy-whore swung his feet down to the dirt floor, kicking and scuffing. He looked very young. 'What, like a home? To live in regular like?'

'Yes. If you please him.'

'Well, then, let's go. I ain't never had no home before.'

Locusta smiled and then let it fade. 'But first, we must see that you please him. What is your name?'

'Robin.'

'Robin. You will come with me. I have paid for a lodging room. It is a fine place. You will wait there, and my husband will come to you.' She felt a blush creeping up her cheek – a real one – 'he has strange tastes. But he will come. He will enjoy the night, I think. You will take care of him.'

22

You might have heard of the Duck and Drake. The fine tavern – a cut far above the lice-ridden drinking dens by the river, and even above the fairer taverns of the City – stands in the Strand, itself a byword for wealth. It thus lies in the shadows of all those great palaces, Cecil House, Salisbury House, Durham House, Essex House. None of the great earls or lords would ever have set foot in the place, mind you; but it was there, catering to their gentlemen and attendants, their servants and hangers-on.

But, of course, that is not why you know it.

The Duck and Drake, as all England knew and knows, was the place where Catesby, Fawkes, and the rest of those damned Powder Plotters had met to swear on their bible that they would give the parliament and king a great blow.

Customarily, I wandered the Strand a little, looking in envy at the great houses and considering all the little treasured objects that lay within, just asking to be pocketed. Just before six in the evening, however, I looked up at the tavern's thatched roof and glass-heavy walls in trepidation.

I was safe that much I knew. On my person were two daggers, some stones, and a short, heavy stick. I had not made it to Whitehall. Instead, I had gone to my favourite of Cecil's safe houses in Fleet Street and written up a dispatch detailing the place, the number of men I thought sufficient to surround it, and all that had passed in Westminster Abbey. Both notes, the Abbey note and the invitation to the tavern, I had enclosed with the letter. My own interpretation of the former went too.

As I gazed up at the tavern, I pretended not to notice the men in black coats who stood in doorways opposite, behind fences and in the shadows of rich men's gatehouses. If Locusta were truly in the place, if she really intended to meet me, she would neither win a fight – and I would not fight fair – nor would she be scampering off as she had at Westminster. I stepped lightly across the cobbles, trying not to let my various weapons jangle, and straightened my hat before entering.

Music greeted me. It was decent stuff, too, lutes and other stringed instruments playing courtly tunes and strummed by a whole company of musicians. Every wall was either panelled or dressed, and round tables stood about. Privacy was provided for those who wished it, by virtue of several wooden screens. These private supper spaces, I noticed, were all empty. I imagined that one of them had been used by the plotters, and now no one wished to be seen seeking private discussion in the Duck and Drake.

Give it a few years, I thought. In a few years, the curiosity seekers would come, perhaps after the king's time. Then they would demand to be seated where the wicked men had sat, demand to be served off the same plate and drink from the same cups.

But the baker of Southwark will not be amongst their company, will he?

A few drinkers stood about, but most appeared to be in the dun of service weeds. I crossed the room, winding through the tables, and made for the polished wooden bar. I rapped on it to draw the stout old tapster and, as he smiled and made his way towards me, I drew out my pipe, packed it and lit it. 'Good morrow,' I said, the smoke escaping with the words.

'How do?'

'I am here by invitation.' I stood back a little. The old beggar Georgie's clothes had arrived during the day, but Faith had been too busy fashioning herself a veil to alter them. Instead, I was wearing the redressed suit I'd worn to my audience with Queen Anne. I allowed the tapster a moment to drink it in, to search my face for recognition. He found none, of course, but that didn't mean I wasn't some guest of one of the great men. 'I am to meet Locusta.'

'Oh,' he said. He gave me a look I didn't like. A leer, almost, and I frowned.

'Locusta,' I said again, a little harshly.

'Ay, sir. Room upstairs booked under that name. Your- ah, your friend, sir, is waiting.' He smiled again, and I shook out my pipe whilst he gave me directions to the stairs and the room.

Without thanking him and with the barest touch of my hat

brim, I swept through the barroom and found the staircase. Luxury indeed, I thought – it even had a narrow carpet running down the centre of the wooden steps. I kept to it. There was nothing I could do about the creaking.

At the top of the stairs, the hall gave on to a small number of doors, spaced widely apart. Locusta's was the second on the left, and I crept along the wall to it.

I was no fool. I knew that I might be walking into some kind of a trap. Yet I knew the art of entering an unfamiliar room, where an enemy has the advantage. The thing is not to barrel in, to keep in mind always that they know the ground, the secret spaces, and you do not. And, further, they know that you do not; they expect you to pause, to stumble, to waste time in careful glances about.

I did not knock on the door. Instead, I stood back and kicked it in. It fell easily. I drew back again, expecting the new space to frame darkness. To my surprise, the interior of the room was well lit. Evening sunlight fell in shafts from the glass windows. I fixed my hand on the hilt of my dagger and then drew it out, holding it low and ahead of me as I took tiny steps into the doorway.

'What the hell?'

I started, waving my blade towards the voice. 'What?' I asked. The room was dominated by a good bed, a tester, and on the mattress was lying a spotty youth. In his nightshirt, I noticed – the white cloth hitched up to his knees.

A trap!

I wheeled, the point of my dagger rising. 'Where is she?' I shouted. 'Where is the bitch?'

'You her husband?' the lad behind me squeaked. I didn't turn to him. Instead, I scanned the room. There were no shadows, no hiding places. I jerked back towards the door and threw it shut, lest she be creeping in from another room. And then I returned my attention to the boy. He was sitting up on the bed now, his face hard and set. I ignored him and went around the great thing, shaking its open hangings, kicking at its base. She was not hiding on the other side of it.

'Where is she? Where is Lady Locusta?' I barked again.

'The woman ain't here,' said the boy. He got to his knees on the bed, his fists pressing down into the mattress.

'Who the fuck are you?!' My voice tore out in a ragged gasp. 'What is this?'

He began to clamber over the bed towards me. 'Been sent here for you, sir,' he said. With horror, I realised that his voice was intended to be alluring, a childish approximation of a silky coo. 'So you just do whatever you're wanting to do, sir, and then I'll stay by you, and you give me a place like this to sleep, for all time. You can call me Robin, master. I won't say nothing to nobody.'

'I … I …' was trembling. Confused. Disgusted. Many accusations might rightly be nailed to my door, but a lover of poor, flea-bitten little boys I was not, nor ever had been – except when I'd been just such a boy myself.

At that moment, the door fell inwards once again. I spun, my dagger up, just in time to see the tapster fall into the room. 'Look here,' he said. Disgust was plain in his face. 'This noise. Can hear it. Won't have it, no matter how much was paid.'

I opened my mouth to speak, to protest, to listen, in fact, to whatever confused brabble poured out. But I had not the chance. Faces appeared over the tapster's shoulders, two, three, four. I recognised the black, undressed hats. Cecil's men had entered the tavern, expecting trouble. They, like the tapster, took in the scene.

'It's not … she is not … this boy is no …'

What's the bloody point?

I saw some snickers, some glances down towards the carpet, some fists going up to mouths. And then my host seemed to realise the intrusion, to take in the nature of it instantly. 'I know nothing of this man,' he barked, his pudgy hand circling his throat. 'Honest, gentlemen. I – some lad booked a room. I didn't know it was for filthy practices, sodomy.' More chuckling, more embarrassed glances. I heard the boy begin to swear and hiss oaths from the bed. From one of Cecil's men, I heard the foul insult, 'acorn eater' whispered to another, followed by 'knew it'.

This all seemed to push the tapster further. 'I swear,

gentleman, this isn't that sort of house. We want no more trouble in this place. Take this stranger and his sodomite, please, to your master. Throw 'em in the Clink. They're none of mine.'

I couldn't speak.

There is nothing quite like embarrassment to rob a man of his will. It is, I've always thought, why the bawdy courts so love to parade naughty men and women before their neighbours, to draw them through the streets with papers announcing their adulteries, their vices. I felt my own will depart, like morning mist. I had been caught before in bedchambers, locked in illicit embraces, but then I had been guilty. And I had always been nameless, hiding away in private places. This was of a different order. These men in black were my colleagues. Cecil had, indeed, put me in a position of command over them. And here I was, standing exposed, not simply a man-lover but a boy-lover – a foul slander that they cast upon all of us – before them all.

The tapster prattled on, condemning me, condemning the boy, Robin. For his part, the young fellow gave as good as he got, accusing our host of being a bawd and worse. I let it all wash over me, straightening myself up, looking for sympathetic faces amongst the crowd. I found none.

'I'll go,' I said. My voice was husky, distant. 'Leave the boy. Let him go.'

'You heard him,' said the tapster. 'Take the creature in ward. Let him bend men to his will in gaol, heh?'

I walked from the room, my head bowed, ignoring the continued cries from the boy and the old man. I was content to leave in the company of my colleagues, disgraced as I was and disgusted and embarrassed as they were. Together, we tramped out of the room and down the stairs. The music stilled. Heads turned. Shame blanketed me. And under it, we went out into the street.

'I … the woman was not there. It was a trap. A foul slander.'

'Ay,' said a grey-faced black-coat, the eldest and hardest looking of the bunch. 'I recall, sir … ah, must be twenty years since or more … the old Archbishop Sandys. He was found, sir, in bed naked with an innkeeper's wife in Doncaster, think it was, sir. Of course, his Grace swore blind that a fellow had put the lady there to slander him.' Snickers rippled through the other men.

Finally, a little fire lit within me. I knew that old tale, though it had taken place before my time. It was still good for a laugh amongst the ballad singers, whose audiences were delighted by the thought of a lusty old archbishop suing a man for slander for supposedly dumping a naked woman in his bed. It bore no relation to me, nor what had just happened.

'Would … would I have invited you, fellows, to break in upon the place if there … if I had planned to … with that boy? Would I?'

'I suppose not, sir. Will you be taking anyone to law for it, sir?'

I punched a hand into my fist. 'I – I will find the woman who put that undressed boy in my bed!' This provoked outright laughter, and I felt heat creep up my neck, into my cheeks. 'To hell with you all,' I said. 'His lordship will hear that you … of this.'

I was innocent of dignity as well as of any crime. And I had lost the men, lost any chance to direct or engage them. Perhaps that had been Locusta and her masters' plan, I thought – to ruin me. If it had worked just a little better, I might even have been arrested, locked up awhile until things could be sorted out.

Turning my back on the men, I looked up the street. In the fine glass windows of the great palaces and houses, lights were burning, though there was still heat and warmth and light in the air. Bees buzzed around flowers in the gardens, where gardeners were still singing. I began stomping off, my head high.

'What would you have us do, then?'

Fuck off is what.

I didn't answer.

I was going to break in upon Cecil's evening.

***

I had been in Salisbury House before, though then it hadn't been gifted the dignity of that name, nor its master that title. Even then, it had been a remarkably fine place, set back from the road, with its own private water stairs, galleries facing out to the Thames, and even a bowling green somewhere to the rear.

In addition to the main street door, which led into the kitchens, there was a side door for domestic staff. This I made for, beating on it. I was furious at Cecil, at his men, at the tapster, at Locusta. Being made a figure of fun will breed such aimless, scattered fury in any man. 'Open up,' I cried, stupidly.

The door was opened almost immediately. The chamber groom narrowed his eyes. 'Who are you?'

'Edward Savage of Shoe Lane, servant to Lord Salisbury. I would speak with his lordship immediately. This moment.'

Perhaps my affected accent served my turn; the young fellow said, 'wait here, please,' before darting off. I could hear his voice within, though not what he was saying. Eventually, I was allowed into the room, and passed from groom to groom, from usher to usher, always being questioned, always being delayed. The Lord Salisbury, I was told, was at supper with his cousin and I should have to wait. I knew, in fact, that I was being discussed, debated, as the army of servants decided whether or not I was truly worth interrupting the master.

But I made progress, going from domestic chambers walled with plaster to halls with painted cloths to galleries lined with tapestries. I was, as I had been in the past, going up in the world, approaching the dizzying heights of Cecil's private living quarters. Eventually, I was shown into a shuttered antechamber. The usher did not, this time, accompany me. Instead, once I was halfway across the room, the door slammed.

'What –' I did not have time to finish. Something exploded in my lower back, and I went to my knees. Only by thrusting my hands out did I avoid my face slamming into the carpet. I began to turn, to see what had struck me when a voice cut through the darkness.

'Don't move. Don't try anything.' It took me a second to place it. Verney, the personal escort. In my fury to burst in on Cecil, to spoil his night if I could, I had forgotten that he had private protection.

'No trouble,' I breathed. I let his hands wander over me, relieving my of my stones, my daggers, the small, heavy striking staff at my belt. 'Take it,' I said. Then, because I was annoyed, 'I want it back. All of it, when I leave.'

Verney, sounding quite cheerful, said, 'of course, sir.' And then his hand was stretched out, and he had the audacity to help me to my feet. 'Just a matter of duty. No danger near his lordship. No weapons.'

I almost thanked him, so sudden was his metamorphosis from raging beast to smooth-faced gallant.

Just a matter of duty.

Like informing on a baker with too broad a mouth and too much ale in his belly, I thought. When I'd regained my feet, I brushed myself down and secured my hat neatly on my brow. 'Is he expecting me, then? My lord of Salisbury?'

'Ay, sir. Go in.' And then, as though he still didn't trust me, 'I'll be out here. Right here.'

'That,' I said, 'is such a comfort.' I nodded as he held the door open, allowing me passage into Cecil's gaily lit supper-room.

It was a cosy chamber, octagonal in shape. I judged it must have lain in one the house's stone turrets. Cecil was seated across from Bacon at a round table draped with a rich purple cloth. On it was spread all manner of dainties: wafers, dishes of honey, various jugs, strangely painted little cakes piled up in pyramids. Bacon beamed as I entered. 'Good evening, sir. We were just celebrating Gowrie Day. The feast of his Majesty's delivery from assassination in Scotland. And debating the right governance of Christian commonwealths.' I looked away from him towards my master. Cecil was not smiling.

'What news?' he asked without any other greeting.

I sighed. The anger I had felt, and the strange confidence which rode upon it melted away under the man's hard gaze. I was, I realised – and I knew, of course – just a menial servant, a grubby intelligencer, who had singularly failed and who kept failing to catch an assassin. 'My lord,' I began, 'I have much to report upon.'

Everything that had passed came out, in lurid detail, and in order. Cecil and Bacon each interjected, asking for more on points touching the Abbey note, which my written dispatch had apparently failed to explain properly.

'You truly believe they intend some attempt at Hampton Court, in … what is this? Two days hence?' This was Bacon.

Before I could answer, Cecil snapped, 'we have had creatures try to blow up parliament on the day of its opening, cousin. Monsters grow overbold in these times. Neither my father nor yours ever knew such horrors. Such terrors in this state or any Christian realm. The world is like an apple, growing more rotten each year. Worms and maggots only grow fat on the flesh.' He tutted to himself. 'And this latest, this boy … you interrogated him?'

'I hadn't the time, sir. There was the tapster, your friends- I …' I shifted my gaze to my shoes. I had not been invited to sit.

'A cruel slander,' said Bacon. I looked up, but neither he nor Cecil would meet my eyes. Both, I could see, wished to pass over the matter.

Cecil suddenly became interested in his nails. 'I shall have the palace searched from its stables to its kitchens. If a fragment of dust looks fit to be lit, it shall be swept away. But it must be done privily. I would not embarrass his Majesty before King Christian with the wild ravings and plotting of any foul creatures. Or their minions.'

The word hung in the air: minion – a byword for male love-toys. My chin hit my ruff; its stiff linen folds were more nuisance than comfort. 'Security,' said Bacon, at length. 'Indeed, cousin. Security. If there is some society, they might have men anywhere.'

Cecil's cheek jerked. 'Society,' he spat, as though the word were grubby. 'No reports have reached me of any damned recusant dining with friends, at home or abroad. Yet it will be done, this great search, on the morrow. And the kings will be well girt about with my men on the seventh day. The hall at Hampton Court will be a very strongbox.' He finally looked at me and sighed. 'You have done some good work, Ned. The old man – the coach beast – I have let him go. He cost more in food and beer than he knew. I assume that you handled him.'

I nodded, setting my jaw. 'Smashed the truth from his mouth, my lord,' I said, recalling the slap, the crack of the man's head against plaster.

Cecil looked away, his lips pressed together and working. But Bacon's mouth fell open. 'Such handling – is such handling within the compass of our laws, cousin?'

My master ignored him and addressed himself to me again. 'If you are correct in your reading of this mad verse … well, then, we know what the plotters aim at. Two kings murdered, as we thought, by some secret assassin. And we might take measures to prevent it. But the thing is to find out who these people are, society or not. Who, who, who. Names, names, names.' He punctuated each repetition with a thud on the arm of his chair. 'True names and identities, not Locustas nor Mrs John Johnsons.'

Bacon rose from his seat. The table gave a musical tinkle of plates and glasses. Cecil, I noticed, did not rise or acknowledge his cousin's movement. 'Well, my very good lord,' said the lawyer, 'I must go.'

'Back to your wife, Francis, or your friend?' He accompanied the jab with a smile.

'Lady Bacon, yes.'

A sudden suspicion fell over me. Could Sir Francis Bacon be a man of August, and his child bride dart about London on his command, using the name Locusta? Before the idea could mature, I let it go. I did not know the lady, but others certainly would. No, the creature I had glimpsed in the Abbey, blonde periwig or not, was some other. Some unknown.

'You may go too, Ned,' said Cecil. As soon as the words were out, he began applying himself to a stack of cakes. Sugar paste stuck to his fingers and he frowned down at them. 'Farewell.'

Bacon gave me a brief look of amusement, and I stood back to let him pass. Together, we left the supper room and went out into the dim outer chamber, where Verney handed back my weapons without a word, and I gave him none in thanks. He gave Bacon only a fine lawn coat. 'Well, Mr Savage,' said the little lawyer, shrugging his arms into it, 'I think my dear cousin is a man of a sceptical bent. He does not believe in any secret society of men. Perhaps he is right. Such things belong in the past.'

'Perhaps,' I said.

'Come, walk out with me.' He moved off with a lively, cantering step.

As we descended through the house, Bacon broke off the humming he had begun. 'I say,' he said, 'do you recall I spoke to you of Raleigh?'

'Yes, sir.'

'It strikes me … I recall that the fellow was indeed bruited to lead a brotherhood of men. The playwright Marlowe was one. The rest I cannot recall. Nor do I know if my lord cousin ever found proof of it. Atheists, they were said to be. A secret society founded on wicked and heretical ideas.' He shrugged. We had reached the domestic regions of the house. 'Perhaps it was mere rumour.'

'Raleigh is in the Tower,' I said flatly.

'Of course, of course. Yet he has friends yet. And it is well known,' he said, lowering his voice, 'that the king did reduce him. Or my cousin acting to please the king.'

I considered this. Raleigh had been a prisoner for three years; he had fallen – or been thrown down – as soon as the old queen had died. King James was said to be deeply suspicious of him.

And I had met him.

'I do not accuse the fellow, mark you,' said Bacon. He went silent as a groom appeared and opened the door for us. We stepped out into the cooling evening. The smell of the river and the garden fell upon us in a sweet, hazy, watery cloud. 'I do not accuse Raleigh,' Bacon repeated. 'Yet if there is some society, some group of great men at work – then who better to know of their working than a man who might once have directed such a body?'

As I digested this, the little man touched the brim of his hat and began marching down the cobbled path which led to Cecil's private water stairs and jetty. I watched him shrink before turning in the opposite direction.

The Tower again, I thought, tightening my coat against the coming night.

23

Locusta awoke to birdsong and sunlight, in a room more pleasant than any she had ever known. After depositing the boy-whore in the Duck and Drake the previous night, she had taken up her masters on their invitation to lodge for the night in their inner sanctum. It was a place as fine as any she had ever known. She had slept sweetly, on a good, feathered bed in her own chamber high up in the attic rooms.

Exactly why this honour had been granted, she didn't know and hadn't asked. It was enough to have more than the pallet she had been provided within the City chambers, which were lumpy, straw-stuffed and brought on dreams of her previous life amidst creatures of no account and little skill. The only caveat of the invitation was that she must continue to play her role – the wicked and most cunning assassin – throughout.

That was easy. She had been Locusta the Cunning for weeks now.

The thumps of movement in the house below roused her, and she dressed quickly, silently, using the Puritan Goodwife clothing that she'd had altered to fit. The loss of the wig and veil was a problem. The leader of the Augustans had provided her with quite a number of fine lady's clothes, which had only to be let out a little; the wigs she had had to borrow herself.

The door opened, just as the russet wig slipped over her ears. 'My lady,' said the Augustan. He essayed a bow. A lean-faced man, this one, rather serious and stuffy. 'The master craves an audience with you.' He gave her a look she didn't like. Disapproval? Disgust? It brought heat into her cheeks, and she looked away. His nose rose in the air, and he left. Locusta looked around the room, at the painted cloths, the bed, the coffer, the carpets. And then, hugging her arms around her newly Puritanical body, she followed.

The room to which she followed the Augustan was a large hall, set at the back of the house. To reach it, she had to go through a well-furnished parlour and a room full of books. The delicate tinkling of virginals played with skill came from a distance, played by some unseen figure in some other part of the house. She kept her gaze steady, locked on the thin, bobbing back of the fellow. He paused in the doorway, reaching up to pull down his hood. 'Come,' he said without turning.

Inside the hall, other figures in their black robes were kneeling, facing the leader who stood at the front. Candles were burning, despite the airiness of the room, and the air was thick with the scent of good wax. Instinctively, Locusta fell to her knees.

'Rise, please,' said the head of the society. She did. The man was not masked, but his sack-like hood obscured his face. 'The man Ned Savage,' he said. 'You did as you were bid.' It was not a question.

'Yes, sir,' she answered, anyway.

'We know. He was watched. He left the tavern in the company of men. Men whom we know to serve a great master, though not as great as we fellows acting in concert.' Locusta heard the rustle of silks around her; the other brothers nodding, she supposed. 'And he went straight to a fine home. The Lord Salisbury.' Locusta knew the name, of course, and looked down at the black-carpeted floor. 'It is clear that this Savage, this attack dog, is favoured by the king's secretary. And that together they intend to spoil the merriment we have planned. They will not. This Savage will not. Members of our brotherhood will watch to see where he goes in the City. And it is there you must strike.'

Locusta's chin rose. 'Strike?'

The leader put a hand on her shoulder. It clamped down, hard. His hood turned away. 'Brother?'

One of the other men stood and, without speaking, shuffled over to a corner of the room and bent over something. He straightened, turned. Something curved and shining stood against his chest, seeming to grow from his hands.

'Tell me, have you ever used one of these?'

'No, sir.' Her voice was barely above a whisper. 'Not in any good fashion. I mean, when I was – when we were all – we were made to practice.'

'Quite. There is space in the fields beyond this house. You might try it a little. You need not be a master-mistress.' He leant down, the soft edges of his hood brushing the russet strands of the wig and whispered.

Locusta smiled. 'And then, sir?'

He stood back, then turned away. 'And then? And then we will hear your report of the matter. Go to the usual place when you have struck at your mark. Go now and practice, if you will. But do not take too long. It is a fair way. One of our boats is waiting.'

Locusta held out her arms as the other Augustan handed her the bow.

24

Like the Earl of Northumberland, Sir Walter Raleigh was housed not in a dank cell, but in chambers which might have belonged in any grand house. This the old spy and lieutenant of the Tower, Sir William Wade, had told me when I'd flown up to the Tower with the sun and birds. He did not accompany me to the condemned man's rooms this time, for they were close by.

The Bloody Tower.

I had only passed under it on my previous visit. This time, I was led directly up an outer staircase which gave onto it, a yeoman unlocking the outer door with a jangle of brass and iron.

Sir William had spoken truly. Inside, the prison chambers were brightly lit, lead-lined, barred windows set deep into the stone walls. Those walls were painted white, scrupulously clean, and the floors were covered in rush matting. The ceiling high above was fine oak, and similar good wood appeared to have been used in carving the various cabinets, desks, and shelves which stood everywhere – in the centre of the room, against walls, in stone recesses. Most were covered in papers, books, and what looked like diagrams. It was not his old palace at Durham House, but it was a fine place to be.

Then where is he?

The door closed behind me, silent on its oiled hinges. I was unnerved, lost all of a sudden. I did not think the old man would remember me. Since I had last seen him – then, I had unwittingly been implicating him in a plot of which he was innocent – much had happened. His disgrace, his trial, his loss of freedom. I understood he had even fathered a son whilst locked up, the old goat. Surely, I hoped, I was just one in a sea of faces, drowned out by many others.

I stepped farther into the first room, squinting down at the desk nearest me. Its papers seemed to show plans for a garden, with neat script labelling squares set apart to grow rosemary and mint. Reaching out, I traced one of the squares with a finger.

Was this, I wondered, what the famous voyager, the man who had been to the New World and the Azores, was now forced to do with his time? Plan gardens like a sad old countryman, or an addled cunning woman? What a waste.

I looked around the fine room again. It was still silent. I have heard it said that the greatest punishment one could face is long imprisonment. Endless days, spent even amongst luxury, will wear and pall. Such suffering is considered likely to breed madness and illness, great pains of body and mind.

Rubbish.

Looking at Raleigh's entrance chamber – some of the cabinets even boasted the bizarre curios I knew he favoured – I saw the lie of such claims. Any shoeless urchin out in London would, I knew, give his last tooth to be trapped in such rooms, never to leave them, even, rather than to live free amidst gutters choked with turds and fields barren of anything to eat but grass. Still, perhaps those bred to adventure and to live well in the wide world found it torture.

Still hearing nothing, I moved over towards one of the desks set in a wall recess. Bathed in morning light were all manner of books. I reached for one, drawing it across the polished oak and opening it. The inside page read: *The firste volume of the Chronicles of England, Scotlande, and Irelande: conteyning, the description and chronicles of England, from the first inhabiting vnto the conquest.* There was more, but already I felt my heart begin to speed.

'Good morrow to you, stranger.'

I jumped, the book sliding from my grasp and thumping onto the desk. Wheeling, I saw Raleigh. He had come silently – a remarkable thing, for he had grown stocky – and was standing next to one of the carved wooden shutters which blocked off the first of his rooms from the second. His cool, amused gaze was focussed on my face. I could see the pupils of eyes dart minutely, could sense the engine of his mind turning, turning, searching.

I bent my head, stepping forward, hoping that movement would rob him of the ability to place me. It might be that he simply thought I looked like the dead Essex, as everyone else did.

'Good morrow to you, Sir Walter.' I even did him the honour of removing my hat, though he was just a prisoner, an unperson. 'I am pleased that you would see me.'

'I was not aware I had a choice.'

I coughed, frowning, feeling a half-brain. My hat returned to my head. 'It might be, sir, that you can be a help to me.' The fellow's grey eyebrow rose. He rested on a cane, and he brought it from his side, placing it in front of his body and putting both hands over its gilt top. A neat little barrier, I thought.

I had decided that I would attempt no trickery with Raleigh. He was, to be frank, a far cleverer man than I was. If I tried to play games, he would have a better hand at every turn. 'I represent the king's secretary, Lord Salisbury.' My chest rose. And then it deflated. Raleigh would not be impressed by either of the men who had put him away. He had, it was said, been the petted lover of a queen. 'I come in search of your aid, should you be willing to give it. In discovering the August Plot.'

Nothing. Not a flicker.

'What,' he asked, 'is this?'

I sighed, my eyes sliding to the stone floor. Cecil did not know I was here. I was acting with Sir Francis' guidance, to be sure, but Bacon was a nobody, a lawyer who had achieved little and whose only saving grace was his kinship to Cecil. And yet, under Raleigh's glare, I poured out everything that I knew, from the rumours of Locusta which had sparked the affair to the threats against the two kings I'd perceived to be enacted the following day. I even included my failed attempts to catch the assassin, before laying out the possibility of her being hired by a secret society of powerful men.

'And,' I concluded, 'my lord would find out these men, if they exist, and smash their society. He would have names. He would discover all.' I hesitated. And then I added, 'I am a nothing, sir. Yet, if you can be of any help in revealing how such a society might come to be, then I- I shall inform his lordship of your aid. And he, I am certain, will inform his Majesty. To aid in saving the king's life- it might clear all that has gone before.' I pointedly looked around the room. It was nonsense, of course, but I was hoping that even a clever man might harbour hope – however flimsy – of freedom.

Raleigh, who had listened throughout, never questioning, never asking for points to be cleared, turned and limped over to the wall. Resting his cane, gold head against the white wall, he twisted his shaggy head. He was still a handsome man, as he had been when I'd first met him, little tarnished from what he must have been in the days when he'd rested his head on the queen's wrinkled bosom. 'Why me?'

'It is said that once you were the head of such a company. A brotherhood of men.'

'Ah. That, alas, was a mere rumour. Supper parties with friends only. Watered, fed, and grown by my enemies into slanderous rumours. As you can see, I have no society of friends here. My gentlemen are absent. I craved solitude, and we are quite alone.' He began to trundle towards me. Instinctively, I stepped back, my breeches jostling the desk. But he drew up short and turned to look out the window.

I followed his gaze. Through the polished glass, I could see the courtyard. Nearest us stood the garden dotted with trees that stood near the lieutenant's lodging. 'Ha. In truth, I wish no man to share my burden for too long a stretch.' He breathed deeply of his clean prison air. 'Do you know, this place, these rooms, used to be called the Garden Tower.' His voice, when it got going, was burred with a country accent. It was pleasing, in its way, more lyrical than the clipped snap of London voices. 'Do you know why they call it the Bloody Tower?'

'It is said the princes were killed here. By their wicked uncle, Richard III.'

'You know your history,' he said. I bowed to the compliment. 'Yes. And it has become a bloody place since. A tainted place. Did you imagine I should end up in such a place when last you saw me?'

'I didn't … it wasn't … I was at Durham House under orders, sir.'

'Durham House.' He smiled. 'Yes, that was it. Thank you. I knew I recalled you from somewhere. It has been troubling me.' I cursed myself more than him. 'You came … you forced your way into my chambers. The shadow of Essex that is what I recall. Though, you were not so tall as he was then and neither have you grown. You were with some fool from the parliament.'

'That,' I countered, 'is history.'

'Hm. And now you work for little Cecil. Oh. My apologies. We prisoners are apart from the ever-spinning world and its rising men. You serve Lord Salisbury.'

I smiled, pleased to have one up on him. 'I did then too, sir.'

He frowned. 'Interesting. It was that fellow who helped put me here.'

'And who might help you back out.'

Raleigh's face broke into a handsome smile. 'The day little Cecil does me a good turn, sir, is the day this tower melts in the sun.'

I stepped away from the pool of light. 'My lord serves the king in all matters.'

'As you serve the secretary. In matters of intelligence, I think.'

'Quite.' I was bored with him now, bored of his words. 'Can you help me? I would secure the king's life. Both kings' lives.'

'I will help you, sir. Though not with any secret society. I do not believe such things prosper. The late Powder Plotters, did they not teach your master that brotherhoods of men always fail? There is always one man – at least one man – who cannot keep his mouth shut. And thus the whole house of cards falls.' I opened my mouth to speak, and he raised a finger, silencing me. It was amazing, I thought, how the old fellow – ruined, imprisoned – could still master a room. 'I will school you a little if it pleases you. Come, let us sit by the fire.'

I followed, like a schoolboy indeed, whilst Raleigh regained his cane and led me past screens carved with diamond-bisected shields into the next of his rooms. There, a fireplace glowed red with embers. Two carved chairs sat, facing one another, a circular games table with a chessboard sitting between them. I must have given it a quizzical look for, as he folded himself down, he said, 'my gaolers, some of them, are good enough to play with me. It passes the time. Sit, man, sit.'

I did as I was told, settling my palms on my breeches. I could feel him staring again, and I looked at the little chess pieces. All were made of silver. I decided then and there I was going to steal me a queen. 'Now,' said Raleigh, drawing my head up. 'This is better. You tell me that your lord and master seeks to discover the names of these – what was it? August Plotters?'

I nodded, recalling Cecil's words: Who, who, who. Names, names, names. Though I had not been a part of the affair, I knew that he had been similarly obsessed with discovering the true name of John Johnson. Once he had secured the identity of the unfortunate Guy or Guido Fawkes, the rest of the plot had quickly unravelled, dropping the creatures I now knew he had been watching into his net.

'Then your master,' said Raleigh, 'is a fool.'

I half-rose. I bore no great love for Cecil, but honour demanded a rebuff. Besides, as much as I disliked and distrusted him, I did not think my master a fool. 'Sir, I –'

'Sit, man. I need no feigned outrage,' he barked. I obeyed. 'The who is not important when time presses. The names of these men are irrelevant. If you suspect they will kill – seek to kill – on the morrow, then you need not know who they are. Find out how they plan to strike and stop it. Have a care of their identities only when the victims are secured. Now, I never was any intelligencer.' The last word dripped with distaste. 'Yet I was the captain of the late queen's guard. A noble profession.' He settled back in his seat. 'I know something of matters of security. And I did listen with interest to your tale. Have you any tobacco about you?'

'No,' I lied. I was not about to share my precious store.

'A shame.' He stretched his leg out and tapped the games table with his shoe. It juddered, its little men and women threatening to topple. 'Regard the board. Now, there are customary matters of security; I am sure your master will have the wit to consider. This board is the hall at Hampton Court. Check the thrones for poison, search the place for powder. Be sure that no man or woman who comes to the place has a pistol concealed about them, nor any other weapon.'

'I know this. And his lordship, too.'

Raleigh did not look offended, though I'd spoken curtly. 'All eyes will be on the stage tomorrow—a good time to strike, when men's gazes are placed elsewhere, on the players. Yet -yet … how? From where?' He frowned down at the board, as though, in his mind, it had really become the great hall at the palace. 'In such a space.' Raleigh looked back up at me; his grey eyes were still aflame. 'Concentrate all your men – Salisbury's men – around the hall. And plenty strung throughout, like beads on a chain.' Something seemed to strike him, raising his brow as it did. He leant forward suddenly and reached out, picking up first the king on his side and then – pointedly, I thought – the queen on mine. He set both on the floor, before rising with a grunt.

'What do you mean, sir?' I asked.

'Look beyond the board, Savage.' I shrugged, trying to catch up. 'You tell me these people have advertised a great attack and the place and time – when two kings are watching.' I nodded. 'Why should they announce their plans, even in verse? To force you to look in one place-to secure one place. Whilst their true design lies elsewhere.'

'I have considered it,' I said. I hadn't.

'I suggest,' Raleigh continued, 'there are two possibilities. One: there is a masterful plot set by cunning men – to snap their fingers at all your security and slay the kings under your noses. Though I cannot provide any means by which they might. Two: they plan to distract you and keep you busy in the hall – their true complot, their time to strike, is elsewhere. At some other time and place.'

'You mean – after the plays? Or before them?'

'I should think so. Either way, the two kings must not be left alone at any time. Trusted men must attend them at all times, lest some friends of their Majesties have been bought and turned.'

'Friends?'

He shrugged. 'I do not know of the state of the current court, nor anything of the Danish king's. Caesar was slain by his friends, men he trusted. I can offer no more. Secure the great hall, yes – and every entrance and exit to it. Strip the rest of the palace bare of guards if you must. But be sure that men at all times surround both sovereign lords.' He smirked. 'Even if little

Cecil must go naked. He must spare every man to the king's security. That is what I did in Queen Elizabeth's time – spare my own guards to protect her.'

And look where such altruism got you!

But he was right. All Cecil and I had to go on was what the plotters themselves had suggested to us – or, rather, my interpretation of their suggestion. We assumed they planned to slay the kings as they watched the entertainments on the seventh. If it was a mere distraction, with the planned assassination taking place after when our guards were down…

'I perceive – I have perceived,' I said, 'that we search for men of genius. Of much wit and learning.'

'Hardly,' grumbled Raleigh. Again, he silenced my protest with a wagging finger. 'Hardly, I say. Any creatures who aim to destroy a king are poor thinkers as well as wicked men. Ay and women. A king governs by counsel. For as long as wicked counsellors haunt the court, they will haunt any successor.' He grinned.

'Do you speak, sir, of my lord of Salisbury?'

'I speak, sir,' he said, mimicking only a little, 'in generalities drawn from the history of the world.'

I drew in my cheeks and lifted my chin. 'I shall inform my lord of your advice, Sir Walter. We shall not let our guard down.'

'Please do not,' he said. 'Inform Lord Salisbury of my help, I mean.' I must have shown my confusion, for he waved a hand in the air. 'If this plot exists, and that man learns I helped – even to discover it, to ruin it – well. I have no doubt I shall find myself accused of having knowledge. I know your master, Mr Savage. He will bite the hand that feeds and enjoy the taste of it.'

I did not reply. He was quite right. I leant forward as I made to get up, in a rustle of padded breeches. My hand slid to the stone floor, moving silently.

'For God's sake, man!' boomed Raleigh. I jerked my hand back up. 'Take the damned chess piece.' I could feel twin searing waves cross my cheeks. But the old fellow did not look annoyed. 'Take it, damn you. I recall you trying and failing to steal from me before. I cannot recall what it was.'

Licking my lips, I said, 'a piece of jet, or the like, as I recall.'

'Hmph. Yes. For God's sake, grow up and demand what you wish, without such pathetic subterfuge.'

Just as the man demanded, I leant down and stole the carved chess queen. It would go nicely in my collection, I thought. I did not bother to thank him, but inclined my head and, once the piece was stowed in my pocket, I touched my hat brim. We rose from our seats together, and he walked with me out through his rooms and towards the door. I rapped on it with my forearm. At the muted sound of keys tinkling, Raleigh spoke to me again.

'I wish you fair fortune, young sir. Ay, I do. Pray, come to me again – if you stop this design. Furnish me with news of it. And if any strange complots and riddles come to you in times coming, well, I am here. Always, always here. Such mad riddles and tangled designs- they pass the time.'

***

I left Raleigh to the Tower's tender mercies and made my way to the water stairs, where a wherry took me back upriver. It was a sparkling day, not so hot as it had been, but bright and clear. I stood to debark when the welcoming sight of Whitefriars Stairs hove into view, looking as weed-choked and decrepit as ever.

There was no crowd waiting to take my place, and so I turned to exchange a word with the wherryman. Before I could speak, however, I saw the man's eyes widen. His oar slid from his hand, clattering against the side of the boat and landing across it. 'Look out!' he cried. 'Get down!'

I fell immediately, throwing my hands over my head. The wherry rocked, bobbed, making my stomach lurch. Some Thames water came up over its side as we nearly capsized.

What the?

Something hit the far end of the craft.

'We're being shot!' cried the boatman. I braced myself for another wild dip. It never came. 'She's going!'

For a second, I thought he meant the wherry, assumed that we were going to sink right there by the stairs. But nothing happened. 'What?' I asked stupidly. I tried to stand and found that my legs had turned to jelly. The best I could manage was a stumbling, bent-over lurch. Still, I made my way down to the end of the boat.

There, jutting from the wooden interior, was a single arrow.

'Shot,' I echoed.

'She's gone, mate. I saw her run off.'

I did not answer him. Instead, I turned to dry land, looking at the landing stage and then up the stairs, towards the grey stone houses and buildings which fronted the river. 'A woman,' I said. 'Her.'

It was not a question, but my boatman answered anyway. 'Saw her run off, mate.'

'Get you gone, friend,' I said. 'Some new form of robbery.' I managed to get myself onto the bank and began climbing the stairs. The street snaked away from them, disappearing into the permanent gloomy shadow hidden by the overhanging thatch and slate. People were moving about, of course – men, women, children. I had barely taken two steps when my shoes slithered into something. I hopped back.

Again?

At my feet was a russet wig and a women's kirtle. Either Locusta was now roaming London naked, I thought, or she had carefully concealed some plain clothing beneath this latest disguise. I gathered the whole lot in a bundle in my arms and began marching through the streets. Anger began to flood in to fill the void of numbness and shock the sudden attack had brought.

An assassin – a true assassin – should have had the skill to shoot the prick off a mosquito. This one, this Locusta, was either unskilled, did not intend to kill, or-

Or she is no assassin.

Instantly I thought of the old man's body in Gray's Inn.

What if...

When I reached Shoe Lane, I dumped the wig and clothing in the empty water-butt, closing the lid on it. Inside the house, I found David, Faith, and Nicholas Hopgood. 'What's happened?' asked Faith. Her hand, spoon still in it, paused in mid-air over the brazier. 'Are you hurt?'

'What? No.' I realised my colour must be off, my hat askew, or some such tell. Perhaps she just knew me too well. 'I'm well.

I'm just...' I looked from face to face. 'I just realised that you will be getting married the day after tomorrow, you two.' I managed a smile.

'Yes, sir,' said Hopgood. 'And I'll take good care of her.' He moved to stand a little closer to Faith but stopped short of touching her.

'Where are you to live?' I knew the answer, of course – they were to go into a room above his master's weaving shop. 'How about here?' I asked. A look fell between the couple. 'Not *here* here, I mean … here in Shoe Lane. If I can…if I can end the work you know I've been engaged in – end it well – I should fetch a high price. For my labours.' I was babbling, and I knew it; I didn't, however, know where the words came from nor where they were going. 'I'll buy you a place. Here in Shoe Lane. One of the other pairs of rooms.'

Both Faith and Hopgood frowned. The latter, looking sheepish, said, 'we couldn't … sir, we could not accept…'

Shut up, you!

'You can pay me back when your own weaving trade is great. And you will be nearer to David,' I said, directing myself to Faith. 'You can watch him near as he becomes England's finest player.'

'I …' she began.

'Think about it,' I said, trying to affect a casual air. 'Talk about it, if you will. It's not often I'm generous.' I swallowed. 'You will have the house here to yourselves.' I shrugged, turning to David. 'Little man, you must make yourself ready to be the second sister, gentlewoman, and Lady MacDuff. Sir Edmund Tilney would hear you and the rest of the King's Men before the kings hear you on the morrow.'

David smiled up at me, and I returned it, but only vaguely.

I would go with him to Revels because someone there knew the truth about what had been going on.

25

There wasn't time for Locusta to return upriver to the grand house, even if she'd been asked to – which she hadn't. Instead, she had had to come to the Augustans' City lodgings. These rooms she knew well enough, for she had spent her nights there since first being hired, sleeping in an empty, cell-like place with a cot bed. The society of revels-loving men, it seemed, could afford much. In this great complex of buildings, she had found her masters full of interest in the success of her latest mission.

'He was unhurt?'

'Of course, sir.'

'Good,' said the leader. He turned to the other two Augustans in the room. They stood behind him, one on each side, in the middle of the grand chamber. 'Perhaps he will now think we have aimed first at his credit and reputation and now at his life. Maybe … we must hope … yes. Yes, he will think that he has discovered our true plans and that we tried to stop him for fear.' A smile spread over the man's face. 'What mirth. What merriment. What a fool. And what he believes, the kings will believe, and the secretary will believe.' A murmur ran through his fellows. As if to stifle it, the man continued. 'He will be fair convinced that he knows what is afoot. Perhaps he will even be frightened off from his intermeddling. All such parasitic intelligencers are cowards who will look to their own skins.'

Locusta understood none of this. Her mission had been simple – as simple as the last. All she had had to do was fire upon Ned Savage and do him no harm. In any case, she would never have harmed him. What the man thought was happening, she had no idea. And she was not being paid to think, but to play the role.

'What now, sir?'

The leader turned back to her. 'Now? Oh, yes. Our association is at an end.' He fumbled at his belt, his nimble fingers darting about a stringed purse. Once loose, he thrust it outwards and dropped it. Locusta scrambled to floor. Even by touch, it was the largest amount of money she had ever touched. 'We have no more need of you. You can shed your weeds as you shed your wigs. You are our sweet Lady Locusta no more.' And then the fellow stepped forward. Never had he been menacing before, but something hard came over his face now. 'I suggest that you forget that name. Though, it might be on many lips in the coming days. You never heard it. Nor have you heard of a Mrs Johnson, nor any of the roles you have played. You have done well, and now you would do well to remember nothing, my dear boy.'

Locusta-no-more got to his feet and nodded. The act was over. He had lived as a woman amongst these men for so long; he still moved with a short-stepping grace. He backed away from the room, leaving the Augustans who had hired him to their secret conference, the purse of money growing hot in his hand.

Passing along the hall outside, he paused.

He had promised himself that he would find out what games he'd been involved in. From the very beginning, he had been promised that all was revelry – a great entertainment being played out with the knowledge of the king. Yet when Ned Savage had become involved, when she – he – had had to begin tricking him, pushing him down, and now firing upon him, it all began to look darker than mere entertainments and interludes.

Padding on his soft woman's slippers, he crept along the wall, back towards the doorway into the Augustans' great hall. Their voices drifted out, echoing in the large room.

'– and the whole pack of dogs will be busy about the great hall when the strike comes. They will see nothing amiss,' said the leader.

'I still say he will be too well guarded to kill,' said another.

Kill, thought the fellow formerly known as Locusta. Kill!?

'Bah! Our true assassin will accomplish it,' rumbled the third voice. 'All eyes will be on that foolish fat Dane. He is the novelty, the toy.'

'And the plays, of course. I understand there is to be some trash about Denmark, Scotland, and Italy,' said the leader. 'The Scotch one falls in the middle—about a killing with daggers. King Duncan, slain by Macbeth. Then. Then is the fitting time.'

The second voice spoke again. 'If only there were some other way.'

'There is none,' snapped that hard third man. 'He should have died long since. I still say our murderer might have done it privily already.'

'No,' snapped the head Augustan. 'This is not wild vengeance. This way is safer. Now that the Lady Locusta is well known and suspected. Has been seen by Salisbury's own man. Struck at him, even.' Some grumbling met this, too low to be made out clearly. 'Ay,' chuckled the leader, 'a shot in the street or a hole driven into the barge. Have you no love of history, the theatre of the world?' His voice was gently mocking, edged with mirth. 'Caesar's assassins chose the Curia. We have chosen Hampton Court, and this we will stick by. All agreed. Not before the stage is set, opportunity or not. Be patient. He dies on the morrow when we manage that stage. Our assassin strikes then and only then.'

The second man, who sounded the least confident, said, 'it is the only way to end his filthy grip on this realm, is it not?'

The leader let out a windy sigh. 'I fear it is so. It is no crime to rid the realm of an evil creature who would destroy it. Who, would destroy the very name of England. On the morrow, then, during this *Macbeth*, the end comes.'

Fear crept up the eavesdropper's neck in hot, tickling, itchy fingers. He fled.

26

‘How many children had Lady Macbeth?’ asked Hal Berridge.

The whole company sighed. Mr Shakespeare’s balding head descended into his hands. He was sitting on the edge of the stage, prompting the players and watching them deliver his lines. ‘These lines, these lines I have to say,’ Hal muttered, ‘“I have given suck, and know … How tender 'tis to love the babe that milks me.” Where’s the babe?’

‘It *died*!’ snapped the playwright. Some laughter rippled through the chamber. Berridge, I noticed, had arrived late and given trouble from the first, forgetting some lines, questioning others. He was not fit to be the principal boy, I decided.

Nor will he be.

Nevertheless, the rehearsal continued, Sir Edmund Tilney dozing contentedly in his cushioned seat opposite the little stage. I cast another look up. Hal was stuttering his way through a speech under the furious gaze of Richard Burbage. The boy was dressed in a fine black gown with a white ruff, the only concession to Scotland being a plaid shawl about his shoulders. Burbage was clad in purple garments that would befit an earl. ‘Bring forth men-children only!’ boomed the great tragedian, cutting over Hal’s lines. To the rest of his company – and me, and the sleeping Tilney – he cried, ‘it isnae fit that any man should have sic a wife!’

‘Perhaps we should take a short break so that young Berridge can recover his wits,’ said John Heminges. Scattered muttering greeted this. Hal looked fit for tears. ‘Mr Savage, you have read the play. Do you not think it fit that we can proceed with it? That it is fit and proper food for a prince?’

I folded my arms, noticing that the writer was staring at me intently. I felt my lip curl. ‘It is fit, yes. Mr Shakespeare, you are indeed to be commended as our finest maker of tragedies. Why, truly, right from the opening lines of this play, I wished to see everyone in it die.’

I did not get the laugh I'd hoped for. Instead, another outbreak of angry words erupted between the players. I left the arguments onstage and slid across the rush-strewn floorboards of the playing space to the only real woman present. Mrs Cole, the seamstress, was standing with her arms folded, chewing on the inside of her jaw. 'Might I speak with for a spell?' I asked. 'Outside.'

She gave me a careful look. And then she shrugged and led me towards the door. In the hall of the office building, we stopped. 'What is it now, Ned?'

I smiled at her familiarity. Once, years before, she had helped to disguise me as I prepared to raid a house full of evil men. She had guessed then that I was in the secretary's service. As far as I knew, despite her blabbering reputation, she had not betrayed me to anyone.

The question was, who else had she been disguising?

'You have made them all up well,' I offered.

'The players? Hm. I did what I could. Your boy – the weird sisters – I'd have liked to put them in blue, make them creatures from the sea. Sea witches – such was my thought. But what can you do?' Her elfin face crinkled. 'But that's not what you're after, is it? Come on, Ned. I've told you before; I know something about the work you do. Was engaged in it myself, in my young day. Did I ever tell you I had to disguise myself as a manservant? That was in –'

'I was attacked earlier today.' That shut her up.

'You were hurt?'

'No. A warning perhaps. Or a bad assassin.'

The old woman sucked air over her teeth. 'What can I do?'

'I … this isn't the first time. I've been searching for a woman. Calls herself Locusta.'

'I've heard the name,' said Mrs Cole. She was a little woman, well into her fifties, but her eyes glittered with intelligence. 'It was the news a couple of weeks back. That a wicked woman called Locusta was abroad in the town.'

'The same.' I reached up and kneaded my brow with the ball of my fist. 'Yet … the creature has been near me twice. And both times discarded clothing, wigs. When I saw the second wig today- a russet thing, it's the type of thing you use in the playhouses.' I described it to her and the other, the blonde one left behind in Westminster Abbey.

And thereafter, old Mrs Cole told me quite a tale of the fellow who had asked her to let out fine clothes – finer even than the usual stage stuff, and much of it new – as well as borrowing a couple of wigs. It seemed he had borrowed one of the suits of clothing – the type used to dress stage kings – and lost it. That explained the playbill, I thought, found in the dead man's suit which I'd made my own. 'After that, I wouldn't give him anything else of ours. He already had the wigs. He promised me those fine gowns he had me let out – for the company, he said, when he was done with them.' I wished she would shut up for a minute and let me think. Georgie's fine suit, which I also now owned, had come from elsewhere. So had the Locusta gowns. The plotters, therefore, had a real woman amongst them, connected to them.

Luisa Mendoza!

Penelope Devereux!

Queen fucking Anne!

'You won't hurt him, will you?' she asked. I returned my attention to her. 'I … I think he's an innocent. I know a bastard when I see one. I think he was being used. He reminds me of one of my boys. That's why I helped him.'

I said nothing.

And then I felt her grip on my arm. It was hard. 'Ned – Mr Savage. Ask him questions if you have to. I don't know what this business is you're involved in – don't want to – but handle that poor lamb gently.'

I shook her off. She left me, going back into the staging room. As the door opened, I heard the lilting Scotch accents of the actors, just for a moment, just until she banged it closed again. As the rehearsal thundered on, I remained out in the hall, smoking until my throat burned, and my pouch of tobacco was finished.

Eventually, the thing was at an end. Sir Edmund exited first, his eyes bleary. 'Christ Jesus, Savage,' he said. 'What have you done to the air out here? Never mind, never mind. It is late. I am going home.'

'The play, sir?'

'What? Oh. Yes, yes, all good, fine, nothing to make any man quake. They can play it on the morrow, yes, yes, quite.' He shuffled off, yawning, one hand on the plaster wall. And then came the stage-wrights, Shakespeare and Burbage at the head of the troupe, their heads bent in conversation. I could tell by the playwright's face that he was displeased with something or other. In his hands he carried the script, all bent out of shape with various folds and splotches of ink about it.

At the rear of the group came David and Hal, both dressed in their own clothes. My boy was smiling, but his friend looked troubled, preoccupied. 'You'll do good tomorrow,' David was saying. 'It's just the night before.'

I plastered on a smile and launched myself off the wall I'd been leaning against. 'Yes, Hal. It is the mark of a good player that he can convince the penny-payers he is not all a-tremble. The same goes, I should think, for performances before kings. You have played before the king before, have you not – in your old company?'

'Yes, sir,' the boy answered. He didn't meet my eye.

'Are we going home now, Ned?' asked David. 'I want to be up early and … to say my words again. Just in case.' I reached down and squeezed his arm, pulling him away from Hal. I kept dragging him, all the way to the front of the Revels Office, which was lit by candle trees. The windows outside gave on to darkness. Some of the players were still standing about, enjoying the light, pulling on coats.

'Mr Heminges!' I called. The fellow turned. I lowered my voice. 'Would you take David home? Shoe Lane. It's on your way.'

'Yes, I – of course.'

'Good man.'

'Aren't you coming, Ned?' David asked. His eyes were wide.

'Soon, son. Soon. I have to see this place locked up, keep worse men than players out.'

I almost pushed the pair out into the night, and then darted into one of the unlit side offices. I watched as the damned actors continued chatting, arguing, laughing.

Go and get drunk, you stupid dogs!

Eventually, they did begin exchanging their extravagant farewells, kissing one another's cheeks, clapping backs, promising a better show before the kings. And then the rump of them began filing out.

Hal Berridge, who stood back from his fellows, made to follow them. The moment I saw his back framed in the doorway of the building, I leapt forward, snaking an arm around his neck. He did not have time to yelp as I yanked him back into the place.

'You're going nowhere, you little shit!'

***

Having dragged the choking boy all the way back into the staging room – which I knew to have only one doorway, I threw him down and closed us in. There was no lock, but I did not intend to let him get past me if escape was on his mind.

He did not; I noticed as I turned back towards the room, attempt anything. He simply lay on the floor next to Sir Edmund's empty chair. At length, he began whimpering.

'What?' I snapped.

'I'm sorry. I'm sorry, I'm sorry, I'm sorry!' The words became more hysterical each time. Tears accompanied them.

'Locusta. It was you. Don't deny it. Don't you dare lie to me, you sneaking little bastard.'

'They paid me. They paid me to do it. To be the Lady Locusta the whole time.'

'They paid you to be a killer? I saw the old man's body.'

Hal's eyes widened. 'The old … he died. They told me to find an old beggar and dress him up. I did – I did – but he dropped dead. I – I had to jump out the window. I was all in a panic.'

He seemed to be telling the truth. 'Why should you dress up a beggar?' I asked, crossing my arms over my chest. I didn't want to beat the boy, but I would.

'A game. It was all revelry, they said. They – they paid me to play the lady and to spread word of her. A wicked woman, an - an assassin. But it wasn't real. I didn't kill anyone. I never would, Ned. It's like playing Lady Macbeth – it's just playing, just pretending. I promise. I promise.' He began to dissolve into sniffles again.

I threw my hat to the ground and ran a hand through my hair. 'Who is this "they"? Who are these men? Men of August, plotters – who are they?'

Hal looked up at me through huge, red-rimmed eyes. 'They,' he whispered. 'Not August. Augustans. Brothers of Augustus.'

The name sank in, and I cursed myself for my stupidity – no, for the blockheadedness of the old drunk Georgie, who had fed me the name. Augustus, the peace-making emperor of Rome. That was about all I knew of him. 'Who are they?' I asked again. 'Their names, boy.'

'I don't know,' he said. But I thought I saw his eyes flick to the ground.

Liar.

I stepped closer to him, and he cringed against the chair. 'I promise! They're great men, they are. I thought – I knew the greatest, he's like their king, I knew him from the court. He was sometimes at court.'

I paused, mid-step, my boot crunching down on nutshells discarded by Tilney, who had munched merrily before sleeping. 'Then, you know his name.'

'I don't! But … I know where they meet—the house of their – their society. And the great house too – I slept in it last night. Before I – before they took me on the boat to Whitefriars to … to attack you.' I moved towards him again, and his stream ran on. 'But not to kill, no, to miss, to miss!'

'Do you expect me to believe,' I hissed, 'that you have been living as a fucking woman for days, weeks, doing the bidding of this group? And that you know nothing of them but where they meet?'

'It's true! They wear masks and hoods most of the time. There are a whole lot of them. They … they run the world. They know everything. They know who you are – that you're in the service. And …' He licked his lips and began to pull himself up. Again, he looked away from me, into the shadows of the room. 'I … I thought it was all games. Sometimes I was the Lady Locusta, and sometimes a Goodwife, and a maidservant. Sometimes a page. They said you were spoiling their games, their –

merriment, the man said. But then today- today … after they paid me and told me I could go …'

'What?' I fought the urge to kick at him.

Handle that poor lamb gently.

'I listened.' He looked up at me, and the terror was genuine. 'I listened to what they said.' I waited, one eyebrow arching. 'I … I think they're going to kill the king. During the play. Our play, the Scotch one. On the morrow. I listened, I swear, and they said they would kill the man when,' he frowned, his smooth brow wrinkling, 'when eyes were on the Danish toy. Whatever that means, I don't know. But they said, clear as day, that he would die when it was fitting, when Duncan was done to death with daggers. And you – you, they said, would think you knew what was going on. But you wouldn't, Mr Savage, you wouldn't truly.'

I felt my breath desert me. Too many thoughts swirled, too many ideas, each fighting the other. 'What else?'

'Um … um … something about the man who would destroy the name of England. How he'd die. One of the men said he pledged it.'

That foolish union flag rippled and fluttered in my mind's eye. I could almost hear again the irate ramblings of the tapster Rooks, who descanted upon being born an Englishman and expected to die a Briton. King James's darling, the smashing together of Scotland and England into one Great Britain. The man who would destroy the name of England.

Then Locusta – Hal – was never the true assassin. He was a decoy, a lure, something of that nature. The real assassin was amongst this company of Augustus.

'You said, you know where they meet. Where they live.'

'I've been sleeping there; I have – since they made me Locusta and bid me live and do as her.'

'Take me there. Now.'

I reached down and yanked the boy up. He was weightless. Possibly, I thought, he was heavier when buried under wigs and gowns and bows. I kept a tight grip on him as I blew out the flames on the sconces which were already burning low in the staging room. And then, together, we went out into the hall. As we neared the door and I began to extinguish the candle trees, he started whimpering again.

'What is it, you fool?' I hissed.

'David will hate me now. Everyone will hate me.'

'I'm sure whatever they paid you will buy you new friends,' I spat.

'I didn't want this, none of this,' he whined. Tears were threatening again.

'Then you should not have agreed to play their games or their Locusta.'

'I didn't know. I didn't know what none of it meant, not till I heard them today, I promise—kings and killing. I'm not yet sixteen. I'm from Hackney, for the love of Jesus.' He was sliding, protesting under my grasp.

'My advice is that you get the hell out of London for a spell. Far, far away. And don't come back – not as Hal Berridge or Locusta or anyone.'

I had misjudged the words. I had awoken fear. His arm stiffened under my grip, and he whispered something under his breath. I turned and glared down. His face was impossible to read now, in the dimness. 'What?'

'They'll kill me,' he said. And then, louder, the words edged with madness, with terror, 'they'll kill me! They'll kill me!' He bucked suddenly, like an unruly colt, and as I fought to keep hold of his arm, something slid downwards towards my head.

I had no time to cry out. The iron candle tree, its dozen flames thankfully extinguished, toppled, striking the side of my skull. My disobedient hand relaxed on the boy and, as I waved my arms about, trying to catch the tree, I heard his voice. It was moving towards the door. 'They'll kill, they'll kill me, they'll get me!'

A rush of cool night air blasted in just as the iron clattered to the stone floor. Already I was on my knees, leaping up and towards the door. Panting, I fell into the night. 'Hal! You fool! Hal! Come back! Take me there, take me, show me, I'll protect you!'

My words were lost to the prowling wind.

Hal, Locusta, Mrs Johnson – the infamous female assassin

who was neither assassin nor female, but a used, mindless player – was gone—vanished into the streets of Clerkenwell, into the maze of London.

And with him went my only chance of finding the men who had hired him.

27

I wonder about time sometimes, at how hours can drag by or pass in a flash, depending on one's humour, though the seconds themselves are indifferent to our moods. The morning of August the 7th was one of those interminable ones. I did not leave the house on Shoe Lane but, since rising at 6 am to the sound of St Bride's distant bells, I dressed in my Revels livery and was content to pace about my bedchamber, growing annoyed with things. Since running out of tobacco, I found that I grew short, nothing pleasing me.

At what felt like five in the afternoon but was in truth only seven in the morning, I opened my door to find David and Faith busy. The boy was darting about, as though fire licked at his heels, whilst his sister was again bent over a table now fit to buckle under its weight of flowers.

Tomorrow.

'How fares the bride to be?' I asked, forcing levity into my voice. She looked up, a bashful smile on her freckled face. 'This is your last night as Faith White. Tomorrow you are Faith Hopgood.' The name sounded foolish to me. 'Goodwife Hopgood.'

'Yes,' she said. 'Ned, I …' she began, darting a look at David. 'I spoke with Nicholas. About your offer. We don't think we could … I mean, it's so kind but…'

I swallowed, trying to find fit words. I would not plead. 'Do as pleases you, of course, you must. Only,' I added, moving over to her brother and letting my hand fall on his shoulder, 'I thought you should like to be nearer to the lad. Who knows what trouble I'll get him into if you are not but a door along the street.'

'You're not going to give this plan up, are you?' she asked.

I grinned. 'No.'

'I'll speak with Nicholas again,' she said, looking back down at her flowers. Draped alongside them, its edge hanging off the table, was a bridal veil. It was none of it expensive or grand. I should, perhaps, have given them more money than the purse Luisa Mendoza had provided. But no matter – the lease of a house would be my real gift. It was, of course, wildly extravagant, but I didn't care. A strange thing: I had no trouble expending vast sums, yet the waste of an individual penny was a dagger in my heart. Faith's stubborn little chin lifted again. 'I mean it – it all depends anyway, doesn't it? On … your work.'

My heart sank. During my fitful sleep and since rising, I had been trying to consider the dangers which lay ahead and to forget them. I should, I knew, have written a dispatch to Cecil describing the discovery of Locusta, the creature's true identity. More, I should absolutely have written, or tried to find him in person, to warn him about the assassination attempt Hal had claimed would take place that night, during the performance of *Macbeth*.

But I did neither.

I had failed again, and I could not face discoursing at length on how I had had one of the plotters – or an instrument of the plotters – in my grasp, quite literally, only to let him escape. Again. Nor could I explain how the fellow had known exactly where the Augustans – not the men of August – kept their lodgings and planned their wicked deeds. I could almost see the cold, narrow-eyed frown that would greet that.

'You had their minion and his headful of knowledge, and you let him run.' A tut, a frown, a glance down at his nails.

No, I would not tell any of the previous night's discoveries to Cecil until I had to. He would only demand that I found the creatures, that I continued to find them and name them. I had no intention of doing that either, not for the moment. Raleigh's words were my salvation.

The who is not important when time presses. The names of these men are irrelevant ... Find out how they plan to strike and stop it.

Nominally, I was still in charge of Cecil's sprawling army of agents, or at least those who haunted the capital and court. They no doubt thought me a fool and worse, after the disaster at the Duck and Drake, but I could command them at least. My goal was to make Hampton Court's great hall my chessboard and to surround it with the black-coated creatures. Every entrance and exit would be guarded. Aided by the king's guards, if necessary, they would admit no one once the entertainments began and would let no one leave. I would be in the hall myself, walking its length, keeping an eye on the royal family and the crowd of courtiers which would throng the place. I would, in short, thwart the plot.

Then, once the evening had passed without incident, might I turn my attention to the who, who, who. The how would have been either discovered and destroyed or die before birth.

I hoped.

A knock at the door interrupted my thoughts, and I jumped. David sprang across the floorboards silently, throwing it open. Expecting his little friend, I supposed, who was hopefully well gone from London.

Framed in the doorway was not Hal Berridge, but another pair of players: the squat little comic Robert Armin and John Heminges, who had escorted my boy home the night before. 'What news?' I snapped.

'Mr Savage,' chirped Armin. 'What a fine house you have. Who dressed it, Guy Fawkes?'

Arse, I thought. My house was plain, but it was neat as a pin, thanks to Faith, and it was certainly no dingy under-croft. 'What do you seek, Heminges?'

The man swept his hat off and stepped into my front room. 'Oh, do come in,' I said.

'Disaster, Mr Savage. Disaster.' His voice was pure Theatre English, high and loud. His palm flew to his forehead. 'All is lost.'

'Unless,' said Armin, bouncing in behind him and dropping to one knee before David, 'we can find us a lady.'

'What?' asked David.

'That fool boy Berridge,' said Heminges. 'He has not come to us. And after his weakness last night … we fear some mischance. He was to meet with Mr Burbage this morning. You know how Burbage demands perfection in all things. The boy has grown a fear of playing before the kings, perhaps, or some like mishap. He did not come. Mr Burbage is in a fury. And

Berridge was to be the Danish prince's sweetheart and Macbeth's lady tonight. The pretty Celia in *Volpone* too. If he does not come, all is lost.'

'I –'

'David will do it. He will be Lady Macbeth.' I turned to him. 'You know her words, do you not? You heard them from Hal?'

'I … think so. I can try.'

'By the mass, then, we might be saved!' cried Heminges. I rolled my eyes and Armin began a jig.

Christ, I do hate these players.

'I can't do the other,' said David frowning. I put a hand on his shoulder again. 'The Danish – Hamlet's sweetheart. Or Celia. I don't know them.'

Heminges waved this away. 'Fear not, we have found a boy who has played those parts before. He will come back to us for the first tragedy and the comedy. Alas, he is past twenty and bearded, but … it is a very yellow beard, very pretty. And there is time yet for him to be barbered. He shall know *Hamlet* and *Volpone,* and you shall know *Macbeth.*'

Armin laughed – a quite natural laugh, unlike his stage cackle. 'Mr Shakespeare says,' he cleared his throat before mimicking, '"no longer do I play!". Yet Berridge was to play others as well as Macbeth's wicked wife. We shall have our master play-maker as one of young David's weird sisters.' I pictured the portly poet, his brown beard fanning over his chest, his wiry remnants of hair stark against his spreading brow. 'We are having him write some new lines.'

'Nothing blasphemous,' I said, smirking.

'By God, never,' said Armin. 'No. Some lines about the sisters being bearded and man-like. That should explain one of their company being an old man.'

Heminges scoffed. 'He rather likes the idea, does our master poet. Spoke of the play discoursing on the strangeness and – what was it? – the porous nature of borders. Between sexes as well as spaces.'

Armin gave a little cackle. 'Poets!'

Turning my back on the players, I hunched down before David. 'Are you happy with all this?'

He smiled. His little face was reddening, but his jaw was determined. 'Yes, sir. I'll do whatever they want.'

'The lad is a true actor, a company man,' said Heminges, clapping his hands.

'Mm,' I said. 'And I trust that shall be put in writing and he shall be paid as such. For his extra labours.'

Armin laughed again, smacking his fellow on the back. 'Our David has himself an agent to argue in his cause,' he said. 'Ay, sir. David, you are a King's Man tonight and for all nights hereafter, if it pleases you.'

'If it pleases the king and the company,' added Heminges. 'But we shall do what we can.'

I turned to Faith, who had remained silent throughout. She was staring at the players with a mixture of suspicion and dislike, her lip petted. I could read her mind, more or less: though she had accepted David's choice of occupation, players, musicians, and anyone involved in entertainments would always be a little soiled. 'Mouse,' I said, 'let us celebrate with a drink. To David's successes.'

Suddenly, warmth spread across her face, her white teeth emerging. She was looking past me, and I turned to see Nicholas Hopgood in the doorway, his hat in his hands, hanging back. He was looking at her, but the sight of two strangers seemed to be giving him pause. A weak young man, Hopgood. She would have her work cut out manning him.

'Christ Jesus,' I barked. 'It is getting like Cheapside Cross in here. I bid you kiss my tail and get out, if you don't live here, nor are marrying one whom I love. Don't jump, Hopgood, you're allowed. Gentlemen players, we will drink together when I have seen some written proofs of my boy's contracts. Until then – bugger off. I shall see you this evening.'

I pushed the two men out of my house and beckoned Hopgood in. 'The husband-to-be,' I said. 'Come, come.'

'I'm sorry to come so early, sir, to intrude like this.'

'It's past seven,' I said.

He sucked air over his teeth. 'Oh, I know – I feel just terrible.'

Was ever there a creature so wet?!

'What is it, Hopgood?' I asked.

He cleared his throat. Ummed and ahhed. I was on the point of telling him to spit out when he said, 'your offer, sir. Your most kind offer. Did Faith yet speak with you to tell you that we accept?'

I turned and frowned down at the girl. She was looking at her man with wide-eyed … what? Her lips were moving in silent rebuke. 'No,' I said. 'Not yet.'

Hopgood looked between her and me, confusion suddenly distorting his features. 'But sweetheart, darling,' he mumbled, 'I thought we … a good opportunity … to start our own trading, in time, I …'

Something cold and hard formed in my gut. Faith, I realised, did not want to be beholden to me, a dependent, forever trapped by my side. And after all I'd done for her. I felt the hairs on my arms prickle under my sleeves. Her evident embarrassment seemed to be transferring itself, like the pestilence carried on bad airs, to me. 'I mean … we didn't absolutely decide anything, really, sir. We just -we thought …'

'Ned,' said Faith, finally rising from the table. 'Your offer is kind. And it would be a good thing, it's true. To be near David and you.' She put out her hand to me, but I stepped back. 'Only … to make our own way in the world. And not rely on … your open palm. Nor David. I'd … we'd … like him to live with us.'

Hopgood appeared to retreat into himself. I sucked in my cheeks. It was not that I couldn't understand their desires, but that they seemed, at the moment, to be a personal insult. And she was not taking David anywhere. 'You can decide after you're married,' I said. 'But … I say only … Faith, you're my family. And David. And you, too, Nicholas, if it pleases you. There's no charity in family.' I could hear my voice growing querulous and reined it in. 'I've asked for very little of this world and, God knows, that's exactly what He's given me. I'm asking you, now, to consider my offer.'

The young couple moved to stand beside one another. Seconds began to tick by. 'I'd like you to be near here,' said David, his voice small. 'But … this is my house. Here.'

See!?

Hopgood smiled and suddenly looked less serious. 'Well,

sweetheart. If the little man wants it.'

She gave a wan smile. 'I'm going to fight all of you.' Then, more quietly, 'we'll talk later, Nick.' I didn't like the sound of that. Talking later undoubtedly meant discussing me: whether I was a reliable man, an honest man, a man fit to keep the charge of her brother whether she lived next door or in Holborn. In truth, I had been neither of those things to Faith in all the time she'd lived under my care. 'For now … hadn't you better be getting to the king's palace?' This was addressed to the boy and me.

'Already?' I asked.

'For David to practice or whatever your people call it. If he's to speak new words.'

I inclined my head—a good idea. Besides, the earlier I was at Hampton Court, the more time there should be to secure the place, to help search it, to set up the chessmen. 'Your sister speaks fair, lad. It will save us a fare if we take a wherry together.' The palace, I knew, was some miles upriver, beyond Richmond, beyond even Twickenham. 'Let's go.'

As we were pulling on our coats, Hopgood smiled again. 'By my good night, I do envy you. In a great big palace, right before the king and his family. What an honour.' He struck an absurd pose. 'Blades in your hands, fighting on the stage!'

I froze, though my lips moved of their own volition, mumbling, 'ay, an honour, come.'

No clear idea struck me then, no hard suspicion of anything. Only something vague and nebulous, something about blades being provided in that hall for the use of the players.

As we left the house and went down to the river to catch a wherry, the feeling of unease, of dread, hardened. The prow of the little craft plunged into the crystalline blue, knifing it, cutting a wake through it, making it bleed angry white caps.

Throughout the long journey, the subject of facades, deceptions, Trojan horses – call them what you will – was much on my mind.

28

Hampton Court, set well back from the Thames, reminded me of Queen Elizabeth. When I say that, I mean it struck me as the stone and glass equivalent of an ancient dame trying her best to look youthful and fresh. The place was a sprawling, red-brick complex of towers, gatehouses, courtyards, and turrets. To my annoyance if not my surprise, it housed a small and excited army of people, most in the domestic service. I deposited David in the Buttery – with a player in tow, I was hardly allowed to use any of the main entrances – and then began a tour of the grounds.

Standing in the first court – or Base Court, as it was described to me by an usher – I could see out to a bridge over the moat which guarded the front block of the building. On every side of the enormous courtyard, windows winked down at me. Too many windows, I thought—too many places for someone to be lying in wait. Royal guards had already been stationed at the farther gatehouse across the way. I passed under the enormous archway, the clock-face above looking like a miniature, counterfeit sun in its true brother's beams, and put my back to the wall. A whole network of rooms and chambers lay to my right. The best that could be hoped for was that guards – royal ones and Cecil's men – could patrol them, perhaps one to every pair of rooms. To my left lay the real heart. The place of greatest danger, I thought. Already it had been searched for powder, over and under. I made for it.

The great hall, where the plays were to be staged, could be accessed by two means: the Buttery stairs, which the domestics – including the players – and household officers used, and the southern stairs, which the courtiers and invited guests would climb. I went up by the latter and emerged at the foot of the vast, sweet-smelling space.

I felt very small, suddenly, looking out into that cavernous room. It had been filled with chairs and scattered cushions, and at intervals along its length, candelabra were already lit, just far enough from the furiously colourful tapestries to be safe. A number of voices bounced up to the hammer beams, some laughing, some coughing, some muttering. I began striding down the hall, keeping to one side, towards the low wooden stage about a third of the way down. The men crowding it were not players – they were all in black, their unremarkable black hats standing tall.

I coughed to gain the attention of Cecil's rogues. Heads and hats twisted in my direction and I trod along the carpet, nudging cushions away with my feet. Before I reached the stage itself, I could see beyond it, to the raised part of the hall, the great dais. Here sat two enormous thrones, liberally painted in gold and red, rising at the top into spearpoints. On either side of each were smaller versions, their triangular tips not reaching as high.

I turned back to the men on and about the stage. 'Good morrow, gentlemen,' I said. Some titters greeted me. I frowned. These men were scum, filth; the lowest riff-raff-rascals Cecil could raise up. This was probably the first time they had ever stood on carpets, never mind been inside a king's great hall. I searched the hard faces for one I recognised and settled on one of the fellows who had accompanied me downstairs in the Duck and Drake.

Better than nothing.

'You, sir,' I said. 'What's your name?'

'56,' he said.

Well, I thought, there is to be no familiarity, no friendship in this matter. 'Then I'm 710. Some of you might know me.' More laughter. I fronted it. 'From my work as one of Lord Salisbury's chief friends.' I let that sink in. 'You will then know that he has set me to lead you in this matter of the two kings' safety. A murder plot has been laid, and together we must stop it.'

Nothing, no fear, no grumbling, no shared looks of nervousness. They all glared back at me, their faces set. It pleased me that collective look of ruthless efficiency. My master knew his dogs.

Wasting no time, I turned my back to them and pointed, not just back down the hall but upwards, into the shadows. 'Minstrels' gallery,' I said. 'A good place for a villain to creep with a weapon. Two men, one on each side. Whichever of you have the sharpest eyes or the least blindness about you. Go.'

Two fellows detached themselves and began marching the way I had come. 'No one to be allowed in. Detain anyone who tries – who isn't a musician. And search the musicians!' I called after them. I had time only to hope they had a good understanding of the word 'detain' before they disappeared. I turned back to the rest, dividing them up in my mind, recalling the places I had seen. 'There are not enough of us,' I said. It was true. Even if they joined forces, as I intended that they should, with the king's guard, it would be impossible to defend every window, every entrance and exit to the palace. I held up a finger. 'Not for this whole palace. And so we must instead have some wit. The two kings will sit yonder,' I said, jabbing towards the thrones. 'In this chamber. And so we must have a care to make sure that this chamber is secured and remains so.'

56 coughed. I nodded at him. 'We're keeping the servants locked downstairs. Under their – clerk – what's he called, big man – rich-like?'

'The Clerk of the Green Cloth,' I said. 'Good. And the lower servants, see them kept down under the Clerk of the Kitchen.' The fellow did not go off himself, I noticed; instead, he nodded at another pair who did his bidding. I cursed silently. I did not wish for a turf war with a bloody black-coat. 'Now. Four men in the great watching chamber, which lies behind the thrones. No one allowed in or out when the kings are here. Two in the great hall court, which lies next to this chamber. A man at each entrance to this hall.' I pointed, 'down there. And,' I said, realising I had run down my complement, 'I wish two of you to be always walking around. Detain anyone you encounter on your patrols. Is that clear?'

56 stepped towards me, a little closer than I liked. 'What about the master?'

'What?'

'The master. Some of the lads here are his own special escort. They go with him always, under Mr Verney. Not you.'

I felt my fist ball. 'Today and tonight you are under me.' I regretted the words instantly. The remaining company, led by

56, began to smirk and chuckle. I felt myself colour. To dispel it, so as not to lose them, I laughed too. It seemed to work; I could see them slouch a little, relax. 'Lord Salisbury will have his armed escort, as always. He needs only one man tonight. The rest of you are needed to protect greater men.' I jerked my head towards the dais. 'The work we do tonight here might save four nations from falling, gentleman. I suggest we do it as best we can.'

It wasn't much of a speech, but I supposed that the great hall would be ringing with better ones in a short time. It worked, too, as the men began to saunter off. As 56 brushed past me, he mumbled, 'fair words, lad. Have care. It begins.' His final words were overtaken by a commotion at the bottom of the hall. The two men I had sent to the minstrels' gallery had their daggers drawn and were arguing with a company of men. I stepped down from the stage and moved towards the scene. Gradually, it resolved itself.

'Let them pass,' I shouted, my voice bouncing, like a tennis ball, about the huge room. 'It is only the players. They have our leave.'

The King's Men, David amongst them, descended in a noisy, singing, careless mingle-mangle. Beside the stage, I saw, was a small curtained room – a makeshift tiring chamber. Before the players could reach me, I darted over and pulled back the curtain. The whole thing was really just a tall box frame, with curtains around four sides. Pulling one back, I saw that it was empty and exhaled relief. Then, as an afterthought, I bent and looked under the low, scaffold-like stage. It was clear too. Burbage's voice caught me in the act of rising.

'What is this, creeping about mine palace at Elsinore?'

Hamlet, now, I thought. Bloody idiot.

'Young Berridge did not then appear?' I kept my voice as steady as my gaze.

'No,' said David. 'What's happened to him, Ned, do you think?'

Heminges spared my having to invent an answer. 'He had better be dead of ague or stricken with a fever to leave us thus. He shall never work in London again.'

Good.

'Well, you have my boy. He will carry the thing off.' I smiled. 'Please, go about your business. Ignore me. I am here only to represent Revels.'

They did, even David, who again adopted the serious look that only the young seem to have mastered, his pink tongue protruding when his mouth was closed – which was not often because he appeared to be mouthing his lines to himself. The jocularity, the wit, the attempts at badinage faded as the stage-wrights set to work. They had dragged trunks in with them, and immediately I set upon one myself. Opening it, I saw the cache of weapons: daggers, swords. I lifted one. 'No to these,' I said.

Hopgood's stance, his words, repeated. These actors would stand between the courtly audience and the two kings, with naked steel in their hands. But, I thought, as I lifted one, it wasn't steel. The thing was light as air in my hand. I dropped it and grasped at the others—all false.

'Worried, sir,' said Armin, 'that we might give each other splinters of wood about the breast?' He hopped up onto the stage and began miming thrusts at no one.

'These other coffers. What are they?'

'Our dresses,' said Heminges. Burbage, standing next to a chest, kicked at it. Shakespeare was standing with another boy, tugging at his beard. The rest were unrolling a cloth carpet over the stage. All quite usual, all correct. 'All the stuff needful to give the kings good cheer.'

Unwilling to embarrass myself further, I stepped away. 'Oh, hurry up and make yourselves ready. David … you will be the finest amongst them.'

I did not leave the great hall but spent the rest of the unravelling afternoon walking its length, miles and miles it seemed, of walking, checking behind tapestries, looking upwards to see if the minstrels' gallery – it filled quickly with musicians – retained its pair of black-coats. There was nothing else I could do. An air of unreality descended, not helped by the jittery, pre-performance wittering of the players, cursing one another and cheering one another, chalking markers on the stage (I guessed that Hal Berridge had left them chalk enough after daubing 'VENGEANCE' on the wall of the George Inn), and adjusting one another's costumes.

And then the guests began to descend. I hurried to the end of the hall and stood by the doorway which led from the southern staircase, keeping my eyes peeled as a living arras, a glittering rainbow of golds, purples, tawnies, blues, and reds washed past me and pooled on the chairs and cushions before the stage. Amongst them flitted a handful of ushers and grooms of the chamber, acting under the eye of the resplendent Lord Chamberlain to direct the noble flock to ranked places. The women, I noticed, took the chairs. It did not seem to be gallantry that drove the men down onto the cushions; the latest ladies' fashions prevented them from sinking downwards, even if they might wish to. At the end of the procession came Cecil. He gave me only a tense nod, as he strode by alongside Bacon. The cousins sat well to the rear, despite my master's lordly title. Nor was Cecil dressed in finery as the Earl of Salisbury, but sedate in the suit of principal secretary and chief counsellor, the only nod to courtliness a shimmering black cloak pinned at his shoulder. His escort, the brutal Verney, was at his heels like a lean hound.

The room shrank around the influx of noble and gentle garments, each of which had buried deep within it a noble and gentle body. I began moving up the hall towards the stage. The players had retired to their temporary chamber, leaving the stage partly carpeted. There was no backdrop, no curtain, or the like. Aristocratic imagination – however great or small that might be – would have done much heavy lifting, I thought.

The sound of excited chatter and tinkling laughter drifted throughout the hall, and I felt sweat begin to pop out on my brow. I stationed myself in the exact middle, where I could see both the dais and the entrance.

There's nothing more you can do.

As though in agreement, a sudden blast of trumpets flew out over the chamber, lending a festive air to my thought. The hubbub of the great hall ceased, as though every throat had been cut. Looking up, I saw the musicians, still well watched by their shadowy guards. As the fanfare left only a ghostly echo, I turned to the stage and looked beyond it.

From their own private entrance – royal guards flanked either side – came the royal family. King James appeared first, loping across the dais. No, that is not fair. For though he was a habitual loper, he moved before his court with a measure of grace, as a schoolmaster might before an assembly of his pupils. His florid face was unsmiling, I could see. In a handsomer man, such a look might appear stately, magisterial, even severe. In King James, who was neither beautiful nor ugly, it just looked bored. He sank onto his throne, the right-most of the two central ones. Queen Anne, smiling, looking quite pretty despite her nose, followed, her brother strutting after her. He shared the nose but boasted in addition a distinct paunch and a military gait—finally, the twelve-year-old Prince Henry. The little prince was remarkably tall for his age, and very fair, his features all neat and even, his hair a blonde halo. He resembled his parents very little, I thought. Perhaps he had inherited his delicate good looks from his legendary grandparents on his father's side, who were said to have been paragons in their faces if nothing else.

When the royals had settled, the musicians began to play again, their insistent blasts demanding continued silence. And then the players appeared, to begin their *Hamlet*. There was no ribald jig, no opening bawdry to the audience from Armin or any other. Instead, the audience was transported directly to a platform before Elsinore.

I shan't bore you with the details of the performance. Possibly you know the play, which has had a very good run, in its time. The players did well enough, with their old-young boy playing the Lady Ophelia and sundry other parts. Much was cut from what I'd seen, whether because of the sudden loss of an actor or because the full thing would have bored the king I couldn't say. Throughout the curtailed drama, I walked, and I watched, and I walked, and I watched, keeping to the walls and sides of the room. I saw nothing amiss: only some sleeping courtiers, some cuddling and kissing courtiers, a bored Cecil. Whenever I reached near the head of the hall, I looked beyond Elsinore and its walls of words and turrets of iambics. There I saw Queen Anne, leaning forward, her chin on her fist, watching intently;

Prince Henry was in a mirrored pose on the other side of the two kings. King Christian looked either confused or disinterested – I had no idea if he spoke English; King James was sliding dangerously towards sleep, jerking like a puppet whenever his heavy lids fell.

The play's the thing.

Macbeth.

When everyone was dead and risen, there was brief confusion as the players retired. Food – which I had been assured in advance would be well tasted, was brought up the Buttery Stairs and passed amongst the ranks of the courtiers. Again, refreshments came from the king's privy kitchen via his guards at the private entrance.

Not only was I perspiring; now, my heart began to race. Time, so slow in the morning, so sluggish, began to race. It was pressed onwards faster, faster, by more music blasting from the gallery above.

The players began to return to the scaffold-like stage. Only three of them came out at first. The weird sisters, I knew – David was up there now. But I couldn't see him. All three players were dressed in heavy black robes and hunched, like black boulders, waiting for the play to begin.

And then I saw it.

Someone, I could not see who, was fumbling at the edge of the stage, bent over, trying not to be seen.

Of course! The players! A brotherhood! The damned players!

I launched myself forward, a skidding, flying wherry, away from the wall, down the aisle at the edge of the great hall, towards the stage. Just as I reached it, I saw the fellow, the creature, the

Augustan!

In a dark cloak, holding a flame, a tinderbox.

Fire!

I threw myself at him, on him like a gull on a breadcrumb, hitting out, scrabbling for his arm, hissing, spitting.

I was too late.

Whump!

I reeled backwards, was thrown, lifted. The smell burst out

over me, over us both, over the stage, the crowd, the kings. The creature, the assassin, fell with me, was hurled back in a shower of sparks, of flame, of smoke, of fire.

And then the screams began.

29

Screaming filled my ears, sounding distant, very distant, because of the ringing. There followed a muted chorus of oooohhhhh and ahhhhhhh. And then something was slapping at me.

I was, I realised, lying flat on my back just beyond the corner of the stage. I jolted up, ignoring the unseen assault, and twisted my head to see beyond the stage.

The king, is he hurt?

King James, I saw through the thinning smoke, had half risen from his throne, his knuckles tight and white against the edges of its armrests. And his expression, lit in yellow – it was … fearful, excited, leering with a mad kind of delight. I blinked, over and over, before choking again on the foul, acrid smell. Jagged fingers seemed to be scratching their way up my throat.

And then I was slapped again. 'Wha'?' I mumbled.

'What the hell are you about, man?' I screwed my eyes shut this time. Spots of colour danced behind my lids, in the vague, irregular shapes of the flames I'd seen. I waited until they faded before blinking them open again. Robert Armin, the damned fool, was pressing down on my legs. His hand was poised for another strike. I reached up and grabbed his wrist.

'You!' I shook him until his black robe slipped down. It was, I could see, one of the garments the stage-wrights used for invisible work: a blind robe, they called them. 'You!'

'You could have burnt us both, jumping on me like that.' He was whispering hoarsely. 'Taken our eyes out, blown off our hands.'

'What?' I asked again. I swallowed burning, foul-tasting spit.

'The squibs! The firecrackers.'

'Squibs,' I repeated dumbly. And then I heard the words falling down on us from above, sensed the movement of black figures crawling around on the stage.

'Fair is foul, and foul is fair:

Hover through the fog and filthy air.'

I sat up, my head clearing. Squibs, I thought. I knew well enough that the stage-wrights used fireworks and other dangerous effects in their theatres, making counterfeit lightning strikes and thunderstorms, choking fogs and demonic entrances and exits. But I had not thought they would attempt any such trumpery in the palace; I had not even considered it. The other coffers, I realised, must have housed their little stores of firecrackers. Probably also the bladders filled with pig's blood that had been hidden in their clothes for when they slew one another with their wooden swords.

You fucking idiot!

Armin, breathing heavily, began to scuttle up alongside me, still whispering. 'Missed the lightning to see them out, by Christ. But got a good scream. Good terror. Those courtly folk'll remember being on the heath this night.'

Together, we crawled, our heads down and backs bent, towards the tiring room. Once we'd gained it, I brought my fist down on the clown's back. 'Hey!' he barked. 'What do you mean?'

I pushed him again, into the gloomy chamber. Other players stood about, some in the act of dressing. If they set upon me at once, there was nothing I could do but throw myself backwards, tearing down the curtains, the frame, drawing all attention from the stage. And I would do it.

As Armin straightened up, I swept my gaze around the gaggle of stage-wrights. 'What do you know of the Augustans? Tell me.' Brows wrinkled. Eyes narrowed. Glances were exchanged. 'The Augustans,' I repeated. 'The brotherhood. I know all. Tell me.'

'You're having us on,' said Armin, at length.

I breathed out, slowly, my pulse only beginning to calm. 'There is a plot against the king,' I said. 'Set in train by the society of Augustans. I know all about it. What are they to you?'

Silence reigned in the curtained room. From outside drifted the sound of the players – David's voice was amongst them, shrill and gritty. I caught the words, 'Aleppo' and 'Tiger'. I maintained my glare. Eventually, Armin broke into barely stifled laughter once more. 'Society of the Augustans,' he said.

His scorn seemed to infect the others. Smiles broke out. 'You've got the wrong men, Mr Savage.' The rest began to nod.

Two of the others – Condell and Cowley – echoed his words: 'the wrong men, ay, the wrong men.'

I cursed. 'None of that,' smiled Armin. 'Not allowed anymore.'

'Fuck off,' I spat. And then I turned on them, emerging back into the great hall. Still, the audience was enraptured. Still, the royals were watching, King James no longer bored, Queen Anne holding her hands clasped before her as though in prayer. On the stage, Heminges, in a soldier's helmet, was raving about chappy fingers and skinny lips, as he and Burbage stood over the cringing weird sisters. Their voices rang out, up to the beams, lyrical and melodic.

I was wrong, I realised. Utterly wrong. The players were innocent of all but being tiresome. I smoothed down the front of my livery and began again to stalk the walls. Another look up – the gallery was clear. A glimpse back – the dais still had its pair of royal guards, their halberds at rest.

All was well. All was proceeding without incident.

My back to the stage, I began moving once again down towards the foot of the great hall, ignoring the sea of colour to my left. The courtiers were no longer locked in embraces or secret conversations. This play was new to them, whereas the shortened *Hamlet* had been old, a thing staged again just to complement the Danish king. As I reached near the stairwell entrances, I paused, casting a lookout over the rear jumble of seats and cushions. Hats and headdresses formed an uneven landscape.

But there was a gap.

There was Sir Frances Bacon, sitting on a short bench. His cousin, however, was gone. I frowned. It was not like Cecil to leave a place where trouble might be brewing. I took a half-step towards the audience and then stopped. I had no wish to force my way through the crowd. Instead, I continued skirting it and went to the archway leading to the southern stairwell. A royal guard immediately stepped from one side, one of Cecil's men from the other.

I nodded at my colleague. 'His lordship. Where is he?'

The man frowned at me. 'Gone.'

'Gone where?' Something began to needle its way up my back. The hair at my temples rose, ticklish and irritating.

'He got a note. Went off.'

'A note?! From who – where – who?'

The fellow shrugged. 'Mr Verney found it. Must have been dropped or thrown down, I reckon. Dunno.'

'I said no one in or out,' I hissed. But the words, as I heard them myself, were stupid, useless. No one would deny Lord Salisbury anything, certainly not one of his men. 'Where did he go?'

'He didn't say.'

The royal guard coughed, before speaking. 'You might try the chambers south of the Clock Court, sir.' I gave him a sharp look, questioning. 'Oftentimes … when a man seeks a … a little privacy in this place – a great man – perhaps with a lady, sir … he'll take her there. A secret meeting you understand, sir. With a lady. You get my meaning?'

'Thank you,' I said.

I stared out into the dimness of the stairwell. Was it possible that Cecil had sneaked off for some assignation with a woman? Which woman? I had heard rumours in the past that the old dog had quite a reputation for seducing other men's wives – I could only assume his power made him irresistible – but could not imagine that he would let his yard-shaft do the thinking when the king was in danger.

'He's well served,' said the black-coat. 'Verney is gone with him.'

The needling sensation graduated into a tremble. A rush of warmth passed my brow, bringing a fresh wave of perspiration. Voices sounded in my head, a whole chorus of them, male and female.

You've got the wrong men.

The man who would destroy the name of England. How he'd die.

And you – you, they said, would think you knew what was going on. But you wouldn't.

Any creatures who aim to destroy a king are poor thinkers as well as wicked men.

Their true design lies elsewhere.

For as long as wicked counsellors haunt the court, they will haunt any successor.

My enemies are not his gracious Majesty, but the counsel that surrounds him.

The great butcher Lord Salisbury.

'Oh shit,' I said. 'Oh, shit!'

Leaping over the threshold, I fled the great hall.

30

The painted walls and hangings of Hampton Court passed in a blur. I had taken the broad southern stairs earlier, but not committed the rest of the place to memory. And what vague impressions I had taken now fled me, driven out by panic. I simply ran, moved, my shoes flying over carpets and polished wood.

Where did they go?

I had bungled. I had been misled, deceived. Of course, of course, it was Cecil who was to be assassinated. The great Lord Salisbury, who had made more enemies of both sexes than I'd had private-room tumbles with men. It had all been a feint. I'd been sent after a false assassin and set to foil a false plot against the two kings whilst leading my own master to think himself quite safe. And now he was going to die.

I fell out of the doorway and found myself blinking in fading sunlight. To my right, beyond the stone archway, lay the Base Court. The Clock Court was to my left. I stood for a moment, irresolute, fighting the urge to scream.

Bastard Augustans, whoever they were, making a coney of me.

At every step, I had accepted their leading notes, their too-obvious threats. I had even thought myself quite the fox, understanding their pathetic riddle. And in doing so, I had played into their hands. The entire security force – Cecil's own men, even – was concentrated on the great hall, on protecting two kings whose lives were in no danger.

It didn't matter who they were. That could be discovered later. What mattered was saving my damned bastard of a master. I skipped across the shadowy cobbles and into the doorway opposite. It led to another a room on the other side of the clocktower, a large entrance chamber with gilded wooden screens set along it. Pausing for breath, I tried to listen, to think.

I could not hope to search the entire palace by myself. Nor could I rely on the pair of men I'd sent to patrol the place being anywhere near. I tried to construct the layout from memory, but it came only in names, not directions. The ancient cardinal's rooms; the chambers of the late queen's father … these, I knew, lay somewhere across the Clock Court, lost in the shadows of time and the onrushing night.

So what lies ahead?

Cecil was not an idiot, I told myself, not really. Even with his escort, he would not allow himself to be lured into a shadowy, shuttered part of the palace. Nor would a clever assassin try to draw him somewhere which might cause suspicion. Instead, he must have gone somewhere relatively close by, somewhere lighted or clean.

I looked beyond the screens. The chamber led farther into the building. This was the way directly from the great hall's stairs. They would not have struck off into the open courtyards.

You hope.

I proceeded through the room, drawing my dagger. Running was no good. I needed to be able to listen, to see things clearly. I passed beyond the screens and through an open doorway. Open, I thought. Yes, they had come this way. The next room was a smaller version of the first, but rather than screens, it bore cushioned benches along each wall.

So many rooms, rooms going into rooms going into rooms!

Passing from the first benched room into a duplicate, I met a problem. The series of little chambers dead-ended in a panelled wall – a hallway led through an open door on my right; farther down on the left stood another passage.

Shit.

I stood, wheeling on the spot, my dagger swiping at the air.

And then I heard it. Softly at first, and then louder as my ears told me the truth: voices were coming from the darker doorway down on the left. I held my breath a moment, listening. Putting my back to the wooden panelling, I slipped along the hallway, keeping my shoes firmly but softly on the carpet. I did not leap into the doorway but stood beyond it, hopefully out of sight of whoever was hiding within.

A woman?

The soft tinkling of laughter.

I stepped into the doorway.

'Get up! Stand forth!' I cried into the dim stone passage. It was a small place, a shoulder between the great arms of the building. Ahead of me lay a circular staircase, rising upwards.

'I say!' hissed a male voice.

'Get out, you dog!' I cried, a little less surely. For good measure, I waved my blade. 'Come forth or be slain!'

The yelp which followed was certainly a woman. From the shadows beneath the staircase, she emerged first: a short tent of a creature, her dark green dress stiff and round, its bum-roll and drum askew. The yellow tassels lacing her front were loose, the curve of her bosom circling over the lacing. Only her standing ruff remained stiff. As her little hands began fiddling with her frontage, her friend emerged: a moustachioed, bearded fop, his breeches, sleeves, and chest impossibly broadened with bombast. 'What the devil?!' he cried, in a voice too small for his padded frame.

'Whit dae ye mean, knave?' cried the little lady.

I stood, gawping, blinking like a dullard, before giving myself a shake. 'Where is my lord of Salisbury? Did he pass this way?'

'No,' said the man. 'Be off with you, dog. And say nothing of this.'

I was in no mood to be put in my place by a peacock. 'His lordship is in grave danger and like to be murdered,' I said. 'Where did he go?'

The fellow paled. His mistress, however, stepped forward, her arm raised up over her bosom in an attempt at dignity. 'The Lord Salisbury?' I inclined my head. 'We heard … the now … no' long since. Men's brabble.'

'Where?'

She pointed over my shoulder. 'Doon there. We hid.'

'We hid, sir, fearing some danger,' said the man. 'No other reason.'

His lady had the grace to look abashed. I gave her a brief nod and then spun, jetting again down the passage from which I'd come. The other door it must be. I was upon it in seconds.

The passageway I had earlier ignored led into another chamber, this one spreading to my right. Here were portraits, cushions, stools: a waiting room of sorts. At the other end, a door led into yet another hallway, this one stretching far ahead, the whole length of what I realised must be the southern range of the Base Court. Doors were set in intervals along the left-hand wall.

Only the first was open.

I did not creep this time, but lunged for it, swinging left, my dagger again upraised.

And I froze.

Lying on the carpet was Cecil, one arm twisted over his head.

Over him leered Richard Verney, his own blade held high and poised to strike.

31

I didn't think. I sprang, leaping from the balls of my feet. Verney was a tall man, but more rangy than stout. It was a foolish move, however. My arms circled his neck, but my dagger fell to the carpet, settling into its weave.

My grunts matched the assassin's. Keeping one hand around his throat, I pulled up my legs and wrapped them around him like a child being carried by his father. He went forward, nearly toppling down onto Cecil, who had not moved, who didn't react. And then the brute righted himself, throwing me up and back. I clung on, fly-like. With my free hand, I reached out, trying to reach his forearm, his wrist. His dagger – iron, it looked like, lethal, the handle made of lead – flashed in the candlelight.

And then the room was spinning. Arrases and paintings, panelling and plaster, all went by in a whirl as Verney spun, rocking me, trying to throw me. I squeezed hard, jerking my arm up and into his throat. That blade rose again, and he made the mistake of trying to slash backwards. I feared that razor-sharp edge, feared what it would do. But the soft white of his wrist, emerging from the cuff – I forced my hand to grab at it, to circle it and hold it away.

Verney ceased spinning, although the room didn't.

'Ow!'

The cry came unbidden as pain shot up my back.

'You little bastard!' the creature hissed. Again he stepped forward and then threw himself backwards, into the wall, crushing me between it and his back. Air was pressed out of me. My head began to lighten as it clattered against his greasy scalp.

Stop him!

Just as he moved to smash me into the wall again, I threw my head forward, my mouth falling open. I snapped my teeth shut over the soft flesh of his ear, first bending it and then biting through skin and gristle. His scream tore across the room. He went forward again, away from the wall. I felt him sliding under my grip. My thighs began to strain, to protest. I was going to lose him, going to slip to the ground. I tightened my grip once more, clamped my teeth hard, and jerked my neck.

I fell to the ground, gagging and retching, spitting the severed ear onto the carpet. I stared it at it dumbly for a moment, fighting the urge to vomit. The tang of iron had invaded my mouth. My stomach rebelled against it, my eyes against the glistening, slimy fold of flesh. His screams brought me to my senses. Verney had spun. One hand was held up to the side of his head, blood already dribbling from between his fingers, and he was looking down at the carpet with the same revulsion that I felt.

Before he could recover, I dived forwards, grabbing his lower legs and pulling them back. One held fast to the ground, but the other buckled, and the man slid. As he was falling, I rolled, looking, searching, hunting,

the blade!

His iron dagger was closer than wherever mine had fallen, and I stretched out, my fingers closing around the handle. Triumph surged through me, laughter threatening. The sudden grip tightening around my ankle stopped it. And then I was being yanked, dragged back. I rolled again, onto my back this time, just as the brute was getting to his knees. Fury and pain were written across his face in streaks of blood. He grunted, raising his hands, his eyes trained on my throat.

I pulled my own together, like a man readying himself for prayer, just as Verney fell on top of me. Instantly he cried out, realising his mistake.

The dagger, which he had ignored in his rush for angry vengeance, had remained in my hands, its lethal tip pointing upwards. The base of its hilt was pressing into the pit of my gut, driven down by the sudden descent of his body. But the blade itself sank through his black coat, his black doublet, into his ribs.

His face was close to mine. Surprise had fallen over it. Blood dripped onto my cheek. And then I cried out, like a whipped child. I shifted and twisted under him, desperate to be free. He fell, eventually, off to one side, and lay on his back, the dagger still protruding from his middle. He coughed. More blood bubbled up from his lips. I reached over and pulled the blade free.

And then I brought it down again, and again, and again, screaming and crying.

Die, die, die! Stay dead!

Stop!

Die!

'Stop, Ned!'

I fell away from the body, trying to turn, the dagger still in my hand, still dripping blood. Gallons of the stuff seemed to have washed over me. I could feel my hair wet with it. My hat was gone, lying clean across the room, next to

Cecil!

'My lord! I – he was going to kill you. Your own escort, here, here in the palace, I found him, I stopped him.' The words came shaking and shivering out of me, hot and cold and excited and quite, quite mad.

Cecil had drawn himself up and was sitting, cross-legged, looking like a small, badly formed child with an old man's face. 'You killed him.'

I looked at the dead Verney and felt my stomach churn, though more with fear than horror at what I'd done. I'd killed before, but never in such a company. 'He was the assassin, sir.' My mouth had dried. I badly wanted a pint of beer. 'He would have killed you.'

Cecil seemed … I could not read it. There was an embarrassment, I thought, at his having allowed himself to be lured like a fool. But it seemed to be hurt dignity that troubled him the most. He could not meet my eyes, not from his seated position on the floor. Without his great desk, his flock of attendants, his imposing chairs, he was nothing – just a vulnerable old man, over forty and looking twice his age. I swayed, nearly falling prone once again. 'He struck me,' he said, his voice full of wonder. 'He laid hands upon me. Knocked me down. I … was insensible.' A shiver ran through him, making him quake.

''You … you got a note.'

'Hm?' Cecil looked at me. And then he looked away quickly.

'Your mouth.'

I lifted my hand and touched my upper lip, the rough nap of my chin. My fingers came away sticky and red. 'I bit his ear off,' I said. The words sounded strange in my own ears, muffled by a rush of blood in my head. Laughter threatened again.

'Christ, Jesus. Help me to rise,' croaked Cecil.

I wobbled to my feet and offered him a hand. He took it and let me haul him to his feet, before grumbling what might have been a word of thanks. And then he looked again at the body, before closing his eyes. For a man who had sent a good many to a bloody death, I wondered if he had ever actually seen it.

'The note,' he said at length. He fumbled inside his doublet and pulled out a piece of paper, passing it to me.

I took it and read, 'the villain is found in the southern range, locked in the lodging chambers. Come immediately. 710'.

'710,' I mumbled. 'I didn't send this! I mean … I was in the hall, sir, the whole time before you left.'

'I did not see you,' said Cecil. 'When the Scotch play began, the note came. I did look – I had Verney look – but you were gone.'

'Shit. Sorry, my lord. I – I was with the players. I- made a mistake in suspecting them. And then I realised. The whole thing, all that these creatures have given us sir, it was all to distract us. To make us watch the two kings, all of us, all night. Whilst you … whilst your lordship was…'

'Assassinated,' said Cecil. He smiled without the slightest trace of mirth. He was realising, I thought, not just how foolish he had been, but how hated he was. I might have told him that myself and for free. He raised a finger and put it in his mouth in a bizarre, childlike gesture which struck a chord in my memory but which I couldn't place. Withdrawing it, he said, 'I can scarce believe it. My own man, a Catholic assassin.'

Catholic?

'Sent by the plotters. They've done this, my lord.'

'The men of August,' he said.

'A sham, as you thought, my lord. There is no society. Just scattered plotters. This creature their chiefest instrument.'

'And what else are they but a band of Catholic intriguers?' He moved over towards a wooden seat and eyed it, as though eager to sit. He apparently decided against it, but he remained with his bent back to me, one-shoulder utterly defeated. 'It would have been an easy thing. The creature might have slain me. And then…'

'And then wounded himself, I suppose. Some slashing about his hands. A jab in the gut. And then he might tell the world that Locusta did it and fled.'

'The mysterious Romish lady murderer.' He turned. 'But you saw her. You saw a woman.'

Hal Berridge's stupid face rose into my mind, looking young, looking foolish, looking scared. 'She is dead, my lord. She was this creature's lover.' The lies, when they began, flowed easily. I saw how he would believe them. He was certain that a band of Catholics were at work. 'She attacked me on the river, my lord. The woman. I regret that we fought. She fell. Was lost.'

'Who was she? One of the Spanish wench's imps?'

'No. Only a trull of Southwark. Lover to this creature. They must have plotted this affair. They and their papist friends. To make us think a female killer roamed the streets, looking to kill the two sovereigns. A coney for us to chase whilst this brute slew you, my lord, and for her to have the blame of it. Though doubtless she, she … would be gone back to their bolt hole, seen about Southwark. Had I not rid the City of her.'

He seemed satisfied, but I knew that my invention would be questioned when his wits were returned. 'You will write a dispatch, Ned. Put all this in writing. And then we might … we might be more mindful of the recusants.'

I bowed. 'As you wish, my lord.'

'And this … have my men clean this up. Quietly. Privily. I do not wish his Majesty to be troubled by it.'

Do not wish for the king to know you're a fallible figure of hatred.

'Yes.'

'I will return,' he said. 'All must appear to be in order.'

'Wait, my lord.' I stepped towards him, wiping my fingers clean on my breeches. He shrank back a little as I got close. And then he simply stood, looking off to one side, whilst I straightened his ruff, brushed down his front, and slid the silver brooch which secured his cloak back into place.

'Thank you,' he said gruffly after I'd finished playing the manservant. He began to move heavily towards the door, not looking at the body. He stopped on the threshold, framed by the low light filtering in from the windowed hall beyond. He turned his neat profile to me. 'You saved my life, Mr Savage. I should have been dead. At this moment, my soul might have returned to my dear wife.' I didn't answer this. 'You will be rewarded, Edward Savage. I thank you.'

32

The bells tolled wildly in the steeple above St Andrew Holborn, jangling my nerves. I stood back, amongst the crowd, watching and waiting, my hand on David's shoulder. The previous night, after saving Cecil, I had helped the rest of his men destroy all evidence of Verney's life and death. The creature and his ear had been carried away – I ordered both slung into the Thames. It had been a long night's work, not helped by the sudden appearance of rain, which turned the river into a noisy, protesting snake. I had sent my boy home with the players, trying to smile at the excitement, the energy, which seemed to flow through him after his turn as the wicked Scotch queen.

I looked down at his unruly redhead. He must have sensed my look, for he smiled up. Though he had washed his face, there were still traces of paint about his lips. He was no witch or evil queen now, but in the best and smallest suit I owned. I was in my own best: a white doublet and cream hose, my ruff well stiffened. We owed it to Faith, I felt, to give her a good showing on her wedding day. I looked down at my hand, still resting lightly on the boy's shoulder. It had come clean much more easily than his lips. 'Look, look,' he said. 'They're coming!'

I turned from our position near the porch to look down the street. Sure enough, Faith was marching towards us, a garland of flowers around her red hair, her dress white and trailing. Two of Nicholas's sisters attended her, both shiny-faced and plain as pudding. My heart caught in my throat. On a day of scattered clouds and the night's castaway puddles, she provided her own light.

Faith marched onwards, looking nervous, to take up her position in the porch – beside Nicholas, of course, who stood ready, looking about as good as Nicholas Hopgood could look. His horse-faced parents were in the crowd and his master the weaver with his family. He had quite a showing, I thought, compared to Faith's brother and myself. The vicar appeared, his black robes brushed, and stood before them in the doorway of the church, mumbling through the lines of the service with none of the skill or diction of a player. Faith and Nicholas made their protestations accordingly. When the ring and the bible appeared, a ripple of cheerful chatter passed back and forth through the crowd of us outside the building. And then the priest stood aside, ushering in the couple. That was our invitation too, should we wish to take it up, to see them blessed at the altar steps. Nicholas's sisters went first, followed by his parents and then the assembly of his master's family. When David stepped over the churned mud of the street, I remained where I stood.

'Coming, Ned?'

'No. No, you go on in.'

He frowned. 'But…'

'But me no buts. There's something I have to do. It shan't take long. You go and see your sister married. I'll be at the Hopgood place shortly. And remember,' I added, winking, 'you stay living with me, and that old married pair come down to Shoe Lane and lodge by us.'

He smiled. 'Right!'

I watched until he had disappeared into the church and then stood awhile, gazing up at the blocky building. Other people, the nosy bunch who can't miss a wedding, began to return to their business.

'Oh, weren't she looking right pretty?'

'Is that the weaver's girl?'

'Do you know her?'

'C'mon, I could eat.'

I bit at my bottom lip, before glimpsing up at the sky beyond the line of thatch and stone. Scudding clouds went racing by, the sun fighting a good fight to be seen. I might use that, I thought, later, at the bridal feast. Perhaps I might say something about the weather betokening a marriage of sunshine and storms. Or perhaps not. I had time to think of a better jest. I had work to do yet.

***

I knocked on the door inside Fulwood's Rents. It opened almost immediately, and I stepped in, not waiting to be invited.

Sir Frances Bacon looked ashen, though his eyes were still bright. He said nothing as I strode into his sitting room and began rummaging about in one of the shelved cabinets. 'I am looking,' I said, not turning to him, 'to borrow a book, sir. By Master Holinshed. A history of the world, with a missing page.'

I turned, eager to see the effect. Bacon was not looking at me but at the closed door to his bedchamber. He was still wearing a nightgown, with his furry robe hanging about his shoulders. Returning his attention to me, he said, 'has my cousin sent you?'

I sighed. And then I took a seat by his desk and gestured for him to sit. He obeyed, moving warily. 'I understand this place will not be getting its porter back.'

'Verney is dead,' he said without expression.

'My lord told you what occurred when he returned to the play?'

'No.'

'I see,' I said. But Sir Frances had presumably guessed that the plot had failed when Cecil came back alive. 'The Augustans. Who are they?'

He was silent a good while, as though organising his thoughts. Eventually, I tutted. 'Sir Frances, if I intended to betray all I know to my master, I should have done so already. I haven't. And I might not. If you are honest, sir.'

This seemed to give the little man pause. At length, he shrugged. 'There is no such society. A mere trickery.'

'That stinkard Georgie – he saw men.'

Bacon took a deep breath, sucking on the air as though it might be his last chance. 'Perhaps it is better if I show you,' he said. 'Would you wait whilst I dress?' I nodded as he pushed himself back up from his chair and went to the bedchamber. He slid inside, barely opening it.

Instantly I was on my feet and sliding across the room. I did not know if there was some escape from within, some window or other door. Nor did I know if Bacon was the type to run. In truth, I had come to realise that I knew nothing of the man except that he was a deceiver – and for reasons, I still could not understand. From inside, I heard a muffled discussion, the words too low and indistinct to make out. When I heard footsteps approach, again I stepped away, back into the centre of the main chamber. Bacon slipped back out, dressed and booted. He seemed, too, to have regained something of his good cheer and kindly, sparkling demeanour.

'Come. Walk with me a little. I would speak with you honestly. As a friend.' I chose to let that word pass without comment and let him lead me out of the room, downstairs, and into the morning light. He led me down the street, away from the direction of Holborn, both of us stepping over scattered puddles. The street opened into a cobbled courtyard, and he turned right. I picked up my step until I was alongside him, and we passed through an alley between buildings. Ahead lay the chapel and its courtyard, the place I had inspected the body of the fellow who had apparently been earmarked for use in the plot and died before he could be of service. In the yard, some young men – students, I supposed, with nowhere else to go during the recess – were kicking about a pig's bladder. Bacon saluted them before turning right and hopping up a low step into a building adjoining the chapel. 'Just in here.'

'What is this place?' I asked when we were inside. My voice echoed around the room. Paintings stood up on the walls, which were partly panelled and partly plaster, and graced too with fine glass windows set high.

'The hall,' he said. He closed the door behind us. 'So you know something, then. Or suspect it.'

'That your Mr Verney, the porter you gave to my master, was an assassin. Sent to kill his lordship whilst we – his men, I mean – were alert to an attack on the two kings. Sent by you, Sir Frances. Sent by you to assassinate your own cousin. I ask you only this: who was amongst your company? Raleigh? The Lady Penelope? The wizard earl?'

Bacon's brow wrinkled. His eyes shone with their usual humour. 'What?' And then he laughed. 'Oh dear, Mr Savage. You shoot wildly. Blindly.'

I was in no mood to be mocked. 'The truth, Sir Frances, or I will tell him. I will. All that I suspect.'

Bacon shook his head slowly, raising a finger to dab at his eyes. 'Ah, Mr Savage. No, none of those people were amongst my company. There is no Society of Augustus. Those fellows you saw out there kicking their ball – they helped me a little, providing bodies. They knew nothing of what they were doing.' He sighed. 'In my time, I have written many masques and interludes to be performed at the Inn. The Society of Augustus, the Brotherhood, call it what you will … it was just another.'

'To sow doubt. To sow fear.'

'A game,' he said, quite firmly.

'And who else? Mr Verney was in on your plot, of course. A conspirator.' Another idea struck. 'And that chaplain – what was his name?'

'Mr Sturrock. Yes. But he did not know the true design. Only Verney and I did. I promise. Mr Verney was my gun. My dagger. He cost less than the coach. It is me you seek, alone.'

A lie, I thought. I smiled. 'And pretty Mr Roger Delamere.'

Bacon frowned, folding his arms over his chest. 'Nothing. Nothing. He knew nothing of any of it. He is innocent.' My regard for Sir Frances Bacon rose. He was lying through his teeth, of course, but it was an admirable thing. Concern passed his face. 'You didn't harm the boy, did you – young Berridge? He was truly an innocent. I knew of him from his old company. Did as he was told, played the lady with skill. He knew nothing of what we – what I – intended. He believed utterly that we were all a great society of his betters. Playing games, no more.'

'The boy is unharmed. I sent him from London.'

Bacon relaxed. He looked around the room with an expression I couldn't read. 'So … does my cousin suspect me yet?' I shrugged. 'He will, though. He will think on how I recommended Verney to him and then his diseased little mind will hum and turn.'

'He believes the man to have been a Catholic,' I said.

Bacon laughed again. 'Oh. Then the papists will suffer the more. I am sorry for that.' He began moving down the hall, slowly and deliberately, his head bent. Over his shoulder, he said, 'and my good cousin lives to do more harm.'

'What?' I asked.

He paused, turning. 'Mr Savage … you have named several people. Raleigh, Northumberland, the Devereux wench. And there are many more, sir. Essex, whom you resemble a little.' Something crossed his brow. 'My friend. Whom little Cecil and the old queen bid me help destroy for their own amusement. My own cousin caused the man's fall. Drove him stark mad. And then had me dress his passage to the block. My friend.' He shook away the memory and looked at me again. 'Tell me, what do each of these creatures hold in common?'

My lower lip jutted. 'A hatred of my master.'

'And why?'

'I'm not here to talk policy,' I said.

He shrugged. 'You have been searching, all this time, for a villain. For some villainy. Oh dear, dear, dear, Mr Savage. Did it not occur to you, as you saw prisoners, a woman in disgrace, even that Spanish papist … did it not occur to you that you are the very agent of villainy?'

I made a fist and was prepared to use it. 'Don't get clever with me. Not now.'

He held up his doughy white hands. They looked like starfish. He would melt under a beating, I knew. 'I mean no clever words. I speak the truth. Did these people cry upon the evils of the king or the evils of my lord of Salisbury?' When I didn't respond, he went on. 'When the old queen died, we all looked forward to a time without fear—a rebirth for England. And we find instead that the state continues as it was under this king. Oh,' he waved his hand, 'I say nothing against his Majesty. The cancer is my cousin. Such creatures infect what they touch. And must be cut away.'

'You cut nothing away.'

'No. Because the villain's henchman stopped it, your master has risen high, Mr Savage. First to the privy council, then Essenden, Cranborne, Salisbury. He collects titles as a magpie collects silver. And at what cost, Mr Savage? How much blood do you think he has spilt? And will, in the future, in his suspicions and his avarice?'

'You're jealous,' I said. And then I laughed. 'You're jealous of your cousin.'

Bacon did not grow angry. Instead, he turned fully to me and looked down at his boots. 'If I examine my soul … perhaps …

I see a little envy. I find that rewards in this realm go by favour and not merit as they did in the late reign. And what stands in common between that queen and this king?' He looked up.

'My master,' I supplied. 'Of whom you are so envious.'

He smiled weakly. 'I was doing my duty to the state.' The words fell like thunderclaps, like powder blasts. 'As poor little Berridge was doing in serving his betters. As you fool yourself you are doing when you dirty your hands, I should think. You should have been free of him, Mr Savage. Free of spying and informing. Free of sending men to die and killing on his behalf.'

'Free of the riches and rewards,' I said.

Bacon threw his head back and gave a genuine laugh. 'Spoken like a true villain, sir. Riches and rewards … and my own little complot so cheap.' He gestured around the room. 'This place for our use. My house at Twickenham. Even my poor wife's wardrobe was raided to serve the Lady Locusta. All that cost me was the making of a coach. And that should have been recompensed. I should not have had to buy my cousin a New Year's gift this December.'

I had no idea what to say. He was not ashamed. He was not frightened. He did not even think of himself a villain. On the contrary, he believed himself a hero of sorts. 'You failed,' was all I could manage.

'Yes. So it seems. Yet I failed to do the right thing, not the wrong one. Do you see? My cousin is above the law, as no subject should be. There are no legal means to be rid of him. That is no right thing for any commonwealth, to have such a man in it. I intended it for England.'

'My master, too, has a care for England,' I said. As much as I distrusted Cecil, I thought that true enough.

'As long as it serves his turn,' countered Bacon. 'As long as it enriches him. Can you think that right, Mr Savage?'

'How should I know what's right or wrong? I'm not a Greek philosopher. But I can see what's before me well enough. My master dead, slain. And the king induced to see the dead man's cousin. A man overlooked. Little valued. Fit to be raised. Intelligent.'

Bacon smiled again into his beard. The little look of

amusement faded. 'I am sorry I lied. And sorrier still that I had to touch your reputation, your credit. But there was never any danger to your life. Nor to anyone's, save that wicked creature.'

'You lied,' I said. 'I don't care. Lying is great. I lie all the time; I lie every day.' This seemed to startle him, and it was his turn to be lost for words. 'Such men as we are surviving, Sir Frances, by lying in our teeth. Ay, and in our hearts.' I dug inside my fine white doublet and pulled out the little miniature of the saint I had taken from Luisa Mendoza at the Spanish embassy. 'Here,' I said, holding it out.

He took it and his face puckered. 'What is this?'

'Put it in Verney's lodgings,' I said. 'One day – possibly this day – my master will have had time to think on the evening. He will send men to search. Better they find something that confirms what he wishes to think. That Verney was a secret papist. Even if he dislikes you, he doesn't – I think he doesn't – suspect you of popery.'

'Poor Mr Verney.'

'He played, and he lost,' I said.

Bacon's hand closed over the miniature. 'Why … why are you helping me?'

I sighed. 'Because I wish this to be over.'

'Then you might betray me.'

'You are his cousin, Sir Frances. Not a great or much-loved one, I think – but I've no wish to meddle in my master's family. Keep the thing. Use it, as I've said.' I smiled. 'I find that there is greater joy in using things than having them. Ay, and to give more than to take.'

'Thank you,' he said.

'No, thank you, Sir Frances.' At his puzzled look, I added. 'It strikes me that a man of … my tastes. My past. I might one day have need of a man at law: expensive things, lawyers. But I shall never have to pay; I don't think. No, not even for a good one, a strong counsel. No matter what falls out in the future.' I waited whilst he inclined his head. 'Good. We are agreed, then. Verney was a papist villain who hired a trull from Southwark to play the lady assassin. All else was either unknown papist plotters or … or else fond imaginings. And so the affair must die.' Bacon nodded, a little morosely. I stepped forward and grabbed him by the front of his silk doublet, making him jump. 'And no more, Sir Frances. No more. Remember what I know and consider it if – if you ever think to do your duty again. My master is well fenced and hedged. No more foul plots, no more mad rhymes and false trickery.' I released him and he stood back.

He attempted another smile, but it died on his lips. 'I confess I should leave the poesy writing to the stage-wrights. Any … any scribblings in the poetic vein I will keep to this hall.'

'You do that.' I turned my back on him and began to walk through the hall, past the paintings, past the hangings.

'What are you going to do, Mr Savage?' he cried after me. Fear edged his words, I noticed with satisfaction.

Without turning, I said, 'I am going to a bridal feast, where I intend to get drunk. It is a fine thing to end such an affair at a wedding.'

Author's Note

On the 22nd of March 1606, Londoners rose to alarming reports that King James had been assassinated. As the morning wore on, panic spread through the City and beyond, and in the palace of Whitehall, Robert Cecil, Earl of Salisbury, hastily took charge, readying the Tower against a rising and securing the persons of Queen Anne and Prince Henry.

Gradually, however, it became clear that the rumours were false, and based on nothing more than an escaped criminal having ridden through the countryside, at which sight various countrymen had cried, 'treason!' That word, more dangerous than ever before in light of the recently-foiled Gunpowder Plot, began a whole slew of wild tales all hinging on the king's murder. Happily, of course, the truth came out. Nevertheless, James himself was compelled to abandon his hunting trip in Woking and return in person to assure the people that he was, indeed, alive and well.

A largely ignored episode in the reign of James VI and I, these reports of a royal assassination were hot news in the early part of the year. Amongst the rumours were claims that the king had been stabbed, smothered, or even set upon and killed by a party of Scotsmen dressed as women. The incident even sparked dedicatory verses from Ben Jonson. James Shapiro's *1606: William Shakespeare and the Year of Lear* (2015: Faber & Faber) recounts the incident. In the novel, I have presented James and Cecil as having engineered the whole thing, but this is merely a creative choice.

Shapiro's excellent study of the year also provided much of the background for the visit of King Christian IV of Denmark, who arrived – later than expected – for the first state visit England had seen in many years. The triumphal progress through the City which the royals made can be found in the printed record, *Entry of Christian IV, king of Denmark, into London* (London: 1606), which has been digitised by the British Library. From Shapiro, I also found the inspiration for Savage's visit to Westminster Abbey. As odd as it might seem, the cabinet of life-size effigies was indeed set up to dazzle the

Danish king, who visited with Prince Henry on the 4th of August. As Peter Quennell (1997: History Today) notes, Elizabeth's effigy was amongst those on display (the others were Edward III and Philippa of Hainault; Henry V and Catherine of Valois; and Henry VII and Elizabeth of York). The late queen's tomb was also completed in 1606, although it is unknown if this was done by the time of Christian's visit. In the novel, I have decided to have it ready, as it seems to me that James would have had it finished prior to his brother-in-law's tour of the Abbey; and, as Shapiro notes, Christian was expected earlier in the year than turned out to be the case.

One thing that is certain is that Shakespeare's company, the King's Men, performed three (unrecorded) plays at court on August the 7th. Tradition holds that *Hamlet* and *Macbeth* were amongst the three staged. However, it should be noted that the first recorded performance of the Scottish play is found in Simon Forman's journal in a 1612 entry. Nevertheless, the weight of scholarly opinion remains on the side of the play being written in or before 1606, with a court performance in August seeming likely. Ben Jonson's *Volpone* had also been written by this time. That it was the third play performed that night is my own invention.

Hal Berridge is almost certainly fictional, but he is not my invention. Rather, an apocryphal tale deriving from the pen of Victorian essayist Max Beerbohm holds that on the night *Macbeth* was to be performed at Hampton Court, the boy actor, Hal Berridge, fell ill 'of a pleurisy'. Disaster! Young Berridge was to have played Lady Macbeth. Thankfully, the show went on with none other than Shakespeare himself donning the wicked queen's weeds. In reality, however, there was no such person as Hal Berridge. The story has nevertheless gained such traction and been given such an association with the alleged bad luck the play brings that it seemed a shame not to include Hal in this modern fictional take on that night. It's worth reading Richard Huggett's *The Curse of Macbeth and Other Theatrical Superstitions: An Investigation* (1981: Picton) and *Murdering Ministers: A Close Look at Shakespeare's Macbeth in Text, Context, and Performance* (2016: Cambridge Scholars).

Naturally, *Macbeth* itself is worth a read – as is Jonson's *Volpone*, which I've had the privilege of teaching – and find that people still find it witty! The world of Shakespearean Apocrypha exploded following the Romantic period. Readers might enjoy Laurie Maguire and Emma Smith's *30 Great Myths About Shakespeare* (2013: John Wiley).

A figure far less written about than Shakespeare is Luisa de Carvajal y Mendoza, a well-born Spanish lady who came to England at the invitation of Father Garnet, who lost his life in the wake of the Gunpowder Plot. Luisa was a crusading Catholic missionary and a prolific letter writer. She took up residence in the Spanish Embassy, from which she attempted to win souls away from the English Church. Amazingly, she was only imprisoned a couple of times (in 1608 and 1613). Her letters can be found in Anne J. Cruz's edited collection, *The Life and Writings of Luisa de Carvajal y Mendoza* (2014: Iter).

The Gunpowder Plot itself has been endlessly written about and made its way to the silver screen repeatedly. My favourite study of the subject is Antonia Fraser's *The Gunpowder Plot: Terror and Faith in 1605* (1996: Weidenfeld & Nicolson). A scrupulously accurate fictional rendering, which is also a great read, is Michael Dax's *The Powder Treason* (2018: Carter & Allen).

The Gunpowder Plot – or the Powder Plot, or Powder Treason, as it was then known – had long-lasting repercussions (indeed, we still light bonfires and release fireworks). In the short term, when the big names had all been executed, there remained a number of figures connected with the affair still living in the small community of London. Ben Jonson, for example, was indeed seen dining with the plotters prior to the 5th of November 1605. Henry Percy, the 'Wizard Earl' of Northumberland, remained in the Tower, though no definitive proof was found against him (it was popularly believed, though, that such a plot had to have had a noble backer). Northumberland's sister-in-law was indeed the infamous Penelope Devereux, sister of the late Earl of Essex. Her story can be found in Sally Varlow's *The Lady Penelope: The Lost Tale of Love and Politics in the Court of Elizabeth I* (2007:

Trafalgar Square). Penelope had by 1606 been thoroughly ruined by Cecil, publicly denounced as a 'whore' and worse, and she would die the following year.

Walter Raleigh, too, was still in the Tower in 1606 – and he would remain there for a decade until his ill-fated trip to Guiana in search of gold finally led to his death sentence being carried out. His story is well told in *Sir Walter Raleigh: In Life and Legend* by Mark Nicholls and Penry Williams (2011: Bloomsbury).

By far the most interesting of the figures new to Savage is Sir Francis Bacon. Bacon was and is a puzzle. He was the father of empiricism, a genius polymath, an idealistic philosopher, and a fun-loving writer of educational Inns of Court revels. However, he was also ruthlessly ambitious, open to financial corruption (as were many important figures in the period, of course – but Bacon's would ultimately see him prosecuted by parliament) and accused of pederasty (having sex with his much younger male students). He married the twelve-year-old Alice Barnham in 1604 when he was in his forties. Almost certainly this was for her dowry, though he claimed to find her the most appealing of her father's daughters. My favourite biography of Bacon is Daphne du Maurier's *The Winding Stair* (1976: Virago). It is outdated now but naturally remains as readable as any of her novels (although she flirts with the idea that he wrote the plays attributed to Shakespeare, as was then the vogue). Bacon had Twickenham Lodge in 1606, but he would pass it to the countess of Bedford in 1608. Du Maurier notes that he was living in a place called 'Fullwoods' for part of the decade, though she doesn't identify it with Fulwood's Rents, a street of lodging houses running between Holborn and Gray's Inn. I've placed Bacon here in the story.

In closing, I'd like to thank everyone who has read this far. If you enjoyed the book – or didn't – I'd love to hear from you. You can reach me on Twitter @ScrutinEye and on Instagram @steven.veerapen.3. As always, I'd greatly appreciate it if you could leave a review on Amazon or Goodreads, and hope that you enjoyed this trip into Jacobean England as much as I did.

Printed in Great Britain
by Amazon